TO KILL IS NOT ENOUGH

The Ghost of Flight 666
A novel
By
Christopher L. Anderson

I0539259

Christopher L. Anderson

To Kill Is Not Enough

The Ghost of Flight 666

ISBN-13: 978-0692371893
(Thor's Grog Induced Publications)
Printed in the United States of America

THE GHOST OF FLIGHT 666

Christopher L. Anderson

PROLOGUE: Windows

Air Force test pilot Jeremiah Slade hated his given name. Most people just called him Slade, but not Jay or Jerry, and never Jeremiah. Rather like the Johnny Cash ballad, Slade grew up not only hating the name but developing a cold, impenetrable exterior to deal with the ridicule.

That armor never left him.

Today was no different. As Slade left his squadron operations building at Edwards Air Force Base to conduct a high level test mission, his test engineer, a DARPA guy who was good but chatty, needled him. "Lots of Congressmen and Senators watching today's test flight Jerry—you nervous?"

Slade didn't answer as they stepped out of the air conditioned building into the blast furnace heat of the flight line. The tarmac shimmered. The smell of jet fuel, exhaust and asphalt was stifling. Neither the heat nor the test engineer appeared to bother Slade. Topping six feet, at an athletic two hundred and ten pounds, Slade walked with an easy, almost panther-like stride. As a rule he was serious. His most demonstrative action was to brush back the lone forelock of his dark hair from his lean, gunfighter face with its piercing eyes.

"Jeez, you really are touchy about your name aren't you?"

No answer. Slade saw no reason to waste words on the obvious.

"You do know how important this mission is don't you— Slade?" the engineer asked, now getting nervous. His butt was on the line as well. "Those guys from D.C. will be listening to every word, watching everything via datalink. This is as big as it gets!"

Slade finally answered enigmatically, "Yeah, it ranks right up there."

They climbed into a specially modified F-15E Eagle and performed their preflight, including a lengthy routine on the small box connected to a belly pod codenamed "Magic." Everything checked. They started engines, taxied out, and then Slade shoved the throttles up for takeoff. The Eagle accelerated quickly, pushing them back in their ejection seats. The runway markings sped by, and Slade eased the stick back. It didn't take much, the Eagle was sensitive. Half a mile down the runway the Eagle effortlessly climbed into the sky.

The fifty-eight thousand pounds of thrust generated by the engines dominated the cockpit, permeating Slade's flesh, shaking his bones—he loved that, but he would never admit it. The twenty-five ton aircraft accelerated into the hazy blue sky. As the hangers of the flight line disappeared beneath the canopy rail, the test engineer announced, "Approaching the first test point Jay."

No answer.

He cursed and repeated the declaration. "First test point—Slade!"

"Checks," he replied to the unnecessary announcement. "Test point one, three thousand feet; two hundred fifty knots; clean configuration—mark—clear for magic!"

"Magic—on! ALQ nine-seven-two mode alpha engaged," the test engineer replied, adding unofficially, in a bad Scottish brogue, "Cloaking device engaged Cap'n, all systems nominal!"

"Stick to the script," Slade reminded the engineer.

"Approaching test point two!" the engineer announced.

"Test point—hold on," Slade started to say, but he stopped. As the altimeter swept through ten thousand feet the Eagle began to shudder, not violently but conspicuously. Instinctively, Slade backed off the throttle, slowing down. The buffeting stopped.

"What's up; what was that?" the engineer asked with concern.

"I don't know, but it felt like it was coming from the tail," Slade told him, stabilizing the aircraft at 240 knots. He lightened his grip on the stick, feeling for any further vibration—nothing. "We'll approach the test point again—stand by." He accelerated slowly, smoothly, but once again at

250 knots the aircraft began to shudder. Slade felt it in the
elevators via the stick. The rudder pedals chattered,
transmitting the buffet on the rudder into his boots.

"Turn the Magic off!"

"That's not in the test script!" the engineer complained.

"Turn it off!"

"Magic off!"

The buffeting continued.

"That's it," he said sharply, easing the throttles back. The
buffeting stopped. Slade allowed the speed to bleed off,
levelling the jet. "We're scrubbing the mission and returning
to base. Call operations and get a chase ship up here to look us
over."

"You sure Slade?" the back-seater said. "This is as high
priority as a test gets!"

"The test won't matter if we're a pile of smoking metal in
the desert," he replied, leaving no room for argument.

"You got that from a bit of buffet? I think it's just the big
gyro in the pod," the engineer theorized, meaning the heavy
rotating electromagnetic transmitter mounted on the belly.
"We knew there might be turbulence problems caused by the
rotation. It's just the pod deforming in the windstream. Don't
worry, it's stressed up to nine g's; the pod's not going to come
off."

"It's not the pod; it's in the tail not the belly," Slade
reiterated. "Let operations know that we're doing a
controllability check and bringing it in slow; get that chase
ship. I'll declare an emergency with Joshua Control."

"Are you sure?"

"Get on the horn with Ops," Slade told him emphatically.

"All right, but I'm not taking the fall for this! The general
brought half of Washington out here on a weekend to see this
mission! He's not going to be happy!"

"The general isn't in charge up here—I am!" Slade replied
coldly.

As it turned out, the engineer was right. The general was
not happy at all. He was so steamed, that he marched out of

the test control center and left the dressing down of Slade to the Test Wing Commander Colonel McFarland.

McFarland scowled at Slade with knit brows and a clenched jaw, reminding the junior officer, "Captain Slade, you did a Functional Check Flight on this aircraft three days ago—right—no problems?"

"Yes sir."

"Well there better be a problem now! The old man is hot!"

Maintenance took the aircraft and went over it, finding— nothing. Slade told them to check again. Again they found nothing. Colonel McFarland was irate.

"Maintenance can't find anything wrong with the aircraft. Captain, as the chief test pilot of this program you've grounded the aircraft; by regulation my hands are tied. Only you can clear it to fly again. I suggest you take it back up and do another check profile."

"Sir, with all due respects, I think this is a structural problem in the tail. That's where the buffet came from."

"Maintenance buys the test engineers story about the pod being the problem," the Wing King replied impatiently.

"Sir, I'll talk with maintenance; we'll find out what's wrong," Slade replied.

"Make it fast captain, Washington wants these tests done and they want them done now! We have operational missions waiting to go." The colonel hung up.

Slade talked to maintenance. They went through the aircraft with a fine toothed comb. The next morning they got back to him. "Sir, we checked the gear doors, the fairings, balance bays, cables, the pod, you name it. Everything checked out."

"What did you check in the tail?"

"Both stabilizers are at the same trim setting, elevators move fine, hydraulics are within limits—we're stuck."

He hung up, but before Slade could second guess himself the phone rang. It was General Green. He was blunt. "Captain Slade, I don't think I need to tell you how important that jet is. We need to know whether this system is going to work before we commit reconnaissance aircraft to high risk areas—do you understand?"

"Yes sir, and that's part of my reasoning for grounding the aircraft," Slade said. "If the problem is structural there's a chance of losing the empennage. We're risking a unique testbed. It took six months to outfit this Eagle. We can't afford a mishap sir."

"Release the aircraft to another test crew," the general demanded.

"With all due respect, I can't do that sir," Slade replied as tactfully as he could muster. "If I'm right and the failure occurs during takeoff no one gets out and we lose the asset."

"That's not what maintenance says. That's not good enough captain. I need that jet!"

"Sir, we'll get it back to you ASAP," Slade replied, but the line was already dead.

The next few days grew increasingly bad. Everyone distanced themselves from Slade. His test engineer began whispering, "I knew it was only the pod, but Slade knows best! He told the general to shove it; this was his program not the general's!"

Slade knew he had to shake the tree. He called Tech Sergeant Roscoe Chapman. The sergeant worked on Eagles since their initial flight testing and was Slade's crew chief for three years before getting a coveted transfer across the base to NASA's flight test center. No one knew the airplane better.

"Sergeant, I have an Eagle, number 0183, you know the one; it's the Dreamland bird," he said, going on to explain what happened on the mission. "I know you're busy, but I need to another pair of eyes on this. Can you come down and look at it—now—it's in the middle of the program and we have a timeline to keep?"

"No problem captain, I'd still be rotting in that Costa Rican jail if you hadn't sweet talked the Secretary of Transportation into letting me out!" he laughed. "I'm on my way!"

Chapman checked in with Slade on the way to the maintenance hangar, looking through his own personal log of the aircraft; Roscoe kept meticulous records for every aircraft he worked on. "I oversaw the current modifications on 0183 before I came over to NASA. This bird was the first production E model, December of 1986, she's got lots of miles on her."

"What's your gut feeling?"

"The bird's thirty years old captain. Those elevator cables stretch after years of high G forces; it doesn't take much. If there's something wrong I'll find it." He began to walk out, but then he stopped and turned. "Captain, what if I don't find anything?"

"Then I take her up again," Slade shrugged. "If you say the aircraft is sound, sergeant, that's good enough for me." Chapman nodded and got to work.

Two hours later Sergeant Chapman called Slade to the jet. Slade arrived with his squadron commander Lt. Colonel Wilkins and found Colonel McFarland and General Green there as well. They were not in a good mood. Apparently Sergeant Chapman would not report to them until Captain Slade was there.

Slade saluted.

They refused to salute back.

Instead, the general barked, "Sergeant what do you have to say? No excuses. I want to know exactly why I had to send two dozen of the most powerful people in Washington back to the capital with nothing—nothing!"

"Yes sir, but begging your pardon sir, I think I better show you." Chapman led them to the left rear stabilizer. There was a ladder there. Sergeant Chapman pointed to the fin.

"Captain Slade, sir, would you push up on the leading edge of the stabilizer." Slade climbed the ladder under the withering scrutiny of his commanding officers. He knew what he expected to find; the stabilizer must be loose. Even a slight wiggle in the fin at high speeds would cause significant buffet that would inevitably shake the fin apart.

Slade was wrong—dead wrong.

Obediently he pushed up on the leading edge of the stabilizer. It wasn't supposed to budge, but it moved and it didn't stop moving. There was a gasp from the observers. Slade pushed until the left horizontal fin was straight up and down; however, the right fin was still in its horizontal position; that wasn't the way it was supposed to look.

"Holy shit! What the Hell happened?" General Green demanded.

Sergeant Chapman pointed to the stabilizer and replied, "Sir, the horizontal stabilizer is held on the torque tube by a bolt two inches in diameter. The bolt is missing. It had worn through the torque tube until the head could fit through mounting bracket and then it departed the aircraft. That's when Captain Slade felt the buffet."

"You mean to tell me there was nothing holding the stabilizer on the aircraft?" the colonel exclaimed, turning white.

"Nothing sir," the sergeant said, shaking his head. "There's no reason on God's green Earth the fin should still be on the airplane; there's literally nothing holding it on! I don't know how Captain Slade flew the jet and I don't know how he landed it. All I know is that if this jet tried to takeoff like this the stabilizer would have come off. It would have killed everyone on board. They wouldn't have known what hit them."

The commanders strode off without a word. Slade's squadron commander looked after them, cursing, but then he came up to Slade. "Don't worry, I'll take care of everything."

Wilkins stomped off. Slade went and offered his hand to Sergeant Chapman.

"You saved my ass."

"No need to thank me sir, I'm just glad you called. These new techs have no common sense. They don't know how an airplane flies. They checked the rigging, the sensors and the position indicators—everything the tech order told them to— everything was right on. But they never actually touched the tail. I'm glad to help straighten things out." Then he looked at Slade strangely, and hesitantly said, "You know there's no way you should have been able to land that jet."

"I know. Someone was looking out for me," Slade admitted.

"I never knew if you believed in God or not sir."

"Oh I always believed in Him, Roscoe," Slade said, using the sergeant's first name for the first time. "I just didn't know until now that He believed in me."

Three months later, after a successful conclusion to the test program, the fallout kicked in the door to Slade's life.

Lt. Colonel Wilkins called Slade into his office. He entered and saluted. The commander pointed to his chair, and said, "Slade, I put you in for a commendation medal for saving the aircraft and crew of the test flight."

"Sir I appreciate that, but I was just doing my job."

"That's the story of your career isn't it?" the colonel said mysteriously. He reached into his desk and took out a blue leather folder and handed it to Slade. "This is the medal and the commendation; everything went through fine." He laughed humorlessly, adding, "That weasel of a test engineer put in for a commendation himself and got it. If you'd listened to him you'd both be dead!"

Slade took it without any show of emotion. The colonel shook his head, but it was the timbre of his voice that caught the captain's attention. Slade stiffened.

"Damn it captain, you don't get it do you?" the colonel snapped, catching Slade completely off guard. "I've got thirty pilots out there. You're the best of them, but why are you still here instead of in the astronaut program? I'll tell you why: self-promotion!

"You should have rung your own bell like the DARPA engineer did; you would have been right to do so! Who the Hell knows you did a great job unless you tell them? I'll give you an example: one of my line pilots, Captain Barr, has half the time you have and half the credentials—damn it, she scraped the tail off a C-17, a Class A mishap—but she's going to the astronaut program, not you. You thought doing your job exceptionally well should be enough. It's not. You flew under the radar in RF-4's during Desert Storm; you're still doing it! Wake up!"

The colonel got up and pointed to the mandatory row of photos on his office wall. It descended from the President of the United States all the way down to General Green and

Colonel McFarland. "Because you're stubborn and you're good, General Green will get his second star and Colonel McFarland will get his first. If you'd knuckled under to their pressure we'd have had a mishap. The investigation would have stopped the program for a year. The command would have cleaned house—the general, the colonel—even me. We owe you our careers and this is how we repay you."

"I don't understand sir," Slade replied.

The commander slid a file over to Slade.

"I'm sorry Jeremiah, they want you out. You embarrassed them by doing your job to perfection. Your people got promoted, but you got passed over for major. You've got six months. I'm sorry."

Slade got up with his commendation medal and his walking papers in hand. He saluted smartly. The colonel stood and saluted, but said, "Jeremiah, it's been an honor serving with you. Let me give you one last piece of advice: take advantage of opportunities when they're offered. You didn't do that in the Air Force. If you had, I'd be saluting you instead of the other way around. Even if it's not what you think you want, take the opportunity and run with it. When a door closes a window always opens—remember that."

"Yes sir."

Jeremiah Slade walked out of the operations building a broken man. He'd followed the rules, done his job and done it well. This is what he got for it? "I'm done. Twelve years down the tubes. What the Hell do I do now?" He felt the physical weight of bills piling on his head.

Slade went to the Officer's Club and took a seat at the bar, wondering just how he was going to deal with this sudden change of events. He had six months to solve the problem, then the money stopped. What could he do? Slade was a pilot, but he loathed the idea of the airlines. It wasn't an option anyway—the major airlines were all in bankruptcy. With that reminder he got out his wallet.

With a bitter laugh, Slade mocked himself. "Ten days to payday and I haven't got enough for a beer!"

The bartender came over. Humiliated, Slade held up his hand. "Sorry, I can't stay."

A voice from behind him said, "Two of whatever the captain is drinking—on me."

"Yes sir," the bartender said, looking expectantly at Slade.

Slade turned around to see a man in a suit with a government haircut holding a briefcase. He shrugged and motioned to the seat next to him, answering, "Michelob."

The man sat down. "You move fast Captain Slade. I didn't even have a chance to catch you at the squadron before you bugged out."

"I didn't have much incentive to stay."

"That's why I'm here," the man said with a shadow of a smile. He held out a hand. "I'm Joe Wilson. I'm an old friend of Lt. Colonel Wilkins. He called me and told me about your situation—the whole story—I'm sorry. The service hates to lose good men."

"They have a funny way of showing it," Slade replied suspiciously, but he shook the man's hand. Lt. Colonel Wilkins last bit of advice rang in his head.

Wilson shrugged. "The Air Force's loss is the CIA's gain. That's who I work for."

"The CIA? Why would you be interested in me?" Slade said as the bartender set down two bottles. "I'm a pilot. I don't have any training in whatever it is you guys do."

"We always need pilots—good ones—we challenge our people," Wilson said, tipping back the Michelob. He looked at Slade with a penetrating all-knowing expression. "You're more than just a pilot though Slade. You're an expert marksman; you earned your black belt; you earned a Master's degree and your loyalty factor is off the charts. You're what we call a suitable candidate."

He paused and took another swig of his beer. Turning to look at the soon to be ex-Air Force officer, the CIA recruiter put the question to Slade. "What if I were to tell you that your service to your country didn't have to end here?"

"I'm still coming to grips with my career spiraling down in flames," Slade said with a sigh. "Do you need an answer right now?"

"Let me put it to you in a practical sense Captain Slade," Wilson said firmly. "Windows only stay open for so long. We want, no, we demand dedicated individuals. The reasons are obvious. We have needs, but so do you. Your—lifestyle—isn't cheap Captain Slade. Your salary barely covers expenses. What's going to happen in a few years? Well, by my reckoning, considering your responsibility oriented character and your special needs, well your expenses are going through the roof."

"You know a lot about me," Slade admitted.

"Our file on you is fairly comprehensive."

"You're right," Jeremiah sighed, but then he glanced at Wilson and his eyes narrowed. "Money isn't much of a reason for loyalty. Wouldn't that make me even more of a risk?"

"If that were all there is to it we wouldn't be talking," Wilson replied dryly. "You're the kind of guy who takes pride in serving your country. You demand responsibility; hence your money problems. You also need the adrenaline rush."

"You know about that do you?"

The man nodded. "On one of your missions over Bagdad you flew over an Iraqi helicopter at Mach 1.2. The report said you overflew him by less than twenty feet."

"Ten—my wake turbulence caused him to depart controlled flight," Slade smiled thinly. "I got credited with a kill; the only one by a Recce pilot that I know of."

"You have courage with a splash of nasty thrown in for good measure," the agent said.

"I was frustrated because I was flying an unarmed Recce bird in the middle of a shooting war," Slade sighed.

"Yet you still did your job," the agent smiled, swigging his beer but not taking his eyes off Slade. "We can use men like you." His expression turned deadly serious. "Understand me Slade, this isn't James Bond and Specter. We're in the middle of a war on terror. These people are not as sophisticated as your Hollywood villains, but they are crueler than you can ever imagine. Your job will take you into hostile territory."

Slade shrugged and said, "As long as I have a good life insurance policy, we're set."

"May I take that for a yes?" the agent smiled, holding out his half empty bottle toward Slade.

Slade thought about it. "To windows," he muttered, and then he reached over and clinked the bottom of his bottle with Wilson. The deal was done.

CHAPTER 1: Sowing the Seeds

A decade later, on the island nation of Malaysia, Abdullereda Hussein was late to the hospital. It wasn't because he'd landed late. Although he was an A380 captain for Malaysia Airlines he hadn't been flying; he'd been whoring.

During his latest visit to the brothels outside of Kuala Lumpur, his favorite being a walled estate overlooking the Strait of Malacca, Hussein received an urgent phone call from his son Abdulla. His wife Safrina was in the hospital with severe abdominal pains.

"It cannot be labor yet," Abdullereda complained. "She's only six months pregnant. She's simply got morning sickness that's all. Why is she in the hospital; that sounds expensive?"

"As expensive as your whores?" the seventeen year boy asked viciously. The sound of the intercom in the hospital made it hard to understand his son's words, but it wasn't hard to understand his feelings.

"You will not talk to me that way!" the airline captain said angrily, defensively. "You have no idea how good you have it!"

That was Abdullereda's excuse for everything; especially his personal failures. He was a rarity in Malaysian society; the upper part of one percent among earners, and he took that seriously. The fact that his wife and children did not understand how successful he was, and that they didn't allow for it and so ignore his faults, constantly grated on his nerves.

"Stay away then, you'll probably do more harm than good," his son said and hung up.

Furious, Abdullereda left the brothel and drove to town. It took two hours to get to the hospital through a driving rain. His way through the city of Kelang was slowed by flooded streets and snarled traffic, which only became worse when he entered Kuala Lumpur. When the wayward husband finally arrived at the maternity ward, angry at what was obviously an over-reaction by his family, he entered in a huff. His son and daughters, three of them, were waiting at the entrance to the ward.

"You're too late," his son informed Abdullereda. "The baby, our brother is dead."

"What on earth do you mean?" he replied, angry and shocked.

"Mother had a miscarriage," he told his father. "She's lost a lot of blood. She may die. They won't know more until tomorrow."

As he told the news to his father a doctor stepped up, and asked, "You are Mr. Hussein, Safrina's husband?"

"Yes, yes, what happened?" he stammered, still registering the fact that he'd lost a son and his wife was now battling for her life. "Is it her age? Did she over-exert herself, fall—what happened?"

"No, Safrina's only thirty-two and she was doing everything right," the doctor said, and then his eyes grew hard, accusatory. He clutched the pilot's arm, and his voice dropped to a low, angry whisper. "It is for you that I have questions."

"Me, what do you mean?" he retorted.

"I have been told by your family, not just your wife, that you have many relationships beyond you're your marriage. Is that true?"

Abdullereda took the doctor aside, away from his son and daughters. "What of it? What has that to do with anything?"

"How long have you had Syphilis?" the doctor asked sternly.

"A few years—so what?" he sneered.

"You gave it to Safrina and that caused the miscarriage," the doctor said harshly. "It may cost your wife her life. The miscarriage is a hard process for the body to go through to begin with, much like natural birth, but in this case she hemorrhaged severely. She'd lost a lot of blood by the time we got to her." He sighed, and finished, "You will have to prepare yourself. Even if she survives she will never again be able to bear children."

Abdullereda was too stunned to speak.

"So, it was you who did this to her!" Abdulla said from the door, furious, eyes glaring at his father.

"Shut up!" his father told him.

"You pig!" the boy said, using the most terrible way for a Muslim to describe another Muslim. "You pig. You've killed our mother!"

"Shut up boy!" the father shouted, but when Abdulla opened his mouth to speak again he struck him, knocking the teenager to the ground. "I said shut up! You will obey me!"

The doctor and the staff got between them and two attendants ushered him out of the ward. Abdulla shouted at his father, "We hate you! You pig! Go away, far away, and don't you ever come back!"

That was the last time Abdullereda saw his son. When they discharged his wife from the hospital she returned to her parent's home in Borneo. She took the children with her. As much as Abdullereda believed that this was wrong, that a Muslim woman had no right to take his children and leave, no right to make a decision on her own, he could not stop her. Safrina's father came to collect the family personally and Abdullereda could not face his father-in-law.

It wasn't only that. Abdullereda, even in his most angry moments, had no idea how he would face his son.

The next few months deteriorated into long bouts of drinking and angry rants at the world. Abdullereda blamed his debauchery on others, on the materialistic poison of the West. On the sluts in China. On the Jews. On everyone but himself.

The precipitous decline of his life crept into his performance at work. Hussein's chief pilot summoned him to the office. It wasn't the first time his supervisor had seen the effects of a broken marriage on his pilots. The men spent a great deal of time away from their families and there were always temptations, especially for the older men.

"Take a month off Hussein," he told Abdullereda in a communicative but serious tone of voice. "You have vacation coming up; I'll move it so that no one will ask any questions." When Abdullereda began to protest the chief pilot held up his hand and stopped him. "Don't start. Take some time off; solve this before it becomes a problem I can no longer deal with. You should know, that after the Asiana crash in San Francisco the company has made it clear that our pilots are to be held to higher standards."

The supervisor sighed, looking at his desk as if troubled. He let Hussein know, "There is even talk of hiring Western pilots directly into the captain's seats, outside our seniority list, right over you; over all of our senior captains. Don't assume your job is safe. Take care of this now before it consumes you! Go to your mosque, Hussein. Talk to your imam. Put your life back together."

In desperation, Hussein took his chief pilot's advice. He drove straight to his mosque and saw one of the imams. The prospect of losing his job was terrifying. If he were fired from the country's national airline no one would touch him; his piloting skills would be worth nothing. With such a black mark on his name he'd be finished.

That didn't release the fury of his self-induced crisis. Hussein raged to his imam about the Western pilots who would be recruited to replace him. These wouldn't be the best pilots in the West, but those who weren't flying for the major airlines in the United States or Europe. Hussein knew Western pilots, even the castoffs, were considered superior to Hussein and his peers. It was humiliating!

The imam listened patiently, finally telling Abdullereda, "This is a sign of the times. It is the inevitable encroachment of the West on our civilization. This is just the beginning Abdullereda."

"How do we stop it?" he asked automatically, even more furious.

The imam smiled and introduced him to other men, men with similar experiences. Men who were underappreciated, victims of forces they could not control, victims of the West and the decadence of the outside world. "You see how the West targets you first. You are the best and the brightest. If you fall what is to become of the rest?"

Other imams chimed in with variations of the same message: they were not recognized for the great people they were and it was not their fault. It was the West.

For weeks he went to his mosque and prayed, but even though Abdullereda made friends with these men all he wanted was to get his life back; especially his son. He never realized how important that world was until he lost it. He'd do anything to get it back.

When he found that Abdulla left Malaysia he was devastated. Safrina would not tell him where Abdulla was or how to get a hold of him. In one month Abdullereda lost his unborn son and his namesake. The prospect of dying and not having a son to speak well of his father, to carry on his line, was sobering; it put everything in perspective—but how to salvage his life and legacy?

"Perhaps we can help," said his new friends at the mosque.

"Really?" pleaded Abdullereda. "What can you do?"

"We can find out where your son is and what may cajole him to reconcile with you as is proper," they told him. He readily accepted any help they could give him.

A few days later Abdullereda's friends brought a man with them to their daily gathering for talk and tea. The man was an Arab and horribly disfigured, but his friends treated him with great reverence.

"This is Khallida, he has sacrificed a great deal for the cause. He has been fighting America and the West since before Nine-Eleven." Khallida held out his right hand. Abdullereda took it, shaking the cold, clammy, limp thing. It reminded him of a hand cut off by the Sharia swordsman and then sown back on for looks only; it was still dead. Yet Khallida's eyes burned.

"I have talked to your son," Khallida said, taking a cigarette from one of Abdullereda's friends. "He is in Paris."

"Paris! What on earth is he doing there?"

"He is one of our young lions and is set to take apart the Western world from within," Khallida smiled, taking a long drag from his cigarette and blowing out a plume of blue smoke. "Although you are not yet reconciled I can see that he gained a great many positive lessons from his father; you have taught him to honor the jihad. That is commendable for both of you."

"Is he happy and healthy?" Abdullereda asked.

"As happy as he could be without a father to look up to," the Arab said sharply.

Hussein's head hung low. He closed his eyes in shame.

Khallida continued in a softer tone. "I understand also that you have had a difficult time recently; but that you are looking for guidance. Is that so?"

"Yes, yes, I have been lost," Abdullereda admitted. "But I would do anything to win back the respect of my son—anything."

"Anything?" Khallida smiled, which was gruesome, and he segued shrewdly to his point, "I understand you are a pilot."

CHAPTER 2: Hook, Line and Sinker

For the next few days Abdullereda spent a great deal of time with his new friends and Khallida. He found that he could pour his heart out to the Arab, who had heard so many stories like his that Khallida's empathy was like a warm comforting blanket around the shoulders of a shipwrecked man.

He read Hussein's need and offered the solution. "My friend, your life has been one of materialistic debauchery; it's meant nothing to the people you love and it has done nothing to celebrate the glory of Allah. What has it been worth?"

"Nothing," Hussein admitted. "My whole life has meant nothing."

"We cannot let it end that way," Khallida told him. "Look at me. I too have suffered, but Allah is not finished with me. I cannot go to paradise while he still has use for me. Therefore I persevere. I will continue the fight as long as Allah wills it. However, you are a fortunate man, very fortunate."

"How so, I'm miserable, and I see no way to redeem myself in the eyes of my family, most especially my son," Abdullereda complained. "It is too late for me!"

"It is never too late in the eyes of Allah, who can forgive all, but you must serve him," Khallida told the wretch emphatically. "You know who I represent do you not? I do the holy work for al Zawahiri and Al Qaeda. We are always looking for men like you; men who have lost their way but seek the path of holy redemption."

"I do seek that path," Abdullereda admitted. "I cannot continue the way I am. It has been a nightmare; there is not enough alcohol, there are not enough women to fill the void in my heart. Yet I have done such terrible things."

"Terrible sins require a great holy act to reconcile them; that is why I say you are such a fortunate man," Khallida told Hussein, placing his good hand on the airline pilot's shoulder. "I have just such an act that will set you above even the martyrs of Nine-Eleven!"

19

Abdullereda looked up and his eyes glistened. "A martyrdom operation; yes, my son would respect that. What desire have I for the material things in this world anyway?"

"This is not just any martyrdom operation; it is a stake in the heart of Zion!" Khallida said fervently. "You now have a chance to redeem yourself in the eyes of your son, your family and to Allah. You have a chance to go down as one of the founding martyrs of the Caliphate, a name remembered through all history. Will you seize that chance?"

"I will; I must!" Abdullereda said forcefully.

"Excellent, then we may move forward on the operation?"

"Absolutely, I am eager to be of service," he replied.

One of Khallida's men laid an aeronautical chart on the table. It was of Southeast Asia and the Indian Ocean. A small red circle had been drawn around Kuala Lumpur, Hussein's home base. Another red circle was drawn around Beijing, China. "This is your normal route is it not?" Khallida asked. "You can fly this whenever you wish?"

"Absolutely!"

"Good, now, what other airports are within range with the fuel you carry, can you tell me?"

"Certainly," Hussein said, taking the proffered pen. He drew an arc headed west and then south, stopping abeam Australia in the great southern ocean. "This is the range of the A380 with the fuel load we carry to Beijing. As you can see we can go anywhere within the circle, from Pakistan, the Chagos Archipelago in the Indian Ocean and south to Indonesia—anywhere."

"You're certain the aircraft can do that," Khallida asked, shaking his scarred head. To emphasize his point he gestured with his burned right hand. "We need the aircraft to be seen turning west and then south. The assumed crash site must be in the deep south around Australia to throw the capitalists off the track."

"Trust me the A380 can do it without thinking about it," Abdullereda said fervently, nervously, as if applying for a job interview. In effect, he was. "The Westerners may be decadent but they build good airplanes. The A380 is a beautiful aircraft."

"Are you certain *you* can do it?" Khallida said sternly, touching the man's chest with his permanently frozen finger.

Abdullereda shuddered involuntarily. "Of course," he gasped, glancing over at the Al Qaeda guerillas Khallida brought with him. "I've been doing this for twenty years."

"That is not what I meant," he said, the normal half of his face grimacing but the burned half staying flat and expressionless, which made Abdullereda even more uncomfortable. "I do not question whether you can fly the airplane. Abdullereda, you must understand that phase one of the operation involves hijacking this aircraft for our uses. That means you will pilot the aircraft and fly the profile; however, we cannot afford to take a chance that your Malaysian crew or the passengers will interfere."

"What could they do? I will be locked on the flight deck. The passengers and flight attendants can do nothing but go where I take them."

"Unfortunately, experience taught us otherwise. The harsh lessons of Nine-Eleven were clear: the passengers of Flight 93 interfering with the mission to destroy the American capital; and a single pilot, the CIA's Crusader, killing our entire team and saving the American White House. Yes we have learned from those hard lessons. Allah does not accept arrogance or complacency. The passengers and crew must die."

"I am a pilot; I am unfortunately not a fighter," Abdullereda admitted humbly.

"Not to worry," Khallida said with a grotesque grin. He took out a cigarette and lit it, looking over to one of his men. "You will have help. This is Muhammad. He has recently come from Iraq; he even has his own video," Khallida chuckled, leaning toward the pilot and adding, "Muhammad was not the lackey standing behind the executioner yelling Allahu Akbar! No, he has blood on his hands and plenty of it." Khallida looked at the pilot as if gauging his courage, taking a drag from his cigarette, before saying, "We will have three brothers there to help you—one is Muhammad, and the other two are Iranians."

"Iranians—Shia?" Abdullereda said with surprise.

"This is a new era of cooperation," Khallida told him, although his tone held reservations. "A new Caliphate is coming; a new age is coming. This is the first step in that new age. The Iranians are supplying more than muscle in this operation. We must be meant to work with them for we cannot achieve our goal without their aid. We are supplying the aircraft and pilot; they are supplying the cargo."

"Very well. Will they be passengers; how do I make contact with them?"

"The Iranians will be passengers. Muhammad will be travelling as a replacement pilot to Beijing, you pilots have a special term for that, what's the word?"

"Deadheading," Abdullereda said flatly.

"How appropriate," Khallida nodded. He turned back to the map and continued. "The three brothers will help you take the aircraft."

Abdullereda plucked up his courage, trying to be helpful, and pointed to a cross-hatched line over the ocean. "We transition between these Air Traffic Control Zones here, between Malaysia and Vietnam. Sometimes the High frequency radios are hard to understand. If we take the aircraft here, in the transition area, it will cause confusion and delay in Air Traffic Control."

"Excellent; that will keep the Westerners from realizing that something is wrong with their beautiful aircraft." Khallida pointed to the Indian Ocean. "We have given you the locations of multiple airfields; you will practice them. Specifically, you will ensure that your computer at home shows that you practiced them. It is part of our deception plan," Khallida paused and shrugged. "We too have learned from the Americans. If you wish to strike them you must not look in that place; then you must give them a reason to look elsewhere."

"Where do you want me to land?" Abdullereda said.

"Here!" Khallida circled an airport in Indonesia.

"But that's a very busy airport," Abdullereda argued. "We can't avoid their radar, and even if we could enter their airspace undetected there is absolutely no chance we could land there without the controllers knowing about it!"

"Of course they'll know," Khallida smiled.

"You mean they are in on it?"

"No, that would put far too many people in the loop, so to speak," Khallida chuckled dryly. "They don't need to know the particulars, they simply must be told what to do. What you do not appreciate, Abdullereda, is that Indonesia is the largest Muslim nation in the world. It takes very little persuasion to get a few dozen people to ignore a single Malaysian A380 coming into the airport; we simply talk to them."

"What do you say?" Abdullereda stammered.

Khallida shrugged, and said, "We offer them money of course, along with the opportunity to follow the will of Allah. For those who are still troubled we furnish them a helpful visit from some of our more zealous holy warriors; a visit that will affect their entire families. That way they understand where they fit in the scheme of things."

"I understand," Abdullereda swallowed, sweating at the thought that he too had a family and now, like it or not, they were inextricably bound by his choice.

"Good!" Khallida smiled, patting him on the back. "Don't worry about the airport. The controllers will be expecting you. Be assured we will have our people in every facet of the Air Traffic Control System. The people you will be talking to will be our people; their schedules will be set up for the operation. Anyone else will have been spoken to already; they will not interfere. So play your video games and leave the rest to us."

"When will the operation take place?" the captain said nervously.

"That you do not need to know," the Al Qaeda boss replied firmly. "You will know when to implement the plan when Muhammad shows up for your flight." He handed the captain an envelope. "Give yourself another two weeks of vacation before going back on duty. Here is the flight plan. You need not ask any questions. You simply need to be able to fly it, understood?"

"Understood."

"Good, now I must leave Indonesia for a few days to attend a very important meeting. This operation will encompass many of our active groups, not just Al Qaeda and Iran, but even the upstarts in Syria and Iraq, ISIS," he said soberly. "All of our organizations are preparing the way for a greater entity; one that will wipe away the stain of Zion and Christianity throughout the world!"

"Allahu Akbar!"

CHAPTER 3: Another Day in the Office

A day after Hussein's meeting with Khallida, Jeremiah Slade, now a Company veteran, flew low over the Iraqi desert in a rattling old OV-10 Bronco. Slade hadn't changed, nor it seemed, had his companions. Over the interphone his friend Delta Force Captain Abe "Killer" Kincaid joked with his team.

"We'd like to thank the Delta Force for flying Spook Air! We hope you've enjoyed your flight into former Iraq; now the 7th century paradise named after the fetching Egyptian Goddess ISIS! There's some irony for you!"

Mentally shaking his head, Slade concentrated on maneuvering the twin turboprop Bronco low through the nighttime desert. The Bronco was a Special Forces mule. That meant there was nothing in the aircraft that wasn't required; no creature comforts whatsoever. The Bronco was so loud the two men in the cockpit and the four men in the back couldn't hear a thing over the roaring, rattling, shaking machine unless it was over the interphone. Looking like a cross between a pregnant P-38 and a monstrous insect it was perfect for these sorts of missions and Slade had a few thousand hours in it—all combat time.

That's how the Company normally used Slade, having him fly SEALS or Delta Force troops into hot spots and picking them up. However, over the past years the Company found Slade was more than just a pilot; he could be a useful and deadly field agent. Slade turned out to be a very instinctive and accomplished killer.

Today was a case-in-point. This was a "Cobra" mission; so named because their job was to hunt down leadership and remove them; cutting the proverbial head off the snake. The CIA, unlike Slade, was not averse to some black humor. His tasking read, "The mission is to interdict a meeting between ISIS, Al Qaeda and the Iranians. You and your partner Barret will be uninvited participants."

Barret was Slade's Barret 'Light-Fifty' sniper rifle. The Company had excavated hidden talents Slade never imagined he had. This was one of them. Slade was likely one of the top three shots on the planet and he never knew it.

"We should have been doing this a year ago before they ever ventured out of their stinkholes in Syria!" Killer commented.

"We're here now," Slade replied coolly.

Twenty minutes later the GPS told him they were approaching their insertion point: an abandoned village six miles from the target area. He picked out the silhouettes of his landmark hills through his night vision goggles, commonly called NVG's.

"Prepare for landing," Slade told the Delta Force team. "Strap in tight, it looks kind of rough."

"The new management doesn't fix potholes!"

Banking between the two hills and lining up on a relatively straight stretch of desert, a dirt road that led into the village, Slade prepared to land in what was now the first Islamic Caliphate since the Ottoman Empire.

"Hold onto your butt's guys!" Killer warned his team from the observer's seat in the Bronco. "You know how these Air Force guys land!"

"That's the Navy!" Slade corrected, pounding the desert into submission with the five ton Bronco and throwing the props into reverse. A cloud of dust and sand swirled in front of the machine, effectively hiding them.

He taxied down the narrow street and then around a ruined building. Slade eased the aircraft between that building and another, parking it in the sandy, rocky alley between them with the nose pointing back toward the street. He shut the engines down and switched off the multiple glass displays that the Bronco used for flight controls, navigation and weapons delivery.

With the systems powered down, the props stopped spinning and the aircraft grew silent except for the inevitable knocking of metal parts as they started to cool. The Deltas in back were already out of the plane, dragging a camouflage net up onto the roof of the abandoned mud and brick dwelling. They slung the net over top the Bronco, obscuring the aircraft from unfriendly eyes.

In five minutes the Deltas were ready. Killer asked Slade, "So how does it feels to be back in Iraq?"

"You're the one who got shot," the grim faced Slade reminded Killer.

"Are you sure, I thought that was Columbia?" Kincaid recalled with a shake of the head. "Damn, I'm losing track. I must be getting old."

"You're twenty-eight Killer," Slade growled, hefting the Barret over his shoulder. The "Light-Fifty" was anything but light, weighing in at almost a pound for each one of Jeremiah's years. He grunted perceptibly.

"You're coming up on forty grandpa; do you want someone to carry that schwein-stucker for you?"

The four Delta grunts chuckled.

"I didn't hear you complain when I hauled your ass out of country over my shoulder!" Slade retorted.

"Course not, I was unconscious!" Killer said dryly. Turning to his men he saw that they were ready and waiting for his word. His expression settled into the serious nature of their mission. People were about to die and they were in a hostile country. There would be no extraction. Their only expectation would be having their heads slowly sawed off by trench knives; all the gruesome details would be available to their loved ones on video.

"Okay ladies it's ten klicks to meet our contact. Let's go!" Killer waved them forward. They fanned out in a ragged patrol line, searching the hills and horizon with their NVG's; weapons carried comfortably ready at ready.

Two hours later they arrived at a house on the outskirts of a small village. The house was identified by a small infrared reflector mounted at the angle of the roof. It was invisible to the naked eye, which was the only safe way to mark a house in this very unsafe country. Still, they approached the house with care. Killer set up his two teams to provide covering fire in case he and Slade had to beat a hasty retreat.

"Our contact is a local named Sulla. He's a Sunni, so he's as safe as you can get and still be an Iraqi," Jake whispered. "He used to be very high up in Saddam's world. Now he's nobody again." They'd stopped at the ramshackle shed across from what served as a back door. The back windows were open. One of the curtains was drawn up. There was a light on. That was the signal.

Slade was wary. "He's got no reason to love us. We ruined his world."

"Maybe, but we got his two sons out of a Shia prison and we pay him ten thousand a year. He was set before ISIS came out of Syria. You think we put a crimp in things, these ISIS boys have the locals terrified. Sulla contacted us about this meeting between ISIS, Al Qaeda and the Iranians."

"What's he get in exchange?" Slade said.

"We've already got a new coalition Shia-Sunni government forming. Sulla is going to get his old job back and his family gets to move back to Bagdad," he said, blowing a silent whistle. "That's how things work out here."

Killer keyed his mike. "Okay, we're moving into the house."

They made their way quietly through the yard and into the house through the back door. The back room was a kitchen. The sound of a TV could be heard coming from the front room. There were two other ways into the kitchen beside the back door, the living room entrance and a dark hall leading to the bedrooms. Killer turned off the single light. Now the only illumination was from the room up front, the living room.

As Slade covered the back hall, Kincaid went to the window and gave a thumbs up signal. "Fox in the henhouse."

The Delta team covering the back of the house acknowledged. "Bravo copies; fox in the henhouse."

"Alpha has the front of the house. There's no activity."

"Fox is making contact," Kincaid informed them.

Slade still had his Barret slung over his shoulder but he had a KRISS Super-V for anything that required up close and personal combat. The .45 caliber Bullpup packed a big punch

28

at close range. He checked the dark hall with his flip down NVG's—nothing. He gave Killer a thumbs up.

The Delta Force commander nodded and stepped up to the living room entry. For a moment there was no sound but the TV. Then Killer said quietly, "Salaam Sulla!"

There was an excited gasp from the living room. Slade noted a woman's voice as well as at least one child, probably a girl. Words were exchanged and Killer backed into the kitchen. He motioned for Slade to join him. He did, positioning himself so that his back was to the kitchen counter and he was facing the hallway.

Sulla turned the light on and came into the kitchen with his hands held out, showing that he held no weapons. He was not a tall man, but he was stoutly built. By the looks of him, Sulla could handle himself. He was not some desk hugging bureaucrat.

To Slade's surprise, Sulla came in with his family. Joining him were his wife, two young men and a little girl. Slade swallowed hard, confiding his anger to some deep, dark place. The mother and the little girl, maybe twelve, were both horribly burned on their faces by what could only be acid.

Killer had filled him in previously, but seeing it caused a visceral reaction—rage. Sulla's wife was a school teacher in a girl's school. Her daughter was her pupil. Then came ISIS. It was the fundamentalist answer to women's rights in the wonderful world of Sharia. Slade couldn't help but think, "So much for glass ceilings, reproductive rights and the "War on Women.""

Sulla smiled. "Hello Captain Kincaid! You see, I bring my loved ones so that you may know that you are safe here in my home."

"We appreciate that," Killer told him. By bringing his family Sulla put them in the crossfire of any treachery. It was a big chunk of collateral.

Sulla sat down heavily. His youngest girl clutched his arm. Her skin might be burned but her eyes were alive; she was both frightened and curious. Slade didn't know if she was frightened of them or something else, probably both.

The Iraqi was blunt. "How long we are safe is anyone's guess. No one is safe with those murderers on the rampage, the ISIS swine!" Sulla's anger and disgust were apparent. "They soil the name of the Sunni even worse than the Al Qaeda scum! Sadam would have nothing to do with such animals. They are so much worse than he was, so much worse even than his sons! Now they are rampaging against Kurd, Sunni and Shia alike!" He hugged his daughter and nodded to his wife. "They are animals!"

"We've heard some things about them," Killer said carefully. "There are reports of mass executions, mass beheadings, and mass rapes—are they true?"

"They are all true," Sulla nodded. "Anyone found with the army, the police, anyone who might have worked for Malaki or the Americans—no offense intended—is summarily executed. Even Shias who took no part in any of this are being herded out, loaded into trucks and shot. That's not the worst."

Sulla closed his eyes as if in pain. When he spoke it was with a thick, guttural voice laden with emotion. He showed them pictures on his iPad. "When they took one of the bigger towns they took exception to the playground for children. It wasn't Allah's way, so they said, so they beheaded the children and set their tiny heads on stakes around the playground. It was a warning to the other children. It's barbaric, even for the Al Qaeda scum!"

Sulla frowned, paging through his iPad. He found what he wanted and handed it to Kincaid, saying nervously, "That's just the beginning. They are truly demented these ISIS pigs. They are servants of the Devil; it is the only way to describe them."

Those were strong words coming from a Muslim.

Kincaid looked at the iPad, turning it so that Slade could see it as well. It was a photo of a poster stapled to a telephone pole on a dusty street. The poster informed all inhabitants of the town that they were now part of a new Caliphate and thus subject to Sharia Law. In addition they were expected to support the jihad. Specifically, all unmarried girls between the ages of twelve and thirty were to be brought to public

30

buildings so that they could be married off to the jihadi warriors. If they failed to comply the full weight of Sharia would fall upon their shoulders.

Sulla held his little girl, telling the two Americans, "So under pain of death fathers are to take their little girls, just like my darling Adara, to them so that those animals can rape them! I cannot believe it! I simply cannot believe it!"

Kincaid downloaded the contents of the iPad to his phone, but told Sulla, "We'll do what we can, Sulla. However, you know as well as I that the current administration is not eager to interfere militarily—in anything. The chances of American boots on the ground in force is nil." Killer sighed, and shrugged, "This is all you're going to get. It's your ball game Sulla. I wish I could do more."

"Then the President is simply going to allow this caliphate, this terrorist state to exist?" the Iraqi exclaimed, clearly dumbfounded.

"We're going to supply the airpower and Special Forces support, but we're hoping that the locals will provide the muscle on the ground—you're just as good as these guys—you'll be fighting for your homes and families," Killer said gravely.

"Our men need to learn anger instead of fear, but you are right, we must fight these devils ourselves."

"My advice is that you get your family to Bagdad. That's still the safest place in country; or I could get you out of the country seeing as you've been an asset."

"I will not leave Iraq to these animals—these degenerates who want jihad for the sake of jihad—all they care about is blood, plunder and rape. I must fight them in any way I can, even if I spend my sons and daughters. If I can't raise my children in a country without fear then I must fight for that country."

"We will do all we can," the Delta commander repeated. "That's why we're going to interdict that meeting tomorrow. We hope to isolate ISIS. We don't want them making any deals with the Iranians or even Al Qaeda. The goal is to build distrust between ISIS and the other players and then systematically take out their leaders."

Sulla turned to Slade and looked at him and the Barret slung over his shoulder. Smiling, he said, "So you brought your father to do that work for you?"

Slade smiled, but it was a deadly, mirthless twist of his thin lips. It was not a pleasant expression.

"He may be old Sulla, but he's also one of the best operatives in the world," the Delta Force commander reassured the Iraqi.

"I am only joking my friend," Sulla said, patting Slade's arm tentatively. "I have a great deal riding on you Americans. We all do."

Slade's expression softened. He nodded toward the little girl. "I have a niece Adara's age," he told Sulla. "I'll do everything I can."

"I do not doubt that, but when it is all said and done we must defeat this scum ourselves," Sulla agreed. "With Allah's help we will do so."

Killer nodded, but he reminded his host, "The longer we stay the more danger you'll be in Sulla, so let's get down to business."

Sulla took back the iPad and paged through to another screen. Laying the tablet on the table, he showed them a diagram of the village. "Here is the house where the meeting will be taking place. It will occur tomorrow at three, tea time, in the back room," he said, pointing out the various tactical situations.

"The house is on the outskirts of town, but they will not have many guards. This is necessary because if you brought two rival factions like ISIS and Al Qaeda in close proximity you would be guaranteed a bloodbath; the hotheads would egg each other on until there was a full blown war. That would be good for us but very bad for their plans. Therefore there will be only four guards apiece. The ISIS guards will cover the street entrance, the Al Qaeda guards will be on the back terrace."

"And the Iranians?"

"They will stay in their vehicle!" Sulla said with a laugh.

"What's over here, do the sheppard's graze their flocks in these fields?" Killer asked, pointing to the open area beyond the veranda.

"No, no one uses those fields," he said, his finger thumping on an area about a kilometer south of the house. "This is a low ridge with a dirt road beyond. The road goes south but is seldom used even by the shepherds." He glanced up at Slade and his Barret. "It is a perfect spot for someone with a nice long rifle and a good eye!"

"About twelve hundred yards—perfect," Slade said.

Killer held up his hand and his face turned suddenly grave.

Slade heard Alpha report over their comlink. "We have a small group of civilians approaching the house. Two adults and a bunch of kids; it looks like a family. They're all worked up but we can't tell why."

"There's nothing else?" Killer demanded.

"Nothing—hold on—it looks like a group of Tango's are entering the north side of the village about two hundred meters behind them. There are a dozen Tangos armed with automatic weapons, but I don't see any support trucks or troops. They might be a patrol."

"Keep me informed," Killer ordered. He told Sulla what they'd seen. There was the unmistakable sound of voices outside the front of the house and a sudden, urgent pounding on the door. Sulla's wife had gone to the door and opened it. Sulla turned off the kitchen light and rushed to the front room.

Killer and Slade melted into the shadows, listening to the strained voices of men, women and children from the front of the house. The conversation was too fast and agitated for them to discern much, but Sulla returned a moment later with a man.

"Things are not good," he informed them. "This is Hamad. He and his family are friends, Shia from the next village. The ISIS animals are raiding the homes, killing the men and raping the women and girls they find regardless of who they are— they have a Fatwa from a Saudi cleric as their justification— Allah help us! The Shia and Christians are being slaughtered.

"Hamad fled here, hoping to find refuge with us as my family did with him when Malaki's people were rooting out former Sadam supporters." He wiped his brow, obviously nervous. "I don't even know if I'm safe with these scum! What are we to do?"

"There's only a dozen of them so far," Killer told him. "We can't afford to compromise the meeting tomorrow. So whatever we do we'll have to do it quietly. For now, keep them here and keep them quiet. We'll play it by ear."

As the refugee family settled in the dark of the kitchen, looking hopefully at the two Americans. Killer got back on the line with his squads, keeping tally of the ISIS group's movement. The news wasn't good. "They must have marked where the family was going, because they're coming here."

"What do you want me to do?" Sulla asked.

"If you can talk them out of this it would save a lot of trouble," Killer sighed.

Sulla went over to a cabinet and got out a Quran. He took a deep breath and sighed. "I will try."

"Don't worry Sulla," Killer told him. "We've got your back. Try to bribe them. Make the best deal you can. If they don't want to deal then we'll take care of this the old fashioned way—permanently."

Killer talked to his squads over the radio, "We'll cover the front yard through the windows. I want Alpha high and Bravo down low covering the flanks and rear."

"Alpha has a good view from the roof across the street," reported the team leader.

"Bravo ready," reported the other team leader.

Moving through the new arrivals, their eyes wide with surprise and fear at the sight of Killer and Slade armed to the teeth, they chose a window inside the small front bedroom. It was just to the right of the front door. Slade went to the south side of the window, opening the curtains just enough so that he got a good view of the yard and the street.

He could hear the ISIS group approaching, and then he saw them, advancing south toward the house. They were either undisciplined or more likely they feared nothing from the villagers. They were talking and yelling but they weren't paying any attention to their flanks or the rooftops. Every door and window was closed. The fear was palpable.

The first few terrorists pointed at the house and crossed over the yard to the door. Slade caught only a little of what they were saying, but the AK-47's made their intentions clear. Before they got to the door Sulla opened it and met them outside holding the Quran.

"You're hiding some of the Shia swine in your home," one of them said tritely. "Give them up; it's no use hiding them."

"By this holy book you shall not have them!" Sulla told them firmly, holding up the Quran. "They are Muslim, loyal to Allah, why are you pursuing them? What wrong have they done you?"

"They are Shia dogs, do we need another reason?" said the first.

A second terrorist motioned at Sulla with his rifle, and said, "Bring them outside. We will shoot them and be on our way; we have many more to track down tonight. Do it quickly or it will mean trouble for you and your family, not just the Shia!"

CHAPTER 4: It only Gets Worse

The ISIS terrorists were insistent, but Sulla stood his ground waving the Quran in their faces. "I cannot give up my guests! They are Muslims. They sought my aid in good faith. I would be violating all we hold dear."

"They are going to die!" the terrorist told him firmly, motioning his men forward, shouting to two of them, "Go around back and see that none escape."

Two of the terrorists headed around the corner of the house to the back door. Slade heard Killer whisper in his mike, "Bravo, two Tangos coming to you—quietly!"

"Bravo!"

As the rest of the ISIS party approached the front door, Sulla tried desperately to bribe them. That caught the terrorist's attention. "They are a middle aged man, his young son, wife and three girls; what possible threat could they be to you? I will pay for their safety!"

The terrorists talked it over amongst themselves. While they did so Slade heard Bravo team report in a matter-of-fact way, "Tangos are down."

At that moment the ISIS party made their decision. Four terrorists pushed past Sulla and forced the door open. They were met by screams and shouts. The head terrorist told Sulla, "We will take your money for the lives of the woman and girls. They will satisfy my men, but we will let them live. The man and boy we will shoot!"

"You cannot shoot the boy!" Sulla objected, tearing at his beard. "How can you say such a thing; he is only fourteen!"

"We have fighters already his age," the ISIS terrorist said, yanking Sulla out of the way as his men shoved open the door. "Besides, what do you care; he is Shia? Do you have some love for these dogs?"

Slade heard yelling in the next room, screams from the women and girls, and guttural curses from the ISIS thugs. Calm and cool, Killer's voice came over his headset, "Easy boys, no one makes a move until they get outside and we have a clear line of fire. I don't want a firefight inside the residence with all these women and girls—steady now. Shooter's got the triggermen. Everyone on his mark!"

The KRISS Super-V was already steadied in the corner of the window. The room behind him was dark, so Slade was invisible to those outside. He had a perfect view of the entire area in front of the house through his red-dot sight. It wasn't a scope, but Slade didn't need one at twenty meters. He could have placed a round up the lead bastard's nose without leaving a mark.

The ISIS terrorists dragged the man and boy outside. The father was pleading for the life of his son. The boy was skinny and gangly at that age; awkward and stumbling. He was in shock. His eyes were round and staring at the ground, not registering what was happening. For Slade, his deep seated rage turned him to ice—everything slowed down—he was in complete control. The entire scene unfolded as if he were a movie director editing the film, frame-by-frame, picking his time and his spot.

The boy was thrust to his shaking knees, falling almost prone before the ISIS scum yanked him viciously upward, shouting, "On your knees boy! I want your father to see you die!"

The father's voice was one long drawn out wail. Every pair of ISIS eyes looked at the boy, lusting for the slaughter of the innocent. A short rumble of automatic fire split the night air. It was just a burst, a split second long, and the boy flinched, his hands spasmodically jerking toward the back of his head as a spray of blood splattered over him.

The blood erupted from a ragged hole in the ISIS thug's face. Three forty-five caliber slugs slammed through the sweaty, greasy flesh at the narrow isthmus of the uni-brow, punching into the festering, diseased brain and blowing out the back of his skull. The material not exiting the crater in the terrorist's head sloshed back forward in a fountain of blood and chewed up brains, exiting through the hole like sludge from a sewer pipe.

Before the terrorist's knees began to buckle, Slade had already shifted his sights to the ISIS thug holding the father. The KRISS finished its slight recoil, bucking up almost imperceptibly thanks to its delayed blowback mechanism. He centered on the shocked expression of the terrorist and pumped three bullets right up his nose.

The terrorist's head snapped back, certainly breaking his neck, and he collapsed like a rag doll, dropping his pistol. The father reacted instinctively, leaping across the space and tackling his son, smothering the boy beneath his own body to protect him from the incoming hail of bullets.

That fire came swift and deadly.

To his consternation, Slade didn't have an opportunity to get in another shot. The Deltas were strikingly efficient and deadly, dropping the other eight terrorists in short, concentrated bursts of fire. The firefight was over in seconds. When the last body dropped to the ground Killer's calm voice penetrated Slade's earpiece.

"Alpha is everyone down?"

"No more Tangos," Alpha said calmly.

"All right," Killer said tersely, "let's get these bodies in the back. We don't want ISIS to know any of this happened."

Slade walked back out to the front room. Both families were huddled together, sobbing, praying; happy to be alive but frayed. As the Deltas dragged the bodies out back, Sulla was already speaking to Killer, his voice still heavy with excitement.

"When ISIS finds out these men were killed here they will slaughter everyone in the village—everyone!"

"Now Sulla, we'll put them in the desert," Kincaid told him. "No one will find them for days—if ever. You're going to have to bug out by then anyway."

Sulla argued that his neighbors would have to face the repercussions, but surprisingly it was one of the neighbors who provided a solution. He'd watched the firefight from his window and hurried over to Sulla's afterwards, afraid for the same reasons.

"I drove from the village north of us today, just ahead of the ISIS dogs. There is a place only a few kilometers from here on the road where we can get rid of the bodies," he said eagerly. "No one will ever know they attacked our village and died."

Slade wondered why today was any different than any other day on the road, but Killer just shrugged. Sulla and his neighbor got their cars and the Deltas loaded up the bodies. The Deltas and Slade piled in while Sulla's family packed.

"Don't worry, the ISIS scum won't bother us anymore tonight," the neighbor said. "These pigs were after this family. The rest are too busy raping and celebrating—some warriors of Allah!"

Killer was riding in the front bench seat with Sulla. The back seat of his white Renault had four bodies stuffed into it. When Sulla and his family fled they were going to have a disgusting time of it. The ISIS thugs stank in life but dead they smelled like the Devil himself crapped on them.

The neighbor drove an old battered station wagon. It was a rocking, rolling ride as Slade rode on top, lying prone in the luggage rack. One Delta rode in the front seat with the neighbor and the refugee father, leaving Slade and three others on the roof, two facing front and two facing the rear. The back was filled with dead ISIS terrorists; stacked like firewood.

Slade grimaced at the Delta Force soldier next to him, a twenty year old kid nick-named Johnny Bravo. Bravo grinned from ear to ear. "Didn't you ever want to do this as a kid?"

The sniper gave him a sour look, and answered in his best deadpan voice; that is, his normal tone of voice, "What are you talking about Johnny; we didn't have cars when I was a kid."

The Delta's laughed.

The heavily laden station wagon led the way, bouncing across the pothole scarred road. After ten minutes they slowed down. The headlights groped ahead in the darkness. Slade peered through the night, picking out a rough area next to the road. Something was in the shallow ditch; it stretched on for about twenty or thirty yards, it was hard to tell.

They stopped. The night was eerily quiet. There was only a slight desert breeze, pleasantly cool after the heat of the day. The breeze carried the stench of death.

Slade hopped off the top of the station wagon to see what it was in the ditch. Switching on the rifle mounted flashlight caused Slade's already stern expression to grow positively grim. There were bodies in the ditch, dozens and dozens of bodies. Killer went to one of them and then another, examining them. He waved Slade over.

Slade felt his stomach turn as he got closer. Killer pointed out, "They weren't even bound when they were shot. They look like they laid themselves face down and let the scumbags machine gun them to death."

"They didn't even put up a fight," Slade said harshly.

"They died like sheep," Killer agreed, standing up. He jerked his thumb back toward the cars. "Our Tangos probably took part in the killing. Let's hide them amongst the men they murdered. Put them at the bottom; no one will ever know we did them."

The Deltas hid the bodies, but halfway through the grisly chore they got a surprise. A trooper called Killer over. The commander was talking with Sulla and Slade.

"What is it?" he asked bluntly, stomping over to the pile of bodies. "You better not be showing me some of their handiwork! I mean, I've seen everything, but these guys are the sickest bunch of bastards on the planet!"

"No sir," the Deltas said, visibly excited, "We got a live one!"

Killer hurried over and Slade followed. Sure enough, two Deltas were extricating a boy from the bottom of the pile. He was a skinny teenager, Slade couldn't tell how old, maybe thirteen or fourteen. He wasn't strong enough to burrow his way out from under several layers of dead men.

The boy was shaking when they finally got him clear. The Deltas gave him some water and he started talking. Neither Slade nor Killer could keep up with the boy's Arabic. He spat out the story in a frantic spasm of shocked terror.

When he was done, Sulla told them, "ISIS rounded up everyone in the village who was from the military or the police. They broke into the homes, killing any who didn't follow their orders or let them rape their wives and daughters. The boy watched his mother and younger sister get raped—he thinks his sister must be dead because she was so young and so many men brutalized her—Allah watch over her!"

Sulla wiped his eyes, continuing with difficulty. "When there weren't enough police they simply gathered all of them up, men and boys as young as twelve. They herded the men out into the street and picked out the Christians. The rest they ordered into line and marched them to the trucks. They loaded themselves in the trucks and then they were driven out here, lined up in the ditch and told to lie down. Then the shooting started."

"Bastards!" Slade cursed.

Killer sighed and grimaced, "We got about fifty or sixty men and boys back there—I've got to report this. I mean, this needs to stop. ISIS is on the offensive and out in the open going from village to village."

Slade shook his head, "B-52's loaded with cluster bombs and the problem disappears."

"They'll never go for it; it sounds too much like war," Killer said scathingly. "Unfortunately, it'll have to wait until after the meeting tomorrow—that takes priority."

"Wait—what about this man's son?" Sulla asked, pointing to the refugee father who was picking through the bodies, searching for someone.

Killer nodded, and then he turned to Slade. "He's searching for his eldest son. The son was shot while they were fleeing, but he was still alive."

"And he left his son back there?" Slade whispered incredulously.

"Yeah, damndest thing isn't it?" Killer said. "Anyway, he wants us to go back to the village and take a look. Maybe he's still alive."

"It's a little late for parental concern," Slade replied coldly.

41

"We'll go take a look, but if there's any signs of ISIS still in town we're out of here," Killer said. "I can't compromise the mission."

An hour later they were in a ghost town; a movie set from Hell. Bodies, furniture and trash were strewn over the streets and barren yards. Burning houses lit the place up with an evil, flickering glow. The street was lined with dozens of men and women—even children—hung on makeshift crosses, trees and telephone poles; the ISIS terrorists crucified the village Christians. It seemed as if no one was alive, and indeed, that's what they found when the father led them to his house.

The door hung half on its hinges. The family's main room, where they watched TV, entertained relatives and otherwise lived their lives was a room of horrors. The refugee father saw his son bound to a chair, slumped over—dead.

On further inspection, death was a release. The young man was clearly tortured. The father was distraught, asking, "Why, why would they do this? Even when I was a soldier in the Iran-Iraq war we never treated our prisoners this way. We'd shoot them—yes—but quickly, mercifully! Why would they do this; I don't understand?"

All Slade and Kincaid could do was leave. They didn't understand this either—any of it.

CHAPTER 5: The Operation

Abdullereda was having second thoughts. He felt like a trapped animal, but there was really very little he could do about it. He wasn't dealing with a local gang of thugs. This was Al Qaeda. Any squeamishness on his part would result in his ignoble and painful death and the death of his estranged family as well. He had no illusions as to who he was dealing with.

The would-be terrorist found himself sweating, shaking, opening a bottle of whiskey—one hidden deep in his cabinet and only brought out when the blinds to his windows were shuttered—he didn't remember how much he drank.

Sometime the next day, feeling miserable and guilty, Abdullereda found himself in front of the American Embassy. He didn't like America; he hated Americans and everything they stood for. However, America was perhaps the only place in the world that might take him in, perhaps even his family. The Great Satan was his only way out of this devilish conspiracy.

"Can I help you sir?" the marine guard asked him.

Funny, he thought, how the American's were always polite, even with people who hated them; especially with people who hated them. Far from being "Ugly Americans," Abdullereda found Westerners were always ready to help; the more you hated them the more eager they were to spend money on you trying to make you like them. Strangely, despite their depravity, they were less decadent than the imams who railed against them, imams who preached that rape of women and girls was all right so long as it was in the name of Allah; imams, who on one hand whipped the crowds into frenzies to hang or stone gay men to death, and on the other hand encouraged their Holy Warriors to bugger each other when there weren't any women to rape.

The more whiskey he drank the more these thoughts infiltrated Abdullereda's besotted mind. He wondered, could it be because this was American whiskey? Was that why he suddenly doubted his course of action? If it were, then the Americans were clever.

So Abdullereda stood there dumb, with a torrent of thoughts going through his head, and the marine repeated the question. "Can I help you sir?"

"I want asylum," he prepared to say, but out of the corner of his eye he caught sight of two men who seemed to have no other business than to stare at him. Al Qaeda! The shock jarred him out of his original intention and right into self-preservation. He had enough self-control not to look at them, and instead pretend to be talking with the marine. He shouted in broken English, "What are you doing here; you're not wanted."

Abdullereda began to rant at the marines, who simply watched impassively. That spurred real anger and Abdullereda was able to carry off his act convincingly—or so he hoped—finishing by spitting at the marines. They levelled their M-16's at him and Abdullereda wisely backed away.

Striding purposefully, angrily down the street, he passed the two men without even looking at them, muttering to himself. One of the men called out to him from behind.

"Brother, wait for us!"

Hussein froze, looking back at them, and trying not to show he was frightened. Indeed, he was terrified they'd found him out. "Salaam brothers, salaam!" he said trembling.

"You seem troubled brother, perhaps we can help?" said one of the men. His voice was friendly, but it had an edge to it.

"I'm sorry, do I know you?" he replied carefully.

"No, but we know you as a brother," the man said.

"Come, you need some tea! That will settle you down!" the other man said, guiding Hussein firmly toward the café across the street from the embassy.

Khallida was sitting there at one of the outside tables. He smiled that gruesome Death's head grin of his.

"Salaam brother Hussein, salaam!"

"Salaam brother Khallida!"

Khallida motioned for Abdullereda to sit, but it was more like the two Al Qaeda men forced him into the chair.

Khallida reminded Hussein, "The captain of a Malaysian A380 should be careful not to draw attention to himself; especially from the Americans. They are ignorant and weak, but they are still dangerous. It is unwise to highlight yourself."

"I understand," Abdullereda sighed, sensing their suspicion. It was a dangerous moment for him and for his family. That spurred a thought. Hussein he got out his phone. Safrina sent him pictures of his girls—that might save him. He showed Khallida the three girls, all in Western type clothing. "I am so angry! The Americans polluted the minds of my family, driving them from me! Look at my daughters in American blue jeans—blue jeans—like they were saloon prostitutes! I burn for vengeance; holy vengeance!"

Khallida's voice became more soothing. Even his grizzled minions looked upon Abdullereda with what might be construed as compassion. He said, "We understand all too well; thus the need for the warriors of jihad to steel themselves to the accomplishment of their mission. We have only two choices: martyrdom and paradise or failure and the fires of Hell. There is no escape for the holy warrior."

"Nor should there be," Abdullereda lied.

"That's the spirit," Khallida said with his hideous smile. "Come, we will have tea with you and then walk you home. It's the least we can do for a brother."

Abdullereda knew better than to argue, or even appear to argue. He simply nodded and drank tea with them. When he reached his home he knew what he had to do. Khallida was right. There was no turning back. He would never have a chance to escape again. The possibility of returning to his old life, reconciling with his wife and starting anew was nil; he'd end up on a beheading video alongside his family.

The only way to escape the Hell he'd boxed himself into was to do the Devil's bidding. He sat down at his computer and Abdullereda returned to flying flight simulations to dozens of islands in the Chagos Archipelago.

Three days went by. Abdullereda was fastidious, flying hundreds of approaches to the small airfields carved onto the atolls. After checking with Khallida, he put himself back on flight status. Malaysia Airlines happily assigned him a Beijing flight.

On the day of the flight, Abdullereda went through his pre-flight routine, packing his bags and driving to the airport with a firm resolve to do nothing that would highlight himself. He was resigned.

When he got to work and entered flight operations, a young man greeted Hussein. It was his first officer, Jaren. Hussein had flown dozens of trips with him. Jaren was a Christian, not unusual in Malaysia, and had the cheery disposition and chronic fatigue of a brand new father.

"Well, how does it look Jaren?" Abdullereda asked, glancing at the paperwork.

"Nothing much to worry about, just some turbulence over Vietnam from the evening thunderstorms, nothing out of the ordinary." He handed the captain the flight plan with a smile, "Suri is the lead flight attendant. She's already talking about what a good time you two had in Beijing last time you flew there!"

"She's a sweet girl," he smiled sheepishly. "Yes, we had a good time!" They both laughed, but then Abdullereda saw an extra name on the manifest. A thrill of fear coursed through his veins. His smile turned to a frown of confusion. "Who is this?"

"Oh, we have a deadheading pilot," Jaren told him. "He's at the plane already."

The name wasn't familiar, Abdullereda calmed down. There were always pilots deadheading around the system, replacing pilots who got sick during trips or gaps in coverage for crews. It wasn't Muhammad, so this didn't mean anything.

Forcing himself back into the routine, he asked, "So how's the new baby Jaren?"

"I'm hoping to finally get some sleep on this layover," he admitted.

"I'll take care of the girls then; you're still married and in love!" Abdullereda laughed.

After going over the paperwork, checking the weather, signing for the aircraft and approving the fuel load and flight plan, the captain handed the stack of papers to the first officer and picked up his hat.

"Let's go!"

The terminal at Kuala Lumpur was a bright, airy and incredibly busy place of steel and glass. As the twelfth busiest airport in the world it fit in with the tall modern skyscrapers of the city but contrasted sharply with the squalor away from the financial district.

Similarly the airport didn't fit the passengers. While there were men and women in business suits a plenty the majority of passengers were the shabbily dressed and poorly washed masses setting off on might be the only trip of their lives to visit relatives in China, Indonesia, India and any other place on the planet. Fifty years earlier Malaysia had virtually no ties to the outside world, now it was trying to become a player.

Abdullereda approached the gate with an easy manner, looking forward to the boring, easy flight to Beijing. There was the usual busy atmosphere of the passengers waiting to board and the customer service agents trying to deal with their innumerable questions, many of them spoken in Chinese or broken English since most of the Chinese didn't speak the many different languages and dialects of Malaysia.

The senior agent stopped working with her Chinese customer in order to show Hussein the final manifests. "Good evening captain, you will have five hundred and twenty-seven passengers tonight. Everything is on time so far." She held out the documents.

"Thank you," he smiled, reaching for the paperwork. He looked beyond her to survey the passengers. There were a lot of Chinese, in fact the majority of the passengers were Chinese. He was about to comment about that when he marked two familiar faces. The two Middle Eastern men stared at him with coal black eyes; their expressions grave with intent. It was the two men who accosted him at the

47

American Embassy a few days ago; the two men with Khallida. They must be the Iranians!

Hussein started. It must be coincidence, he lied to himself. They might be travelling to Beijing to meet with their Turkic Uighur counterparts. Yes, that must be it.

"You also have a deadheader sir," she told him, pointing to a man in uniform. A shudder coursed down Abdullereda's spine when the deadheader went over and talked with the Iranians. The deadheader was none other than Khallida's man, Muhammad.

"Is everything all right captain?" the gate agent questioned, a concerned look in her eyes. "You just turned so pale."

The moment was upon him, and there was nothing to do but go with it. He snatched the manifest from the agent and walked into the jetway without answering her question.

His footsteps thumping in his ears, blood rushing to his head, Abdullereda had to gather himself, to focus on the minutia of the job. He didn't look ahead, that was too hard; he had to concentrate on every aspect of his job no matter how routine.

"Hello Captain Hussein, nice to see you again," said a woman's voice.

Abdullereda looked up and saw Suri. She smiled knowingly at him. The recollection of their time together chilled his blood. Soon, this sweet, attractive twenty-eight year old woman with her whole life before her would be slowly choking to death.

"Stop it!" he scolded himself silently. There was no point in thinking about it!

He forced a smile. "Good evening Suri, good to see you too." Hussein found refuge in his routine. "It's going to be five hours and fifty-three minutes. Weather should not be a factor but there's a chance for some turbulence over Vietnam, the normal things. We'll wait a few hours for our meals but coffee would be nice."

Footsteps followed behind. He looked back to see Jaren with the deadheader coming up behind—he'd completely forgotten about them. He pointed back at the deadheader, and started off to the cockpit, saying, "He's coming along so take good care of him!"

The extra pilot smiled at Suri, "Don't worry about me, I'll just sit up front tonight."

"What, all that way?" Suri asked. Pilot's as a rule didn't want anything to do with the cockpit if it wasn't to fly the airplane, especially on a long flight. "Wouldn't you rather sleep? We have seats in the back."

"I'll be fine, thanks," he said, following Abdullereda and the first officer up front.

The captain listened to the exchange, but did not interfere. He led the way to the cockpit. Passing the galley, he exchanged pleasantries with the flight attendant in charge of their meals and repeated his order for coffee. The important part of the flight being taken care of—getting the coffee going—he entered the cockpit and stowed his bag to the left, beside the first observer's seat.

Sliding into the captain's chair, Abdullereda started to load the flight management computer, the "box," entering the flight plan, aircraft weight and takeoff data. The printer started spitting out the information he requested over the ACARS, the aircraft's datalink system: weather, takeoff data, aircraft loading and clearances amongst other things.

As he did the preflight programing the first officer left the cockpit with his flashlight to do the walk around inspection. That left Abdullereda alone with Muhammad.

"You seemed nervous when we got to the gate," Muhammad said softly.

Abdullereda snapped angrily, "How many times do you think I've done this before?"

Muhammad reddened, admitting, "Never, of course; all right I get it. Just be yourself."

"Is there anything special I should be doing?" Hussein mentioned, turning back and punching data in the box.

"No, keep everything normal," he replied. "Everything should go just as it always does. Don't do anything you wouldn't normally do."

"What about Jaren? He's not in on this is he?"

"A Christian?" Muhammad exclaimed softly. "Are you kidding? Of course not!"

"What are we going to do about him?"

"That's why I'm riding up here," Muhammad said.

"What are you going to do with him; he's an innocent kid," Abdullereda said with a hint of fear in his voice.

"He's not Muslim; he's not innocent," Muhammad replied roughly. "None of them are!"

"By Allah!" Abdullereda felt his resolve weakening.

"Calm down!" the terrorist warned, but he stopped short of saying more as someone was coming up from the galley.

Suri came up to the cockpit with their coffee. She looked at them with a worried frown. "Is everything all right? You two look so serious. Captain are you feeling well?"

"Just tired Suri, just tired, that's all," he said quickly, taking the proffered coffee.

The deadheader thanked her as well, trying his best to seem like everything was fine.

"You're sure that's all?" She didn't look convinced.

Abdullereda pointed to the instrument displays, and explained, "We had a momentary malfunction in a hydraulic pump. It would have delayed us. Last week the company docked a captain a month's pay for too many late departures! Fortunately, I recycled the pump and it came back on. We're fine now; we're good to go!"

"A month's pay!" she started. "That would make me nervous too! Okay, as long as everything is all right. Let me know if you need anything else!"

"Thank you Suri!"

She left. The captain sighed and wiped the sweat from his forehead.

"Well handled captain," Muhammad nodded. He seemed as relieved as the captain. "Remember, everything should go as normally as possible."

Abdullereda chuckled grimly to himself, "Yes, like you know what normal is up here!" The captain's momentary sense of superiority swept over him and then disappeared as quickly as a surfer's missed wave, leaving him frustrated and anxious. Whatever his technical superiority over the Al Qaeda thug it was the uneducated terrorist who controlled the situation and Abdullereda's life.

He finished programming the route. In the alternate routine, called "Route 2" in the Flight Management Computer, Abdullereda was able to program his mission. This gave him the ability to switch from one route to the other by executing a few keystrokes.

He trembled. A few keystrokes and his life would be irrevocably different. No—he reminded himself—that wasn't true. As soon as he contacted these people his life was set upon an inevitable course. He had no choice. His only solace was that his children would be taken care of, no, he couldn't think of that now. The Al Qaeda agent was noticing his nervousness. Fortunately, before he spoke up Jaren entered the cockpit again.

"I hate to break up your little plot but the jig is up," he said seriously. His eyes narrowed and he pointed to Abdullereda. "I know all about it captain; I know everything."

CHAPTER 6: The Play

In Tehran, Iran, as Slade caught some sleep, nestled beneath a bush with his Barret, and as Hussein slept prior to his flight to Beijing, the personal envoy of American President Oetari waited for his meeting with the President of Iran. Freddy Waters knew President Oetari's mother back in the sixties, when they ran around with radicals and protested the war. Decades later Freddy became a sort of older brother and mentor to the young Oetari, showing up now and again to tell young Patra of the struggle, smoking joints and instructing him on the rules of the game for radicals. Now Freddy was in Iran on business for his protégé, the president.

President Aliaabaadi of Iran walked into the well-appointed room. He was tall and gangly, striking many as a sort of comedic caricature of the American President Lincoln. He thought of himself in the same manner, a great man, ever since he stormed the US Embassy in Iran and kidnapped the Americans. That moment crystalized his future.

Aliaabaadi had a taste for power. Unfortunately, he wasn't educated in the right manner to go via the religious road, he got into the university only because his father worked for the Americans. He was thought of as a scrub by his fellow Iranians, an Arab, not a Persian. In 1979 he betrayed his only friends, taking them hostage, and that got him noticed. The betrayal was the perfect springboard for a political career. So politics it was.

After the necessary pleasantries, Waters was blunt and crass. "Mr. President, the nuclear issue is a media generated problem. Frankly, we don't really give a damn whether you have nuclear weapons or not." His expression showed that he meant it. "You have your own reasons for having them—fine. The president' opinion is that when Iran does acquire nuclear capability it will balance the power in the Middle East. However, we need political cover."

"Yes, I imagine that would make your Democratic contributors in New York angry," Aliaabaadi replied, sipping his tea and sitting down, looking rather like a complicated folding chair while doing so. "He's got his second term, but Oetari likes to raise money and these New York Jews will think twice before showering him with gold if I do attain these weapons—which of course is not my intention—although it is my right."

Aliaabaadi grinned and sipped noisily.

"Half the Zionists in New York don't give a damn about what happens in Israel," Waters said brusquely, ignoring the shudder that ran through the president's angular frame every time he cursed. He sipped his own tea, wishing he could somehow slip a bit of scotch into it to spice it up. "That's not a concern. We'd like to come up with a deal that will push this down the road past the Mid-term elections."

"I want the sanctions off for a year," Aliaabaadi said firmly.

"That is consistent with the president's wishes as well," Freddy nodded. "We will continue to promote a deal, a deal which will move incrementally forward. However, we would like something more concrete; something that will shut the conservatives up."

"Such as?" Aliaabaadi said, his eyes almost disappearing beneath his bushy eyebrows.

"One of the sticking points in the negotiations is the amount of enriched Uranium you possess; Uranium that is enriched but still not to the standards of being weapons grade."

Aliaabaadi nodded and picked up his phone. "Please send in Doctor Feruud." Turning back to Freddy he sighed, "You touch on a very sensitive subject. The only manner in which we can proceed is with inspectors—correct?"

"Unless we can come up with a better mechanism," Freddy admitted. This was one subject where he was legitimate. Freddy hated nuclear weapons. He had no problems with the violence of the sixties, but nukes he hated. That made his present mission somewhat problematic, but he satisfied himself with the thought that the only way to disarm the Israelis was to disarm their adversaries. First, though, the adversaries had to be armed and that meant Iran had to have nukes.

Dr. Feruud, a man in his late fifties or early sixties entered. The President asked Freddy, "How much enriched Uranium do you think we have?"

Waters came ready with his numbers. "We estimate that Iran has somewhere around six tons of Uranium enriched to three-point-five percent—that's enough to make everyone nervous. That's why the United Nations wants to keep tabs on it with inspections."

Aliaabaadi knit his bushy brows and countered, "What if, instead of inspections, we were to voluntarily place half of our enriched Uranium in a United Nations vault; as a token of our good will."

Waters started. This was good beyond his wildest dreams. "That would be perfect! If you were willing to do that it would open the door for the complete relief of sanctions!"

"Would the remaining three tons be enough for our research Dr. Feruud?"

The nuclear physicist sighed and said, "Three tons is enough for our research and possibly enough for a small prototype reactor."

"Very well Mr. Waters. We have already been working on the deal. The UAE has agreed to help both parties. We will transport the enriched Uranium to the United Arab Emirates for storage in a United Nations vault. Your inspectors may observe the loading of the containers and escort them to the ship. I expect and welcome a United Nations escort across the Straits of Hormuz to Abu Dhabi. Will that be acceptable?"

"Absolutely!" Freddy exclaimed, too pleased with the victory to wonder how it came about. "That will give the president the cover he needs and give you the flexibility to move forward with your peaceful nuclear research. The president's goal is to settle the international agenda down so that he can pursue his domestic agenda. If Iran can calm things down in the Middle East then we don't need to spend any time or energy here."

"By that you mean Hamas," President Aliaabaadi said carefully.

"And ISIS," Freddy inserted. "Hamas and their unrelenting rocket attacks on Israel, as justified as they might be, are eventually going to push the Israeli's to retaliate. You're one dead kid away from all-out war in Gaza."

"Hamas is Hamas," Aliaabaadi shrugged. The Americans had no cards to play and he knew it. "They are hotheads. They are run by teenagers and young men with axes to grind. They think firing a few rockets and strapping on some suicide vests will change the world; let the Israeli's kill them. It is propaganda for us, for you as well, as I know President Oetari looks for any excuse to distance himself from the Zionists. Let it play out Mr. Waters."

"Yes sir, but the ISIS situation is in some respects even worse. The Hawks are playing up the loss of American troops in securing Iraq after Sadam—something that gave you increased leverage here—without Sadam you're the big dog on the block. This ISIS group isn't following the "Arab Spring" playbook. It already looks like we've lost Egypt. We can't lose Iraq as well."

"ISIS is Sunni, Mr. Waters; Iran is Shia," he said simply.

"The American people don't look at it that way, Mr. President. The Islamic State's brutality to Christians is largely ignored by the press; but their predation on other Muslims shocks even the media. The almost daily beheadings, now of women and children, it makes it impossible for the president to represent Islamists as reasonable partners in the peace process," Freddy countered.

"Then bomb them," Aliaabaadi told him simply. "You have my blessing!"

Now it was Freddy's turn to put the screws to Aliaabaadi. With a twisted smile, he adjusted his small pig eye glasses, and said, "It might start that way, but bombing is just the opening move. Do you really want American boots on the ground in the Middle East again?"

"No, I admit that is not in my best interests."

"Mr. President if ISIS is faced with muscle, real muscle like Iran and the threat of Iranian intervention, they'll crawl right back into their foreskins."

Aliaabaadi grimaced at the analogy, but he pursed his lips and nodded. "I agree that they must be reined in. Such brutality in the Prophet's name does no one any good." He paused, sipping at his tea before saying, "Perhaps you do not know this; I am also concerned with ISIS, so much so that I have directed my own chief of security, Colonel Nikahd to speak with the ISIS field commanders. He is in the Islamic State as we speak, and at great personal risk, I might add."

"Do you think he will have any luck?" Freddy said with real frustration. "We are not opposed to the goals of an Islamic homeland to balance out Israel, but their brutality makes it impossible for Americans to buy the whole "Religion of Peace" line!"

"That is only half the problem," Aliaabaadi sighed. "They are forming a government in competition with the Muslim world instead of in concert with us. They have a revenue stream through their Syrian oil wells on the black market. This is no longer a phantom menace Mr. Waters. President Oetari's refusal to deal with ISIS when they were vulnerable has put us all in a difficult position."

"We are not the world's policeman," Freddy Waters said firmly, as determined as Oetari that America should not flex its military muscle. "Those days are over."

"Someone must fill the void Mr. Waters," Aliaabaadi said with equal candor, spreading his long fingered hands out wide. "That is the reason ISIS exists. You did not create it but you allowed it to grow and become strong. If the United States will not do it then we must secure our own interests. We cannot allow a group of autonomous thugs who enjoy rape, murder and mayhem to become a nation much less *the* Caliphate."

"You do not have any plans to engage them militarily?" Waters pressed.

"We are attempting to instruct them on the bigger picture of things to come," Aliaabaadi assured him. "We want them to see a future and not just the pleasures of the present."

"Pleasures?" Waters smirked unpleasantly.

"Mr. Waters when you are angry at the world nothing is more pleasurable than taking out your anger on others. These ISIS scum claim to be establishing the Caliphate but in reality they are simply using that as an excuse to feed their lust and their thirst for blood and revenge—against anyone and everyone, Muslim, Christian or Jew—they don't care."

"Whatever you can do to tone them down will help all of us," Waters told Aliaabaadi. "Remember, we want you to succeed Mr. President. Your support will be vital for President Oetari's political future."

"Really? I thought President Oetari already won his second term; that is, unless he wishes to really discard the Constitution as his adversary's claim," Aliaabaadi said, standing up and indicating that the interview was over.

Waters stood as well, explaining, "He'd love to rewrite it himself, but that's not in the cards. American's love their mythological Constitution with its mythological Founding Fathers. Even Oetari can't change that, so he's not going to try."

"What is he running for then?"

"Something far more meaningful to him and to you than his temporary post as President of the United States: the Secretary-General of the United Nations."

Freddy followed Aliaabaadi's lead to the door, espousing his own dreams if not the president's. "After Oetari finishes tearing down the imperialist power in the US, he'll go on to his true tasking and his ultimate goal of establishing a much more global hierarchy through the UN; a hierarchy where the old colonial powers are simply member countries in a greater more equal world."

"Well that is ambitious," Aliaabaadi smiled. "I must ask, however, why I should support such an ambitious man? What is in it for me?"

"Well, you know the affinity the president has for the work you are doing," Freddy told him. "Previous presidents were just staunch supporters of Israel; they viewed the Persian and Arab states as second class—afterthoughts."

"And this president has repeatedly told us that he understands our people; our struggle. That is good rhetoric Mr. Waters, but words are simply words," Aliaabaadi stopped at the door, tilting his head to the side thoughtfully. "That is, unless President Oetari allows us entry into the most exclusive club in the world?"

"Of course," Freddy assured him. "When *your* Caliphate is established it will bring stability to the Middle East. When that Caliphate is armed in such a way as to bring balance to all continents of the world then we can truly pursue our dream of world equality."

It took a man who wanted to rule the world to recognize another man who wanted to rule the world. "Very good. Assure President Oetari that he shall have our support."

"Thank you Mr. President," Freddy said, shaking hands. The aides escorted him out.

When the door closed Aliaabaadi shook his head and said, "Poor President Oetari; he dreams of his happy worldwide utopia! Let him plan on his New World Order. In time his election to the UN, though he thinks it inevitable, will not matter. It will be his undoing. We shall take the international structure he has fabricated and use it to quickly establish the eternal Caliphate throughout the world."

He turned to Feruud and asked sternly, "Will three tons of Uranium be enough?"

Feruud smiled and nodded.

Aliaabaadi grinned. "Excellent! ISIS will supply us with the diversion, Al Qaeda with the delivery vehicle and we will supply the means to destroy Zion. By the time the West figures this out Israel will be no more and the Mahdi will have established a new Caliphate. We will establish the New World Order; the final world order."

58

CHAPTER 7: The Disappearance of Malaysia 666

Both Abdullereda and Muhammad looked at each other, sweat beading on their foreheads. The Al Qaeda terrorist reached inside his pocket.

The captain swallowed and asked, "What is it you think you know Jaren?"

The young man laughed and pointed his thumb back at Suri, who was bringing him coffee. "Suri told me all about your dinner plans in Beijing. I hate to be the one to ruin them but I found something on my walk around. We have what looks to be a bad tire," he reported. He slid past the fuming Al Qaeda terrorist and slid into his seat, completely oblivious of the effect he had on the two terrorists.

"It is a split across the tread," he explained, meaning the tire. "There are two red cords showing. I'll write it up, but it will take some time to change it." Jaren brought up the maintenance reports page in the ACARS.

"No, we'll write it up in Beijing," the captain replied firmly. When Jaren looked at him in surprise, he qualified the statement. "Operations already let me know about it. Maintenance caught that during the walk around but they don't have a tire. We'll get it in Beijing; they already know about it."

"We don't have a spare tire?" Jaren said incredulously.

Abdullereda stiffened with real anger, and bristled, "Are you questioning my authority as captain or as a Muslim?"

The first officer didn't look satisfied, but he didn't dare argue with the captain. In Asia that was simply not done. There was a strict caste system even amongst pilots. When Korean Air 007 flew into Russian airspace both first officers were well aware that their captain had erroneously programmed their Flight Management Computer, but neither of them had the courage to violate the cockpit protocol. They flew right into a Russian missile, fully aware of their captain's mistake but too smothered by the caste system to violate tradition.

Malaysia and Korea were worlds apart, but where their artificial caste systems were concerned they were hauntingly similar. Beyond that was the overt and covert oppression of the majority Muslims over the religious minorities in the region. It wasn't always that way in Malaysia, but with the rise of Al Qaeda and the indifference of successive American and European administrations Muslim power and influence increased. Jaren said nothing. He went about his business sullen and silent.

Their checklists complete, the tug pushed the big jet back from the gate. Twenty-three minutes later the captain shoved the power up and the million pound machine lifted into the warm, moist air.

"Positive rate, gear up," the captain ordered, easing the nose up to almost twenty degrees high. The landing gear whirred and clunked, folding itself in the fuselage. The aircraft accelerated quickly.

"Climb power," he commanded. The first officer hit the switch which then lit up with a bright golden light.

"Engaged," Jaren said mechanically.

"Flaps to one, flaps up!" Abdullereda called as he accelerated through the flap retraction schedule. "After takeoff checklist."

"Gear off; flaps up, after takeoff checklist complete,"

Abdullereda reached up and pressed the center autopilot command switch. Unlike Western pilots he didn't hand fly the airplane any longer than was necessary. Like most Third World pilots he was almost completely dependent on the automation of the jet.

They climbed out of three thousand feet, heading north over the island. The first officer switched from departure control to center. Center directed them, "Climb to and maintain flight level one-nine-zero."

"Climb to and maintain flight level one-nine-zero," Jaren parroted, confirming the cleared altitude of nineteen thousand feet. Passing six thousand feet he leaned forward and changed his altimeter setting to the standard high altitude setting of one-zero-one-three Hecto-Pascals, a common altimeter setting that ensured all aircraft in high altitude airspace were flying at the desired altitudes.

As he leaned back in his seat Abdullereda saw movement out of the corner of his right eye. His head snapped that direction to see Muhammad, who'd been standing behind Jaren and looking out of the window, suddenly grab the first officer from behind, cupping his left hand around the young man's chin. Muhammad's right hand disappeared behind Jaren's head, but remerged holding something that flashed in the cockpit lights, something metal.

Jaren cried out in surprise at the unexpected assault, but his voice changed in an instant. He gave a short, sharp cry that changed into a horrible keening, gurgling wail. Muhammad's right arm ripped back viciously. In answer, a fountain of blood splashed the first officer's flight instruments. His white shirt turned a bright crimson. Jaren reached out instinctively for his neck, but then grappled for the flight controls, flailing wildly. The autopilot clicked off and the aircraft lurched to the left.

Abdullereda grabbed the stick, but the aircraft kept bucking to Jared's spasmodic inputs. It wasn't until he punched the override that Hussein could bring the big jet under control. The stricken first officer and father grew weaker, his eyes impossibly wide, his skin turning pallid. The dying first officer grabbed the throttles either by accident or instinct and pulled them back, perhaps a desperate desire to get back to the ground.

Muhammad wrapped his arms around the first officer's torso, pinning them to his side. As Abdullereda shoved the throttles back up—his stomach heaving at the sensation of the warm, wet, slick blood of his first officer on the plastic handles—he stared dumbstruck at the young man.

He was no longer human. Jared was a marionette jerking and gasping. His white eyes vacuous, it was obvious that the young man's brain was no longer processing information, it, like the rest of him, was slowly dying. The blood pumping out of his ripped throat completely covered his shirt and the terrorist's arms, but it was coming out ever more slowly. Finally, with a gurgling rattle Jared slipped into unconsciousness and death.

"Allahu Akbar!" said Muhammad triumphantly.

Abdullereda felt sick.

"Quick! Inform the brothers! Get them up here!" he ordered.

Automatically Abdullereda cycled the "No Smoking" signs off and then on twice. A moment later there was a chime. The flight attendant was calling the cockpit.

"Answer it," Muhammad told him, adding with a macabre laugh. "The first officer is busy going to Hell!"

Swallowing hard, Abdullereda answered the call. It was Suri. "Is everything all right up there? You didn't mention any turbulence."

"We hit someone's wake," the captain replied. Just like hitting the wake of another boat on a lake aircraft caused invisible waves in the air that could rock a following aircraft. The explanation apparently sufficed. Suri told him two other men wanted to come up into the cockpit. There was a note in her voice that asked for an explanation. This was unusual, but Suri was not about to question a flight officer and a male.

Whatever Jaren's hesitancy due to the Asian caste system the gulf between men and women, both in Asian and especially Islamic culture, was much greater and fraught with more dire consequences.

"It's all right, they are sent by the company, and talked to me about it earlier. I should have let you know. I'll let them up," he told her soothingly. He turned the door switch to "UNLKD." An electronic switch clicked and the door opened. Two men tumbled in and quickly slammed the door shut behind them.

For a moment, the captain's bearing returned to Abdullereda and he put the horrifying events behind him, but only for a moment. As soon as he got the autopilot back on and the aircraft back on its flight path he looked over to see the terrorists unceremoniously dragging Jaren's body from the seat.

The young man's dead eyes looked at him, damning him, or so he thought, and then they were gone. They dumped him in the back by the door, leaning his dead body against the doorframe. Jaren's head slumped over his crimson chest like a disjointed doll.

Muhammad slid into the wet first officer's seat and the other two terrorists strapped into the jump seats. They all donned their oxygen masks. Abdullereda followed suit. The Al Qaeda leader nodded to him and said sharply over the interphone, "Implement the plan!"

They continued out on the flight planned route. The flight plan called for them to cruise at thirty-three thousand feet. Hussein requested and was granted a higher altitude, and they levelled off at forty-one thousand feet. As the peninsula disappeared into the darkness the last Malaysian controller—unaware that the aircraft had been hijacked—said goodnight and passed on Malaysian flight 666 to Oceanic Control.

"Good night," said Abdullereda, but instead of calling oceanic he turned off the transponder.

"Now they cannot see us correct?" asked Muhammad.

"No, their radars can only see us through what we call 'skin paint.' That means they have to see us by bouncing radar off the aircraft, but civilian radars aren't designed to do that. They're designed to ping us with radar which triggers our transponder to reply with position, airspeed and altitude."

"Only you turned that off right?"

"Yes," he assured them.

"Good, very good. Continue with the operation!"

A calmer Abdullereda selected "Route 2" on the FMC and executed it. The aircraft began a turn to the left, heading out from Malaysia and into open sea. He was in control now and that made him feel better. Abdullereda took a deep breath, reached up and turned the Cabin Altitude switch clockwise to manual.

"Go ahead, we are on Oxygen; we are ready," Muhammad told him, nodding. His wild eyes and bloody clothes were made more macabre by the proboscis of the Oxygen mask. He looked surreal and terrifying.

Reaching up to the Cabin Altitude Control knob Abdullereda touched the smooth, cold plastic—he'd never killed anyone before—he'd never even contemplated it. As soon as he turned the switch five hundred people would die of Oxygen starvation. He couldn't even comprehend that number.

"Do it!"

Abdullereda turned the packs off first, stopping the aircraft from pumping in preconditioned air. Then he shut off the engine bleed valves. Now the engines would not supply pressurized air to the ducts. The last step was to let the air pressure inside the aircraft escape into the atmosphere.

The airplane was like a balloon. The air pressure inside was greater than the air pressure outside; it wanted to get out. However, like a submarine the airplane's hull was sealed, keeping the air pressure inside the hull and thereby keeping all of the people inside alive. People could survive at ten thousand feet or even twenty thousand feet, but there was so little Oxygen at forty-one thousand feet that most people would black out in a matter of seconds. Death would take longer but no one would be awake to experience it.

Turning the Cabin Altitude Control Switch clockwise, Abdullereda opened the pressure relief valve. He felt the lightening of pressure on his chest. It wasn't an explosive decompression but it was noticeable and uncomfortable. At once a red alarm light illuminated and a horn sounded. The air pressure kept dropping, as the interior of the airplane spit out all of its air, naturally flowing outward through the open valve and trying to equalize the inside pressure with the outside.

The temperature dropped. An EICAS message informed him that the Oxygen masks in the back had deployed. He pointed to it and hacked his clock. The second hand started running, smoothly five hundred and forty-four people, passengers and flight attendants, had left to live.

"The passengers have twelve minutes of Oxygen," he said through the intercom.

"We will stay up here long enough to ensure they are all dead," the Al Qaeda terrorist told him.

The twelve minutes were among the longest of Abdullereda's life. The chime from the back, the flight attendants desperately trying to call the cockpit, never stopped. Someone was pounding on the door. Abdullereda could hear a woman yelling, screaming, pleading through the door—Suri. Even after the twelve minutes were up it didn't stop.

"I thought you said they only had twelve minutes of Oxygen?" Muhammad asked scathingly.

Abdullereda's mind whirled. No answer came to him. It wasn't until he heard the sound of metal pounding on the door that he understood. "There are walk-around bottles," he said quickly. "There are five or six bottles of Oxygen as well as a few fire-fighting hoods. They won't last long at this altitude though, not with them expending themselves!"

One of the terrorist got up and looked through the peep hole. "He is right," he said, lifting his mask to shout out what he saw. "There are four or five women—" he slumped to the floor, dropping like a stone.

"What happened to Fariz?" came the surprised voice of the other terrorist in back.

"The idiot took his mask off!" Abdullereda shouted over the intercom.

"I will put it back on!" the other terrorist said, leaning over and struggling with the inert body of his companion.

"Be careful! At this altitude it only takes a few seconds to black out without your mask!" Abdullereda warned. It was no use. In his effort to save his companion, who was already turning purple, the other terrorist twisted and pulled at his Oxygen mask just enough to break the seal of his mask. He could still have saved himself when he felt the first wave of light headedness or nausea hit him, but instead he continued to struggle with the mask of his comrade.

The end result of his stupidity was that he fell out of his seat and onto the prostrate form of his partner.

"Do you want me to descend or repressurized?" Abdullereda asked desperately, thinking maybe, just maybe he could at least save Suri, who was still pounding weakly at the door.

"No! If it is Allah's will that they die as well then they will be martyrs!"

They stayed at altitude for another half an hour. The banging on the cockpit door grew weaker and weaker and finally disappeared altogether. The cockpit grew colder. Finally, a shivering Muhammad allowed the captain to start the air conditioning packs and descend. He pressurized the cabin and descended to ten thousand feet; that would keep them out of radar coverage. Then he turned south, heading toward Indonesia.

When they finally reached ten thousand feet Abdullereda took off his mask. The stench of shit and piss from the two dead terrorists mixed with the sharp metallic smell of blood. Looking back over his shoulder, Abdullereda saw the ashen face of Jaren looking disapprovingly at the two terrorists who'd collapsed on his lap.

He threw up into the pubs bin next to his seat.

Miserable and tired, Abdullereda flew the flight plan to Soekarno International, Jakarta, Indonesia. He didn't make a single call, but he switched to approach frequency and heard the controllers vectoring people around, clearing the airspace so that he could come in and land. He felt like a robot, not trusting himself to land the airplane but instead hooking up the autopilot to fly the ILS into the airport.

After landing he followed a truck across the field and into a hanger. At long last Abdullereda shut down the airplane. Even then it wasn't over. It took both of them to move the rigid bodies away from the door so that they could open it. When they did open the cockpit door Abdullereda was met with Suri's dead eyes.

She lay back against a pile of other flight attendants. They were all huddled by the cockpit door. The Oxygen mask was still on her face. She stared at the door as if still wanting an answer as to why—why?

He had to climb over her to get to the aircraft door, trying not to look back in the cabin which was eerily silent and yet stank of death. Reaching the door he had to clear another few bodies away, and then he almost forgot to disarm it, but he remembered, and threw the latch.

Abdullereda was exhausted, but unlike a normal flight he didn't go to a hotel. He was given a cot in a cold room with a concrete floor. On the floor next to the cot was a cup of cold tea and a Quran. He collapsed onto the cot still in his uniform which was stained with sweat, blood, urine and vomit, ignoring everything.

CHAPTER 8: Rogues Gallery

The meeting took place in a nondescript brick and mud house just inside the Syria-Iraq border. There was a single large table made of local wood, old beyond knowing, with rough edges and a top worn smooth from innumerable hands, clay bowls, and the like.

The owner of the house, a large structure for the area, furnished tea for gathering and otherwise tried to play host. It was an important opportunity for his future and his family, but it had its risks as well.

There were three groups of players gathered in his dining room, chosen because of the large size and the large window overlooking the outside terrace. Light was more important than security. This far north into Iraq and this close to the Syrian border meant there were virtually no security risks.

One of the groups present, a knot of four men, strangely they were literate, even well educated, but arrogant and brutal, represented ISIS. The ISIS killers wore their loose fitting clothing with proud rusty brown stains, bragging of how many non-conforming Muslim heads they piled on the side of the road or played soccer with. They appeared to have purposefully left civilization behind; they were grimy, unwashed, their teeth were yellow and their fingernails had suspicious detritus packed beneath them.

Brutal beyond understanding, vicious to the point where they had even the hardline Al Qaeda operatives nervous, they were the new burgeoning power in Iraq and Syria, but their goals were much larger.

Even the Al Qaeda terrorists, the pathfinders in the macabre art of internet friendly beheading had some semblance of awareness when their blood lust cost them more than it gained. The ISIS boys, as they whispered, fearful that they too would end up on the lists, were nothing more than blood drunk murderers.

The third group present were the most nervous of the lot; they were the Iranian Shia, and it was their people who bore the brunt of the Muslim-on-Muslim slaughter. They had a right to be nervous. As incoherent as their policies and actions were there was at least a façade of legitimacy. At least when the Iranian Shia hung their homosexuals by cranes during lunch there was a maniacally driven, terrifyingly self-righteous and completely irrational Fatwa behind it.

"I am Colonel Nikahd," announced the only man, an Iranian, in a military uniform. Unlike the others, his demeanor was neither maniacal nor nervous. He was calm and in charge. "Welcome brothers. I send greetings from Ayatollah Hayayi and President Aliaabaadi of the Islamic Republic of Iran."

He introduced a young man from the Iranian party, explaining, "Although he is in our company this young jihadi is not of Iran but of Turkey."

"Turkey!" the ISIS and Al Qaeda terrorists objected. "Turkey is NATO; they work with the West! They are traitors!"

"Calm yourselves brothers," Nikahd said smoothly but forcefully. "Have you never heard of Taqiyya? What worth is it to have an ally so deep in the enemy's camp?"

"Can they be trusted?"

"I put it to you; this man is the personal emissary of the Turkish president, his very own nephew. Now do you doubt his sincerity? If that is not enough think of your recruits from the West itself. How do they get here? They come through Turkey, of course, and they come freely without fear of being interfered with."

The terrorists calmed and allowed Nikahd to continue.

"Finally, the Grand Mufti Aziz of Saudi Arabia also sends his regards," he raised his finger as if lecturing. "He reminds us all that whatever our differences we must unite behind Allah the Merciful and combat the decadent West. Separately we can hurt the West, but together we have the ability to bring the infidels to their knees!"

"Smooth talk brother, so you say," remarked Fahd, one of the ISIS terrorists. "Yet I have seen what you Shia do to my brother Sunnis. Ever since Saddam was overthrown by the Americans we have suffered. We are gaining our revenge; are you dictating to me and mine that our revenge is unjustified?"

Colonel Nikahd lit a cigarette and waived aside the concern, refusing to take the bait of this angry young man with an AK-47 slung across his back and a bag of gold teeth at his belt. "What you do to the vermin that cooperated with the Westerners I do not care. They have already insulted the Prophet.

"Had they sought to simply deceive the Americans and so come to power—fine—I would have no trouble with them. Yet they sought to implement the American ideals. Justly so their lives, wives and fortunes are forfeit." Nikahd then leaned forward, a hungry look in his eyes. "Besides, we need the eyes of the West fixed on Iraq. The operation Brother Khallida will brief you on is very sensitive—very sensitive. It will required the cooperation of the Sunni and the Shia states, but when it is successful it will cripple the Zionists. We will thereafter push the Zionists into the sea!"

Their murderous vocation protected, their lustful needs approved and their theft condoned, the ISIS terrorist nodded and said, "We are willing to listen."

Nikahd motioned to his Al Qaeda operative, introducing him, "This is Gamel Khallida a very experienced man as you can see by his holy wounds. He has been involved in every major operation against the West since before Nine-Eleven. He is here to brief you on the part of the operation that pertains to Syria and Iraq."

Khallida thanked Nikahd and was about to speak when the ISIS man interrupted him. "We want to ensure that this, none of this will prevent us from establishing our Sharia state, our caliphate in Syria and northern Iraq," he said bluntly, as a young punk will who is trying to pick a fight.

Nikahd held up both hands, soothing the ISIS phantom concerns, by saying, "Far from it brother. In fact, we *want* you to establish your Caliphate. The Grand Mufti and Ayatollah Hayayi have already laid the groundwork for a Caliphate to extend from Iran, through the Arabian Peninsula and into

Egypt. We hope to establish it as far north as Turkey—we are in negotiations with the Turks at this very moment—so you see, what you are doing is in keeping with our overall goal."

"We are not going to take directives from the Grand Mufti in Saudi Arabia!" the ISIS representative said loudly.

Nikahd leaned back in his chair and replied, "The Grand Mufti is already in contact with your Imams; it will be up to you as to whether you follow their guidance or strike out on your own."

The ISIS party looked perturbed, but at the mention of their imams they restrained themselves from further outbursts. Nikahd reminded them that despite their personal animosity, the ISIS imams supported working with their allies.

Khallida built upon this, reminding the ISIS fighters, "It is up to you whether you want to continue to have us fight amongst ourselves and so do the West's job for it," he said, and he spread his hands wide with resignation. "Their blood will remain unspent, their gold will remain in their coffers while we battle amongst ourselves. They will wait until we have bled ourselves white and then bomb us back into oblivion."

"They have no such will," Fahd said. "Their president is a coward or he is secretly with us. They will not interfere."

"Certainly not while we are slaughtering each other," Nikahd said sedately. "Now that doesn't mean we wish you to stop, no, not at all. You are attacking American trained forces; the only forces the West can count on besides their own troops. We have to kill those men to get at the real targets: the Westerners."

"Go on," Fahd said evenly.

"Picture this my brothers, our Caliphate stretching from Africa to Asia to Europe, giving the West no foothold in the Middle East," he said fervently. "We control their oil, their dependence even as we expand our Caliphate—a Caliphate not just established by arms and negotiation but by holy decree—one is coming to unite us, unite us all. We must be ready. Then, when he comes, then we will take our arguments to their proper places."

Nikahd stared at the ISIS men. He stood, looming over them, and asked them, "Do you think your operations in Syria and Iraq are glorious, stamping out the little Christian communities and beheading Sadaam's troops—no!

"When we take what is rightfully ours we will send you, you men sitting her at the table, we will send you to Paris, to London to Berlin! You may plunder the vast wealth of the churches of Europe. You may have your harem of pale skinned European girls, ready to service you at your leisure. Once you are done with them they can be brought here to market and you, as the fighters will always be provided with fresh young women for your every need. Europe will fall; Africa is already falling under the onslaught of Boko Haram and the Somalians. Our day is coming. Be a part of it!"

The ISIS terrorists nodded for Khallida to brief them. When he was finished they agreed to sign on to the plan as it allowed them to do everything they were already doing. Nikahd brought out his iPad and showed them the document. He signed it with his electronic pen, telling them, "It is gratifying to use the West's own tools against them!"

After he signed and Khallida signed he handed the iPad to the ISIS terrorists, saying, "Your Imam's signature is already on the document—right there," he pointed to an illegible scrawl. "We have signed for the Republic of Iran and Al Qaeda. It but remains for your signature to guarantee your gains in this jihad!"

One by one the ISIS terrorists signed the iPad. When the last had done so he handed the tablet back to Nikahd.

The colonel smiled, and told them, "Congratulations, you are now part of a larger, greater Caliphate—boom!"

Before Nikahd could finish a loud concussion sounded in the room. The plate glass window shattered. The leader of the ISIS terrorists rocked back in his chair, a small hole in his forehead. One of the terrorist's behind him took the spent bullet in the throat; it nearly decapitated him. Chunks of grey matter and vaporized blood sprayed the, blinding the terrorists, freezing them with terror.

Boom, boom, boom, boom!

Screams and shouts filled the room as men ducked or ran for cover. There was a pause, and Nikahd shouted, "Sniper! He's reloading!"

The terrorists ran for the door.

Boom, boom, boom, boom, boom!

Bodies crumpled to the floor in plain view of the large dining room window. Khallida and Nikahd escaped—that was all. For a moment all was silent but for the groans of the dead and dying.

From the tangle of bodies one terrorist raised himself painfully on his elbows, whining for aid. The owner of the house appeared at the doorway—shocked, pleading to the heavens—he reached for the stricken man. Boom! One last shot split the air. The terrorist's head exploded, drenching the owner in blood. He fled from the room.

The next morning the bodies of the slain had been removed and buried. The window was boarded up. The only other indication that something had gone wrong was the presence of the owner's head nailed over his front door.

CHAPTER 9: Extraction

Jeremiah Slade put his final shot right through the terrorist's right eye. The Barret "Light Fifty" sent its .50 caliber shell unerringly over the half mile through the now smashed windows, through the eyeball, into the brain and out the back, making a much larger hole on exit than on entry.

To his grim satisfaction the blood and brains of the terrorist sprayed the owner of the house.

"Nice shot!" Killer Kincaid chuckled, looking through his standard Delta Force issue binoculars. "I think you're getting to like this way too much; you're shooting for dramatic effect!"

The thought had already occurred to Slade. It was one thing to get the job done, even to the point of adding a bit of extra terror to the lives of the enemy. It was quite another to enjoy it. He'd enjoyed every minute of that shooting gallery; everything except letting Khallida and Nikahd walk out alive. The Company put a "no-kill" tag on them, but Slade didn't have a need to know, so they didn't explain why.

Killer, told his men, "Alpha team you are cleared in, Bravo, you have their back. We have high cover!"

While Alpha team infiltrated the building to retrieve the iPads and any other intelligence they could dig up in a hurry, the other team took up a flanking position to cover the house.

Killer cursed.

"Problem's?" Slade asked, scanning the area through his powerful scope. "I don't see squat!"

"That's just it," Killer replied. "As soon as these jack rabbits hear a rifle shot that's not theirs the find the nearest burkha and hide underneath it! The bastards are brave enough when it comes to beheading a man with his hands tied behind his back!"

Slade grunted, and then asked, "I'm the one whose supposed to be keeping secrets—that's the CIA's job—so you going to let me in on why I didn't get to pop the Colonel or

Khallida? Damn it, we've been after that bastard since Nine-Eleven!"

"Damned if I know. Maybe we'll get debriefed on it in Kuwait City."

"Kuwait!" Slade growled. "That's not my favorite place, or don't you remember?"

"I'm sure they've forgotten it all by now Slade," Killer laughed. "Besides, you were only *scheduled* to be beheaded. I got you out of there didn't I?"

"Being led to execution square counts as being "scheduled?"" Slade retorted.

"Come on, show some backbone," the Delta Force Captain laughed. "Look at the bright side. In Kuwait you can legally buy western slave girls for your harem!"

There was sporadic fire from down below. Slade saw movement off the corner of the building. He heard over the radio. "We've got runners heading west bound!"

Two men appeared, sprinting across the dirt street toward a house, firing blindly behind them. The door of the house opened for them.

Boom! Boom!

The men flung their AK-47's in the air, falling like disjointed marionettes into the dust.

"Bravo team shows all Tangos down!"

"Alpha team reporting, sir, we've cleared out the guards but we've found a package in one of their trucks. The package speaks French sir!"

Killer chuckled, "Well I'll be damned, just as Intel thought! The Al Qaeda people were bringing the ISIS folks a present!"

"Damn!" Slade cursed out of the blue.

"What is it?"

"Look at the Tangos I just took out," he told Killer, who whipped up his binoculars. "They're using like an eight year old kid to retrieve the AK's and ammo from the dead Tangos."

"Where's Child Protective Services when you need them," Killer growled. "Your call boss."

Slade let the kid go, but not before splashing both of the terrorist's heads like melons all over the child. "Hopefully that'll teach him not to get killed!"

Killer's voice tightened up, "We have company. A five man patrol coming south along the street on the left flank. Idiots, they're walking right into the sun!"

"Alpha team be advised we have Tangos—about one hundred yards. Coming to you Bravo team! Alpha team bring that package as fast as you can!"

"Bravo team has the Tangos. You want us to take them out?"

"Hold on tight," Killer ordered. He glanced through his binoculars, and said, "You want them Slade?"

"Got 'em," he whispered, already set in his breathing pattern.

Killer waited and waited until finally he asked, "You going to fire or what?"

Boom!

The five man patrol, advancing furtively, nervously toward the house froze as one of the men turned a sudden somersault in the air. It looked like a circus act but for the splash of vaporized blood as the fifty caliber shell tore through his upper chest.

The bullet wasn't done though.

The piece of metal splashed out from the terrorist's torso and hit the man next to him in the stomach. There was very little resistance to the bullet in the abdomen. The misshapen projectile tumbled through the guts, tearing the stomach, the intestines and the viscera of the second terrorist, sending him to the ground clutching his belly.

Still the bullet wasn't done.

With the impetus of a handgun it burst through the kidney and burrowed into the third terrorist's groin. That unlucky terrorist faced a long, ugly death as the bullet completely disintegrated in his bowels after blowing off his privates.

"They shouldn't be walking so close together!" Slade chastised them. Boom! Boom! The other two terrorist's fell before they could find cover. Slade said dryly, "No point in letting them teach their friends what they learned."

Kincaid chuckled in a gallows humor manner, and said, "You were waiting for them to line up; a triple! Uncle Sam's going to be very happy you're saving the taxpayer money!"

"Alpha has the groceries and the package; we're bugging out!"

Slade and Kincaid covered the egress of the Delta Force squads. When they were all gathered they hot footed it from the ridge where Slade set up his sniper station and headed southeast.

"You set up the booby traps?" Kincaid asked the Alpha team.

"Couldn't," he said. "There were kids in the house; we could hear them."

"Damned terrorists hiding behind civilians!"

They jogged out of the engagement area. The French hostage wasn't in the same kind of shape as the Deltas so they purloined a bicycle and stuck him on top, trotting on either side of him. It was ninety minutes before they reached the little road. A hundred yards further on was the abandoned village.

"Boss, there's a dust cloud coming from the direction of the target village," one of the men warned.

Slade scrambled up the shoulder of the ridge and turned his scope north. "Killer we've got company!" Slade announced. "Four vehicles heading our way; they are a two thousand yards and closing. It looks like we're compromised!"

"Bravo plant me some Claymores along the road! Slade, give me the Light Fifty!"

Slade unslung the Barret and handed it to Killer.

"Get the bird warmed up. We'll be hot on your heels!" Kincaid said, taking the sniper rifle and steadying it atop a boulder. "Alpha, escort the package. Bravo you're with me!"

Killer and his two man team set up shop at the edge of the ridge where the road turned to the right. As they hunkered down behind the available cover the convoy of trucks appeared at the far point of a shallow valley five hundred yards away. They gunned their motors in a cloud of dust.

As the men set up a few rows of Claymores to cover their egress Killer began sending fifty caliber rounds at the drivers. Finished with their mine-laying, the other Deltas joined their commander and let loose with their SCARS, sending a hail of 7.62 mm rounds at the enemy.

Killer hit one driver in the throat. He took his hands off the wheel and flung them instinctively over his wound. The shell nearly decapitated the terrorist; his head lolled grotesquely to the side as he slumped over the wheel. The terrorist next to him tried to grab the steering wheel, but the dead driver's arm caught in the spokes as he slumped over. The truck turned hard left, spilling the dozens of terrorists crowded in the back onto the desert road. Many of those were run over by the following trucks, who avoided hitting the tumbling truck but not the men scattered across the road.

"Grenades!" Killer shouted.

Two volleys of three grenades flew through the air. The remaining trucks made it through the hail of bullets only to endure the explosions of the grenades and claymores. One truck veered off in flames. Terrorists leapt from the back, some were on fire. Two trucks made it through.

A growing roar behind them caught Killer's attention. "Time to go boys, bug out!"

#

Slade sprinted around the corner and headed toward the parked aircraft. Between the buildings underneath a camouflage net sat the OV-10 Bronco. He didn't need to tell the Deltas what to do. As he clambered into the forward cockpit they cut loose the netting so that it wouldn't foul the props. Then they loaded up the hostage and took their places in the rear, weapons pointed out the open back of the aircraft.

He primed the engines and hit the cartridges; the motors coughed to life amidst two black clouds of gritty, acrid smoke.

Checking to either side, Slade cleared his path, making sure he wasn't going to chop up a friendly Delta; seeing nothing he pushed the throttles up. He didn't worry about checking with the Deltas in the back; those guys could take care of themselves.

The Bronco started forward at a brisk pace, heading out of the narrow opening between the two dilapidated buildings and out into the street. He stopped, keying the mike and transmitting, "Killer are you ready to mount up?"

"Coming up behind you!" replied the testy voice of Killer. "They're hot on our tail!"

Looking in his rear view mirror, Slade saw Killer hustle his men to the Bronco. As they closed Slade shoved the throttles up, moving the twin turboprop ahead at a brisk walk. Dust spiraled out from behind the OV-10, providing effective cover, but the first tracers were coming out of the growing cloud.

The Deltas piled in. As their fields of fire cleared the Deltas already on board began pouring fire behind them. They couldn't see their targets, but unlike the terrorists they weren't firing blind. The tracers gave them a good idea where the firing was coming from. The bark of the SCARS and the ripping fire of the light machine gun made the Bronco shudder.

"All right go, go, go!" Killer yelled through his mike.

For Slade that meant everyone was secure, and he jammed the throttles up to the firewall. The Bronco leapt forward, spitting dust and gravel behind it. The aircraft bucked like its namesake. Slade kept the stick forward, keeping the pressure on the nosegear to give him better steering over the rough terrain.

Twenty-five, thirty, forty knots; the airspeed climbed quickly. All he needed was another forty knots and they'd be able to get airborne. Tracers flashed around the aircraft but Slade hadn't felt any impacts. A blur of movement on his left caught his peripheral vision. One of the trucks was careening over the field, closing in on him and trying to cut him off. They were only forty yards to his left and the truck had a head of steam. The back of the truck carried about a dozen rag tag terrorists, swathed in loose fitting clothing and black schmaugs. One even carried a black flag with "spaghetti noodles" in dirty white.

The terrorists on the truck were firing, or rather they were trying to fire at Slade. In his determination to cut Slade off, the driver floored the gas pedal without regard to the terrain or his cargo. Every furrow, every hole, every hillock caused the truck to bounce and rock wildly.

The terrorists in the back should have been able to draw a bead on the Bronco as it accelerated, but the truck's passage threw them around so violently they fired everywhere but at the aircraft.

One terrorist tried to steady himself with one hand on the plank rail of the bed and fire his AK-47 with the other. He almost had the automatic rifle steadied on the cockpit—Slade prepared to swerve—but the truck's front right tire disappeared halfway down a hollow and then popped back up again, driving the front right quarter of the truck airborne. It came down with a crash, bottoming out the tire and digging the fender into the sandy soil.

All the while the terrorist squeezed the trigger of the AK on full auto. He sprayed his entire clip into the sky and even behind his shoulder as the truck bottomed out. He caught the flag bearer, shooting off the terrorist's right arm at the middle of the forearm. The flag tumbled from the truck and into the dirt with the hand still attached to it.

The impact bounced two terrorists right out of the truck—it would have bounced a third—but he was manning the fifty caliber machine gun mounted on the bed of the truck. He held onto the gun for dear life, flying like a pennant in a violent wind. When the truck bottomed out he hit the deck hard. The force ripped his hands from the gun and he inadvertently fired off another burst straight up into the sky.

"What I wouldn't give for a couple of JATOs right now!" Slade swore, meaning the old, old school way of getting an aircraft off the ground through disposable rocket assist engines.

"What?" shouted Killer, who was climbing into the back seat and was now on interphone.

It didn't matter. The terrorist driver's heavy handed tactics slowed the big truck down enough for Slade to pull the surging Bronco ahead of him. He watched the terrorist yank the wheel to the right, driving the truck through a line of shrubs and a shallow ditch next to the road.

"A present coming your way gentlemen," Slade barked.

The driver of the truck apparently accepted that he wasn't going to catch up to the Bronco over the fields; cutting the Americans off wasn't going to work. So he opted to get back on the road and chase the aircraft from behind. It was a good plan. Even if the truck couldn't catch the Bronco the road would give the terrorists a much more stable platform to shoot the Americans down.

Unfortunately, the terrorists hadn't counted on the Bronco's rear door still being open, giving the Deltas a perfect field of fire. The truck bounced onto the roadway but before the terrorists could get off a single shot they took the combined firepower of a very angry Delta Force right in the chops.

Slade heard the Deltas let go en masse. That was followed shortly thereafter by a large explosion. As he pulled back on the stick and labored into the air, Slade glanced back to see the ugly smear of black smoke amidst the bright flashes of flame.

"Now that's a beautiful sight!" Killer laughed.

Pulling away from the killing fields and heading south toward friendly territory, the Delta added, "Okay boys, buckle up! I hope you enjoyed our free tour of the cultural hot spots of today's new Caliphate. Feel free to enjoy our complimentary pork rinds and bacon bit chips!"

Slade shook his head and flew the airplane, ignoring the banter of the younger men. Their job was over. He still had to get everyone home safe and sound; he took that seriously and it showed.

Three hours later they landed in Kuwait City. Slade took the headset off his Aussie slouch hat and opened the canopy. The extreme heat of the cockpit gave way to the extreme heat of Kuwait. Soaking with sweat, he unstrapped, now feeling every hour of the mission. Exhausted, Slade started to lift himself out of the steel seat, Killer stopped him.

"Hold on Slade, we're going to get a picture," he said. Kincaid waved his troops to the side of the aircraft, calling down to one man. "Tommy! Tommy hand the Light Fifty up to Slade will you?"

Tommy, whose last name Slade didn't know, smiled and lifted the heavy Barret up to him. "Nice shooting sir, but I bet you miss your flintlock!"

Another chimed in, "He's gone from horses to airplanes. Just think of the changes you've seen since the Civil War!"

"No it was the Revolutionary War wasn't it Slade?"

"He fought with the legions under Caesar, Shakespeare said so!"

Thus it went. Slade took it in stride. For the Deltas to joke with you was their way of accepting you. If they didn't Slade couldn't have gotten a colder shoulder from an iceberg. As it was, Slade was part of the photo; he was part of the team.

Slade took part in the debrief and the traditional after mission drink, but as the young guns recounted the adventure, all he could think about was how tired he was and how good it would be to be home for a while.

CHAPTER 10: The President is now the Man

President Patra Oetari, the first non-white President of the United States, whose father was a nationalist from Indonesia, had just gotten off the phone with the President of Turkey, Mustafa Ataturk. The president, an ardent Islamist and notoriously uncooperative NATO partner, was outraged at the assassination of his nephew. Oetari, who sympathized with the Islamists and was hardly any friendlier with his NATO allies was horrified; especially when it became clear that young Turgut was assassinated in an American Cobra operation.

"Who the Hell authorized this?" Oetari demanded of CIA Director Gann and General Mertzl.

"You did sir," Gann told him calmly. "We had no idea Turgut Ataturk associated with terrorists. Certainly we had no idea why he was at that particular meeting."

"Your sniper didn't recognize him?"

Gann and Mertzl looked at each other. Gann's expression made it clear that it was Mertzl's turn to placate the president. The bulldog of a man, Archie Bunker in a crew cut and horned rim glasses, said forcefully, "Our sniper identified the two Tangos he was not supposed to eliminate and did his job sir. I doubt very seriously if he could have identified the young man if asked; certainly I couldn't."

"I have met Turgut several times," the president complained, sitting heavily behind his desk. "He was a vibrant young man; full of life."

"Associating with the absolute scum of the Earth has its dangers," Mertzl commented bluntly.

Oetari seethed, but his political savvy saved him from betraying any more of his political philosophy than he had to. As much as he hated the military, Oetari still had to take care not to completely alienate his generals. He needed them.

Instead, he got up and paced the room. In reality, President Ataturk and Oetari were kindred spirits. They did not so much deplore ISIS as its brutal tactics. They both thought an Islamic

Caliphate was the right of all Muslims, who they considered a marginalized people courtesy of capitalism and the West. They also thought a nuclear Iran was a much needed counterbalance to the Zionist state of Israel. Iran could, if the mullahs were properly mollified, check Israel and bring stability to the region.

That was Oetari's conclusion based on a career that until his inauguration included absolutely no foreign policy experience whatsoever. The problem was, after over five years of on the job experience Oetari still held the same views. He'd learned nothing at all about the world.

So, the president forged ahead with his ideologically based policy. Oetari's trick was getting that policy implemented by using or not using American power. It was a policy that had no chance getting support in the military or from the American people. To be realistic, it wasn't a policy he could talk about openly with his party; it was too radical even for Democrats to consider it viable. It wasn't that the world Oetari envisioned was necessarily bad, it was simply that his utopian view of things was not supported by the behavior of the people who had to live in that world.

So Oetari pushed it behind the scenes, and he played a very careful game with his military brass. He allowed them to think of him as a pacifist—even to the point of being phobic—while he hid his true intentions. Oetari dreamed of worldwide equality, forced if necessary, and he needed the military's help to get it done.

That made his tightrope act very touchy indeed. The rough and tumble Chairman of the Joint Chiefs of Staff was not one of the president's favorite men. He and the directors of the FBI and the CIA were ardently serious about their duties and independent thinkers—dinosaurs of the Cold War, Vietnam and Desert Storm. President Oetari had not yet the opportunity to replace them with internationalists instead of outdated patriots.

He took a deep breath and put on the thoughtful mask of an ardent pacifist, which he was.

"This tragic event is why I am dead set against using American military might—period. You can't make apologies to a dead man."

"No, but you can make a celebratory call to the President of France," Gann told him. When the president looked up in surprise, Gann informed him. "Our military forces rescued a French hostage, coincidence, but our team was there to take advantage of it."

"I don't remember that being part of the operation."

"Our teams deal with locals and the locals are in the know. The team took advantage of the opportunity. Unfortunately, they also uncovered more atrocities by ISIS: mass killings, organized rape parties—and this," he handed the president his iPad. The president's brows furrowed as he read the translation of the poster.

Gann explained, "These signs have been posted at every street corner of ISIS occupied cities. The local populations have been directed to bring their daughters ages twelve and above to ISIS Islamic Centers so that they may," he swallowed hard but his expression stayed calm, if cold, "So that the girls may service the Holy Warriors of jihad."

Carrabolla turned white as a ghost.

"This is insane; this is not Islam," the president muttered.

"It certainly is Islam according to the Fatwas put out by their mullahs," Mertzl commented brutally. "Their opinion of Islam matters more than ours."

FBI director MacCloud, agreed. "Sir, this is what the Islamists call 'Conquest by the Right Hand.' It is how they subjugate societies: taking their women, making them pay the jizya tax, restricting their rights, outlawing worship of other religions. It is documented to be taking place in Europe as we speak and we have seen traffic on the internet describing the same thing here in the United States since 2005. There are no doubt small rings of jihadists that have practiced this here already, albeit on a small scale."

"That cannot be true," the president said emphatically.

"It is true Mr. President," MacCloud said in a tone that clearly unnerved the president. "In Dearborn, Michigan the

Islamists are allowed to demonstrate but the Christian community is not. In New York City Muslim prayers block the streets every Friday—let the Catholic Church try and get away with that—and yet nothing is done."

"They are showing their faith," the president protested.

"Director Gann is absolutely right. If the Jews, Catholics, Protestants, anyone but the Muslims showed the same faith the media would be all over them," Mertzl objected. "It's a damn double standard."

"There is no double standard," the president insisted.

MacCloud insisted, "There is a double standard Mr. President and it's getting dangerous. Mr. President, your attorney general has issued orders to me banning the terms "Islamic terrorist," "honor killings," and "jihadist." He has interfered with investigations, with your blessing, to classify obvious terrorist acts as workplace violence to desensitize them.

"Mr. President, the beheading of a fifty-three year old grandmother in a bakery by a man yelling Allahu Akbar is no more workplace violence than the massacre at Fort Hood. Mr. President—let me be blunt—we do not need to be protecting people who by their own admission are trying to kill us."

"Enough!" Oetari snapped. "There is no domestic terrorism problem! There is no Muslim terrorist problem—period! I'll have no more discussion along those lines. Such talk is bigotry and I will not have that in my administration!"

"Then what would you like to do about the ISIS fighters and their—expressions of faith—Mr. President?" Mertzl asked frigidly.

The president glowered silently, muttering to himself.

Mertzl took a step forward and scowled. "Mr. President, you agreed that we could not allow ISIS free reign to expand their terrorist state. Thousands upon thousands of lives are at stake. Remember the civilian casualty figures from Fallujah and Mosul. Hundreds of thousands of civilians have been murdered, enslaved or become refugees. We have a responsibility to stop this."

"History teaches us that adventures like this only inflame the Muslim population," Oetari replied in an equally blunt tone of voice, but he would not meet Mertzl's gaze. He retreated to the window, looking out over the White House lawn. "The world is a messy place. These kinds of things have been happening for years; Al Qaeda beheaded dozens of people on video after we invaded and occupied Iraq!

"I'm not sure why there's such a hue and cry now, but the polls don't lie, the American people want blood. With the Mid-term elections coming up in a few months I had to give them something; now I regret it. This is what happens when you seek a military solution."

"Mr. President, with all due respects, it only takes one side to require a military solution," General Mertzl insisted. "ISIS does not give us any other choice. You can't negotiate with terrorists!"

Oetari turned on the chairman. "So you favor escalation; after this fiasco? The nephew of the Turkish President is dead at the hands of American forces!"

"Sir, he was consorting with terrorists and murderers," Gann reminded the president. He added carefully, "This incident highlights a possible connection between a trusted NATO ally and the growing terrorist state in the Middle East. That is highly disturbing."

General Mertzl piggy backed on the director's comments, insisting, "We need to do more. The Iraqi's are wholly incapable of meeting this threat, the Kurds are barely hanging on, and the Turks are simply watching ISIS slaughter innocent men, women and children. If we do not intervene ISIS will expand its so-called caliphate to encompass Syria and Iraq, maybe south-eastern Turkey."

The general furrowed his heavy brows, adding gruffly, "If left unchecked, they will pursue their goal of absorbing Jordan and the Arabian Peninsula as well. Thousands more will die and millions will be persecuted."

"A Caliphate is their heritage, and as long as it doesn't cause war with Israel or NATO I don't see why it's any of our business. Violence only begets violence." Oetari reminded

General Mertzl, glancing up at the block of a man with clear dislike. "I agreed to this operation because of the Iranian connection. I agree that we don't want these people working together. However, that's as far as I go!"

"Our profiles of the ISIS players," Gann began, but that's as far as he got before the president interrupted him.

"Profiles? Are you kidding? Profiles!" Oetari barked with disdain. "I grew up with these people in Indonesia, I understand them. Their entire lives, indeed for almost fifteen hundred years they've been held down by the West. Why don't they deserve a caliphate, their own 'Rome' if you will? A united Muslim world is a dream of every Muslim, and why not?

"Certainly Christians have the same wish. Why should Muslims be treated with less legitimacy? I think it would be easier for us, the West, to deal with a proud Muslim world instead of an angry Muslim world." He shook his head vehemently, adding under his breath, "You people simply don't understand how the West has infuriated people all over the world!"

"How so Mr. President?" the general asked, seemingly genuinely mystified and miffed, but then the general was always angry at something.

"Desert Storm?" the president remarked hotly. "You do remember the invasion and occupation of Iraq don't you?"

"I certainly do Mr. President," the general replied.

"Where were the weapons of mass destruction?"

"Mr. President, you know very well that there were weapons of mass destruction: over five thousand chemical munitions were found!"

"Chemical munitions!" Oetari said with disdain.

"Chemical munitions are classified as weapons of mass destruction by the United Nation and for good reason," Mertzl reminded the president. "Saddam Hussein used poison gas on the Kurds, his fellow Muslims, killing thousands. He not only had weapons of mass destruction, he used them," the general replied with a partial dry laugh. "He was working on nukes.

The United Nations decided that was too big a risk for the Middle East and approved Desert Storm."

"On false data supplied by this country," Oetari pronounced with particular vitriol on the word *country*. "We're always throwing our weight around, meddling in the affairs of others. We, the United States, always know best. It's been the same since Rome; only the West knows the meaning of civilization. People in other parts of the world know nothing!"

The three members of the military/intelligence community exchanged glances. They knew what they were up against— that was their job. President Oetari's obvious bitterness over the West could be understood by his upbringing.

The president made no secret of it. He boasted being the product of a hippie, communist, counter-culture, activist mother who fled the United States after a stint in the domestic terrorist group 'The Motorcycle Men.' His mother was famous for lauding the Manson murders, writing that the rich pigs got what they deserved.

That kind of rhetoric made her a target for the "Man," and for the rest of her life her son got a steady dose of that angry ideology. She schooled her son in Marxist, anti-capitalist ideology as well as pointing out the evils of world powers like the United States. Oetari always said that gave him a broader view of the world; a more empathetic view than the traditional colonial view; a view that had the United States looking down on all other nations as inferior.

On the productive side, she taught him globalization, and preached that the day of the superpowers must end in a New World Order that brought equality to all nations. That was productive because it spurred a young Oetari on to make something of himself. He cultivated friendships and through his mother's academic friends, former members of her Terrorist cell now embedded in liberal academia, he received an invitation to Harvard. The young Oetari took advantage of it.

Backed by money, academia, a progressive generation in the media, Caucasian guilt and a gift of easy charm, Oetari translated Harvard into Harvard Law School and thence into politics. After a brief stint in the state legislature and one term in the Senate, his sponsors thrust the handsome, charismatic, articulate ideologue upon the scene as the answer to the stodgy, entrenched political stalemate that was Washington.

He took the political world by storm and even middle of the road conservatives—the American breadbasket—welcomed the change with curiosity and really some relief that the old dogmas were getting tossed out.

Yet in politics as in love some things never change.

Now the people against the "Man" were in power; they were the "Man." Oetari made it very clear he didn't want to play the same games. He wanted to do things his way and only his way. That made moments like these, rare though they were, decidedly uncomfortable for everyone. Oetari absolutely hated to be forced to do things he didn't like.

"The Middle East should be left alone," he grumbled. "We should never have gone into Iraq."

"I agree with you Mr. President." Mertzl replied calmly.

Oetari's expression of surprise demanded an answer.

"I'm a military man Mr. President. I think in a strategic sense," Mertzl explained. "The overthrow of Saddam Hussein was strategically a mistake and put the Middle East into turmoil. While he was in power Iraq was a check on Iranian expansion as well as theological terrorist groups like Al Qaeda and ISIS; all of which are far more dangerous that any Iraqi adventures."

"So you would have left Kuwait in the hands of Saddam?" Ms. Carrabolla, Oetari's National Security Agency advisor said, opening her mouth for the first time. She was out of her league with these men and she knew it. As the president's former campaign advisor and for a time his Secretary to the United Nations, Carrabolla saw the world through the eyes of an ideologue. She was completely ignorant of the real world, and willing to say anything, true or not, to further the Administration.

Carrabolla was responsible for throwing the military and Intelligence community under the bus on more than one occasion—even as the president had—and thus the military men viewed her with suspicion and contempt. She returned the favor.

Mertzl laughed. "Kuwait had no value strategically, it was purely an Arab argument. Using the president's own logic, it was none of our business, why interfere?" When Carrabolla was caught off guard by the remark, searching for a stinging response, he added, "Besides, why would a civilized nation support Kuwait, a country that is considering legalizing the enslavement of women; particularly Western women just like you, Ms. Carrabolla?"

She gazed at the general with shock, astounded that this military dinosaur so thoroughly and efficiently trumped her in rhetoric.

The president actually chuckled at the pointed criticism, sitting down at his desk. He sighed and spread his hands wide. "Justified or not, the Muslim world reacts emotionally to events. I'll be the first to admit they are not driven by logic or debate; you simply cannot reason some subjects in an open forum without risking violence. That is especially true if you are crossing the imams; I remember that all too well.

"That being said, the more we interfere—rightly or wrongly—the more we stir the hornet's nest of jihad. These people want their caliphate. Who are we to stand in their way?"

"That's true Mr. President, and I think the American people would go along with you but for the brutality of ISIS," Carrabolla said, trying to regain her standing amongst the national security team. "We need to act but not in a heavy handed manner which involve us in another protracted war like Vietnam."

Her point was made, but to her surprise, Mertzl nodded and said, "Ms. Carrabolla is right Mr. President."

"You agree with her?" the president said mockingly, amused that the general should side with someone he so obviously disliked.

"Yes, we risk the same results as Vietnam if we're not careful; no one wants to see that."

"So you admit that Vietnam was a mistake," the president exclaimed. "Wonder of wonders, I should declare a national holiday!"

"Any time you fight a war not to win it's a mistake," the general said firmly. "But to gain peace in the region and then pull out lock, stock and barrel as we did in Vietnam is a mistake. Shortly after we left the North Vietnamese communists slaughtered two million of their fellow Vietnamese in cold blood. We watched and did nothing. The same thing is now happening in Iraq; it is the byproduct of leaving the world to terrorists and communists."

Oetari was beside himself, but Carrabolla interjected herself into the sensitive discussion. "We are not abandoning Iraq. The president approved this Cobra operation. We are effectively striking the senior leadership of ISIS just as we did during the surge in Afghanistan and Iraq."

"I agree, we still have time to correct the situation, but we need to be more aggressive," the general advised. "We need to expand the Cobra operations to all aspects of the ISIS leadership. We also need to begin sabotaging their infrastructure, cutting their flow of money."

"Anything else?" Carrabolla asked coarsely. "Can you be specific or is your only answer to carpet bomb everything and everybody."

Director Gann stepped in, telling the president, "There is a surgical method of degrading and eventually destroying ISIS that does not involve carpet bombing, but we have to be committed to it."

"I'm listening," Oetari said with icy reserve.

"For example, ISIS is starting a campaign of transforming significant buildings into visual confirmation of their power and control, painting them black and designating them as ISIS government buildings. That works both ways. We should target every single one of those buildings and send a laser guided two-thousand pound bomb down their chimneys. That would humiliate ISIS in front of the local population; they're helpless against air power."

Oetari nodded gravely, saying, "I don't really have a problem with that. The visual might be effective on the evening news. That might slow ISIS recruitment here." He glanced up at FBI Director MacCloud. "Director, you've been unusually silent. Do you have any suggestions on the Homefront?"

"We have a list of the mosques, madrassas and organizations within the United States that have, may have, or may someday provide support for ISIS and or Al Qaeda. Every single one of those institutions should have their assets frozen immediately. The FBI should raid them. I guarantee our suspicions are nowhere near as bad as the truth."

The president looked stunned. He had agreed to a single Special Forces operation, but that only made the military hunger for more. He had visions of a full scale war on his hands. Oetari the Nobel Peace Prize winner, the president who ended wars was on the verge of starting his own complete with a domestic crack down not seen since World War II.

"This is an all-out war on Islam."

"No sir, that's what we're trying to prevent," MacCloud said firmly. "However, getting rid of terminology, ignoring terrorist acts as "workplace violence," honor killings as "domestic violence" and allowing madrassas to teach kindergarteners that Jews are "pigs" and Christians are "dogs" does not stop jihadists. Putting them under surveillance, cutting their funding and forcing them to live by our laws not only stops the jihadists, it allows the majority of peace loving Muslims to live free of fear, to pursue the American dream. Isn't that what we want?"

"If we allow the peaceful Muslim population to rise from under the thumb of the radicals we defeat them without firing a shot," Gann added. "The last thing the jihadists want is Muslims in America who are free from fear and thriving."

"If they can't coerce their fellow Muslims, if they lack funding or propaganda their recruitment it will dry up."

"We can keep the military operations overseas, but they need to be swift and devastating! Dead jihadists rotting in the desert isn't much of a recruiting tool either," General Mertzl told the president. "Defeating them decisively will stop the flow of foreign fighters to Iraq and Syria."

MacCloud stepped forward and emphasized his point. "We don't have to make this noisy. It doesn't have to be on the evening news. When a hundred of the worst mosques are raided, and we know who they are Mr. President, they'll get the message. When CAIR has its assets frozen because of their relationship with the Muslim Brotherhood then all other Muslim organizations will take notice. Take out the big offenders and the small operators will actively discourage their membership from recruitment and covert aid to the terrorists."

"We need to nip this in the bud Mr. President," Mertzl insisted. "We missed out chance when ISIS moved out of Syria. We may not get another chance to crush them without a full scale involvement. The longer we wait the more this will cost in blood and treasure!"

"You want another surge! There is nothing that corroborates that theory," Carrabolla snapped. "The president is right. We have rocked the boat, but that's enough. ISIS will not be defeated by yet another surge."

Oetari looked at military and intelligence men, and said, "I agree with Ms. Carrabolla. It seems like that's what you're calling for gentlemen—another surge. The previous war didn't work; what makes you think another one will?"

"Sir, Iraq was at peace before we pulled out. It was stable."

"There was no reason to stay," Oetari said.

"Sir, the point I made a year ago is still true today," Mertzl reminded the president. "We left a force in Germany after World War II not simply to prevent the Germans from falling back into their evil ways but to preserve Germany from Russian domination. The same was true with Japan and Korea where we still have troops today."

"At great cost," Oetari reminded the general.

"Yes sir, it would have been nice if we hadn't had to leave troops at all, but look at the price we paid in Vietnam when we pulled out: two million Vietnamese slaughtered, our prestige diminished, our soldiers lost in vain. Mr. President we can't let that happen again."

"But who is to say this will be a success?"

Director Gann of the CIA said firmly, "Mr. President, during the surge in Iraq Al Qaeda admitted defeat. They broadcast to the Muslim world: "We are defeated here, do not send any more fighters!" We also have significant statistics showing the numbers and effectiveness of the IED campaign decreasing in proportion to our Cobra operations against Al Qaeda. The constant reminder of their leaders being assassinated definitely hurt the morale and effectiveness of the Al Qaeda fighters."

Oetari turned to the FBI. The director shrugged, and said, "Our data suggests the same thing. Recruitment became much more difficult when the surge was decimating the terrorist fighting force. However, as of late, as we have relieved the pressure, the home grown jihadist recruiters parlay that as victory, as America retreating, as weakness, and that has led to a spike in jihadist recruitment as well as 'lone wolf' terrorist operations like the Boston Marathon bombing and Major Hassan's terrorist attack at Fort Hood."

"That was a situation involving workplace violence, not terrorism," Carrabolla interjected.

Director MacCloud stroked his mustache with caustic deliberation, allowing the tone of his voice to accentuate his derision. He continued, "Successful bombing and especially ground campaigns may not make us friends but they have proven remarkably effective at stopping the flow of recruits. The equation is simple: young men will not sign up for a lost cause! We've created a problem by relieving the pressure before the threat was annihilated."

"You're talking about another ground campaign," Oetari protested. "I ended this war. I will not begin another."

"We may have ended our part of the war but the enemy has a say in whether the war's over, Mr. President," General Mertzl said gruffly. "When one side quits while the other side is still fighting that generally means the quitter has lost the war."

"I will not commit boots on the ground in Iraq!" Oetari said harshly. "The Iraqi's and the Syrians will have to solve this themselves."

"Does that mean we leave the Christians and the Shia to be slaughtered?"

"These are isolated incidents," President Oetari shot back. "That behavior is grievance driven; it is not a central tenet of Islam, even of Al Qaeda and its offshoots."

Director Gann stated brutally, "The matter is summed up for every person alive: Either submit, or live under the suzerainty of Islam, or die. Does Islam force people by the power of the sword to submit to its authority—yes!"

"Where did you come up with that?" the president demanded.

"It's a direct quote from Osama bin Laden," he replied tersely.

"You simply do not understand these people," Oetari insisted. "Islam is a religion of peace and it is you and all the West that want to see it as a religion of war."

Oetari went behind his desk and sat down. The expression on his face was thoughtful. He said aloud, though as if to himself, "These people are not the people I grew up with. Their fury for past grievances has pushed them to this; however, that is not an excuse for this barbarity, this perversion of Islam—it's not even Islam."

The president looked up suddenly, feeling the weight of the military men's eyes. He cautioned them, "Don't remind me of the actions of Muhammad! That was the seventh century; it was a completely different time! We need to deal in the here and now."

"Then what are your orders Mr. President?" General Mertzl said, waiting patiently.

"We cannot put boots on the ground—period," Oetari replied emphatically. "However, we will respond. I want a limited air campaign, enough to degrade ISIS capabilities both militarily and economically. As distasteful as it is, I see no other alternative than to continue with your Cobra missions.

"As far as the Homefront is concerned, the FBI needs to root out the radicalized elements recruiting our young men to Syria to fight with the jihadists but I do not want mosques raided, is that understood? Go after individual recruiters but leave places of worship alone."

He looked directly at General Mertzl. "I'd like the Air Force's recommendations for targets by this afternoon. Ms. Carrabolla and her NSA staff will look them over and approve the target list and numbers."

"The target lists and air campaign plans are already drawn up Mr. President. The staff can brief you on specifics at any time," General Mertzl replied. "However, am I to understand that Ms. Carrabolla is going to have the deciding factor on the actual targets to be hit? With all due respects, Mr. President, she has no military experience whatsoever."

"She has political experience and she has restraint; something the military does not have," Oetari replied coldly. "The meeting is over. You have your instructions."

The men and woman headed toward the door just as White House Chief of Staff Jeffries came in. The last thing they heard from the Oval Office was her updating the president's itinerary.

"Here is the speech you need to give at 1:50 pm this afternoon; it's expressing your heartfelt condolences to the family of the beheaded journalist. This is important, the press feels empathy for the family; this is one of their own. You need to be both angry and sympathetic."

"All right," he said in a distracted sort of way. "At least it's short."

"It has to be, you have a 2:00 pm tee time, so you're giving the address in casuals with the presidential blazer."

"Okay," he grimaced, then his eye brightened. "Has Freddy called? They should be done with the meeting."

"Not yet sir."

"Put the call through even if I'm on the golf course—hold everything else—this is important."

The president turned and left hurriedly.

Mertzl, Gann and MacCloud glanced at each other with concerned surprise, but then all three men automatically looked at the younger Carrabolla. She was the president's man, so to speak. Their accusatory glances asked her silently to justify the president's actions. She blushed and turned down the hall away from them. It was the opposite way she intended to go, but Carrabolla couldn't answer them, and they knew it.

CHAPTER 11: Rebranding

Being the captain for the operation wasn't so bad. The Al Qaeda people did their level best to create a premature paradise for Abdullereda on Earth. They stuck him in a proverbial garden flowing with wine and virgins, some of each gender; they appealed to Abdullereda's mortal desires—vice.

He had as many women as he wished: Western women kidnapped in Europe and the United States, some as young as twelve; Muslim women who volunteered themselves for the jihad; Muslim women of the wrong sects or proclivity whose families were slaughtered but they were allowed to live because of their youth and good looks; African women and girls captured in schools or villages, or simply swept off the street because they had no chaperones.

Women, girls—he was offered boys, but declined—alcohol, whatever he wanted Abdullereda got. After a few weeks it became somewhat routine. He wondered why they were doing this, not that he was complaining, but he did wonder. At the conclusion of one of his five daily prayer sessions, a cleric informed him why in no uncertain terms.

"If you do not successfully complete your mission you will assuredly go to Hell," he told a stunned Abdullereda.

"But I thought this was to prepare me for Heaven," the dumbfounded pilot replied.

"Some of it is certainly," the cleric agreed. "The virgins will be there, but the Dhimmi certainly will not be. They will be in Hell with you however if you fail."

That caused Abdullereda some concern. The difference between the beautiful but sullen, drugged, half-alive Western girls—none of whom performed except out of fear—was in marked contrast to the Muslim volunteers. Those girls felt like they were doing their part in the jihad, which Abdullereda appreciated; they were very thorough and very motivated to please.

The cleric cautioned him, "The Westerners are largely too fearful in this world, but beware! When they are in Hell with you they will seek their revenge." He looked down at the pilot's crotch.

Abdullereda was especially fond of blow jobs, and the cleric knew that. What he insinuated was terrifying as it would be repeated throughout all eternity. He nodded to the pilot, and said fervently, "The price of failure is severe and not limited to the fires of Hell. Your family will suffer through more than dishonor; they will be complicit. You have children do you not?"

"Yes," he said carefully.

"Do not let your sins fall upon your children," the cleric told him. "The one way, the only way you can fully expiate your sins now is to follow through with the operation and conclude it successfully. Do you understand?"

"I understand," Captain Hussein answered. He gathered his things and made to leave the bordello, telling his spiritual leader, "I must go to the simulator and practice the mission."

"Excellent," the cleric told him.

Abdullereda headed back to his quarters where he had a very advanced version of 'Flight Simulator' hooked up to an Airbus A380 control mock-up. The jihadists were very thorough in their preparation. As he sat down at the controls the Malaysian felt the need to purify himself, but not through prayer.

He called his son.

"Hello?" said the voice on the other end of the line, seemingly far away by the connection.

"Abdulla, it is Abdullereda, your father," he said. "How are you son?"

"Do not call me that!" Abdulla exclaimed, confused. "I thought you were dead. I rejoiced! How is it that you're not dead? I heard it all in the news. Mother called me, trying to tell me to be sad, to grieve. I could not. After all the times you abandoned us I was ready for an end to it—now this!"

"Abdulla, I understand how you feel; I understand you are not proud of your father. I am trying to change that," he replied.

"How are you going to do that?" Abdulla asked, sounding angry and yet like all children desperate for their parents to be someone they could look up to, to respect.

"I know I can never make it up to your mother by being a good husband, so I will free her of myself and make sure that she is taken care of for the rest of her life," he said.

"By faking your death; that is a coward's way out is it not?" the son said, rejecting the explanation outright.

"No, I will not be faking my death," Abdullereda said resolutely. "I have learned something from my son. The son has taught the father an important lesson."

"How so?" Abdulla demanded.

"When your mother told me that you had emigrated to Paris to join the jihad and topple the West from within I was shocked. I had always sympathized with our jihad; but here was my seventeen year old son doing something about it! You took action while I, your father, who should have served as the example for his son, was polluting my soul in search of money and flesh; just like a Western whore! You shamed me Abdulla; you shamed me as your mother's tears never could. So I have finally found my courage and done something about it."

"What have you done?"

The son's voice held just enough hope in it for Abdullereda to continue, to reach for reconciliation. "You know your mother is taken care of financially now; the airline will pay her more than she needs. So I hope to gain forgiveness from you. I have not taken this airplane for me or for your mother but for our holy jihad. I cannot give you the details, but you will see it in the news soon enough.

"There will be great destruction Abdulla. The Zionists will suffer a great defeat, a defeat that will bring about their total annihilation. You can say with pride that it was your father that committed the great sacrifice that began their downfall!"

101

"You will martyr yourself?" the boy asked breathlessly, hoping against all his experience that his father was being truthful now. "I can't believe it. After all your lies how can this be true?"

"The testament to my martyrdom is already in the news," Abdullereda told him. "They know I was the captain. It's in all the papers, but you know I am not dead as they think. I did not crash the airplane. I slew the dog Christian that was my first officer and took the airplane," he did not mind stretching the truth for his son a little bit. Abdullereda had a lot to make up for in his son's eyes.

"What then father, what then?" the boy pleaded.

"Allah be praised it is paradise itself to hear you call me father!" Abdullereda said with tears in his eyes. "I have commandeered the aircraft for the jihad; but my mission is not complete until I take down Zion itself!"

"My father the lion of Islam will strike at the heart of Zion itself!" Abdulla rejoiced.

"My son, I will," Abdullereda said with heartfelt emotion. "All I ask is that you forgive me. Let me hear it with my mortal ears before I enter into martyrdom."

"Father with all my heart I forgive you! I celebrate you! Your name will be on my lips with pride!"

Tearfully father and son parted. Abdullereda threw himself into his work. He had sinned enough. His son ensured that his heart yearned for martyrdom. To redeem himself in his son's eyes was a greater gift to Abdullereda than any harem or hoard of gold.

CHAPTER 12: Idyll

Jeremiah Slade was tired. The long flight from Kuwait City to Paris and then Paris to Washington D.C. took more out of him than the mission. He wondered how the airline pilots did it day after day, month after month, year after year.

He pulled into driveway of the turn-of-the-century Victorian outside of Langley, Virginia in his decade-plus silver Jaguar XK. It was used of course, very used, just like the house, but it was Slade's. It was a reminder to him of good advice about open windows.

In front of him was the lifestyle the CIA recruiter reminded him about so long ago. Slade didn't regret the lifestyle; he embraced it. He was a man who always wanted responsibility and this fit to overflowing.

Throwing his bag over his shoulder, Slade climbed the steps to Victorian farmhouse with a picturesque round tower complete with witch's hat. The broad wrap-around porch shielded the front rooms from the harsh eastern winters.

The residual tension of his mission washed away under the eaves of the house—which was not the source of agent Wilson's concern either—like the Jag, Slade bought the house cheap and brought back to life through years of labor. It served its purpose.

Before Slade could reach the front door it opened of its own accord. Helen, his cousin, appeared in a comfortable print dress and apron, as if from the set of "Leave it to Beaver" or "The Andy Griffith Show." She smiled and greeted Slade at the door with a hug, sliding her shoulder under his arm and snuggling closely. She gave him a long, appreciative squeeze and led him into the house.

"Hello Jeremiah, how was the trip?" she asked, her bright blue eyes smiling beneath tousled blonde hair. She was the only person in the world, his parents included, who called him Jeremiah. She'd been through so much he let her have that.

"Boring but productive," he answered. As far as Helen was concerned, Slade worked for the government at the State Department; a logical follow on from his military time. She had no idea his business was as dangerous as it was violent; but then, Helen didn't care. She owed Slade; at least in her mind she did. One night, thirteen years ago she returned home from a weekend visit to the nursing home where her mother lived to find that her husband had left her.

He was gone with all the furniture—even the baby's crib. Their six kids, ages four to six months, were sitting on the bare living room floor huddled in a blanket, watching a small twelve inch black and white TV—dad had taken the big color TV with him. Helen couldn't be shocked, she couldn't panic, not in front of her children, three from their marriage and three adopted from her sister, who succumbed to breast cancer, but all of them were her kids. They didn't realize what had just happened. Helen insulated them from the travesty and dealt with it privately. She was Mom.

At least the bastard left the food in the refrigerator and pantry. It was a good thing. She soon found that he cleared out the bank account and hadn't paid the bills in months.

An eviction notice was posted on her door the next morning. The power was shut off. The water was shut off, and Helen had to sneak buckets of water from the neighbor's hose. She wasn't working, she'd barely recovered from a hysterectomy a few months before.

Helen was destitute with six children.

Helen had literally no one to turn to. Her father was dead; her mother was in a nursing home, her sister's husband had remarried and they hadn't spoken in two years. All she could think of was to call her cousin Jeremiah. They'd been close. Secretly, she'd always regretted they were cousins, especially when he went into the military like her father did. Helen didn't want a great career or to party; she wanted what her mother had: to raise a family, live in a comfortable house and be a wife to a steady, caring man.

That dream ended that snowy day when her husband left her in Duluth, Minnesota. As proud as Helen was, she was desperate. She called Slade at midnight, having stared at the phone for days trying to get the courage to call.

He took emergency leave and showed up the next day. In an hour they were eating a family dinner at Perkins and then it was off to a comfortable hotel with a pool. The next day they flew to California, where Slade had just been assigned to Test Pilot School.

A few days later they picked out a cinder block house on base and moved in. Helen and her kids had a home again.

Slade took it all in stride, but Helen, whose empathy for people was a true gift, knew that the timing of her crisis was especially bad for Slade. Test Pilot School was a grueling year long program that demanded complete commitment, but Slade never said a thing about it.

Helen grew up in a military family. She knew the routine. She knew how military schools and assignments worked. She instinctively took on the role of running Slade's household so that he could concentrate on his job. She made sure he was fed, his uniforms were always ready, and his house was clean, his coffee was fresh at four in the morning and that he had a gin and tonic when he returned at six in the evening; six, so that he could unwind with a drink but still have his regulation "Twelve hours; bottle to throttle."

Helen took care of everything.

Slade was actually embarrassed by the effort Helen and the kids put forth to show their appreciation, but Helen sat him down and explained things to him.

"Jeremiah, when no one could or would help us you were there. You rescued us. You are supporting us; me, the kids, all of us. They have a roof over their heads and enough to eat; and they don't have to worry about being abandoned anymore. We need to support you, and we will."

It had been that way ever since.

Slade gave Helen and her kids a home. In return, Helen and the kids gave Jeremiah a family.

She was concerned, however, and she brushed his forelock of dark hair, just starting to get streaks of grey, saying, "You look tired. I know it's hard on you over there. Why don't you hop in the shower? I'll have a drink waiting for you on the back porch."

"That sounds like a good idea," Slade sighed, heading to his bedroom. Slade slept on one side of the house in the guest bedroom off his office. It was purely practical. He didn't need much. Helen had the master bedroom upstairs and the kids had the other upstairs bedrooms.

As he walked down the hall, the old oak floors creaking with every step, a chorus of, "Hello Uncle Slade!" greeted him—the kids, now ages thirteen to seventeen, wouldn't think of calling call him Jeremiah. That was for their mom.

"There are my rascals; how's school?" he inquired, or tried to. Helen intervened.

"There will be plenty of time for catching up," she chastised them all. "Your uncle is tired. It's been a long trip. Let him relax for a while."

"All right mom," they relented, returning to doing what they were doing. Welcome home Uncle Slade!"

"Now Helen," Slade softly chided, "You know I don't mind. I miss them too you know; don't tell them that of course! I don't want them to get soft."

She turned him by his shoulders and pushed him toward his bedroom. "You need to go relax and get washed up. You know the routine. Let me welcome you home, you've done your job, let me do mine."

Slade's room was like stepping back in time. A few hours before he'd been holed up in a mud and brick hovel with death all around him. Now he was in a period wall papered gentleman's room furnished with dark wood, twin leather chairs and bronze fixtures. Everything, absolutely everything, was in its place. Helen took her job seriously.

Walking into his closet, Slade opened a hidden panel in his wardrobe. The rack of suits and sundry other clothes swung aside to reveal a flat black panel. Slade pressed his hand against it and a red light came on, scanning his face. The combination fingerprint, facial recognition scan and retinal scan opened up the inner panel.

Inside was a small arsenal of weapons. Storing his sidearm, he undressed, heading for the shower. The bathroom, like the rest of the house, was done as a comfortable Victorian era cottage. It wasn't overdone; it was tasteful.

Stepping into the shower, Slade allowed the hot water to seep into his sore muscles, letting it wash away the last vestiges of Iraqi sand as well as the even deeper, hidden stains of blood and death. He purposefully turned his mind back, away from the last mission, thinking of home; recalibrating himself to domestic life.

It was a careful but necessary balancing act. It was easy, tragically easy to get lost in Slade's world. The adrenaline rush, the power, it was addictive. It was a simple thing to lose that sense of right and wrong when your entire working life revolved around doing wrong so that right would triumph. He'd seen it happen. So he turned that thought process off and thought about home, hearth and family.

Turning off the shower, Slade dried off and dressed in comfortable clothes that had been laid meticulously on the chair at the foot of the bed. He opened the door onto the back porch and sat down on the porch swing, looking out over the tree lined acreage to the slow moving river.

Helen brought him his drink and the kids joined him, filling him in on their lives since he was last home.

Jeremiah Slade was content, swinging idly on his porch, sipping his gin and tonic with a sedate smile on his face. He purged his mind of the images of burned children, slaughtered civilians and the red blossom of vaporized blood resulting from his bullet when it slammed through the fevered brain of a jihadist.

When those thoughts threatened to creep back into his mind a single word dispersed them. It was Helen, calling, "Dinner!"

Christopher L. Anderson

CHAPTER 12: The Daily Brief

Normally the president took his daily intelligence briefing remotely by iPad. That allowed Oetari to read the report at his leisure, which meant that more than half the time the President of the United States simply blew off the report and depended on the world performing according to his view of it.

The insistence of Director Gann briefing the president in person on the disappearance of Malaysia Flight 666 was both irritating and surprising. The president walked past the directors of the CIA and FBI and toward the Oval Office with Chief of Staff Jeffries, Ms. Carrabolla and Freddy Waters in tow.

Director MacCloud stiffened as Freddy passed him. Freddy, for his part, turned beet red. "Come in gentleman, come in," Oetari said, but then his secretary interrupted him.

"I'm sorry sir but President Ataturk of Turkey is on the line. Do you want to take the call now or later?"

"I'll take it now," the president told her. "Excuse me gentlemen." The president entered the Oval Office alone and closed the door. He put the president on speaker. "Mustafa my friend what can I do for you?"

"Oetari my friend, salaam," Ataturk said using the common Muslim greeting.

"Salaam," Oetari replied politely.

"We have a problem Patra, a very large problem."

"I'm listening," the president said, knowing what to expect.

"It is the assassination of my nephew," Ataturk told him gravely.

"I understand Mustafa," Oetari said quickly, trying to sooth the sensitive situation. "No one regrets the action more than I. Yet how could I, how could even my troops have known that he would be there with the ISIS people, Al Qaeda and Iran? Not only did we have no way of knowing but there was no possibility of expecting such a thing. Regardless, you have our heartfelt condolences."

"I know you are sincere in that Patra, and you are right, there is no way to expect that Turgut would be there—he was an impetuous boy, always impatient for the next great thing," Ataturk sighed. After a pregnant pause his voice dropped down a grave octave. "However, you know our people. You understand our people."

"I do," Oetari said quickly.

"Then you understand the emotions involved. My family has been attacked. My relative has been attacked. My family demands Qissas, the law of equality in punishment; a life for a life. That presents a problem."

"Surely that is for a premeditated killing Mustafa," replied the president, who having grown up in Muslim society knew the customs well. "This was an accident."

"Your sniper sending a bullet through young Turgut's eye was no accident," the president said bluntly. He sighed audibly, and then with a still serious but more understanding tone, said, "Put yourself in my place. No matter how much guilt Turgut deserves for putting himself in harm's way do you really think in the present atmosphere that my family, or my country, will view this in any other way?"

"What about forgiveness?" Oetari asked. "The United States will pay the Diyah, blood money, to wipe away the Qissas."

"Again, do you really think anyone in the Islamic world is in a forgiving mood right now?" Again there was a long pause. When Ataturk spoke again there was a heavy sense of gravity. "If this were a personal situation it would be solvable; I can control my family. However, this is more. It is a political situation. The Islamists faction is much stronger than the secular factions in the Grand National Assembly.

"Normally the Constitutional Court would intervene with any anti-secular party—they are no longer doing so. There are now Islamists on the bench and the secular judges are, quite frankly, frightened. The Islamists and jihadists are a problem in my country."

"Is that why your tanks are sitting on the border with Syria and watching ISIS slaughter the Kurds?" Oetari snapped, irritated at being lectured by a fellow president.

"What do I care about the Kurds?" Ataturk replied bluntly. "They are a problem here as well. Let ISIS kill them, and then we can kill ISIS."

"So you will help against ISIS?"

"After the Kurdish problem is solved—yes. However, we first have to solve this problem with Turgut's assassination."

Oetari paused, but finally asked, "What is it you want?"

"I want the name of the man who pulled the trigger."

"You're not seriously thinking of sending your people after him are you? Convict him in absentia. He will never go to Turkey—would that satisfy you?"

"I do not need to involve Turkey in such a way with a NATO partner; you need not worry Oetari. Your sniper targeted other people in that meeting. They are just as interested as I in knowing who the killer is. The beauty of it is they have already threatened your military personnel."

Oetari thought for a long moment. "I cannot give you the name, of course, that goes without saying."

"Then, as I said, we have a problem."

"Mustafa, you are asking me to expose an agent on assignment."

"Patra, it is done all the time. The world is our chess board. We barter these warriors like pawns."

Oetari was very careful in his choice of words. He had Ataturk's attention. "This is too important a matter to deal with over the phone. I will send my personal confidant Mr. Waters to you."

The President of Turkey understood perfectly. "I will try and defuse the situation here," Ataturk told him, satisfied for the moment. "However, if Mr. Waters comes armed with only an apology I will have no choice but to be very public with my comments. Things will take a decidedly bad turn."

"I understand."

#

Director MacCloud glowered at Freddy Waters. Waters for his part avoided the FBI Director's eyes and hid behind Jeffries.

Gann sidled up next to MacCloud, and said, "We've fallen a long way, having a domestic terrorist in the White House with access to the president. But you look like you're taking it personally."

MacCloud clenched his teeth and scowled. "It's very personal. I'm the reason he's here."

Gann's expression was enough to spur MacCloud to continue. "We had Waters dead to rights for murder, terrorism, plotting a violent overthrow of the government—everything."

"He got off on a technicality—I remember—the FBI mole was not operating on a warrant so all of the evidence was flushed."

"Waters was the worst they had. He had a grand plan for a global communist world, including the elimination of those who couldn't be re-educated. Marx was his Jesus. He wanted to implement that game plan to the letter, even if it resulted in millions of people being—eliminationed."

"We've both dealt with scum like this all of our careers," Gann asked. "What about Waters rubs you so raw?"

"I was the mole," MacCloud told him.

Gann was astonished, but there was no time for further consideration. The secretary announced, "The president will see you now."

#

Oetari called his secretary to let his cabinet members into the Oval Office. As they entered he reorganized his thoughts, reminding himself of the subject of the meeting. "So the Malaysians have lost an airliner. Not to be unsympathetic, but why should I care about an aviation tragedy? Regrettable as it is, what is it you want me to do? There are already recovery operations ongoing."

"Mr. President we've briefed you concerning the captain of the aircraft," Director Gann reminded the president. There was a hint of reproach in his normally calm voice. "He is an Al

Qaeda sympathizer. We've discovered that a deadheading pilot was not employed by Malaysian Airlines but was actually a plant, an Al Qaeda operative. There were also two Iranians travelling with stolen passports. The aircraft disappears and there is no wreckage. That constitutes a potential situation."

"First I've heard of it."

"If you'll consult the daily briefings of the last week you will see we touched on it repeatedly," Gann said diplomatically.

"If it's important then maybe you should do more than "touch on it" Director Gann," the president complained. "Obviously you didn't prioritize the information, but go on, what about the captain and the Iranians? Do you think they pulled an Egypt Air?"

Director Gann bit his lip, not mentioning the cost of the CIA brief in sweat and blood—quite literally. He knew his president. Oetari, for whatever reason, was not one to read the intelligence briefings but at the same time he didn't want anyone to realize he hadn't read them. Therefore, Gann had to tread carefully in order to get his point across and more importantly in order for the president to approve any and all necessary actions.

"Mr. President, I would be only happy to report that we had another suicide, but I'm afraid we're looking at a more sinister scenario."

"Which is?"

"We believe there's a strong possibility that the aircraft was hijacked."

The president didn't hide his surprise. "What on earth for? We haven't had any hostage demands—nothing. The airplane simply disappeared." He shook his head and chuckled without humor. "I know it's your job to be paranoid about certain things but really Gann, aside from a captain with questionable politics, someone getting a free ride by impersonating a pilot and two poor Iranians just trying to get out of Malaysia, and really who can blame them, what do you have to go on?"

Gann laid three sets of photos on the president's desk. He pointed to the first photo, which showed a group of about a dozen men sitting around a simple table. They held iPads, which seemed out of place considering the obvious rural Middle Eastern furnishings. Two of the men's heads were circled.

"The photo was taken in northern Iraq a week ago by a Cobra team. The man in uniform is Colonel Nikahd, the head of the Special Operations branch of the Iranian Republican Guard. The other man, the one with the burns," the president interrupted him.

"Khallida—right, one of the masterminds of Nine-Eleven and the follow-on operation "Wave of Allah," correct?" When Gann nodded, the president pointedly said, "I know you guys don't think I ever read those briefs, but on occasion I do."

"Yes sir," Gann replied, but before he continued, Oetari held up his hand, an ashen look on his face. He put his finger on the chest of a young man in tribal garb.

"That's Turgut! This is the meeting where he was murdered!"

"Yes Mr. President, we've spoken about that; he was unfortunately collateral damage."

"Collateral damage my ass," Freddy Waters muttered under his breath.

Everyone looked at him. Freddy shrugged, but Director MacCloud couldn't restrain himself anymore. "Mr. President, I must protest the presence of Mr. Waters. He doesn't have the clearance required to discuss national security matters of this nature. He does not have the need to know."

"I say he does." The president said, glancing up at MacCloud. "Do you have a problem with Mr. Waters being here?"

"I do indeed Mr. President," MacCloud asserted. "He is a known domestic terrorist, a murderer and an enemy of this nation. I absolutely protest his presence!"

"He is one of the most respected members of this nation's academia Director MacCloud," the president said icily. "He demonstrated against the Vietnam War, as did many people, and his actions were directed toward peace not violence. That is possibly why he shows distaste at the "collateral damage" Director Gann so blithely points out. It was a human life snuffed out unnecessarily and tragically."

The president thought for a moment, and then, cocking his head to the side, he turned to Gann. "That reminds me," Oetari said, a scowl crossing his face. "This Cobra snafu still doesn't sit well with me. It was a Delta Force operation, but wasn't that the sniper was one of your men Gann?"

"Yes sir."

"So it was actually CIA that assassinated the nephew of President Ataturk—correct?"

The room grew thickly silent.

Gann turned ashen. "It was a clean operation sir."

"Who was the triggerman?"

"Sir, every target was properly vetted," Gann insisted.

"Who was he?"

After a long pause, Gann said, "I cannot mention his name for obvious reasons Mr. President. The information is in your briefing."

Oetari paged through his iPad. He found a picture and waved Gann over, "Is this him in the airplane holding the rifle?"

"Yes sir."

"He is over zealous," Oetari frowned, making a note on his desk. "Director Gann this isn't a James Bond movie," the president said impatiently, "Perhaps this agent should be assigned something more benign. He's sitting in the airplane's cockpit, does that mean he's a pilot?"

"Yes sir."

"Well then assign the case of the missing Malaysian jet to him. There's nothing to it. Maybe, it will keep your agent from murdering anymore innocent civilians."

Gann steamed, but all he could do was accept the assignment. "Yes sir, but I haven't finished briefing you on the importance of the missing aircraft."

"I'm sure your agent will uncover the nefarious plot behind the crash. Goodness knows aviation accidents don't happen without some kind of terrorist plot behind them! Brief me when you've figured that out." He stood up. "That will be all, ladies and gentleman," Oetari said. As they began to file out, he looked at Waters. "Except for you Freddy."

Gann and MacCloud exchanged suspicious glances but they had no choice but to leave.

The cabinet members cleared the Oval Office. Oetari got up and went over to the window, looking out as he often did over the well-manicured lawn. He said simply, "You need to fly to Ankara and pay my respects to President Ataturk. I need to make sure our NATO ally understands how seriously we take the murder of his nephew."

Freddy Waters walked over to the president's desk. While the president's back was turned he took out his iPhone and snapped a picture of the screen. It was a photo of a group of men gathered in front of an OV-10 Bronco. In the cockpit was a man holding a sniper rifle. The names of the men were printed beneath their photos.

"I will be sure to express my sincere condolences to President Ataturk, Mr. President."

"Your meeting with the President of Iran appeared to go well," he ventured. "Aliaabaadi is willing to consign half his enriched Uranium to a United Nations storage facility in Abu Dhabi—correct?"

"He understands the gravity of the situation and is willing to provide the Uranium as collateral for their peaceful intentions."

"He seems rather quick to give up half his proposed arsenal," Oetari mused. "I didn't expect that." He thought for a moment, then glanced at Waters, who had already finished his espionage and put away his camera, just as the president expected. Oetari frowned. "What do you think he's up to?"

"I think he's sincere Mr. President," he replied. When Oetari's expression turned incredulous, Freddy added, "Oh, I'm sure the Iranians mean to finish their nuclear research and as President Aliaabaadi put it, "Join the club." That's fine. They need that capability to counterbalance Israel."

"That's obvious," the president replied tersely. He looked outside again. Aloud, he summarized his view of the Middle East—his sincere view—one he simply could not articulate publicly. "When the Iranians, the Turks, Pakistani's, Egyptians and Saudis clean out the scum like ISIS and Al Qaeda and form their Caliphate we will finally have stability in the region. Whether Israel is still there remains to be seen. Considering their nuclear arsenal I don't think they're going anywhere.

"Still, the Muslims will then have a stable civilization. This terrorism that pervades Islam will disappear once they have something to counterbalance the West. Aliaabaadi and Hayayi in Iran are the key players. That means they can either build this Caliphate or destroy it. I'm nervous about Aliaabaadi. He's ruthless. I can't be certain he's being straight with us about this Uranium business."

"What could he possibly do with three tons of the stuff when it's not ready to be put in a bomb?" Waters noted. "The Uranium is worth nothing as a bomb now; it is worth more as collateral to him because it gives him time to jockey for position. He's got to get all these nations in line and the Islamists are not helping."

"The Islamists are an aberration," Oetari said firmly. "They will fade away and be forgotten." He turned back to Waters and nodded. "For the time being we must placate the Islamist factions. President Ataturk needs our help. You'd better go now; the situation in Turkey is nearing crisis mode," Oetari told Waters. "Have a good trip Freddy.

CHAPTER 13: Georgetown

Slade loved the opera almost as much as Helen did. It gave them a chance to dress to the nines, have a fancy dinner and listen to music—it was a date night—they looked forward to it.

Tonight it was Don Giovanni. As the last haunting lines of Mozart's damnation faded to applause, Slade and Helen joined in the ovation and took their time exiting the opera house. As usual it had been a pleasant, relaxing night; they both looked forward to the next night out—another three months away.

"Thank you for taking me Jeremiah," Helen told him, latching onto his arm. "It's very sweet of you."

"It's all about my ego dear," he replied. "I love to be seen with the most beautiful woman in the theater on my arm."

"We make a good looking couple," she smiled.

"My sister told us that twenty-something years ago after we went skinny dipping," he teased.

She colored, slapping his arm playfully. Then she sighed.

"What is it?"

They were stepping into the elevator with a lot of people. Everyone else was talking about the opera. Helen waited, hugging his arm closer.

A couple twenty years their senior looked at them and smiled. They must have assumed Slade and Helen were married; they both wore rings. The lady ventured, "Out for an evening without the kids?"

"Yes," Helen smiled.

"How many dear?"

"Six."

"Six, oh my you do need a break," she laughed. "I was done after four!"

The elevator door opened. She touched Helen's arm as they exited first, "You're such a sweet couple. Maybe we'll see you at the next opera. Good night!"

Helen and Slade walked to the Jaguar in slow measured steps. She finally answered his question. "We're not a couple Jeremiah."

"That bothers you?"

"It should bother you," she said.

"Why?" he replied.

"Because you're still young," she said. "My life is my children. You still have the possibility of marriage and your own family."

"So what are you and the kids?"

"I'm your cousin and they are my children," she said heavily. "We can't change that fact as much as I want to."

"You're determined to ruin our evening," he told her stoically, opening the car door for her. She got in, and Slade went around to the other side. After he was in, closing the Jag's door with a satisfactory thump, he put his hand on her knee. She covered his hand with her own.

"Helen, my dear, you are as loving to me as any wife. The kids treat me as their father. For God's sake the youngest three don't even remember any other father. What more could I want?"

He started the car and pulled into line to exit the parking garage. She patted his hand, but said, "You are a man who has always followed the rules, except when it came to me."

"I did what was right. That was more important."

"You did the chivalrous thing and rescued the damsel in distress and all of her baggage," she admitted.

"I hope you don't consider the kids baggage; I certainly don't," he said seriously.

"Of course not, and I love you for how you treat the kids. I just wonder, I'm concerned that it's not enough for you. Jeremiah, you deserve a woman you can call your wife."

He squeezed her knee, then he turned his hand and held hers. Gently he picked her hand up and put it to his lips, a gentle gesture from someone everyone else called cold.

"Oh Jeremiah!" she sighed.

The phone rang.

"That's the office," Jeremiah growled, instantly losing his warmth. It was reflected in his voice, but he didn't hesitate to answer. "Slade here!"

It was Director Gann himself. "Agent Slade, something's come up," the director said in a deadly serious.

"Yes sir?" Slade didn't deal with the director except on very rare occasions. This was unusual, but not as unusual as the director's request.

"You're downtown D.C. by the JFK Center—good! I'm just leaving the White House. Meet me at 1510 26th Street Northwest in Georgetown—got it?"

"Sir, I'm just leaving the opera with my date," Slade objected.

"You date?" the director started. "Your pretty cousin Helen won't like that; don't go Don Giovanni on me Slade."

"No sir, it is Helen," he answered.

"Then bring her along. I'll see you there in about five minutes."

"Yes sir," he said and the line went dead. Slade let out a deep breath. Helen was looking at him.

"Well what is it? What's up at work that they need you at midnight?"

He turned onto Potomac Parkway heading north. "That was my boss; you're about to meet him."

"Is that a big deal, they're just bureaucrats," Helen said testily, obviously unhappy that their conversation was interrupted.

Slade understood. Helen had been trying to talk seriously about the subject for years—literally. He always avoided it. Something always, always came up. Now there was this. "My boss is a bit higher up than that. He's quite high up in fact."

"Well who is he?"

"Why are you so sure he's a he; he could be a she?" Slade chastised her. "Your lady friends aren't going to be very happy with your assuming my boss is a man."

"Jeremiah Milton Slade, you're avoiding the question!"

Slade pulled in front of a white nice white brick house with black shutters and a black front door. He got out of the Jag and

119

walked around to open her door. Holding out his hand, Helen took it but not without some consternation. As he closed the door she whispered harshly in his ear.

"Are you going to tell me what's going on?"

"Helen, dear, there's no time to explain. We'll have a nice talk afterwards. I promise you a nice long back rub."

"You'll be honest—about everything?"

He let out a deep breath. "Yes—everything."

They started to the door, but Helen stopped. "I'm not about to meet your secret family am I; there's not another wife and kids on the side?"

"No, I am quite fulfilled with you my dear cousin!" he told her, leading her to the front door.

It opened for them. A large man met them. He was wearing a black suit and tie. "Agent Slade, Ma'am, the director is waiting for you. Please come in."

"The director?" Helen whispered. "So it's not the Secretary of State?"

"No," Slade said, nodding to the man. "Thank you!"

Director Gann was waiting in the living room with a tall distinguished looking woman; his wife Gwen. She was as much a Washington insider as he, she had to be. This was D.C. Gann smiled stiffly when he saw Slade and apologized.

"Slade, I'm sorry to interrupt your evening, and you Ms. Sanders. As I'm sure Slade has told you, I am Jacob Gann and this is my wife Gwen."

They exchanged greetings and Director Gann immediately invited Slade into his office. Gwen took charge of Helen, "Would you care to sit outside in the garden dear, it's a lovely night?"

Helen accepted, not knowing what else to do. She followed Gwen out through the white rooms through a pair of French doors to the back garden, a narrow but lovely place of flagstones and green areas. She motioned to some outdoor furniture. "Have a seat dear, can I get you anything to drink?"

"No thank you, I had some champagne at the opera."

"How was the performance?"

"I loved it; I always love the opera and the symphony," she said.

"So do I, maybe we can see a performance one of these days. Jacob speaks very highly of your husband, but then in their line of work you have to be careful mixing business and pleasure."

"I'm sorry Gwen but we're not married," Helen corrected her, embarrassed.

"Oh that's right, you're his cousin," Gwen smiled, shaking her head. "I'm so sorry. I forgot. That's right, Slade took you and your children in. That was very gallant of him; there aren't many men these days who would do that. But then you are a very sweet thing and so very helpful. I know that Slade appreciates it."

"I'm sorry Gwen, I don't mean to seem rude, but how do you know so much about me and my family?"

"Gracious me, dear, that's what we do," she smiled.

"I'm sorry I don't understand," Helen said, now completely confused. "What does the State Department need to know about Jeremiah's home life? Is he in some sort of sensitive position?"

"The State Department?" Gwen laughed. "Dear me, do you mean to tell me that Jeremiah Slade hasn't let you in on his little secret?"

"What secret?"

Gwen leaned close to Helen and whispered with great pleasure, "He's a spy dear. My husband is the Director of the CIA. Jeremiah works for him. He's one of the very best agents we have."

Helen looked at Gwen with shock, but finally said, "That explains a lot. I was afraid he had another family somewhere."

Gwen patted her hand, "You know, you're taking the news a lot better than I did when I found out."

"You mean Jacob didn't tell you?"

"My dear, men never tell you anything until they get caught at it," she laughed. "We were married fifteen years before I found out; I missed all the excitement!"

#

Director Gann's office was a large modern room with an electronic fireplace and one wall devoted to half a dozen large flat screen panels. He got straight to the point.

"You did a nice job in Iraq Slade, but unfortunately it's come back to bite us." He put up a picture of the meeting.

"I left Khallida and Nikahd alone sir, just as ordered, though I still don't know why. They would have been my first two marks."

"Mine as well," he said, circling another man standing next to Nikahd. "That was the order, however, and you carried it out. We think Nikahd can be useful. Khallida is someone we want to track. That leaves us this man—do you know him?"

"No sir."

"You're sure?"

"Absolutely—who is he?"

"He is the man who is trying to ruin your career, maybe your life Slade."

"He's dead sir. I splashed his brains all over Nikahd."

"That's the point," Gann sighed. "That man is, was, Turgut Ataturk. He's the nephew of President Ataturk of Turkey; President Oetari's fishing buddy."

"He was with ISIS and Al Qaeda sir," Slade said steadily. "I didn't have a chance to interview all the attendees of the meeting to see whether they or not I should shoot them."

"I understand that, but the president does not," Gann told him. "Therefore, the president wants you off the Cobra missions and on this." He activated a display showing a Malaysian A380.

"You want me to look for the missing jet?" Slade shook his head. "Isn't that Agent Wolfe's territory sir? I mean, he's an airline pilot. It's a perfect reason to use him."

"The president personally suspended Flint Wolfe, who is, as you are, far too efficient in his work. Of course, Wolfe goes off the reservation on occasion, he did this occasion big time, so I couldn't protect him." Gann poured himself a drink, as if the mere mention of the Company's most notorious agent necessitated such a remedy. "If there's one agent the president loves to hate it is Wolfe. Flint keeps killing his buddies.

122

"We're trying to avoid getting you in the same cauldron of boiling water. Truth is, the president wants to give you a dead end assignment. Strangely enough, he may have unwittingly put you right in the middle of something important."

He activated the rest of his displays, shaking his head in obvious consternation. "The president didn't want to hear any of this. He is a political animal with his eye on a different prize. A missing airplane and its five hundred passengers are not on his radar. However, there's something about this A380 that has me concerned.

"The transcript of the meeting—the meeting you interdicted—details discussions for Al Qaeda-Iran-ISIS cooperation. One specific subject of the meeting that caught our attention was the collection of radioactive medical waste, obviously for use in dirty bombs. ISIS thereafter captured Mosul, the fourth largest city in Iraq, and one of the first things they did was to clear out all the radioactive material in the hospitals."

"So they are planning on making dirty bombs with medical waste; how do they plan on transporting it and what is the target?"

"That's what I want to know. It may all be connected." Gann pointed to the second picture and then the third. "This picture was taken in Tehran several weeks before the meeting: it shows Colonel Nikahd in the company of two Republican Guardsmen, the same two Iranians who boarded Malaysian 666 with stolen passports. The other photo is of Khallida at a café in Kuala Lumpur. The man sitting at the table with him is Abdullereda Hussein, the captain of Malaysian 666; the other man masqueraded as a deadheading pilot on that flight."

Slade frowned. "So the jet was hijacked with the cooperation of the captain. They would have to land somewhere after they hijacked it. The people would have had to be quartered. It's one thing to hide a few hostages but almost five hundred people?"

"Unfortunately, we think the passengers are dead," Gann said heavily. "The flight path clearly shows Malaysian 666 climbing up to forty-one thousand feet and staying there for a prolonged period of time. That was not their flight plan. There was no reason to go that high, especially if all they wanted to do was evade the radar and disappear."

"So they climbed that high to kill the passengers."

"Their supplemental Oxygen would have lasted twelve minutes for the passengers and twenty for the flight attendants with walk-around bottles. During that time it would be impossible to even attempt to storm the cockpit. They would be tied to their Oxygen masks until the generators ran dry. Asphyxia would have happened quickly at that altitude."

"That leaves us to find where they landed. Is it on some remote atoll in the Indian Ocean? If it didn't crash where do we start looking?"

"Sir, why does it have to be somewhere remote? Why not Singapore or Jakarta?"

"Go on Slade," the director said, bringing up a map of the region with all the principal airports. Superimposed was the last known flight path of Malaysian 666 and the radius of its fuel range.

"Sir, the region is predominantly Muslim and has a large number of active Al Qaeda cells. Every institution in the country is infiltrated with active members and sympathizers. Even if the air traffic controllers or control towers staff were not sympathizers it would have been easy for the Al Qaeda operatives to intimidate them into staying quiet."

Gann nodded. "We have unfortunately seen their brutality all too often recently. We're talking about maintenance people, tower controllers and radar operators—normal folks— when threatened with the rape and beheading of their families I can see why no one would have said a thing. Al Qaeda is an unfortunate everyday reality to those people."

He walked up to the map and tapped two airports. "Singapore and Jakarta are both controlled by Soekarno, the most powerful industrialist in the world. He controls a network of cooperative enterprises, a cabal if you will, otherwise known as the "Magnificent Thirteen." Together they control thirty-three percent of the world's economic activity."

Gann turned away from the screen and approached Slade. "Up until now, Soekarno has not undertaken any agreements or activities with known terrorist groups. This may constitute a change. I want you to go to Paris.

"Why Paris sir?"

"There are three things involving this mission in Paris right now: Airbus Industries headquarters. I want you to go get a briefing on the aircraft. Fly the simulator, get to know the specs; you know the drill. The second thing is Khallida and Nikahd. They're in Paris right now. Find out what they're up to."

"The third thing?"

Gann put a picture of the Malaysian captain posing with his family. He pointed to the young man standing in front of his father, smiling. "That is Abdulla Hussein, the son of Abdullereda Hussein our captain. The father became a drunken whoremonger, disgracing the family, and that may have been how Khallida lured him into the plot. His son left home to win back the honor of the family name. He joined the jihad. He's in Paris now as well."

"Do I have a contact in Paris sir?"

"I've alerted the bureau chief there. She knows you're coming. As far as the French are concerned you'll have to tread lightly. They have a huge Muslim problem there already. Jean Brueget works for INTERPOL. He's been our closest contact there since Nine-Eleven. If you need anything he's the man to deal with."

"Yes sir, I'll head out as soon as possible."

"Slade, one more thing," the director said, stopping him. Gann seemed uneasy, and Slade waited patiently. "I shouldn't be concerned, but I am. The president is taking a personal interest in you; a very personal interest. After the assassination of Turgut Ataturk that makes me very uneasy. You remember what happened to SEAL Team Six?"

"Their chopper was shot down," Slade nodded. "Someone leaked their presence to the Taliban and put them in an old Chinook with no countermeasure protection."

"There was no investigation," Gann said. "Even Mertzl couldn't get an investigation started. The IG is Oetari's man." He paused before adding, "Slade, you need to watch your back."

"I'll do that sir."

The director walked him out. Exiting the office they saw the two women talking out back in the garden. "So, any plans to marry her? You make a good looking couple. You're going to Paris after all."

"She's my cousin sir," Slade replied.

"Right, you might have to go to Kentucky to get a license." He patted Slade on the back. "Good luck. Report to me directly on this, do you understand? The fewer ears on this outside the Company the better; and I don't trust all the ears in the Company either. There are too many people gunning for my job."

"Yes sir."

The girls rejoined them. Gann said politely, "Well, we're done. Did you have a nice chat in the garden?"

"I filled Helen in," Gwen said.

"Oh!" Director Gann exclaimed. He took a long drink from his glass. Helen walked up and took Slade's arm, a knowing expression on her face.

"We have a lot to talk about Jeremiah," she said to Slade.

He looked confused.

"Sorry about that Slade," Gann shrugged. "They always find out. Good night!"

A few hours later in the hot tub, Slade was rubbing Helen's shoulders. She hadn't said much after they drove back home, so he hadn't asked. After years of cohabitation Slade knew enough about his cousin to no force anything out of her. She'd talk when she was ready.

She sighed, "If we were married, really married, I would be very upset with you right now."

"What makes this different?" he asked, not stopping his massage.

"Jeremiah, I don't have the right do be angry at anything you keep to yourself," she said, stopping only when he made a clear exclamation of contempt.

"You have every right; you always have!" he said. "Don't get into this rescue crap again. You rescued me as much as I rescued you. What makes you feel so guilty about that?"

"I've always regretted that because of me, because of the kids, you didn't get to have a real life."

"What, you think I wanted to go play the field?"

"Didn't you?" she replied. She turned her head to look at him out of the corner of her eye. "You're a spy. You could be in the hot tub with three twenty-something's with plastic boobs instead of a nearly forty-something with Caesarian scars and a hysterectomy."

"I wouldn't trade you for the Swedish Bikini Team," he told her.

She patted his hand, and said, "Really that's sweet, but you're a strong virile man Jeremiah. You don't have to be true to me. There's no reason you should be."

"I have every reason to be true to you," he told her.

"Why?"

"You make me happy; I couldn't imagine my life without you or the kids," he told her with that specific inflection unique to Slade. She knew how serious he was. "Did it ever occur to you that you and the kids are the balance to my life? The only balance I have to my life?"

"Aren't there other things you want; other things you need Jeremiah?"

"Helen," he said, hugging her close and kissing her neck. "There's nothing I need that you can't satisfy."

CHAPTER 14: Treachery

The following day Freddy Waters got off a US government jet and entered an embassy limousine. The driver took him directly to Çankaya Köşkü, the presidential palace. That this was Freddy's second Middle Eastern leader in the week meant nothing to him. In his world view these men were small fry to be swept away. His heroes were largely gone, excepting the seemingly immortal Castro, but enough of the old infrastructure remained. The regime, led by Oetari, would crush these cockroaches in the New World Order.

Freddy was a die-hard communist. He always had been. The fact that he lived as a very wealthy capitalist was not hypocritical to him; it was the crux of Freddy's Marxist ideals. Freddy was an elitist, an ideologue who truly believed that the masses should be equal but that they should also be controlled by the intellectuals of society. No one could expect the Homer Simpsons of the world to enjoy life or to appreciate their equality if someone wasn't telling them what to do.

There were people who enjoyed responsibility and there were people who enjoyed power. Freddy fell into the latter category. Whether it was brow-beating his fellow terrorists in the sixties or brain washing his students at the University, Freddy relished power.

Freddy couldn't dictate to President Ataturk, however. As he handed a hard copy of the photo he got from Oetari's iPad, he had to admit that exposing those people who disagreed with him was almost as good.

"The circled man is the trigger-man Mr. President," he told Ataturk, giving away his fellow American without a sliver of remorse. The pigs deserved what they got. "The rest of them helped him get the job done. They're a little bonus."

Ataturk picked up the eight-by-ten photo, pleased to see the names and addresses where neatly printed below each man's face. "Very good, this will satisfy the more ardent elements in both my family and my government. Thank you Mr. Waters."

"You know, I've had problems with these military pigs since," Waters began, alluding to a personal story, but the president waved his hand.

"That will be enough. Good day," Ataturk said brusquely, turning his back on Waters and heading toward his desk.

Two aides moved between Waters and the president. The former terrorist was momentarily confused. The aides made things plain. After Waters gave the president what he wanted there was no more need for him. Freddy was not who he envisioned himself to be; he was just a messenger.

Even Freddy's maniacally twisted brain burned at the slight, but he'd been down a long road to get back to the coat tails of power. Freddy was patient. Towards Ataturk, he projected the thought, "You and all of your little sand-flea kingdoms will disappear in the new history we're creating. I'll make sure you're nothing more than ass wiping camel jockeys before I'm done with you."

He left for his hotel. During the drive he put in a call to the embassy, telling them that he would be available to have dinner with the ambassador. The aide told Freddy that unfortunately the ambassador was unavailable. An irked Freddy looked up the ambassador's general file.

"Bush appointee—I should have known—I'll have the bastard shot," Freddy growled. He went back to the hotel and ate dinner alone. While sitting at the table enjoying a five thousand dollar bottle of wine at the taxpayers' expense, Freddy sent a text to the president. "Saw Pres. A. and passed him the info. Paris next."

#

As Freddy pulled into the hotel, a posh, modern place wedged between government administrative buildings and frequented by diplomats and their families, the hotel across the street became a beehive of activity. It wasn't upscale like Freddy's hotel but it served a clientele just as varied, from just as many places around the globe. It was an ISIS transit point. Recruits flew into Istanbul or Ankara from all over the world to join the jihad. They stopped here before being funneled south to the border villages and into Syria.

The Turkish government knew all about it, but they did nothing to stop it. As long as there was a Kurdish presence in Syria and Turkey they were more than happy to allow this stream of jihadists to use their facilities and infrastructure.

In one of the two large conference rooms dozens of desks had been set up. Passports, bus tickets, money; virtually everything a fighter needed was set up as an orderly military style reinforcement depot. It was correspondingly busy. There was a tactical desk set up for the depot commander and he was at that moment intently staring at his computer screen.

An aide in the president's office had just e-mailed him a bombshell.

"Allahu Akbar!" he breathed, shaking his head in wonderment. Amazingly enough, he didn't have to contact his superiors, he didn't have to hold a conference. All he had to do was to forward the e-mail to the mosques in the United States.

He typed in, "Search for these soldiers, find their towns. Here are their photos and the addresses. Then show up and slaughter them." Below the simple paragraph was the group photo of Slade and his Delta Force team.

The terrorist hit send and the message went out to a long list of mosques in the United States who either overtly or covertly supported the jihad. There were hundreds of them.

#

Johnny "Johnny Bravo" Garret was out on the balcony of his small apartment. He was off for a few more days after the operation in Iraq against ISIS. He got his nickname from the swath of blond hair at the very peak of his crew cut and his James Dean good looks. "Honey, the grill's ready. I'm going to throw the steaks on!"

He slid open the tempered glass door and walked directly into the kitchen. Opening the fridge, he reached for the tray with two marinating steaks. The doorbell rang. Johnny grimaced, almost calling for Sherry, his pretty young wife, to get the door so he could get the steaks on the grill. He changed his mind and shut the fridge; Sherry was six months pregnant.

Her back was hurting, her feet were swollen; no, he'd save her the trip across the apartment.

"I got it," he called to the bedroom where she was relaxing in the rocker in front of the air conditioner—she had hot flashes too. Johnny Bravo crossed the living room and opened the door, still wearing his grilling apron and holding a large two tined fork. He opened the door.

Three bearded men stood outside. All three shot him in the chest and abdomen with pistols. Johnny Bravo crumpled to the floor. The men rushed inside, dragging his body into the living room, leaving a bloody smear across the cream colored tiles.

A cry of alarm sounded from the bedroom, "Johnny!"

The terrorists dropped Johnny on the shag carpet and looked up. Little Sherry, barely five feet tall and a hundred and twenty pounds—even pregnant—stood in the doorway of the bedroom. The men put away their guns and drew hunting knives, advancing on her.

Johnny Bravo went in and out of consciousness. He couldn't quite recall what was happening, only that he needed to get up, get going—danger! Instincts and training forced him to fight for consciousness. Screaming, pain—danger!—a realization that he was failing. Get up soldier! His eyes fluttered open to a bleary world. There were blurs above him and a sickening flowery smell of sweat and perfume mixed with gunpowder and the brassy stench of blood.

The cold, sharp sensation of a knife blade against his neck rallied him. It started sawing through the muscle and sinew on the left side of his throat. Johnny Bravo surged. His right hand still had the barbeque fork wrapped around his wrist by the leather thong. Johnny Bravo stabbed upward toward one of the blurs. A shriek answered his action. He pulled the fork out and stabbed at another. There was a gurgling howl. He stabbed again, blindly, knowing there was nothing else he could do but go down fighting.

Then sirens.

Finally darkness, a long corridor and a bright white light.

#

131

It was one in the morning when the sedan pulled onto the curb in front of Slade's suburban house. Unlike most guests, the three men who got out took great care to close their doors quietly. One remained behind, keeping the car running. The men furtively but quickly crossed the lawn and climbed the steps, speaking in whispered tones. The gleam of knives could be seen from the street light.

One man went to the door while the other two crowded right behind him, showing anyone that might be watching that they had no tactical training and little common sense. The man at the door tried the latch—it opened—he nodded to his friends.

He threw open the door and all three rushed inside the front hall, shadows disappearing into a darkened house. The door remained open, but the only thing that escaped the house was the hard to be recognized sound of heavy objects falling to the wood floor.

Outside, the driver waited impatiently. Secretly, he was glad he did not have to go in. He was excited that he was taking part in the jihad, but the prospect of facing American Special Forces in their own home made him nervous. Then there were the kids. The information said that this Jeremiah Slade had six kids. His fellow jihadist's had joked about the horror they'd inspire in the neighborhood when they awoke to find the families heads all lined up on the front porch rail like Halloween Jack o lanterns.

He laughed along with them, but the thought of sawing off the head of a little girl or little boy was revolting to the naturalized American citizen. Better that he drive the car.

"What's taking them so damn long?" he said out loud. His increasingly agitated voice carried a distinct eastern accent. He needn't have asked, and he swore at himself for a fool. The answer was obvious. It took time to slaughter a family of eight.

Taking a deep breath he calmed himself, dutifully checking the engine and gas. As he glanced back to the house the sound of his door opening startled him. One of the jihadists—they were all true blue jihadists now—was pranking him. A heavy blow to his head stopped any further thought.

The sensation of cold water roused him and he awoke suddenly, sputtering. "What? What the Hell?" he exclaimed, his eyes snapping open. He was in a room. The jihadist tried to rise but he was duct taped to a non-descript grey institutional chair. There was no other furniture in the room. Ignorant though he was, the young jihadist knew that his career was over. He'd been caught.

"Allahu Akbar! I will tell you nothing—nothing!" shouted a hoarse voice from the room next door. Was it Ahkmed? Muhammad, or the other Muhammad? He couldn't tell.

An answering voice replied testily, "Suits me buddy. It saves us space in Guantanamo!"

A strangled cry was followed by silence.

He began to sweat.

The door opened with a bang. He started, his head snapping to the opening. A man was standing there, a tall man with a mustache, Director MacCloud of the FBI. Two other men came in with him. MacCloud dragged another chair into the room and noisily set it before him, turning it around so that when he sat down he was leaning on the back.

"So Abdul, you're answering the call to jihad," he said in a condescending hard Texas drawl.

"My name is not Abdul! I want to see my lawyer! That's my constitutional right asshole!" he retorted angrily.

The man simply smiled. "Your jihadist playbook doesn't exist with me *Abdul*," he said with derision. "You're in the big leagues now."

"You are the police. You have to follow the rules," he insisted. "I want my phone call and my court appointed lawyer right now—do you understand?"

"I'm not the police. That means I can do any damn thing I want to you."

"It will never stand in trial," he sneered. "No matter what you do to me nothing I say can be used in trial. You haven't even read me my rights! You are so screwed; I'll sue your ass for false arrest and police harassment!"

One of the two men with the director back handed him across the face and then grabbed him by the hair, yanking his head back painfully. He sat there stunned, unable to believe the police could actually do that to him. "You are so screwed. I'm not going to tell you a damn thing until my lawyer is here. Then I'm going to have your badge."

"Funny, that's what the last guy said; the one who broke into Agent Slade's house with a butcher knife."

"Did he succeed? Did he kill the infidel?"

"Why don't I let him tell you himself," the director shrugged. "Andy, would you please bring Abdul-One in here?" The man left the room and came back—with a severed head—only it wasn't the infidel, it was one of the Muhammad's. The agent tossed the ting onto the jihadist's lap. Blood started seeping out of the wound and through his pants onto his legs and crotch. Muhammad's dead eyes looked up at him. His mouth was open in seeming protest. To the young jihadist's horror Muhammad's severed cock was in his own mouth.

MacCloud pointed at the head. "He didn't want to talk. If you don't want to talk—fine—I got your other two buddies in the room next door. Maybe after I put your head on their laps they'll be more interested in telling me what I need to know."

"How, how could you do this?" he stammered, slipping toward a gulf of hysterical terror.

The man who brought Muhammad in, picked up the head and shoved it against the jihadist's face. The wet blood and saliva smeared his face. The soft, fleshy remnants of the corpse's cock nudged his cheek like some flaccid ghoulish tongue. He felt the urge to retch.

MacCloud told him, "Get it through your thick skull Abdul, I'm not a cop! I'm government! We are at war Abdul; at war with your ilk! Now, since you're people already violated the articles of war I don't have to follow the Geneva Convention. You know what that means? It means I do with you whatever I want. Here are the rules: you talk, you live; you don't talk, I send you to Allah in pieces; and trust me, I won't begin with your head. You're going to Allah as a eunuch!"

The jihadist trembled uncontrollably. "This cannot be happening. This cannot be happening!"

"You bet it is, Abdul. You are now in the deepest, darkest hole in this United States of America! No one knows you're here; no one knows you exist! The only way you leave this room alive is by answering my questions—do you get it Abdul?"

The jihadist stared at the glazed eyes of his High School friend, part of his mosque gang. A week ago they were making out with girls at the senior party—now? How could this be happening?

The director's voice was a low menacing growl. "I'm about to let my boys here have you." He waited, but there was nothing except the young man's teeth chattering. "Well, are you going to talk?"

The jihadist couldn't speak; he couldn't take his eyes off of his friend's cold, dead face.

"All right Andy, show Abdul we mean business. Cut off his balls."

The big man took out a wicked looking trench knife. The sound of the blade rasping out of its nylon holster got his attention. The knife moved in front of his face, the point caressing his cheek, and then down. He gasped in terror, instinctively sucking himself back into the chair, away from that awful blade, but there was nothing the driver could do. His ankles were taped to the legs chairs. The big man took the knife and slit open his trousers at the crotch. He felt the edge slice his skin.

He howled, "No, no please you can't do this! Don't do this!"

MacCloud held up his hand and the big man stopped, holding the knife up so that the blood running down the blade was inches from his face.

MacCloud's tone became gentler, more like an understanding mentor. "That's what it's going to be, or you can tell us what we want to know. You're not giving anything away; we'll find it all out eventually. When we're done here, I'll have you transferred to Guantanamo Bay. You've seen the

135

news reports. They're well treated. You can sit there until the war is over and work on your tan. Afterwards, well, you didn't kill anyone so who knows what will happen. You could be out raising a family in a few years and this will be nothing but an unhappy memory."

"Or," and the directors voice sank to a menacing growl again. "Or you can say nothing and die like your friend here, without striking a single blow for your jihad. That means Hell buddy. You didn't die with the blood of an infidel on your hands. You check out with nothing!"

That was enough. He couldn't talk fast enough.

#

After the prisoner's statement, MacCloud came out of the interrogation room. He had already been on a quick conference call with Gann and Mertzl. He called them again.

"It's confirmed," he told them. "They got the information from an e-mail forwarded to their mosque. We're raiding the place as we speak. If this checks out with Corporal Garret's attack then the common thread is the hotel in Ankara."

"We followed up on that," said Gann. "The hotel is an ISIS staging depot. It will take some digging to find out how they got the information."

"Ankara—Turkey?" the gruff voice of Mertzl asked.

"Yes, that's where the trace led us."

"Our pal Freddy Waters is in Ankara," Mertzl informed them. "One of the Mobility Commands VIP jets is at his disposal. He landed in Ankara yesterday. He's leaving for Paris today—if this is on him, I'll have his ass. Corporal Garret is in critical condition. They raped and beheaded his wife. She was six months pregnant," the general paused before finishing. "They cut out the baby and beheaded her as well."

There was a long pause while the three men digested the situation. MacCloud broke the uncomfortable silence. "I think we all know Waters is behind the leak."

"That ties it to the president."

"This is SEAL Team Six all over again," Mertzl growled.

"Gentlemen we have to tread very, very carefully with this president."

"This is treason!" Mertzl exploded, putting it right out there in the open.

"It is," Gann agreed. "However, we've all been in this game long enough to know how pawns are used. That's what the president is doing."

"Waters is on the board now; he's fair game," MacCloud said. "Just as young Ataturk found himself in the wrong place at the wrong time, Waters might not realize what a dangerous world this is. You're ghost saved Slade's family Gann, maybe your man should know that."

"He can make the same mistake he made with the young Turk," Mertzl chuckled mirthlessly.

"Slade is on his way to Paris. That's where Freddy is. I'll see to it that they run into each other."

CHAPTER 15: Paris

Slade landed in Paris tired and in a foul mood. He'd read up on Freddy Waters. The information didn't improve his demeanor. If ever a man deserved the business end of his Special Forces killing knife twisted in his kidneys it was Waters.

"If you leaked the information about our unit to ISIS I promise you, Mr. Waters, you will take days to die!" he muttered to himself.

He gathered his bags and picked up a taxi at the curb. Getting into the Mercedes he settled back into the comfortable leather seat and told the driver his destination

The Hilton was where Freddy Waters was staying.

On the way he got a text. "J. Bravo should pull through. Six holes in him. Good hunting—Killer."

"Thank God for small favors. I hope they keep him out for a while. He's not going to like waking up; I don't know how he'll handle the news. I don't know how anyone could."

He dialed Helen's cell number. She picked up.

"Hey, how are you doing?"

"How am I doing?" she asked with a sigh. "Some guy with a long scar on his face in an airline uniform shows up at the house at midnight and puts us in the attic. Then our boys in black herd us out in the middle of the night and stick us in a hotel under guard. How do you think I'm doing?"

"I'm sorry Helen," he started to apologize, but she interrupted him.

"I'm doing great Jeremiah! Don't worry about me and the kids. The next morning the same guy flew us in first class to Atlantis—Atlantis! The kids are having a blast. I'm drinking a Pina Colada and getting a tan. You should get yourself into trouble more often."

"His name is Wolfe, Flint Wolfe," Slade said with a feeling of relief.

"Who?"

"The man with the scar," Slade told her. "He shouldn't have been there, but I'm glad he was."

"Why, were we in danger or was this a precaution?"

Helen obviously didn't know what went down at the house. He wasn't about to tell her, and Slade didn't have the heart to tell her about Johnny's wife and child—Helen was green to that side of the game—he let her be. "He was just watching out for you and the kids Helen. The Company looks after its own." Slade paused, taking a deep breath before adding, "Have a good time. I'll check back in when I can."

"Jeremiah be safe please. I love you. The kids love you. You know that don't you? We can't afford to lose you."

"Give the kids hugs for me; give yourself one for me too."

It occurred to Slade that he'd never told Helen he loved her. She told him often, always making sure he knew that she hadn't forgotten. He thought that's all it was. Now he wasn't so sure.

They pulled up at the Hilton Concorde Opera, a huge traditional building on a large roundabout. Slade tipped the driver and checked in.

"Monsieur Slade, your company left a valise for you," the concierge told him. He motioned for a valet. The boy returned with a large black suitcase from the back room. "Can I get anything else for you, monsieur?"

"Do you have a schedule for the opera or any concerts?"

"Certainement!" he said, producing a printed flyer. "Monsieur will notice we have Turandot at the Opera House next week, however, if monsieur is available there is a very special event tomorrow night. The organist Monsieur Olivier Latry will be playing Bach after mass at Notre Dame! If you enjoy baroque that is."

"It will be played the Great Organ and not the Choir Organ, I assume?"

The concierge smiled at Slade's knowledge of Paris' great cathedral, announcing proudly, "Absolutely! I will be in attendance myself."

"Please put my tickets and your own on my bill," he instructed.

"Two monsieur?"

"Why not," Slade nodded. He had a mind to invite Jean Brueget, the INTERPOL contact. It would be the perfect place for an unobtrusive meeting. "Oh, one more thing." He handed a photo of Waters and two one thousand Euro notes to the concierge. His text number was on the bottom of the picture.

"OuiSLR monsieur, it will be done. Monsieur Waters is out at the moment, but I will inform you the instant he walks through the door," the concierge said, absurdly pleased that Slade was a patron who knew how things worked without having to be prodded.

Slade went to his room. It was directly above that of Waters. He swept it for bugs and wireless signals; it was clean. Then he unpacked. First he opened the company briefcase. It contained the normal inventory of things: a 9mm Glock with a silencer and three clips of ammunition. Several knives. A broken down sniper's rifle. Two smoke grenades. A garrote. Two small charges of C-4 with a remote and a set of binoculars.

Slade holstered the Glock in his concealed carry shirt beneath his suit. The silencer went in the suit pocket the extra clips went into the other side of his shirt.

His shaving kit included a compact yet efficient surveillance system tied to his laptop.

As Waters was out, Slade took advantage of the opportunity to go downstairs and case the "Motorcycle Man's" room. Getting in was as easy as swiping his CIA 'skeleton key' card over the lock. The catch opened with a light snick! Slade was in.

Waters was a slob. He was also careless. His laptop was open and it took only a generic password to gain access to his files. Slade inserted a key fob into the USB port and began downloading everything on the computer. That took only a minute. In another minute he had the ability to access Freddy's laptop through his own wireless. That would allow him to use Freddy's own camera and microphone to monitor the room.

In case Freddy powered down his computer or put it in its case, Slade planted two camera bugs with microphones. That done, he left the room and returned upstairs. Sitting down at the hotel desk Slade fired up his own laptop and plugged in the fob. The first thing he looked for was Freddy's schedule.

"Well, well, well, Freddy, you're a busy man. You've got a meeting right now with the Iranians, Colonel Nikahd to be specific."

While he didn't appear particularly organized Freddy was fastidious about his schedule. Not only did he have his full day planned out but Freddy cross referenced files and notes with his activities.

He'd been in Turkey and there was a short, terse note describing Freddy's dissatisfaction with the visit. "Met with P. Ataturk—stuck up bastard—completely unaware of what a big present we gave him."

The "present" was a cross-referenced jpg file. Slade promptly opened it and found himself staring at the group photo from the ISIS Cobra mission.

"So this is how we were fingered, but how the Hell did Freddy get this and why did he want the President of Turkey to have it?" He forwarded the file to CIA headquarters, the director's office.

Ten minutes later his phone rang. It was the director himself.

"Slade?"

"Yes sir."

"The photo isn't an original, it's a photo taken by Water's iPhone of the president's iPad, so there's no way to prove the president gave him the information; Waters could have just stolen it and gone off on his own," he snapped, and then he went on without so much as taking a breath. "Now listen and listen good. You've just connected a terrorist act with the White House—do you understand?"

"Yes sir," he replied cautiously.

"I cannot, repeat, I cannot delve into this further at this time. The Company cannot start an investigation on the White House. Do I make myself perfectly clear?"

Slade wanted to say no but he knew the only answer the director wanted to hear was, "Yes."

"Freddy Waters is off limits—do you understand?"

"You're certain, sir?"

"You are not to lay a hand on Freddy Waters. I know Paris is a dangerous place, but there are to be no accidents—do you understand?"

"Absolutely sir," he growled.

"Good, now listen closely," the director said and he paused.

That meant Slade still had a shot at Freddy and the director was going to tell him how.

"We need to keep an eye on Waters. He has stolen sensitive information and possibly—I say possibly—compromised a covert operation. If he has done so then we will catch up to him. Hopefully, we'll get to him before his friends do. We've raided dozens of mosques and taken a couple hundred jihadists into custody. If they think Waters set them up they'll be after his hide."

"Yes sir," Slade replied. "I will keep Waters under surveillance. I'll keep you informed on my progress."

"Good!" the director said.

Slade smiled wolfishly. The green light for Freddy Waters was on, only the method changed. All he had to do was to tip off the bad guys that Freddy set them up and then it was run Freddy, run.

The buzzer on his text went off.

Digging out his phone he perused the text. It was a simple line, "Monsieur on his way up to his room."

Waters was back in the hotel.

There were only two things Slade had to do: activate Freddy's camera, and click the icon attached to his own two bugs. On the screen of the laptop he got an immediate feed for all three cameras. The room and bath were empty. A few minutes later Freddy appeared through the door. He was a bedraggled man, scruffy looking and scrawny. Slade would be almost embarrassed to take him out in a fight, excepting the malignant power of Freddy's brain; that's what made the terrorist dangerous.

He had another man with him. A shorter paunchier man than the heroin chic thin Freddy. Slade sat down at the hotel desk, screwing the top off his bottle of water.

"That Nikahd, I just can't gauge him," said the shorter man.

"What does it matter Alfie," Freddie asked without any interest in the question. "The ragheads are children, their tribal; they don't think beyond that. They want their nukes—fine—let them have them. They'll use them on the Israelis and the Israelis will retaliate. Boom—problem solved."

"That'll mess up the planet for sure," Alfie sighed, digging in the minibar for a beer. He handed one to Freddy. "It'll piss off the environmentalists."

"The environmentalists? Don't make me laugh," Freddy said, popping the top on the beer and taking a swig. "You know that's one of the ironies of this whole deal. The environmentalists worship the president. They think he's a huge supporter. They've never realized that the whole movement was based on telling them what they wanted to hear and not what the truth was. Oetari is screwing the environmentalists worse than Reagan ever did. The only difference was that Reagan told them the truth and Oetari told them what they wanted to hear."

"Is that what we're telling the Iranians or is that what the Iranians are telling us?"

Freddy shook his wiry haired head, a vulture's skull that looked like grey mold or moss spouted from a blotched old rock. His grin showed teeth yellowed from nicotine. "Does it matter?" he laughed. Then he answered his own question. "Either way it works for us. If the Iranians are sincere and get rid of half their enriched Uranium—great. If it's all a scam then they'll use it on the Israelis, again—great. It's a win-win scenario."

Alfie shrugged. "It might be nice to lose the Middle East entirely. There would be no oil and no religion. Christianity, Judaism and Islam would be gone—poof!"

Freddy shrugged, and said, "Islam maybe, I mean if Mecca went away what would be the reason they'd stick with it? I mean really. But Christians, they can be stubborn bastards. They seem to put a lot more stock in Faith than the rest."

"Careful Freddy, you're almost sounding empathetic," Alfie laughed.

Freddy turned on him with surprising angst. "No! They're just stupid; too stupid to be re-educated. That's why Stalin took care of the priests first. He knew there was no hope for them—good old Uncle Joe!"

That seemed to end that vein of the conversation. They talked of dinner, arguing whether they should eat at the hotel or in town. Alfie suggested they hop on one of the barges for a dinner cruise. Freddy was against it. "I've got to meet with Eva Accompando from Soekarno tomorrow on a dinner cruise. Do you really think I want to see this damn city twice from the river? No thank you."

"So Nikahd was serious then?" Alfie asked. "He wants that ship—why?"

"Who cares? He wants it as part of our deal."

"They're up to something," Alfie mused. "Why do they need a special ship to transport the nuclear material; especially that ship?"

"I told you I don't care," Freddie sighed. "She simply needs to get the Iranians that ship."

"What if she balks?"

"I'll use my charm," Freddy smiled. "Come on, the Frog downstairs suggested a restaurant down the street. They're specialty it baked sheep's head stuffed with—something—it's all the rage."

Freddy and Alfie left the room for dinner. Slade thought about it for a while. Using the remote function of his CIA software he brought up the notes Freddy had concerning the meeting. He came to the conclusion that Freddy didn't need to attend the meeting with Eva Accompando; he'd do it himself.

The mechanism to accomplish that was easy. He did it by e-mail. Freddy had exchanged e-mails with Eva already. All Slade did was send Freddie a cancellation and have him in turn send Eva an e-mail describing one J. Slade, who would meet her instead. Eva e-mailed Freddy, really Slade, that was fine and to meet her for the eight O'clock sailing at slip number seven. That done, Slade had a date.

He checked in with the Paris division and they set up a meeting with Brueget at the concert.

After a few hours of half-sleep Slade gave up and walked along the Seine toward Notre Dame. That's where the best free music in Paris. Vespers mass at Notre Dame was not to be missed. The astonishing acoustics of the cathedral, the feel of the place and the singing, not to mention the massive organ were well worth a bit of guilt.

Slade headed out, hoping the three mile walk would clear his head. It was not to be. A bunch of angry young men and women in Burkas were clogging up the river walk waving Palestinian flags, yelling for jihad and calling the Israelis "assassins."

"Jihad in Paris? Oh great, they're pissed that after two thousand rockets the Israelis are finally fighting back!"

At St. Michel's, just a few blocks from the cathedral, the French paramilitary and gendarmes in riot gear cordoned off the demonstrators.

"Jihad-resistance! Jihad-resistance! Jihad-resistance!" shouted a terrorist on the bullhorn with a deplorable French accent.

"Terrorists!" he retorted. The French paramilitary troops knit their brows, and looked at him. He simply raised a brow and asked them, "Quelle serait l'Empereur Napoléon?"

The gendarme looked as if he was going to shove his rifle butt down Slade's throat.

CHAPTER 16: Notre Dame

The gendarme wasn't so much mad at Slade as much as himself. Slade asked a simple question and it cut to the bone of French pride: What would Napoleon do?

One of the gendarmes looked confused, but the other, the angry one replied, "Donnez-leur un relent de à mitraille!"

It was the famous answer Napoleon gave when asked what he would do about rebels in the streets. Legend had it that the general, a master of artillery, answered, "Give them a whiff of grapeshot!"

Slade nodded approvingly and told them, "France is for the French," or in his heavily accented French, "La France est pour les Français!"

They gendarmes exchanged glances, sighed, and nodding their heads, admitted, "Oui monsieur, C'est vrai."

It must have worked, because the next moment a demonstrator got in the gendarme's face, yelling "Jihad! Jihad! Jihad!" The boy's spit flew at the gendarme, who reacted appropriately, smashing his rifle butt in the demonstrator's belly and taking him to the ground. He cuffed the boy, much to the amazement of those protesters nearby, and hauled him to his feet.

As they dragged the boy to the paddy wagon, the gendarme looked at Slade and said, "La France est pour les Français!"

"Vive la France!" Slade responded, adding to himself, "Maybe there's hope after all."

Feeling better, Slade made the cathedral in time for vespers. He went there for the music. The Notre Dame choir was world renowned; it wasn't to be missed. Slade, despite his cold exterior, loved classical music.

After vespers he stayed for mass out of curiosity. Would the cardinal speak about the demonstrations? Slade was raised Catholic, and he'd gone to church with Helen on occasion as they grew up. Then he strayed for a few years; that is, until Helen and the kids moved in. After that, he attended with the family, but only after buying a video recorder for the Vikings games on Sunday.

Now it was easy to tape the games, and Slade still went so as to be a good example for the kids. It ate at him though; his present occupation didn't fit so well with piety, thus his guilt.

That thought brought out Helen's softly chiding rebuke in his head. "All right, I need to practice my French anyway," he grumbled to himself. He stayed for mass.

The Cardinal of Paris was an elder man, robust with glasses. He gave firm, cogent and practical homilies. Tonight was no different. Slade's French was barely good enough to keep up with him, because he was passionate, railing against the evils going on in France and the Middle East.

"Will we sit here while our brother Christians are given the choice of conversion, becoming slaves or death; while they are crucified along the streets? Will we sit here idly while our brother Muslims, those who wish to live in peace with us are slaughtered, left beheaded in ditches, their only crime that they do not wish to follow the path of jihad? Will we sit here idly while our Jewish brothers, and I remind you we are all Jews at our core, Jesus was a Jew and so are we; will we sit idly by while terrorists and jihadist murder their children and send rockets into their neighborhoods?"

The cardinal paused, looking soberly over the congregation. "Will we sit here idly while they shout jihad within sight of these sacred walls? We invited these people to our land and they repay us by insulting our sacred places and defiling our civilization. We cannot allow them to do so. We must be firm in our resolve and patient with our guests, yet like a father to a passionate son we must set boundaries and expect them to live within the law of our civilization as they would expect us to live within their laws if our positions were reversed.

"We must pray, but there is more we must do. We must resist the ignorant who are shouting without our walls. We must tell the jihadists here in our own streets that they are not welcome if they persist in this path of war and intolerance. If they wish to live in peace among us then Amen I say to you;

you are my brother under the Almighty. Yet God taught us to defend ourselves, our families and our Faith. God gave us Charles the Hammer Martel to drive the hordes of jihadists from French soil; who will he give us now?"

Slade couldn't help but like the cardinal. He felt hope after the homily; hope that France might remain French if only the cardinal's voice and other voices carried the day. As he took his place in line for Communion he wondered if his hopes outweighed the reality of the jihadist infection spreading across Europe.

Helen's little voice came on in his head again. He was about to take Communion from the hand of the cardinal. Helen reminded Slade it was not the proper place to be considering violence, war and evil. He whispered, "Dear cousin, you make it hard to do my job sometimes."

The tall man in front of him must have heard his words, for he turned, looking over his shoulder, over the backpack he wore inside the cathedral, catching Slade with a set of dark eyes—almost black.

The old familiar warning bells went off in Slade's head. The man was an Algerian, which was not uncommon in Paris especially. Many transplants from the former French colonies lived in the capital. This man was tall and lankly; the whites of his eyes stood out, almost glowing in the gloom of the dim cathedral. It was his expression that caught Slade's attention; he'd seen it so often in jihadists, the half mad, half doomed demeanor—it set him on edge.

That he was wearing a backpack in the cathedral was suspicious, but many people brought their purses or bags with them, not wanting to lose them in the vastness of the church. No, Slade was profiling. He was suspicious only because the man was almost certainly Muslim. Almost all the Algerians were Muslim, although it wasn't unheard of to see a convert.

He played down his fears, assuming they rode upon the train of his earlier thoughts; hadn't the Justice Department just issued an order prohibiting profiling even in the case of National security? He chuckled dryly to himself, "You're just a bigot Slade—a hater!"

Still, he kept an eye on the man regardless. He could always apologize to the Lord for his suspicions about his fellow man later. Maybe he'd file a report on himself; turn himself in for violating Justice Department policy!

The man reached the cardinal. The cardinal smiled and held up a wafer, saying in French, "The Body of Christ!"

For Slade, it was almost like watching a movie. The man's bearing changed almost instantly. With exaggerated fury he spat at the cardinal. Slade was surprised but ready.

The unexpected nature of the attack was not the attack itself, but that the Algerian took the time to show his contempt for the center of Christianity in France.

"You have kept us down for too long," he yelled, almost incoherent. "Our time has come again. You will submit or die; submit or die! Death to the infidels! Allahu Akbar!" The jihadist finished his tirade and raised his arms. There was a switch in his right hand.

Before the last breath of the terrorist's praise of Allah passed his lips, as the cardinal's face showed complete surprise and horror, as the first screams erupted from the surrounding crowd, Slade's punch connected.

It started at his feet. He crouched, throwing his hips forward in a counterclockwise twist, like a spring unwinding. His torso followed and then the right arm flew, the force aided by the uncoiling of his body. The short, sharp punch connected with the base of the jihadist's skull, shattering the Atlas vertebrae and the base of the skull, shoving shards of bone into the spinal cord and the medulla oblongata.

The punch would at the very least render the victim unconscious, but thrown with the strength of angst and desperate need, the jihadist was dead before he finished his curse.

The body crumpled to the ground. Slade was instantly on top of him. He grabbed the trigger switch from the trembling hand and tore the wires from the box. Ripping open the backpack he found the battery perched on top of the load of explosives and shrapnel. Quickly he yanked the wires out of the power unit. Then he turned the body over and ripped open the jacket.

"You bloody bastard, you're wearing a vest as well!"

Again he ripped out the wires and removed the battery. The dead jihadist was no longer a threat, but there still might be other jihadists around; they would wait for the panic to ensue and guard the exits, massacring the fleeing congregation.

Slade looked up at the cardinal, who was still standing there holding his golden goblet and Communion wafers.

"Father, I need your help; there's no telling if there are more of these jihadists around! Do NOT clear the Church— keep everyone calm—I will get the police and INTERPOL here right away!"

Slade hit his Bluetooth as he grabbed the jihadist by the collar. The head lolled over on the spindly neck, wagging side to side in a grotesque way.

"Brueget!" he barked, keying the number that Director Gann gave him

Slade dragged the bomb laden body out of the vestibule, looking in the crowd for more jihadists. He saw an usher, and yelled for him to open the door out of the south end of the vestibule. The portly man scurried for the door, waving people back, flinging it open. Slade dragged the jihadist outside the church and away from the people.

"Brueget here, how can I help you?"

"Brueget, my name is Slade. We have a meeting set up for tomorrow; I'm going to have to move that up. I'm down here at Notre Dame. Jihadists just tried to assassinate the cardinal and blow up the cathedral. Everyone is still in the church. I need the exits cleared. They may have other jihadists waiting for the people to queue up at the doors!"

"Mon Dieu! I have the military two blocks away at St. Michel; they will be there in two minutes!"

When he got outside, Slade laid the jihadist next to the stone side of the rectory; that would at least partially minimize the damage of any blast. The usher was watching; he waved people back, shouting for his fellow ushers. They effectively cordoned off the area.

Two minutes later Slade heard the pounding of boots. He looked toward the front of the cathedral. Two columns of black garbed troops bearing SCAR assault rifles trotted into the courtyard. Six men rushed down the alley between the cathedral and the rectory. Two levelled their SCARS at the jihadist, two covered Slade and the other two set up posts on either side of the doors.

"Les portes sud obtiennent!"

Slade raised his hands, and said, "I work with Jean Brueget INTERPOL!"

"INTERPOL?"

The usher at the door interrupted, telling the soldiers loudly, "Don't arrest him! He saved the cardinal! He killed the terrorist; I saw it all!"

Nodding, the soldier lowered his SCAR, telling him in English, "It was INTERPOL who called us from the demonstration. Relax, but stay here please!"

The bells began to ring, signaling the end of mass. Slade heard the cardinal's strong voice asking people to file out of the church and praising God.

A few minutes later Brueget and half a dozen other INTERPOL agents arrived with the bomb squad. The bomb squad took over control of the body and bombs. Brueget took Slade inside the emptying cathedral. They exchanged introductions, and then with everything under control Brueget smiled with relief, looking around at the people still filing out of the church. "France is indebted to you my friend," he said. "This could have been a terrible day!"

"We got lucky this time," Slade said, shaking his head. "This could have been Buckingham Palace, the Smithsonian— anywhere. We're reacting instead of being proactive. How the Hell does a terrorist get into the cathedral with thirty pounds of C-4?"

Brueget nodded, and said, "If we do nothing else than what we are doing it is only a matter of time before they succeed."

"Maybe you can help me with that," Slade said. He filled Brueget in on what he was doing in Paris. "Waters has already met with Colonel Nikahd of Iran. Now he's supposed to meet with someone from Soekarno Industries."

"Eva Accompando?" Brueget asked.

"Yes, how did you know?"

"Eva is often in Paris," he explained. "We have taken an interest in her over the last few years. She is Soekarno's international broker and buyer. Her boss does not always desire to buy or sell legal items, shall we say. The only common thread is that everything is expensive. Eva only does multi-multi-million dollar deals. Naturally we are always interested in her activities; especially if they involve a former American terrorist who has been seen with the head of Iran's Special Operations."

"I'm meeting with her tonight in place of Waters," Slade told him. "Would you like in on the deal?"

"With pleasure," Brueget smiled.

A priest came up to them. "Monsieur, if you please, the cardinal would like to see you both."

They entered the vestibule. The cathedral was still clearing, but as Jean pointed out there were gendarmes and paramilitary officers combing the crowd, looking for anyone else. "If they were here they are already gone," he said sadly. "They've probably joined the demonstration at St. Michelle. Who knows what else these vermin are capable of?"

The priest led them through the gates and then right again through the hallway into the rectory. He knocked on a thick oak door. The door opened a crack and he announced himself. Another priest opened the door the rest of the way and motioned them in.

The cardinal was seated in a tall chair in the reception room. Cradling a goblet of wine, he looked up and smiled. "Sacramental wine," he admitted. "It's all we have here, but I think it's for a worthy cause!"

"I'd have to agree Father."

"I am Cardinal Martel; you heard me mention my great ancestor Charles—I invoke him especially at these times. It is for good reason it seems." He stood and held out his hand, taking Slade's warmly in both of his and shaking very firmly.

"Thank you my son for your rescue, not for me, but for all of the people who could have—" he stopped, shaking his head. "Can you imagine how many people would have died, waiting to take Communion? It is deplorable! It is a travesty! Such unrelenting evil and hatred; it is the work of the Devil himself!"

"I couldn't agree more Father."

"We must stop this; we cannot allow it," he continued. "It is one thing to turn the other cheek, but our Lord never intended for us to become lambs for the slaughter. For too long we've sat on our heels waiting and hoping for reason. We must act!"

The cardinal got up and paced around his chair, head down, speaking as if ticking off items on a list. "We face unrelenting evil against innocents. We have tried everything, but now we must be responsible for stopping the evil. We have the strength to stop it successfully. Certainly the evil that way do along the way is less than the evil of inaction—yes, we have the responsibility to act!"

He circled around the chair, seemingly at peace with his decision. Smiling, Cardinal Martel patted Jean on the shoulder. "I am told you are American CIA."

"That's true," Slade answered. "I'm in town on other business."

"We should stay in contact, work together, INTERPOL, your CIA and the Church," the Cardinal told him emphatically. "More importantly, we should get to know each other. This event cannot have happened for no reason. Providence brings us together."

They settled on dinner the following day. For Slade, however, the evening was just beginning. He still had dinner with Eva ahead of them.

CHAPTER 17: Dinner on the Siene

Jean Brueget dropped Slade off at the quays. Slade wanted to have a drink and case the barge out before the meeting. Brueget left to collect his wife and melt into the background.

The boat at slip seven was a long, modern glass and aluminum vessel that seated several hundred people. They'd already cleaned the dining room from the previous cruise and were now accepting those guests with reservations. People were starting to fill the dinner section up, but most hadn't arrived yet. The sailing wasn't for another forty-five minutes and Parisians tried to be as tardy as possible without actually missing their appointments.

Slade walked to the bar and ordered a gin and tonic. Unlike many things in Europe, the bartender delivered his much needed drink with French culinary punctuality. Slade walked around the barge familiarizing himself with the layout and looking for anyone who piqued his curiosity.

There was a singular woman who arrived early. She couldn't escape his notice, or anyone else's for that matter. She was a tiny Asian woman, Phillipino or Indonesia, if he were to guess. She cradled a Manhattan in here slight hand, giving her dark eyes an enchanting expression beneath her long lashes. Her blue evening gown was beautiful and expensive; but it wasn't nearly as expensive as the diamonds she wore around her neck, wrists and fingers. She was dazzling.

He recognized her from Freddy's file.

"Eva?" Slade said with a confident smile. "I'm Mr. Slade."

She cocked her head slightly to the side, "J. Slade?"

He held out his hand. She took it daintily. "Yes, Jeremiah Slade," he said, pronouncing his first name without the usual humiliated hatred that he reserved for it. "I am pleased to meet you Ms. Accompando."

"It's a relief *not* to be meeting with Waters," Eva said firmly, with that self-assurance that meant she was comfortable in expressing her opinions no matter what they were. "He is an odious ideologue, almost impossible to deal with; it's incredible to me that President Oetari can stand him."

"Do you know the president?" Slade asked, leading her to their table and pulling out the chair for her.

She took the act of chivalry in stride, as if she was used to it. Slade thought that was probably understandable on her part. She answered his question as if it were no great thing. "Yes, of course, I've met President Oetari many times. He's good friends with my employer Mr. Soekarno."

"So you are based in Singapore?" Slade asked, sitting down across from her.

"No, although I spent quite a bit of time there. I travel almost constantly between New York, Paris, Honk Kong and Duluth."

"Duluth—Minnesota?" he said with surprise.

Eva sighed, "My husband is a merchant marine captain. He originally sailed on the Great Lakes. When the iron ore business slackened he took to ocean going ships, but he wanted to maintain the family house in Duluth so he could see his beloved Vikings play. That means he spends much of his autumn and winter in the cold and I spend them in Maui."

"I feel your pain. I was born in Minnesota. I have been trying to get the Vikings out of my system for almost forty years."

Eva laughed. "Have you succeeded?"

"No!"

The dinner barge pulled out of the slip and started down the Seine. They passed under the bridge at Point D'Alma and headed toward the golden statues along the bridge named for Alexander III. Beyond they could see the lights for the Louvre.

The waiter took their order, freshened their drinks and departed. Eva raised her glass to her lips. "Now, before we get serious about business tell me a bit about yourself Mr. Slade, or do you prefer to be called Jeremiah."

"No!" he said quickly. "I never go by that name or its derivatives, thank you."

"What if someone wants to be familiar with you?" she asked coquettishly.

"Even my mother doesn't use that name; not unless she's very, very angry."

"Perhaps you should go by your middle name, many people do."

"I can't do that either," he lamented.

"Is it that bad?"

"Milton," he told her reluctantly. "My grandfather."

"Slade it is then," she chuckled. She turned softly serious, looking askance at him. "You said mother instead of wife; you're not married then?"

"No."

"A momma's boy? Do you live with your parents?"

"I'm sorry if I gave you that impression," he sighed. "No, they are out adventuring in Maui. As for myself, the State Department keeps me in D.C. I have a little farmhouse in Virginia."

"No woman though? You're not handsome enough to be gay."

"Thank you for that!" he laughed.

Eva had done enough probing. "Okay, Slade tell me, how is it that you were forced into this deal. Somehow I can't see you as Water's right hand man?"

"No, thank you again," Slade smiled. "To tell you the truth I couldn't be in the same room as Waters. When I was in the military we used to drop bombs on people like him. No, I'm on loan from State, doing some research on the jihadist demonstrations over here."

"What kind of research?" she said with just a hint of suspicion.

He shrugged, and said, "You're a true cosmopolitan Ms. Accompando. You know that what happens in Europe eventually comes to the States. I'm just trying to gauge these groups so that we can deal with them more effectively."

"Such as who amongst the leadership to make disappear?" she jabbed.

"Hardly Ms. Accompando," he complained.

"Eva," she corrected.

"Eva," he agreed.

The waiter brought their dinner. As they ate she began to talk business. "I've seen the proposed shipping order Mr. Slade. The order requires special handling, an open air hull of special design. The *Atlas*, in fact, which is still working on the "Palm" project. Why did you come to me Mr. Slade; we don't own that ship? Can't you talk directly to the company?"

"Unfortunately not," Slade told her. Having read Freddy's brief he was completely aware of every facet of the unique and mysterious deal. "You see the Dutch aren't all that keen on loaning their ship to the Iranians."

"You're here on behalf of the Iranians then," she ventured.

"We have an interest in seeing this deal get done," he said.

"You're allies with the Europeans," she reminded him. "I'm not sure why you're talking to me instead of the Dutch government."

"Let's just say this administration has temporarily degraded the level of trust between the United States and its historic allies," he sighed. "We're in a time crunch. We need to get this done. You are renowned for getting things done. Therefore, we came to you."

"I assume you know then that I come neither cheap nor easily."

"Money is not a problem," he told her. "We simply want the *Atlas* to ferry the cargo from Bandar Abbas to Abu Dhabi."

"Across the Straits of Hormuz? That's a very short distance. What's the nature of the cargo?"

"Sensitive," he said firmly.

"I have to catalogue it, especially these days, and especially from Iran," she said with equal resolve. "You understand that these days there is a great deal of scrutiny on shipments. We have the safety of the ship and the crew to worry about."

"The Iranians will crew the ship and the *Atlas* will be escorted by the United States Navy. There will be United Nations inspectors supervising the shipment from loading to debarkation. You cannot ask for a more secure situation."

"I still need to know the cargo. Do you think the Dutch will lease out their vessel to the Iranians in ignorance?"

Slade sighed, but smiled, "The Dutch are well known for their nuclear disarmament policies. This should make them happy. The cargo is three tons of enriched Uranium which the Iranians are moving from Bandar Abbas to a United Nations storage facility in Abu Dhabi."

Eva whistled. "That's certainly a high profile cargo. However, this is a difficult climate to be working with the Iranians."

"This will help defuse some of the current tension."

"When do the Iranians want it?"

"Then we have a deal?"

"We do; we only have to draw up the contract with all the particulars."

Slade held up his phone. "They're all right here."

Eva bumped her own against his. "I have your information and you have my price. There you have everything you need to know Mr. Slade. Shall we consider our business finished?"

"Certainly."

To his surprise, Eva smiled and stood up. Politely, he stood as well. She patted his cheek, and said, "Good night Jeremiah. It really was pleasant doing business with you. Say hello to Waters for me, but do not wish him well."

She turned and left the restaurant, heading out to the deck.

Since they were in the middle of the Seine, Slade was curious as to where she was going. He followed her out onto the deck. The cool river breeze felt good. Eva, however, wasn't out for a breath of air. She went straight to the rail. There was a yacht keeping perfect pace with the river boat. A gangway was lowered at the rail and Eva stepped off of the river boat and onto the yacht. The gangway rose after Eva stepped on board the yacht's deck. She turned to see him standing at the rail and waved.

"I look forward to hearing the rest of your story one of these days Mr. Slade."

"You make a splash wherever you go—don't you Eva?"

As the yacht sped forward Eva called out.

"Always! Good night Jeremiah, pleasant dreams!"

CHAPTER 18: Leads and Leagues

Jean Brueget and his wife Margareta joined Slade on the rail after Eva disappeared. Margareta was a tall willowy brunette from the south of France. She came from money and had perfectly graceful manners. She contrasted with Jean, who in a well-tailored but slightly disheveled light grey suit, a ginger mustache and unruly hair, looked like an overworked cop—which he was.

Jean shook his head, lighting up a cigarette. "Eva is eccentric and over her head. Yet with a father like she has no one is likely to cause her harm, unless it is the jihadists."

"Who is her father," Slade asked?

"Soekarno," Jean told him. "She is one of the hordes of illegitimate Soekarno children, but he doesn't forget them. They become loyal parts of his global organization."

"Jean, you sound worried about her," Margareta observed.

He shrugged, and told his wife, "Perhaps I am. She is, as I said, in over her head. That cannot end well. It's a pity. He will never release her." Jean flicked his cigarette into the Seine. "Come, let us go back in and have some coffee."

After the cruise, instead of taking Slade back to his hotel Brueget brought him to their apartment. His office had a secure computer setup that allowed Slade to download the contents of Eva's phone. Unbeknownst to her as soon as she passed Slade the conditions for the deal Slade's CIA programmed phone secreted a worm in her device. That worm gave Slade access to everything on Eva's phone and everything connected to it, including her laptop.

The computer screen lit up and Slade went straight to his company icon. "Half a moment," he said patiently. The file that Eva sent him was there and intact. When the anti-virus software finished running its check a question bar popped up. It was a simple request consisting of one word: "Trace?"

Jeremiah stabbed it. At once the software went looking for the sender of the message. Once it had that it pried open a link to the device and every computer it had connections with.

"We're in," Jeremiah said.

Brueget's computer sorted Eva's files according to their interests. Something popped up immediately, causing Slade to comment, "Why are the Iranians dealing with Eva through Freddy when they're already dealing with her in the open. There's Nikahd dealing with her on another account."

"Maybe that account will tell us," Jean said, opening the file labelled *Felis Margarita* and reading the summary. "C'est incroyable! This is interesting. Soekarno is setting up a zoo in the poor section of Jakarta. One of the exhibits is *Felis Margarita*. It is native to Iran and Soekarno wanted Iranian material for the exhibit. Therefore, Eva contracted the Iranians and Nikahd for—listen to this—sand."

"Sand, you're kidding."

"She arranged the procurement of three hundred-fifty thousand pounds of sand from Iran for the exhibit. It is apparently so important to Soekarno that he is using the freighter *Galaxus*. The captain of the ship is a man named Christian Fletcher."

"What's special about him, besides the Mutiny on the Bounty jokes?"

"Christian Fletcher is married to our very own Eva Accompando. He's Soekarno's son-in-law."

"Something's not right," Slade growled. "This can't be what it seems—it's too crazy—for Nikahd to be involved there has to be something else going on. What if Soekarno wants something else from Iran and the sand is just a cover?"

"It would seem to me that's just too much of a coincidence. Look at the dates: the Iranians want to ship the nuclear material from Bandar Abbas on August 28, the same day they arranged for Eva's ship the *Galaxus* to leave port with the sand."

"It can't be a coincidence. The Iranians are up to something; it has to be the Uranium."

"If they ship out on the same day then the whole world will be watching the Iranian's nuclear material transit the Straits of Hormuz."

"Meanwhile Soekarno's *sand* heads off to Jakarta with no one watching."

"You could hide a lot of things in that much sand," Jeremiah mused. "You could have the Uranium inspected by the UN and then simply swap containers."

"While the world watches the *Atlas* go to Abu Dhabi three tons of Uranium are on their way to Jakarta."

"I suppose it's possible," Slade sighed.

"Can it be anything else," asked Jean. "The Iranians are using the sand as a feint!"

"What's Soekarno get out of it? Unless he's the broker for selling it to terrorist organizations."

"There's money in that, and with the sanctions the Iranians are starved for cash. Perhaps the Iranians are simply selling what they can sell through Soekarno, he gets his cut and everyone is happy."

"And three tons of enriched Uranium is suddenly on the world market for use in hundreds of "dirty bombs." Not a very pleasant scenario."

"The answer is in the cargo hold of the *Galaxus*!"

#

Outside the Brueget residence a black Mercedes watched the lights in Jean's windows. Four men inside were speaking amongst themselves. One of the men in back rolled down his window to have a better look at the Empire styled apartment building. He was horribly burned. Holding up a claw-like hand he waited until the man next to him put a lit cigarette in it.

"Just like the last time we met in Paris, INTERPOL is on our tail! He is too close to this business!"

"INTERPOL!" the other men exclaimed.

"Yes INTERPOL," Khallida said softly. "Brueget has been a thorn in my side since the "Wave of Allah" operation— making a mockery of our efforts—it was worse than failure!"

Khallida shuddered visibly, champing down hard on the cigarette and taking an interminably long drag. The red coals sneaked down the white lining toward his trembling claw.

"Hamdi died and it left me," he paused, dragging at the cigarette again. When he finished it was in a whisper. "It left me like this."

"The operation is compromised," said the driver harshly. "Eva has betrayed us!"

"How can she betray what she does not know?" Khallida replied calmly, regaining his composure. "No, as far as she knows this is a noble undertaking for the United Nations. She doesn't know anything but what we want her to know; and as a woman she's simply not capable of discovering anything on her own. The Prophet himself said more than once that women lack all common sense—don't worry!"

"What about Brueget and the American?" the driver said, gripping the steering wheel anxiously. "We should kill him and the INTERPOL agent—now—and his family too! We should send a message!"

"Stay calm!" ordered Khallida. "Don't you think the pro-Palestinian rioters have sent a message already; and don't you think the French have responded? Hundreds of our fighters are in jail now, crippling our operations here—just like you were young Hussein—fools! We are fortunate that the French released those who did not assault the French police."

"I was fighting the jihad!" Hussein complained.

"You are fighting the jihad out of weakness not cunning!" Khallida said amidst swirling cigarette smoke. "We are not yet strong enough to take on the police let alone the military. No—INTERPOL is off limits, but the American, he is different."

"What do you want us to do?"

"What did the Prophet ask when the despicable Jew Abu Afak insulted him, eh?"

Abdulla answered eagerly, "The Prophet asked, "Who will deal with this rascal for me?" And they slew the dog!"

"Exactly," Khallida smiled, letting loose a long stream of smoke.

"I will do it!" cried Hussein. "I will deal with this American; this Abu Afak! Let me regain your confidence."

"Let us be part of the deed as well," the other two pleaded.

Khallida let them wait, looking out the window. Finally, he said, "It is well. You three will end the American's life."

"Allahu Akbar!"

#

Slade spent the morning with Brueget. They worked out of the INTERPOL offices. He then spent several hours at the Airbus Industries headquarters before taking a cab to the rectory of Notre Dame for dinner with Brueget and Cardinal Martel.

"The Holy Father has made it plain that something needs to be done to stop Islamic terrorism," Cardinal Martel told them over a simple meal of pork, spinach and potatoes. "He has agreed that we are in a Just War. The brutality of ISIS and Al Qaeda cannot neither be overlooked nor stopped with dialogue. To do nothing is to be guilty of the gravest sin of omission imaginable!"

The cardinal poured wine for both of them, frowning with a degree of severity that struck them both. "We face a crisis from Islamists not seen since the Muslim invasions after the death of Muhammad and the fall of Constantinople. If you remember, the Caliphs after Muhammad spread Islam East and West. Christianity which had been dominant in North Africa for almost five hundred years nearly became extinct. Millions died in the rampage from the Arabian Peninsula through North Africa up the Iberian Peninsula and even into France itself.

"To the east the Muslim Caliphate scourged India for over three hundred years resulting in over one hundred million Indians being slaughtered. My friends, if Al Qaeda and ISIS are to be taken as the example of modern Islamist dogma then we must assume that they have not tempered their ways. Indeed, it would be irresponsible of us to assume anything else. We cannot live in a fantasy world where the Islamic states will be able to control their more radical brethren.

"Millions, hundreds of millions of lives hang upon our actions. We no longer have the luxury of passivity. We must take aggressive action lest millions of lives are lost. If we do nothing, if we trust to dialogue alone the lives of all those millions will rest on the brows of those of us who had the power to prevent this but did nothing to stop it."

"I'm interested Father in what the Vatican suggests we do," Slade asked carefully.

"The Holy Father will continue to pursue a course of understanding; however, he is about to issue a statement that will condone military action, not total war, but action nonetheless," the cardinal answered. "I spoke to the Holy Father last night. He was deeply troubled by what happened here and sees that it is connected to what is going on in the Middle East. We can expect no leadership from the President of the United States unfortunately. Therefore, he has given me his blessing to pursue other options."

Brueget said flatly, "That says a great deal coming from the Holy Father. I'm heartily ashamed that our government is also a problem. I especially am handcuffed by the new administration which not only wishes that it does not have to deal with this problem but fears stirring the substantial Muslim population into open revolt."

"Certainly not all of the Muslims wish this jihadist attitude on their people," the cardinal sighed. "Yet without a West that is willing to protect them from their fellow Muslims they cannot speak out. Oh what I would give for even a single Imam who would speak out against these Islamists!"

The evening ended on a more sedate note as Cardinal Martel joined Slade for the Bach concert. Afterwards, he accepted a ride home in the cardinal's car. During the ride he noticed two texts: one from the Company and one from his concierge.

"New itinerary. Office in Paris will provide travel to *Enterprise*. Hook up with DT Specter."

Slade was going back to the Persian Gulf where he would be working with Killer again and Specter Team. The second text was almost as interesting. It gave Slade an idea.

"W. will be back at 11:00."

"Excellent," Slade smiled wickedly. "Now for a bit of fun."

Slade walked into the hotel lobby at 10:47. He exchanged glances with the concierge and ducked behind a pillar. From there he could see the front door reflected in the mirrored elevator doors.

At 10:58 Freddy and Alfie came into the hotel lobby. They headed straight for the elevators. They were obviously tired, making small talk, which meant they were complaining about everyone else and commented on how stupid other people were compared to them.

A door opened. Freddy and Alfie shuffled in. Slade followed. Freddy didn't notice him until he looked up from pressing the button. When he saw Slade's face the unrepentant terrorist turned ghastly white.

CHAPTER 19: Ironing

Slade stood there silently with his dark eyes focused on Freddy. The terrorist shrank back with an audible gasp, but he was frozen. He could neither say nor do anything but tremble.

Alfie didn't recognize Slade. He looked up at the tall man in the suit, and said, "He buddy, what's up? You don't like our cologne?"

The warm, sweet smell of urine filled the elevator car. A dark stain grew on Freddy's khaki's. It dripped on his shoe and soiled the elevator carpet.

"Holy shit Freddy; you pissed your pants! Son of a bitch!"

The door opened, but Slade blocked the way. Waters stood there shaking in the back. Alfie couldn't figure what was happening. He looked at Slade and then at Freddy, pleading, "Listen buddy, I don't know what your problem is, but my friend is sick. I have to get him to his room."

"Be careful who you choose as friends," Slade told him.

"What?"

Slade nodded to Freddy. "You're friend there has an interest in photographs. It *will* catch up with him."

"Photographs?" Alfie started.

The elevator door started to close, but Slade stopped it with his arm. He moved aside to allow Alfie to drag Freddy out of the car. They hurried down the hall.

Slade followed in slow menacing steps.

When they got to the door, Freddy fumbled for his key card. He couldn't dig it out of his pocket with his shaking hands.

Slade reached over.

Both Freddy and Alfie gasped and shrank back.

Slade swiped his skeleton key over the door. The lock clicked open. Freddy and Alfie stared at him in horror; no lock was safe.

Slade pushed the door open.

Freddy finally found his voice. "You, you can't touch me Slade! I'm the president's man! Do you get that, goon? I'm the president's man!"

Slade said simply, "Corporal Garret's wife and daughter died. They were beheaded—Freddy."

He went grey, sweating, stammering, "What's it to me?" He rushed into his room. Alfie followed.

#

When they were safe inside Freddy's room, Alfie looked through the peephole and watched the tall man leave. "Shit Freddy who was that guy?"

"He's a spook; an assassin," Freddy said in a trembling voice, going straight to the john and stripping.

"What does he want with you?"

"I gave him up; him and his Special Forces pals. They butchered Turgut Ataturk, the president's nephew, in a Cobra strike against ISIS. I gave them to Ataturk to even the score."

"Shit Freddy, shit! Who was this Garret woman—don't tell me she was," Alfie couldn't finish.

"I think she was one of the Special Forces guy's wife," Freddy admitted, turning on the shower.

"His wife and kid!" Alfie gasped.

"Collateral damage!" Freddy shouted from the shower, regaining his courage now that his own filth was washing off his pallid skin.

"Freddy!"

The shower turned off. Freddy emerged a minute later in a robe, drying his mossy hair. He stuck his glasses back on his nose and shrugged, "What about it? They're pigs. I'll sick the president on his ass!"

Freddy's laptop chimed. He had a message. Before he could reach the screen, while both of them were looking at it, it brightened. The image on the screen was a simple one: a dagger plunged through the Greek letter Delta. It turned slowly round and round on Freddy's computer.

"Holy shit Freddy, you're going to have the whole Delta Force gunning for you!"

Freddy went to the computer and tried to turn the screen off. Nothing worked. The Delta Force icon turned slowly on the screen, ever watchful, ever mindful.

"Freddy, they're never going to let you go—ever! You are fucking screwed man!"

#

Slade checked his files after sweeping the room. The Company was flying him out of Paris tomorrow. He was heading out to the *Enterprise*. There he would link up with Killer's Specter Team again and investigate the *Galaxus* at port in Bandar Abbas.

"A night dive; I hate night dives! That's when sharks feed!" Slade complained, reading the tasking. He was serious. Slade had a phobia about sharks, especially big ones. Night dives didn't help. They were creepy, kind of like being buried alive.

To get his mind off being eaten alive in the pitch dark, Slade ordered a pizza and hopped in the shower.

He had one white shirt, the one he was wearing. Now after two days it was getting ripe. Slade washed it in the sink.

Fifteen minutes later, dressed in his robe and roper boots, Slade hated the idea of going barefoot on the hotel carpet, Slade was back reading the file at his desk, waiting for the iron to heat up so he could iron his shirt. Room service interrupted him. Leaving the laptop half situated, he went to the door and got his pizza. Slade started his ironing and munched on the pepperoni, pineapple pie, wishing he'd ordered extra cheese. A frosted glass of Guinness perched precariously on the ironing board.

Turning on the TV, Jeremiah caught a glimpse of himself in the mirror. He made quite a sight: wearing a hotel robe, chewing on pizza, ironing his uniform, horn-rimmed glasses perched on his oft broken nose.

"The glamorous life of a spy! James Bond eat your heart out!"

Slade was almost done ironing his shirt when the alarm on his computer went off. He swore, and looked over his shoulder but the computer was on the desk behind him and facing away. He swore again; he hated when he was sloppy.

A pass key buzzed the lock. No matter who had it wouldn't work. Slade always changed the lock code for his room with another Company toy.

"You've got the wrong room!" he said irritably.

Boom! The door burst open right in front of Slade, stopping abruptly on the chain. The second hit ripped the chain out of the wall. Three bearded figures rushed in. He could do only one thing: leaping back he flung the hot iron at the first of the attackers—clang! The impact of the hot iron on his attacker's face included a momentary sizzle followed by a scream. The foremost two attackers fell headlong over the ironing board.

The burned attacker fell with his chest on the ironing board but his right leg got caught in the folding metal legs. He fell awkwardly. The result was a resounding snap! Another scream followed and he curled up on the floor clutching his compound fracture with one hand and his burned face with another.

An attacker leapt over the impediment but tripped, falling face first in front of Slade. With a predatory leap Slade was on him, shoving him down to the carpet with his knee and punching the attacker hard in the back of the head. The blow was hurried and at an awkward angle, but it was enough for the attacker to drop his knife and go into seizures.

Slade looked up at the third attacker, a burly, bearded man holding a large knife. He worked his way around the ironing board, yelling in Arabic, "I will gut you American! I will gut you!"

Grabbing the power cord for the iron, Slade yanked it back and began whirling it in a tight circle. As the man lunged he let it fly. Slade didn't try anything fancy; he hurled the hard, heavy, hot object right at the assassin's chest. It struck with a clang and a sizzle; then he yanked it back and started twirling it again. The attacker feinted, hoping to get Slade to commit, risking getting burned again to be able to slip in for a killing blow. Slade whirled his weapon as he would an ancient flail, waiting until the attacker pulled back from his fake, off balance and stationary.

This time he let fly at the attacker's head. The man shrieked as the iron knocked into his head, burning his chin before bouncing off. In desperation he threw his knife at Slade. It was a hurried throw, easily batted aside. The attacker dug in his vest for a gun. Slade charged.

He was only a few meters from the attacker and easily got to him before he drew the gun. Hitting him in the jaw with a palm heel strike stunned the assailant. Another strike to the throat stopped his breath. Slade yanked on the man's shoulder and got behind him, wrapping his arms around the attacker's head. With one swift jerk he broke the man's neck. The attacker dropped like a stone.

With two out of the three out and the remaining attacker writhing in pain from a broken leg and a burned face, Slade took stock of the situation. Looking down the hall revealed no more threats. He quickly closed the door.

Slade rearmed and retrieved a roll of duct tape from his bag, taping the attacker's hands and feet together, ignoring his screams of pain. Hauling the attacker up on the bed, Slade pulled him around by the hair until he faced the chair. He looked down at the attacker; he knew who he was, or at least he guessed. He wasn't Arab, and he wasn't an Algerian; no, the young man was Indonesian or Malaysian.

Slade sat down, thinking, "Maybe I can kill two birds with one stone. He's going to see a jihadist lawyer if they don't outright let him go. I should give him something—Freddy!"

Slade smiled mirthlessly, "You people should be careful who you trust. Freddy Waters told me all about you—everything! I'm just a bit hazy on the details, so we'll go over them now!"

"Die Crusader dog! I will never talk to you!" the prisoner protested, and he spat at Slade.

Slade erupted in anger, grabbing the attacker by the collar and ripping his shirt down to his waist, exposing a lean dark back. "So, you're trying to be funny are you? Okay, two can play at that game! He went to his bag and dug out a bottle. The attacker looked at it in fear.

"What is that, acid? Hah, you can never make a soldier of Allah talk!"

"Yeah, I've heard it all before. The Islamist warrior is very brave, very brave indeed when he is throwing acid in the face of a woman or a girl—I've seen your handiwork Abdul! Very brave indeed!" Slade laughed. He grabbed the young jihadist's head in his hands and tilted it up into an unnatural, painful angle, putting his furious features inches from the now frightened jihadist. "You terrorists hide behind women and children in mosques, slink into hotel rooms and behead people with their hands tied behind their backs—yes, you're brave, so brave!"

He showed the terrorist the bottle. "We're going to see how manly you are! This isn't acid. These are bacon bits; that's right Abdul—pork!"

He sprinkled the bacon bits all over the attacker's back. The man began to shout and curse. Those curses turned to screams when Slade applied the still hot iron to his naked flesh, searing the bacon bits into his back.

"There you go, how brave are you now?" he demanded. "What's your name? Who sent you? Answer my questions and you get to go to paradise as a whole man. Make it tough on me and you'll go there as a eunuch. I'll boil your balls off with this iron. You won't even be able to bugger the little boys!"

The sound of flesh burning mixed with the smell of human and bacon roasting was enough to sicken even Slade, but he persevered. At length, he removed the iron and repeated his questions.

"I am Abdulla Hussein! Khallida, Khallida!" the man yelped. "It was Khallida's tasking!"

"How did he find me?" Slade demanded.

"No, no I cannot, no, I don't know—Aiee!"

The iron hissed.

"How?"

"I don't know, no, no! They don't tell us!" the attacker pleaded. "We hear rumors, rumors of someone in the president's administration. He is Muslim Brotherhood!"

Slade hesitated, knowing this was probably the truth. After a moment of thought, he asked, "Where is your Paris cell located? Who is your boss?"

The door burst open and a chorus of voices shouted, "Freeze!"

It was half a dozen gendarmes. Slade froze.

"Drop the iron!"

"You're sure?"

"Drop it I say!"

Slade shrugged, dropping the iron flat on the terrorist's back.

"Aiee!" the resulting scream was very convincing.

CHAPTER 20: Detective Work

Slade sat cuffed to the metal table wearing his white robe and his black boots, that's all they allowed him. Across from him sat two detectives. They stared at him. He stared back, and sighed, "Gentlemen, let's not waste our time. Let me make one phone call and this will all be cleared up."

The short, heavyset detective with wispy blonde hair grimaced, telling Slade in heavily tainted English, "Monsieur, you are not going to clear up two murders and torture with a phone call."

"Only one of the jihadists died, the paramedics said the other one was still alive," Slade corrected. This was always the frustrating part of things. He wasn't at liberty to blow his cover; that is, he couldn't admit he was CIA.

As far as the detectives were concerned he was an American found in a hotel room with a dead guy, a vegetable and a maimed Muslim with bacon bits seared into his flesh. Worse, he had his CIA case with all the goodies inside. Whatever Slade was, he didn't look all that innocent.

That meant he had to get word to Brueget or the office; they would then go through government channels to get Slade out without blowing his cover.

The detectives, however, appeared stuck on the condition of the terrorists. "I suppose clinically the second man is alive, but he a vegetable," said the other detective; a tall, beanpole of a man with a thin mustache and goatee.

"Monsieur, they invaded my room wanted my head; they're jihadists, you've seen them, they have all of Paris up in arms. Didn't you see the weapons they brought? I don't think they broke into my room to talk about soccer!"

"You make a very good point monsieur," the shorter cop nodded. "They do indeed have Paris up in arms. So much so, in fact that the mayor has become involved."

The taller man continued, "The mayor fears that when your assassination of these young men becomes known—sorry, his words not mine—the entire Arab community will erupt in violence. That would be very bad."

"I'm sorry, but I didn't ask them to break into my room and attack me. Can't I defend myself in France?"

The heavy man shrugged, and said, "Two years ago a man in England shot an intruder. Now it was perfectly clear that the intruder attacked him—perfectly clear—but the court and the jury ruled that he had no right to kill the man. He's in prison now."

"Your point?"

"Our point is that self-defense doesn't work the same in Europe as it does in America," the taller detective told him. "We do not have a cowboy mentality."

"Put yourself in my place. Have you watched YouTube lately? Do you mean to tell me that you'd let those jihadists hack off your head rather than defending yourself?"

The detectives looked at each other and then at Slade. The tall man replied, "You have a right to defend yourself but you do not have the right to take another life."

"Monsieur, even if we convince the mayor that we cannot make you a scapegoat for these hooligans, you say jihadists, and maybe your right, but even so there is the torture and the illegal weapons. That's ten to twenty right there."

"I can explain that," Slade began, but then he gave up. "All right, that's why I'd like my phone call. You can make it for me, I don't mind. Call Inspector Jean Brueget at INTERPOL."

"INTERPOL?"

"INTERPOL," Slade insisted.

"I do not think that INTERPOL will help you with the mayor."

"I'm not worried about the mayor; I'm trying to help you gentlemen out. I don't want you to take the fall for this."

'We are flattered for your concern!"

The tall man got on the intercom. "Philippe, will you call INTERPOL and tell agent Jean Brueget that we have his friend Jeremiah Slade in here for murder?"

"Oui monsieur!"

The heavy man scratched his head. "Getting back to your story. The fight I understand. They break in, you defend yourself, with an iron instead of the many illegal firearms in your possession, am I right?"

"They caught me ironing."

"How did you come into possession of the firearms?"

"I carry them for self-defense."

"Not in France you do not—you know that monsieur— certainly not firearms with the serial numbers filed off," the detective got up with some effort and retrieved a cup of espresso. He raised his brow to Slade. "I assume you like coffee?"

"Thank you."

The detective got him a cup of coffee, really espresso with hot water, and set it down on the table. He sat back down, saying, "Help me to understand Monsieur Slade. This is not New York or Chicago where you spend your time shooting hooligans and dueling with pistols—this is Paris—Paris is civilized."

The tall detective added, "We see that you have been here before. You must like Paris then, oui? Well Monsieur Slade we love Paris; we love our civilized Paris."

"Do you love France?" Slade asked, sipping his coffee.

"Of course we love France!" they said.

"Well then you better start acting French!"

"What do you mean?" they asked together, dumbfounded.

"I love France gentlemen, I really do," he told them firmly. "I love Charles Martel, Joan of Arc, Napoleon and Charles de Gaulle. What do you think they would have done with the rabble in your streets, the jihadists taking over your cities, refusing to become French but demanding that you, their hosts, appease them?"

The detectives sighed, admitting, "Mais oui, the Emperor is rolling in his grave at Les Invalides!"

"But Monsieur Slade that does not explain your weapons or your torturing the young man," the heavy detective told him. "Who are you monsieur? Why would Hussein and his partners want to kill you?"

Slade said truthfully. "I've got a Fatwa on my head." Embellishing a bit, he added, "I write books—novels—they're not flattering toward the Islamists or their prophet."

"So that is why you had the weapons?"

"Yes."

"Why did you torture young Hussein?"

"To find out who ordered the hit on me."

"And did you find out?"

"A jihadist named Gamel Khallida who is in league with an American named Freddy Waters," he added, just to muddy Freddy's name.

"And where are these assassins from?"

Slade sipped his coffee and chuckled, "If your boys had waited another few minutes I could have told you where the Paris cell was and who was running it!"

The door burst open. Outside in the squad room there were shouts. "Jihad, jihad, jihad!"

The detective sighed, "Your wild west lynch mob is here!"

CHAPTER 21: Politics, Politics, Politics

The diminutive Mayor of Paris stormed in with the chief of police and Jean Brueget in tow. Brueget closed the door quickly, but Slade could see and hear the hubbub in the squad room behind.

"Ali Habib and his rabble," Brueget sneered, glaring at the mayor. "Do you have any idea how much trouble this can cause, rousing them like this?"

The mayor turned red, letting them know his displeasure in no uncertain terms. "Ali Habib happens to be the leader of the largest Muslim neighborhood in the city," the mayor reminded them. "It is his job, and mine, to ensure that our citizens are safe from vigilantes like this American cowboy!"

"Habib is the front for the Muslim Brotherhood—a terrorist organization—he personally murdered hundreds of women and children in Afghanistan," Brueget informed him.

"Who are you to slander the leader of the Muslim community in Paris?" the mayor demanded.

"I am INTERPOL," Brueget told him flatly. "So if you want to support a community of immigrants who refuses to adopt the French way of life and favor them over the people of France you will have INTERPOL to deal with, Monsieur Mayor."

The mayor seemed genuinely stung by the remark. He lowered his voice. "Agent Brueget, you must understand the situation. I can anger Parisians and they will do nothing. However, if I anger the Arabs they take to the streets! Mon Dieu, they are already burning cars, marching through the streets shouting for jihad and waving Palestinian flags. They are laying siege to synagogues, disrupting the lives of Parisians, they are affecting our tourism!"

Brueget snapped back, "That is why we have gendarmes and a military; we have a right to defend what is ours, what is France! Just like Monsieur Slade had a right to defend himself from these animals!"

The mayor looked frazzled. "If I do not placate them they will all but burn the city. Monsieur, I have no choice."

The Chief of Police told him firmly, "The Muslims broke into this man's room. He has a right to defend himself. I am not about to throw a man in prison to placate that rabble out there! We have the law to guide us Monsieur Mayor, not politics."

"What is the law but politics!" the mayor scoffed, wedging himself between the detectives, looking at a bored Slade. "Why he doesn't look so dangerous! He's just a middle-aged man. This is our vigilante? Are you sure?"

"You display your ignorance blatantly," Brueget told him with disdain. "Monsieur Slade is a hero of France!" He laughed at the mayor's look of consternation.

"Surely you are joking! He has admitted he killed one man, made a vegetable out of another and was torturing a third with an iron when you caught him," the mayor said. Sighing as if he truly regretted the overwhelming evidence. The mayor added, "Monsieur Slade, it looks very bad, very bad indeed. You're going to have your work cut out for you; that is, unless you want to make a deal that would help me calm the Muslim community here."

"A deal? Really?" said Slade, more than perturbed at the mayor. "You are ruining the most beautiful city in the world, handing it over to the Islamists without a fight. Mr. Mayor are you Vichy?"

The mayor purpled with rage. Before he could speak, Slade hit him again. "Do you know that right now, in your city there are harems of kidnapped girls—daughters of France, your daughters—and they are kept as sex slaves for the Islamists? You know this, but you let it happen—how?"

"I will not let you twist the subject onto me! There will be payment for this vigilante!"

"There will indeed," Slade said.

The Chief of Police whispered an aside to Brueget, saying, "Slade sounds more like the Mayor of Paris should sound than the mayor himself!"

Brueget chuckled quietly, and remarked, "Would that we had fewer citizens who hate France and more Americans like Jeremiah Slade who love her!"

Brueget's phone rang and he turned away to answer it.

The remark stung the mayor, and he stood there like a statue for a long moment. With no renewed attack on him, the mayor regained his composure.

He leaned over Slade and doubled down. "I will give you one last chance to deal monsieur. If you are willing to plead guilty and publicly apologize to the Muslim community, I will be satisfied with, say, ten years. Your government can get you out in five. Think of it, monsieur, murder alone is twenty-five years. You would never see the light of day."

"Actually, no, Monsieur Mayor," Brueget told him, turning back around and pocketing his phone. "This is the deal: release Slade now and give me Abdulla Hussein. He's the man Slade was questioning."

"Hussein? What do you want with that poor boy?"

"Monsieur Mayor, Abdulla Hussein works for a man named Khallida, a notorious Al Qaeda terrorist who is on the terrorist watchlist of France, INTERPOL as well as the United States. He has been implicated on every plot from Nine-Eleven to the current ISIS crisis."

"That has nothing to do with Monsieur Hussein!" the mayor retorted.

"Monsieur Mayor, Hussein is one of Khallida's recruits," Brueget said sternly. "We also think he is involved in the disappearance of Malaysian Flight 666."

"You cannot speak to him," the mayor said firmly. "I will not be dictated to by INTERPOL!"

"This is an international terrorism case," Brueget informed the mayor. "I have the authority to take him into custody and I will not hesitate to do so."

"You are too late, I released him as a sign of good will to the Muslim community," the mayor told Brueget.

"You what?" exclaimed the Chief of Police. "Monsieur, you had no authority to do such a thing! That is my department!"

"I have every authority!" the mayor countered. "This is my city; my police force; it is my responsibility to keep the peace in Paris! I will do as I see fit!"

"We need to get Hussein before he disappears; he can lead us to the missing jet," Slade said urgently, ignoring the mayor.

"I am on it," Jean nodded, taking out his phone and placing a call.

"You will do no such thing!" the mayor protested, red faced with anger.

Brueget put a finger in the mayor's face. "You are interfering with an international counter-terrorism operation—back off Monsieur!"

The mayor refused to back down. "This is my city!"

The mayor got his own phone out, shaking at Sorensen. "You want to play games? This is Paris—my town! I will have you all thrown into prison or deported! There, how is that for calling your bluff?"

"I'm not bluffing Monsieur Mayor; I'm deadly serious. I warn you, you will not win this fight."

"Oh so you want to play politics?" the would-be Napoleonic mayor smiled. "Well my President of France trumps your INTERPOL any day. How do you like that?"

"Game on Monsieur Mayor," he replied. There was a pause, during which the mayor flushed red but became suddenly silent while Brueget was on the phone with his superiors.

"Director, we have a situation brewing in Paris and a possible compromise of NATO security."

"Compromise of NATO security, what the devil is she talking about?" the mayor blurted.

Brueget's eyes flashed in anger. "Our investigation and our agent is compromised Monsieur Mayor, under your jurisdiction—that's an international crime under the NATO treaty—so are you part of the solution or part of the problem?"

"What, I didn't have anything to do with that!"

"Really? I suggest you call your president Monsieur Mayor, you're going to need him."

"How dare you!" he started, but Brueget held up a single finger and the mayor's mouth snapped shut.

"Sir, it's more serious than that," the INTERPOL officer continued. "Slade was ambushed in his hotel room by three assassins. All three have ties to Al Qaeda in Afghanistan, Saudi Arabia, Qatar and Yemen and Malaysia—yes, Malaysia. In fact, he is the son of the missing Malaysian Airlines captain—yes sir, Slade was interrogating Hussein when the French gendarmes interrupted him. Yes, this occurred after he saved the life of Cardinal Martel at Notre Dame yesterday, not to mention saving the Cathedral itself."

"An attack on Notre Dame—what attack?" the mayor blurted. "Why wasn't I informed of this outrageous event?" The mayor was clearly in a panic. The one thing Parisian's loved more than Paris itself was its history and especially *the* cathedral. "Why was I not told of this?"

His aide rolled his eyes, "Monsieur Mayor, you will not take verbal briefings. It was the first item in your electronic brief yesterday! However, if you missed it there, then you might have seen it elsewhere." He handed the morning paper to the mayor. The front page main headline was simple and ferocious: *Muslims try to Assassinate Cardinal Martel and Destroy the Blessed Notre Dame!*

"Mon Dieu!" he sweated. "I was meeting with Ali Habib; trying to defuse the unrest in the city. Why didn't he mention this outrage? Mon Dieu! Mon Dieu!"

Against the backdrop of the mayor's rising panic, Brueget continued, telling the director, "No, Slade is fine. Yes sir, Khallida was behind this. Slade was about to get the particulars on the Paris cell from Hussein when the gendarmes interrupted and arrested him.

"Slade is still in custody, but the mayor let Hussein go. We are tracking him down now. There's more I'm afraid. Our next most pressing problem after recapturing Hussein is that the mayor has seen fit to mobilize the local Muslim Brotherhood factions. Yes sir, the mayor brought them to the police station—yes sir, it's Habib—regardless, we are in serious danger of losing Slade's cover permanently."

Slade couldn't help but admire the way Brueget handled the situation. The mayor was growing paler by the moment. After a moment, he said simply, "Yes sir, we will!"

He put the phone away, and said calmly, "Monsieur Mayor there's no need for you to call the president."

He regained his confidence and smiled, "You see, I told you."

Brueget stepped up to the mayor and lit a cigarette.

The mayor looked at him with disproval, and said, "You can't do that. I signed an ordinance banning smoking in public buildings."

He took a long drag and blew the smoke in the mayor's face. "You misunderstand me Monsieur Mayor. You don't need to call the president; he will call you!"

"He will call me?" the mayor stuttered. "I don't understand."

"No you don't," he agreed. "However, it's about to become all too clear to you."

The mayor's phone rang.

He tapped it and answered with great surprise, "Oh it's you Monsieur President! What a pleasure—what? Yes sir, I'm listening."

As the mayor listened with growing distress to the President of France, who though no hawk, nonetheless was a politician.

Slade leaned over and whispered into Brueget's ear, "How much is this going to cost me?"

He chuckled, and said, "Not this time. Even the Socialist President of France isn't going to buck NATO, INTERPOL and above all the Catholic Church! Politically speaking he'd be dead before he hung up the phone!"

The mayor was now red in the face. He shoved his phone in his pocket and missed. The phone fell to the floor and shattered. The aide scooped up the broken phone and held it out for the mayor, who stared at him and then swatted the offending piece of hardware out of the listless hand.

He looked at Brueget and then at Slade, steaming. In a tightly controlled voice, he said, "You are to be released

Monsieur Slade. It would give me great—pleasure—to invite you to my office this afternoon so that I may, on the president's behalf, award you the Légion d'honneur for your service to France."

The detective had already unlocked Slade, who stood, still in his bathrobe and boots. "It would be an honor Monsieur Mayor."

Turning on his heel, the mayor stormed out of the room and slammed the door. Still, they could all hear him as he shouted, almost screamed for the cops to get every civilian who wasn't under arrest out of the building—now!

The Chief of Police ordered a gendarme to get Slade's cloths. He returned with the clothes and weapons. Slade began digging them out.

"My men are heading to all of the Muslim Brotherhood safe houses," Brueget told him. "If he's still in Paris we'll find him."

"He's probably disappeared like the rat he is," Slade growled. They walked down the back stairs to the courtyard of the Palais de Justice, within which was the Cathedral of Saint-Michel, a small yet stunning example of stained glass gone magnificently mad.

"The car's out on the street," Brueget said, leading Slade through the arch.

"We're never going to find him," Slade growled, there are too many places to hide in Paris."

The sound of squealing tires and sirens caught their attention. Looking up they saw a Renault convertible flying over the bridge toward them; the unmistakable sound of AK-47's filled the Paris morning.

CHAPTER 22: Deception

The first mate of the Iranian oil tanker went out on deck in the early morning hours, purportedly to watch the sun rise over the South China Sea. Why he needed a small gym bag to do that he couldn't have answered but no one asked.

As salmon tinged the eastern sky he went to the rail. After unzipping the gym bag he withdrew a god sized heavy metal object and set it on the deck. It was the same type of Black Box found on all commercial Airbus A380's. There was a cable attached to the box leading to a simple switch. The first mate turned on the switch and noted that a red light shone beneath it.

Taking out a set of earphones attached to a small radio the first officer put them on his head and listened. There was a clearly audible ping! Satisfied, he disconnected the cable and put it back in the bag. The headphones and radio followed.

Lifting the Black Box the first mate heaved it overboard. It fell four stories to the sea below, disappearing into the water without a sound.

A day later a report circulated that the pinging of Malaysian Flight 666 was heard in the South China Sea. The resources of a dozen countries sped to the area but the signal died before the Black Box was retrieved. Speculation on whether the A380 and its wreckage now rested at the bottom of the ocean ran rampant.

CHAPTER 23: General Washington's Kabob

Brueget hopped in the big, black Peugeot and started the engine. Slade threw his case in the back and followed it in. Throwing the transmission into drive, Brueget smoked the tires, trying to nudge the Renault as careened past. He missed, but Brueget kept his foot on the gas, sliding into the street in pursuit, followed by a line of gendarmes with sirens wailing.

There were four men in the Renault, and three of them had automatic AK-47 assault rifles. One of them was Abdulla. The Budda-budda-budda of the Kalashnikov thumped the Paris morning.

"Are they insane? There are citizens everywhere!" Brueget cursed, sliding into a hard left turn onto Quai d'Horloge. The Renault took the next left toward Pont Neuf, and then crossed the Seine, screaming left again against the traffic along the river. The Renault dodged cars and motorcycles, zooming past the Great Canadian Pub's big red maple leaf and trying to make the turn into Saint-Michel—he didn't make it—instead skidding across the plaza, guns blazing, where the Arab population was already gathering for another day of protests.

The Renault plowed through the crowd, with the young terrorists in the back firing wildly, facing backwards. They tried to shoot at the Peugeot, which Brueget swung wide to avoid the crowds, but they seemed just as happy to shoot down people—little realizing these were their own sympathizers.

The Renault was slowed by the multitude of people it ran over, and Brueget was on the point of cutting it off, so the driver steered hard left and headed back over the Saint-Michel Bridge where he started.

Brueget cursed and spun around, gunning it and following. Over the Saint-Michel Bridge they sped, past pedestrians and tourists.

Slade drew his pistols and rolled down his window. He leaned out as soon as he had a clear shot and sent a flurry of

9mm rounds at the Renault. One of the terrorists took a bullet in the shoulder. It spun him around in the seat, but as he was already half standing, he lost his balance and spilled over the side.

"That wasn't Hussein?" Brueget exclaimed.

"No!" Slade replied—thump, thump—Brueget made sure of him.

"Double tap!" Brueget exclaimed.

The heavy car rolled over him, dragging the terrorist for a bit, leaving a bloody smear on the pavement and over the bridge, before the broken man rolled out from underneath as they skidded onto Quai des Gevres, again going against traffic.

The drag of the terrorist had slowed the Peugeot down, but now Brueget stepped on it, weaving through the oncoming traffic, gaining on the Renault. By the time they were close enough for Slade to take another shot they were passing Pont d'Alma. The Renault entered the proper lane and headed toward Place d'Lena on the Avenue du President Wilson. The buildings sped by. As the approached the wide roundabout, Brueget yelled, "He's got to slow and turn right!"

Slade whipped out his gun and shot low. He emptied the clip at the Renault's rear tire. The back tailgate and bumper sparked, and then the right rear tire blew in a cloud of white smoke.

Young Abdulla was not an experienced fighter. He waved the barrel of the AK-47 around like a movie prop, missing the Peugeot entirely. When the tire blew he and his companion clutched the rear of the Renault, just trying to stay in the swerving car. With the tire blown the driver couldn't make the turn. He careened through traffic, bouncing off several cars before running headlong into the concrete pedestal on which rested the equestrian statue of General George Washington. The little Renault slammed to a stop, throwing Abdulla high into the gray morning sky.

The impact tossed Abdulla like a rag doll some sixty feet in the air. He came down on the point of the George Washington's up-thrust sword, impaling himself through the stomach on the symbol of America; the Great Satan. Abdulla hung there for a few moments, weakly clutching at General Washington's steady hand before he fainted.

Jean pulled the Peugeot to a screeching halt next to the statue, laughing. "How apropos," Jean sighed, getting out his phone. "I will get the ambulances on the way. You had better see to young Abdulla! Although I fear he is of no more use to us!"

Slade leapt out of the car and sped to the Renault. The driver was dead, crushed into a bloody pulp with only his wide eyed face visible out of the smoldering wreckage. The other terrorist was flung out of the back as well. He landed on the other side of the statue, just in the street, where the Parisians promptly ran over him a dozen times.

Slade retrieved the AK-47 Abdulla dropped and flipped the clip, chambering a round just in case. He walked around to the north side of the statue where Abdulla's head hung over.

He looked up to the young terrorist, who hung draped over the general's arm; the bloody blade of Washington's sword protruded from the young jihadist's back. Blood and entrails slimed the shaft.

Amazingly young Abdulla looked to be alive—for now. His hands were clutching feebly at the air and his head was twitching, as if he were having some conversation with an unseen companion.

"Abdulla!" Slade called up to him and the jihadist's eyes fluttered open. "Where's your father Abdulla? Tell us and we'll get you down from there in one piece!"

He groaned, but said, "My father will be a great martyr! Zion will fall! I will see him in paradise!"

"Maybe we'll just leave you up there with General Washington," Slade told him. "Maybe he can talk some sense into you."

"No, you must get me down, I must continue to fight," he said breathlessly, his voice wavering in and out of coherence. "You cannot leave me here; you won't. Westerners are soft. You will do whatever you must to save me. You will save me so that I can watch your world fall!"

The smell of fuel alerted Slade to another danger. The Renault's fuel tank burst and the petrol was seeping toward the hot engine block. "Sorry Abdulla!"

He hustled away. There was no choice; he was almost too late. The engine caught fire. The fire swiftly spread through the Renault, searching for the fuel tank.

Abdulla was only partially coherent, but there is something about the smell of smoke that instills instinctual terror on any being unfortunate enough to be around it. He stopped his jabbering, his head lolling from side to side, his eyes trying to see through his puffy, bruised face. When they focused on the bright blur of the flames he started keening, as he was too weak to scream.

His voice became a high drawn out wail—whoomph! The fuel reached the hot engine block. The flames raced back to the breached tank and the trapped fumes exploded, rupturing the tank completely. A fireball of flaming fuel erupted upward engulfing George and his skewered victim in fire and fuel. The flames rose up into a black cloud as the fuel began to burn greedily, licking at the statue and roasting Abdulla on the spit.

"I suppose he's not going to be around when we finally fall," Slade sighed.

Brueget grimaced, "Mon Dieu! He is determined to roast in Hell!"

The young jihadist's wails ended in a single high pitched cry. His arms reached for the sky, hands ending in grasping, burning claws. Then he collapsed and went limp as a fish.

There was nothing more to be done; nothing to salvage from the wreck. The rescue crews came and put out the fire. When it came time to remove Abdulla from General Washington's sword they had two choices: either cut the sword off the monument or cut Abdulla.

The sword remained intact.

As they walked away from the grisly scene something crunched under Slade's boot. It was a cell phone. He picked it up and tapped it. The phone came on.

"It's Abdulla's," Slade told Brueget.

"Incredible!"

They drove back to Saint-Michel. It looked like a war zone. The paramedics were sorting those who were dead, those who could be saved, and those who were going to die. Abdulla and his fellow terrorists killed thirty-three of their own people—amazingly, no other citizens of Paris or Tourists were hurt.

Slade was spirited away to the embassy. Once there, he and Brueget examined Abdulla's phone. The last call from Abdullereda to his son came through a cell tower in Jakarta.

Slade reported direct to Gann.

"Good work Slade, we're getting you out to the *Enterprise* pronto. We need you on the *Galaxus* when the convoy leaves Bandar Abbas. If there's a switch I want you and the Delta's there to nail it."

"Sir, what about the jet. It's got to be in Jakarta."

"I'm heading to the White House to brief the president right now. Get to the *Enterprise* Slade; I want you on the *Galaxus* tomorrow night!"

The connection ended. Jean glanced outside and then at his watch, "Mon Dieu it's six in the morning already. You've made a full night of it—again!"

Slade took the evening military flight from Charles de Gaulle to Abu Dhabi in the United Arab Emirates. It was a little over eight hours on a normal flight, over nine this night since Hamas precipitated a war in Southern Israel and Gaza.

After the Russians mistakenly shot down a Malaysian Airlines flight over the Ukraine just a few days past, mistaking the airliner for a cargo plane, no one had any desire to fly over or near a war zone.

"Malaysian Airline's days are numbered," Slade thought as he read the Company brief. "So are mine. The president wants me dead. He approved this mission because it puts me in shark infested waters during their feeding time. I know it!"

Slade tried not to think of the night dive. He shook his head and failed. "If the sharks don't get me I'll probably hyperventilate because I'm worried about the sharks getting me. I'll get the bends or black out and drown. Then the sharks eat me. Any way you look at it the sharks get me; that ought to make him happy."

He studied his file, but he wasn't happy about it. After landing, Slade transferred to a Navy Hawkeye E2C Hawkeye for the flight aboard the *Enterprise*. It was late morning and Slade met 'Killer' Kincaid in the ready room.

"I'm sorry about Johnny and his family," Slade said, shaking hands with his old Delta Force buddy.

"I was hoping you'd have news of the snitch?" Killer said grimly.

"It goes straight to the president," Slade told him. "I was warned off Waters, but I took the opportunity to put the bug in the ear of the jihadists that he'd given them up."

"Hopefully we'll be seeing his head on the evening news, just his head," Killer sighed. "They offered us an out after the attacks, but the rest of us we wanted to see it through for Johnny Bravo. After what they did to him we have to finish this. I'm only sorry they dragged you out here for such a vanilla mission; there's no one to shoot. It's a standard seaborne insertion and extraction. We're swimming a few miles to the ship, getting on board and ascertaining the status of the cargo—that's it. Not much to it."

"Well, let me tell you what's going on, and what we're worried about," Slade sighed. He told everything that had happened. The further he got the grimmer Killer's expression.

"So we're afraid that the Iranian's may be shipping out radioactive material to Jakarta?" he asked incredulously.

"We think they're going to make a switch after the cargo is checked by the United Nations inspectors," Slade told him.

"Cheeky bastards," Killer shrugged. "All right, let me get this straight, we're checking some Indonesian freighter with an American captain. We're making sure his cargo of sand is just that—sand."

"Sand," Slade sighed.

"It does seem a bit suspicious that the Iranians are going to just give up three tons of nearly weapons grade Uranium."

"Everyone is watching this. They've invited reporters from CNN and MSNBC—our favorite propaganda networks—on board along with the UN to supervise the loading of the Uranium."

191

"If the United Nations is checking the containers going on the *Atlas* what are we looking for on the *Galaxus*?" Killer asked again.

"Radioactivity."

"It's a shell game."

"Right—we're taking a swim in shark infested waters just to make sure the Iranians are sending a bunch of sand to Soekarno for his zoo exhibit," Slade replied. He tried to look unconcerned. "These two things might be unrelated—who knows—maybe the Iranians are shooting straight."

"That's about the only thing we know isn't true!" Killer said sharply.

"Agreed," Slade said, putting on his deepest, darkest scowl. "However, let's just say for the sake of argument that Soekarno's shipment is harmless desert sand and the Iranians enriched Uranium is transported to Abu Dhabi. Where does that leave us?"

"We're back at square one," Killer sighed. "We have no airplane, we have no cargo for that missing airplane, and we're no closer to discovering what the Iranians, Al-Qaeda and ISIS were meeting about in Iraq."

"Let's hope we don't come up empty," Slade said firmly.

Killer shrugged and shook his head, saying, "One thing at a time. We drop in fifteen hours. Come on, get some sleep. We're all packed up and ready to go."

CHAPTER 24: Fatwa

Freddy looked furtively at the only exits of the restaurant. There were swarthy bearded men seemingly everywhere. Their dark eyes bored holes in his sallow flesh. "We can't get out," he said, his voice trembling.

Looking just as nervous, Alfie tried his cell phone to no avail. "We're in the basement. There's no coverage. What do we do?"

"The only line out is the house phone."

"And there's two of them sitting at the bar; we're screwed."

Freddy stood up and took his jacket off. "Get your clothes off." He threw the jacket on the floor and started unbuttoning his shirt. People looked his way, murmuring about what he was doing as Freddy began to pull his shirt off.

"What?"

"Strip now! Do it!"

Alfie stood up and did as he was told. "What are we doing?"

"We're trying to get them to call the police!" Freddy told him.

The bartender looked at them with surprise, yelling over to them, "What are you doing? Put your clothes back on! Crazy Americans!"

"Make me!" Freddy yelled back. "I'm an American. We saved your ass twice last century! I can eat naked anywhere in the world I want to!" Freddy stripped off his underwear, showing off his hairy, scraggly, uncircumcised privates.

The patrons of the restaurant gasped, shielding their children's eyes. The Arabs looked around in consternation, at a loss for what to do.

The bartender still hadn't reached for the phone. Freddy stepped up to Alfie, who was naked now as well, and put his hands on his shoulders. "He's not making the call. Get on your knees and blow me!"

"What? I'm not going to blow you Alfie!"

"You want your head sawed off by these animals?"

Alfie reluctantly got on his knees. Freddy grabbed his frizzy hair and shoved Alfie's face in his crotch.

"Oh God!" cried Alfie.

"Mon Dieu!" came from across the room.

The bartender grabbed the phone. "Crazy Americans! Crazy Americans!" he shouted to the gendarmes. A moment later the sound of sirens wailing came down through the stairwell.

The Arabs left scowling.

"Thank God they're gone; we're all right!" Freddy sighed, collapsing into his chair.

"Speak for yourself!" Alfie groaned, retching onto the restaurant floor.

A moment later the gendarmes arrived along with four plain clothes detectives. One of them, a ginger haired, mustachioed man smoking a cigarette stepped up to Freddy and Alfie.

"I sure could use one of those," Freddy said.

"I'd like one a bit stronger," Alfie commented. "Thanks all the same. Those jihadists were going to behead us right in this bar!"

"Were they?" the man smiled, blowing smoke at the, "I am Agent Brueget of INTERPOL. We have a lot to talk about."

"Such as what?" Freddy asked, irritated.

"Such as why you have consorted with known terrorists like Colonel Nikahd? Why you have photographs of NATO military personnel on your computer—the same photos we found in the jihadist's possession—photos of personnel targeted for assassination. Yes, Mr. Waters and Mr. Alford, we have much to talk about."

The gendarmes cuffed both Freddy and Alfie, not very politely, and not without protest. Then they were hustled away to an undisclosed location. When the INTERPOL agent working for Brueget asked what he wanted done, he smiled, and said, "International terrorists like this can't wait to talk and tell stories. Let them sit in solitary—say, for a month. Then we will talk."

"They're claiming to work for the American president. What if the embassy calls requesting to see them?"

"You're due for vacation aren't you Gerard?"

"Why, yes, but I'm too junior to take vacation at this time of year."

"I will swap with you," Brueget said, slapping him on the back. "Margareta wants to be in Paris during opera season anyway. Process these terrorists into some hole and put the paperwork in your desk. Go to the Riviera and report back to me in a month!"

"Oui monsieur, with pleasure!"

CHAPTER 25: Introducing the World to Taqiyya

Under the bright lights of the Bandar Abbas dockyard three military trucks drove down the docks. They were under escort by a dozen troop trucks loaded with soldiers as well as half a dozen armored personnel carriers. Following the ochre vehicles were the horribly flippant 'baby blue' of the self-obsessed and impotent United Nations. The convoy stopped next to an open hulled ship.

The ship's silhouette was that of a small albeit normal looking freighter, but instead of a deck and cargo hatches the hull was open to the keel and creased along the bottom. The bottom of the hull was actually a huge clamshell door. In practice, rocks would be loaded into the hull and then dropped with great precision on the sea bottom, creating an artificial reef or harbor breakwater, whatever the client desired.

Tonight the ship would transport only one hundredth its normal cargo, but it was a very precious and dangerous cargo.

Under the blaze of the dockyard lights three large containers were uncovered. Inspectors from the United Nations followed Iranian scientists up to the pallets and they examined the containers. Geiger counters were inserted in special breeches to measure the radiation levels of the materials within the containers. The weight of the trucks themselves was taken before the cargo was removed.

The examination was a careful and lengthy process. After an hour the cranes lifted the containers one at a time from the trucks. The inspectors noted the weight of the containers and made their calculations. The radiation levels on the inside of the containers had to match the expected levels of a ton of enriched Uranium 235. The weight of the containers had to match the weight of the Uranium plus the weight of the shielded container. The final calculation was a measure of external radiation levels—some of it always escaped—the Geiger count had to be consistent with a ton of enriched

Uranium 235 secured inside that particular container. Everything matched.

The holier than thou UN inspectors nodded gravely, allowing the press to interview them, ensuring the reporters knew just how important they were, how important their job was and how essential it was that the UN carry out these kinds of inspections in Iran. Inevitably they added that no one, no one, should be outside the purview of the United Nations. It would be to the betterment of the world that they conduct these same inspections in Israel and the United States, so they said, taking a swipe at the two 'colonial powers' of their flawed world.

It appeared for all intents and purposes that the Iranians were playing the game by the rules. The reporters from some networks crowed in triumph, while others were at the very least cautiously optimistic that this might actually be a step in the right direction.

The nuclear containers were loaded onto pallets in the belly of the freighter. They were left uncovered for the short trip across the Straits of Hormuz so Western satellites could maintain a constant vigil. An hour later the ship pulled out of the harbor. The harbormaster departed the bridge and went over the side to his launch. At the harbor exit a dozen Iranian naval vessels escorted the freighter west to Abu Dhabi.

Captain Mustafa of the Iranian Navy piloted the freighter through the Straits of Hormuz. It was one of the demands Iran made of the Security Council and the company was only too glad to comply considering the amount of money the Iranians agreed to pay in order to lease the ship, behind the scenes of course.

Everything went according to the press plan. In live feeds across the Western world the press had a party atmosphere. It was markedly different in the bridge of the *Atlas*. Captain Mustafa was grave, checking, always checking that things were right. His crew had much to do and little time to do it. Although the trip was short it was the most important moment in their careers. At Midnight he looked to his first officer. "Is everything prepared?"

"We are ready sir," he replied, looking at their American invented, Chinese manufactured GPS system. "We are approaching the coordinates."

"Binoculars," the captain asked, and one of the men handed him a pair of German made binoculars. "Let's find our little friends. Helmsman steady as she goes."

"Aye sir."

The captain and the first officer scanned the dark waters ahead. "Time!"

"Twenty-three hundred hours, fifty five minutes and thirty seconds sir!"

They kept scanning. Every few moments the captain asked the time. When the time approached and passed midnight he became audibly nervous. "Where is he? He's late!"

"I don't know," the first mate replied, perturbed.

The captain lowered his glasses, squinting out into the night. "Time!"

"Zero hours and four minutes, twenty-three seconds!"

"Damn!"

"Captain!" the first officer exclaimed. "Twenty degrees to port; I see it!"

The captain trained his glasses on a hardly to be seen speck of light appearing and disappearing against the black waters. "That's him, he's late and a half kilometer off, but's thank the Prophet he's there. Signal him!" The captain went to the control panel and rang the engine room. "Start the operation!"

The engines slowed and the smokestack began pumping out thick black smoke. The captain went out on deck, looking up at the gathering cloud. When it reached a level of opacity that blotted out the stars he nodded to the team of men waiting for his order.

They ran down into the hold and activated airbladders built into the pallets of the three cargo containers. Air hissed and the bladders billowed around the cargo containers. Once the men were out of the cargo hold the captain returned to the bridge.

The first officer reported, "The *Rahman* is beginning its approach. Our support vessels are calling us."

"Tell the destroyers we are having engine problems. We request their assistance. Make ready to tow."

"Yes sir," he said, beginning the busy work of a ship in distress.

The captain was unconcerned. Taking hold of a large lever on the control panel he pulled it back. The whine of hydraulic motors and the groan of steel drowned out every other sound. In the hold the two huge clamshell doors in the bottom of the ship opened. In the normal course of the ship's duties they opened so as to drop tons of rock onto the ocean floor, thereby building artificial reefs and breakwaters. In this case they opened to the sea. The three containers with the enriched Uranium settled into the water, secured by ropes but now floating on the ocean.

The crew dragged the containers to the bow of the ship and held them there. The containers didn't protest; they stayed there, bobbing sedately. For a few minutes that's all that happened.

The ship's crew fell silent, waiting with anticipation, peering into the dark waters of the hold. Finally something appeared, a black stalk pierced the water and rose about two meters above the surface, but it was close to the side of the hold—very close.

A dull metallic clang rang over the ship. It shuddered.

"Idiot!" the captain breathed. "He hit the ship!"

The stalk sank back down into the depths.

Turning to a team of six men wearing wetsuits he motioned them angrily into the water. They frogmen entered the hold. After getting into the water the deckhands threw lines to the frogmen. Catching the lines the frogmen descended into the darkness. Flashlight beams cut the black water.

A few minutes later the frogmen emerged and shouted directions to the deckhands. The men on the starboard side began winching in their lines. The frogmen watched the progress of the work, finally signaling the deckhands on the port side to operate their winches.

The frogmen directed the forward operator to start his winch and then gave direction the aft operator. Slowly a narrow black mass rose from the depths. It was half as long as the hold, a narrow torpedo shape with a trashcan shaped conning tower amidships: a midget sub. On its aft deck were three cargo containers identical to the three containers now floating in the freighter's hold.

The hatch to the tower opened and a man popped out. Two more followed, crowding the small conning tower. With a great deal of yelling and manipulating the winches moved the midget sub to the center of the hold. When it was in place the frogmen activated container's air bladders and secured them with ropes. Then they unlatched them from the subs decking.

The containers bobbed to the surface and the frogmen moved them aside. The old containers were switched for the new ones. It was a seemingly simple process, but between the numbers of men, ropes and floating containers it quickly became confused. The captain of the ship and the captain of the sub shouted incessantly, and finally they got the containers swapped.

With the frogmen holding the containers in place on the deck of the sub the captain ordered the dive tanks blown. A hiss of air could be heard. Bubbles rose to the surface as did the midget sub. The containers settled to the sub's deck and were deflated and lashed down.

With the sub's deck now fully above water the sub captain and his engineer climbed out of the conning tower and onto the deck to inspect the damage caused when he struck the freighter. Squatting on the rounded hull, they looked with concern at what appeared to be a long dent or gash.

The captain of the freighter went down to the deck. As his men secured the containers he yelled down, "How bad is it?"

The sub captain looked up and yelled back, "We're leaking. It's not bad but we'll be limited to periscope depth," he replied. "We need to get going fast. We need the darkness."

"Well why did you run into my ship in the first place?"

"You try berthing that tub blindfolded then you'll understand what we were attempting! Do you know how many times I have done this—once!"

"All right, all right," the freighter captain relented. "Get going then and may the Prophet be with you!"

The sub captain and his companion climbed the conning tower and disappeared into the midget sub. The frogmen cast off the sub's lines. One man patted the side of the conning tower three times. The frogmen jumped off the sub and swam to the ladders out of the holds. As they clambered up the hold the sub began to sink into the ocean.

When it was gone the captain ordered the replacement containers floated to the center of the hold and then he closed the doors. The hydraulic motors whined and the gears turned. With a crunch and groan they closed. Three containers sat in the hold just like before.

Turning back to the sea, the freighter captain waited until the periscope of the sub popped up out of the water a hundred meters off the port bow. That part of the mission done, the captain turned to cleaning up the ship.

#

In the White House situation room the Chairman of the Joint Chiefs of Staff, Marine General Mertzl, was staring at the satellite feed with a scowl on his all too square face. He muttered loud enough for the entire table to hear it, "They're up to something!"

National Security Advisor Carrabolla was twenty years the general's junior with a curly mop of blonde hair and a choir girl demeanor. She sighed, "You always think the worst of people general."

"You think when we have three plus tons of near weapon grade Uranium at risk this is just another political campaign?" he shot back, reminding Carrabolla the reason she got the job had nothing to do with her foreign policy experience. "This stuff is enough for a bunch of atomic bombs or a whole lot of trouble if they're made into dirty bombs. This is real world stuff!"

"That's why we have our Navy ships shadowing the Iranians," she reminded him. "They're not going to pull anything while our ships are there."

"They already are," he told her. "They're doing it right in front of us. Why do you think the freighter has stopped and laid a smoke screen over its location? It's night. Even our low light satellites won't pick up any detail now and our Infra-Red satellite cameras are being blinded by the flares they're sending up."

"Maybe the ship is in distress; did you think of that?" she retorted. "We are monitoring their radio frequencies. The Iranian warships are moving in to assist."

"And you trust these bastards?" he shot back, incredulous. Before she could answer, he told her, "These people love your candy ass view of the world. That means they can do whatever they want. The bottom line is this: in my professional opinion forged over the last forty years of service to this country, I say they're up to something and the president should be informed; he should be here monitoring this in the situation room."

"He's on a fund raiser in Texas," she told him emphatically.

"Since when has greasing the palms of fat cats taken precedence over an international crisis?" he asked testily.

"The wheels of government turn whatever other countries do general," she retorted.

He laughed, and asked, "So where in the Constitution does it say that fund raising takes precedence over—anything?"

"Would you say that if the president was here general?" she challenged him.

"I wouldn't have to say it; he'd be where he was supposed to be!" the general shot back.

Carrabolla looked indecisive. She wasn't happy; but the general had a point. "The president has a responsibility," she started, but the general cut her off.

"He has a responsibility to do the job he was elected to do! He is in his second term. There is no need for him to campaign endlessly."

"If he loses the mid-terms, if he loses the Senate he can't do his job," she argued.

"So the government just stops, is that what you're telling me, Ms. Carrabolla?" he chided, grimacing in a truly frighteningly way. When she hesitated in responding, he continued his point. "Listen to me: the Iranians are bald face lying to the world; which isn't so unusual excepting this time it involves three tons of enriched Uranium. We know the Iranians have met with Al Qaeda; we know the Iranians have met with ISIS; do you really want to see those bastards get their hands on that much Uranium?"

"I don't see the connection general," she replied automatically, immediately realizing she'd said the wrong thing.

"You don't realize the connection between three terrorist organizations—all rivals—meeting with each other and then lo and behold three tons of Uranium goes missing?"

"There is no Uranium missing," she replied patiently. "We haven't heard anything from the Iranians that would leave us to believe anything nefarious is going on."

"You blindly trust them?" he replied emphatically. "Have you ever heard of Taqiyya?"

"I'm unfamiliar with the term," she lied.

The general laughed bitterly, "Well it's the use of falsehood to further ones purposes for the sake of Islam; rather like the political lies told to sell healthcare or target your political foes using the IRS or the attack on Benghazi."

"All right general you've made your point," Carrabolla cut him off. "At this point I don't see anything that would give us any indication of alarm; this is a glitch, these things happen. This isn't the first ship with engine trouble."

"Well then you won't mind if I send in some ships to lend assistance," General Mertzl smiled, turning to Admiral Sampson. "Bob, who do you want to send in to lend a hand to our poor unfortunate Iranians?"

"I have four destroyers and a couple of guided missile cruisers that can be at the freighter in fifteen minutes," he replied calmly. "The Nimitz is ready to put two flights of super-hornets armed with harpoons overhead in five; with full fighter CAP in case any 'unfriendlies' come our way. Just give me the word Frank."

"Testosterone driven Neanderthals!" Carrabolla cursed under her breath.

"What was that Ms. Carrabolla?"

"I said you are exceeding your authority," she replied coldly.

"Ms. Carrabolla only one man in this country has the power to countermand my orders—one man—and he's on the way to a fund raiser," the general answered tersely. "I have a duty to safeguard this operation. Those are my orders. I will accomplish them as I see fit."

"I think you are unnecessarily provoking the Iranians," Carrabolla argued. "As the head of the NSA I object strenuously to this course of action!"

"Ms. Carrabolla, you and your NSA ideologues don't know shit from shinola," he told her. "You're all political hacks. If you listened to your NSA professionals they'd tell you you're full of crap!"

"You leave me no choice but to call the president!" she threatened.

General Mertzl raised his hands in supplication to a greater power. "Hallelujah! That's what I've been trying to get you to do for the last fifteen minutes!"

"That's what this is all about?"

"Good God in heaven do you have any clue about what's going on?" he exclaimed. Burying his head in his hands the general took a deep breath before looking back up at her. "I really want to know how you ideologues think; what the Hell goes on in your brains?"

Carrabolla got the distinct impression he'd like to saw the top of her skull off with the knife he undoubtedly carried in his boots and look in to see what festering disease was rotting her brain—all while she was awake.

Angry, she retorted, "The days of bullying other nations is past general. We're just one of hundreds of nations on this planet; the sooner you realize we're nothing special the longer your career will last. The days of the last superpower are over."

The general glowered at her. The situation room was clearly divided between the military, the CIA and the FBI and the other agencies, President Oetari's ideologues. It was a simmering conflict of distrust, with one side firmly believing the political zealots were bordering on treason and then other side convinced that evolution had passed the warmongers by.

Carrabolla made the call. President Oetari was put out.

"You do realize that I have a very important fund raiser tonight," he reminded her over the speaker phone. "It's not as if I can cancel this because the Iranians are veering off the script."

"Mr. President, we're talking about the security of over three tons of Uranium 235!" General Mertzl said soberly, barely keeping his tone civil.

"The UN's keeping an eye on it, why do I want to go and trample on their turf?" the president replied. Before a stunned Carrabolla or Mertzl could respond the president cut them off. "Listen, I'm doing the party's business tonight; that's the people's business. Iran has to comply with the UN agreement—they signed it—so as long as they comply I don't care how they do it. I've given the UN *my* ships to shadow the Iranians; what more do you want me to do? We are not the world's policeman. As far as I'm concerned the subject is closed—good night!"

The president hung up.

Mertzl was seething. He echoed the president's comment in disbelief, "*His* ships; *his* ships! They are warships of *the United States* and he's just handed them over to the United Nations? Did he really just say that?"

For once Ms. Carrabolla was speechless.

An officer approached General Mertzl. She wore the dress whites of the US Navy. She handed Mertzl her iPad, pointing to the message, "From the *Los Angeles* class attack sub *Key West*. She's shadowing the Iranian convoy."

Her eyes raised and met Carrabolla. They was no gender fraternity there—none.

Mertzl looked at the message and then at Carrabolla. He said nothing.

His silence unnerved the NSA chief enough for her to finally blurt, "What is it?"

"The game has changed," he told her emphatically, pounding the table with his open hand. The sharp, insistent sound made Carrabolla jump. Everyone in the situation room looked at the general with surprise. The room fell silent. "You need to call the president back and get him here right now!"

CHAPTER 26: *Rahman's* End Run

Captain Bashir of the Iranian midget sub *Abd-el Rahman* paced the cramped deck of the submerged boat. The boat was named after the jihadi general whose rampage through the Iberian Peninsula and southern France left so many dead Christians, that in his words, "Only Allah knows how many are slain!"

Bashir and his crew took pride in that. They had the quote painted on the bulkhead of the bridge.

They ignored the fact that Rahman was himself slain and his onslaught crushed by Frederic "The Hammer" Martel at Poitiers. Martel saved Europe, but the Islamists still celebrated the death and destruction Rahman spread.

The captain was nervous, muttering to himself, "Park the boat blind in the hull of a freighter? These clerics and their loyal lapdogs have no idea of the reality of these things!"

"I'm sure the guidance comes from Allah himself," his navigator warned him. The younger man's glance was hard; disapproving of the captain's lack of faith.

As a German naval captain might diplomatically reply to a junior Gestapo officer, or a Russian captain to his political officer, Bashir smiled thinly and said, "You misconstrue my comment. I speak only of my own shortcomings in guiding the boat blindly to a difficult berth. Allah's plans may be perfect, but I am not."

That appeared to placate the navigator for now, but Bashir chastised himself for speaking his doubts out loud. In today's Iran, especially in the military, that could be dangerous, very dangerous. He knew of many friends who had disappeared for speaking common sense; they disappeared along with their entire families.

The image of dozens, hundreds of bodies swinging slowly from the gallows in the Tehran breeze came unbidden to his mind.

Purging his thoughts of such depressing memories, the captain went back to the periscope and watched the approaching convoy. The Iranian ships were being shadowed by the Americans; that's what concerned him. If American ships were out there then their submarines couldn't be far.

"It's time to take her down to thirty meters—quietly!" he told the first officer.

"Ready sir," he replied.

The captain looked sternly at the navigator. "Are we in position; exactly in position?" he demanded.

The navigator nodded, and said, "We are in position!"

The captain sighed, and struck back at the navigator, saying sharply, "We'd better be! Allah will not endure mistakes; not now! Take her down!"

Bashir stowed the periscope as the first officer ordered the tanks flooded and the hydroplanes set down. His orders were repeated much too loudly. It made Bashir wince, the Americans, if they were out there, had to be able to hear them; but it couldn't be helped—shouting was the only way the seamen could hear the orders over the sound of water rushing through the slots in the hull and into the dive tanks.

#

Three thousand yards from the *Rahman*, the sonar operator from the *Los Angeles* class attack sub *Key West*, Seaman First Class Jonah Jameson winced at the same moment Captain Bashir did.

"Holy Moses they're loud," he said. "No doubt about it captain it's a midget sub. He's roughly three klicks at heading three-two-seven, right in front of the convoy, and he's heading down from periscope depth. I can hear the periscope being stowed."

"What's his heading?" asked Captain Mars, a short, black haired graduate of Annapolis originally from Wyoming. He walked over to the sonar station and looked at the various sound patterns on Jameson's displays.

"He's going straight down captain, there's nothing from his propellers."

"Keep me posted on the midget sub," he said. Then he pointed to a louder sound signature, that of the Iranian freighter. "Our job is to keep track of this guy, but why would a midget sub sit in his path, basically waiting for the convoy to pass overhead?" He paced the deck silently, thinking. After one circuit of the bridge he returned to the sonar station and picked up his thread of thought.

"Those midget subs can't keep up with the convoy. He's not shadowing them; still, he's up to something. Let me know if you hear anything, anything at all Jameson."

"Aye, aye sir!"

Jameson kept listening. The midget sub wasn't very stealthy on a good day. The boat was old, rickety and poorly serviced. Everything on it made noise including the crew. They were easy to track. This one, however, was noisier than any he'd ever heard. The sound was strange; something was causing a great disturbance in the water while the midget moved. What it could be he had no idea.

The *Key West* hung in the water at fifty meters; the midget was at about thirty. He guessed that by the way the sounds propagated through the water.

The freighter chugged along. It was another real noisemaker. Jameson and his sonar buddies had never heard anything quite like it. Then again, it wasn't made for the open sea. It was a glorified barge set up to carry rocks. Consequently the doors of the hull, battered and bent as they inevitably were, caused disturbances in the water; that meant noise, and a lot of it.

It also made the ship easy to single out. Jameson backed off the volume on the known ships and highlighted the freighter. That way he could identify any small change, any nuance in the freighter's sound signature. He was defining the signature, breaking it down into its component parts when suddenly it changed.

Something, it sounded like a generator of some kind, started up. There was a low whooshing sound accompanying it. It ran for several moments and then the engine wound down.

"Captain! Captain, we've got something," he reported. When Captain Mars reached his station, Jameson explained what he heard.

"Could be an emergency generator starting up after an engine failure," the captain said.

"The generator went on line before the engine quit," Jameson told him. He shook his head and replayed the sound of the engine shutting off. "There's the power coming to idle and there's the sound of the fuel valve closing—this was a normal shut down—there was nothing wrong."

He showed the captain the sonic signature of the freighter over the last ten minutes, pointing out, "There's no variation, nothing, even when I blow it up. It wasn't a fried bearing, thrown rod, or broken crankshaft; it was a normal shutdown."

"They're up to something," the captain said suspiciously. "The bastards have three tons of enriched Uranium on board—of course they're up to something—but what?"

"There's that midget sub," Jameson said.

"Where is he in relation to the freighter now?"

"One klick at the freighter's eleven O'clock."

"If there's something going on between them then they're going to have to make contact somehow."

A sharp, metallic clang rang through the seawater, bouncing off their hull.

Once again Seaman First Class Jonah Jameson could only shake his head in amazement, taking his headphones off as he did so. "They're not subtle, that's for sure. There's the signal captain; plain as day!"

Captain Mars frowned, counting the sharp, metallic sound of hammer blows on a steel hull. The crew heard it and they counted along. Nine clangs followed by a pause. After three more clangs everyone—everyone—knew what was coming. When they were done the captain sighed and looked over his crew.

His expression was dead serious, and he said, "Nine-Eleven; they're using Nine-Eleven as their signal. Well gentleman, I think you know that the only way to respond to this is going to be with a torpedo up their ass! The only question is when and where!"

#

The sound of the freighter engines chugging to a stop was noted on the *Rahman*. Then came nine heavy clangs followed by another eleven clangs: the sound of a hammer on the hull. Bashir groaned inwardly. Who couldn't hear that even without hydrophones? The sailors resting in their bunks below the waterline could hear the signal kilometers away; but no, the fanatics in charge of the mission knew no tactics, no strategy, only their holy war! Holy idiots, all of them!

"Are we going to answer captain?" the navigator demanded.

The captain closed his eyes, knowing he had no choice. "You do it," he said finitely.

The navigator took out a heavy hammer and rapped on a pipe—hard. The first officer, who was also the engineer, sprang across the narrow deck and grabbed the navigator's arm.

"Idiot, what do you want to do; crack the pipe and sink us?"

"They must hear the signal!"

"You imbecile everyone in the Straits of Hormuz will hear us! Rap more softly, they will hear it, I assure you!"

The navigator complied, but the first officer went to Bashir and complained, "He's served on boats for a year and knows nothing of our job—nothing!"

The captain held a finger to his lips and whispered, "His father is a very influential Imam in Hayayi's inner circle; be careful what you say!"

The first officer swallowed hard, sweating, and said loud enough for everyone one the bridge to hear, "I was only concerned over our sacred mission. The Prophet, Allah bless him, demands all of our skill for his glory and success!"

"Yes, yes he does," the captain smiled mirthlessly. He went to the sonar operator. Bending over the man, Bashir wrinkled his nose at the pungent mix of sweat and perfume—common for the boat—extreme for this man.

211

"Report, do you have a bearing?"

"Yes sir, we should proceed at zero-three-nine degrees!"

"Helm, ahead one quarter zero-three-nine degrees; maintain depth twenty meters!"

The midget moved forward rising slowly, heavily, noisily. Never quiet, the midget sub was burdened more than usual. Cargo lashed to her foredeck marred the sleek torpedo shape and created turbulence in the water; that meant noise.

There was nothing the captain could do. Therefore he paid attention to his approach, growing more nervous by the minute. Every minute the freighter repeated the code. Bashir hoped rather than knew it wasn't being listened to by unfriendly ears. If the Americans could hear it—he shuddered at the thought—then he and his crew would be marked for a deep and watery grave, he had no illusions as to that whatsoever.

The sonar operator honed in his heading until they were almost upon the freighter and he could hear water slapping against the sides of the stationary ship.

"We're close!"

"All stop!" Bashir ordered. "Periscope depth!"

Air hissed into the dive tanks, displacing the water and making the boat more buoyant. When they came to a stop at three meters, just short of the conning tower breaking the surface in the trough of a wave, Captain Bashir raised the periscope. The freighter wasn't in front of them!

"Damn!" he breathed, looking around wildly. He sighed with relief. There it was at eleven O'clock. It wasn't bad, but it made the approach more difficult. In order for Bashir to surface within the hold of the ship he had to be aligned nearly perfectly.

Adjusting the course to line the midget sub up was hard enough, but the freighter was now drifting. Having their engines shut off was part of the illusion, but Bashir had tried to tell the Imams and the army commander in charge of the mission, a Colonel Nikahd, that the current would turn even a heavy freighter with its engines shut down. They ignored him.

Therefore Bashir had to trust to luck and a quick approach to make this happen. He approached the freighter from the front, passed by the port side and then made his final approach from the rear. As the stern of the freighter loomed over him he ordered the midget sub to dive.

Staying at his periscope, Captain Bashir picked up a light that had been lowered in the front of the freighter's open hold. The light glimmered in the darkness of the night waters, making the approach possible, allowing him to line up the sub with the ship. It was a waterproof version of what airline pilots used to park their aircraft, unable as they were to see the stopping points beneath the nose of the aircraft.

When the light flashed red, he ordered, "All stop! Blow tanks; periscope depth!"

Air hissed into the tanks and the boat began to rise. Bashir scanned all around, trying to ascertain his boat's position relative to the freighter. It was impossible to tell. The one light told him how far he was from the front of the hold. Beyond that his periscope was met with inky blackness.

All at once his vision cleared; the periscope popped up above the surface of the water. His first view was of the far side of the hold. He could see men on the catwalk on the side of the hold, pointing at the periscope. The midget sub continued to rise.

"Hold periscope depth!" he ordered, but the sub struck the side of the hold, rolling hard to the left. Bashir clung to the periscope as his feet stumbled on the rolling deck. Several of his men lost their footing and crashed to the steel floor. A resounding clang sounded throughout the boat.

The midget sub popped up from under the freighter, swerving to port and rocking like an angry bronco. There were shouts and curses. The horrible sound of water jetting from a burst pipe—a submariner's nightmare—cut the fetid atmosphere.

"Stabilize our depth at five meters!" he ordered.

The engineer ordered the tanks balanced while he and another man packed a clamp over the burst pipe and shut off the valves. The leak slowed but it did not stop. The mate reported, "We've got a breech in the seam of the pressure hull! Diving is out of the question now!"

"You mean we can't get out of the hold?" Bashir asked.

"I don't know until I examine the damage topside. Maybe we can brace it and get ten meters out of her, but nothing more," he replied.

"Well planned or not, we're here. Wait for the frogmen to straighten us out." They waited, working all the time on the leak. Water soaked the deck plates and stations on the port side of the bridge, gurgling into the bilge.

A slap sounded on the conning tower. "Bring us up to one meter—slow!"

"Conning tower free!" the first officer reported.

"Come on; let's check the damage." Bashir opened the upper hatch. A fog of smoke and salt spray made his eyes water. He coughed, hacking and wheezing as he clambered out into the conning tower. Rushing to the side, he looked over the bulwark at the damage. It was hard to see without the boat fully surfaced, but there was an ugly dent along the port side. It was nearly ten feet long; Air bubbled out of the crease every time the boat heeled over or submerged the foredeck.

A strident voice assailed Bashir. He heard nothing but the tone of the comment, so he retorted, reminding the commentator, the captain of the freighter as it turned out, that this was not a normal maneuver, that he should try it if he didn't like it.

Frogmen and deckhands secured the midget sub in the hold of the freighter. Then began the arduous process of swapping the cargo containers. Each weighed two tons, so Captain Bashir had the engineer slowly flood the dive tanks so that the deck was awash. Inflatable collars allowed the deckhands to float the containers just enough to move them around.

As the business of swapping the containers continued a gangway was lowered to the conning tower and Bashir was taken aboard the freighter. The captain met him with a sober but apologetic manner.

"That can't have been easy; forgive my outburst, the import of our mission must be my excuse," he said.

Bashir nodded, "That is the only reason I would ever try anything so risky."

"How extensive is your damage?"

"There is a breech that will prevent our diving deep; however, we are simply transporting the cargo and not going into battle. I don't foresee anything that would prevent our rendezvous with the—" he stopped when the captain of the freighter put up his hand.

"I have no need to know anything further," he interrupted. "You had better get the cargo on the way before the Americans decide to come and aide us. They have an overdeveloped sense of rescuing people!"

Captain Bashir nodded and left for his command. A half hour later the midget sub disappeared in the black waters. Shortly thereafter a destroyer passed the *Atlas* a line and it was secured. At Captain Mustafa's order the destroyer towed the *Atlas* toward Abu Dhabi.

CHAPTER 28: Swimming with the Fishes

As midnight struck over the Straits of Hormuz the hardly to be heard hum of a V-22 Osprey approached Bandar Abbas with very reluctant Jeremiah Slade on board.

Feeling far too old to be doing something like this, Slade sat in his wetsuit at the aft end of the Osprey. Slung over his shoulder was a KRISS Super Vector .45 caliber assault rifle and other gear.

Leaning against his right leg was a torpedo shaped underwater sled complete with radar, infra-red cameras and lights as well as munitions. The sled was invaluable when they had miles to cover underwater, but as Killer jokingly told Slade, "It can't outrun a hungry shark. Sorry buddy."

"Get ready to drop!" the loadmaster shouted.

The hydraulic squeal of the cargo doors was clearly audible over the muffled engines. Then the airstream drowned them out. The air became cool and damp with a salt tang over the smell of jet fuel, oil and the sickeningly sweet smell of hydraulic fluid.

The loadmaster motioned them up, three men on each side of him. Slade stood up and shuffled to the back door, looking down at the black water. The breakwater of the port was ahead of the aircraft; the dimly illuminated cargo bay faced out to sea.

Standing at the edge of the cargo bay Slade glanced at Killer to his right. He wasn't afraid of the ten meter jump, but Slade had a very visceral concern over entering a world where he was no longer the top of the food chain, especially at night.

Killer knew this, and shouted, "Time your jump to land between those two big ones! Mind the teeth!"

Slade had no time to retort. The loadmaster slapped him on the shoulder as the small green light illuminated.

"Go!"

Training took over. Slade could not have stopped his jump even if he wanted to. His body was so thoroughly trained to respond to that situation, to that command, that his muscle memory took over. He was a passenger in his own body. Before he knew it the cold, dark water closed around him, filled as it was with hidden, hungry things.

Fighting that momentary urge to panic, Slade exhaled— training again—that cleared the regulator and allowed him to slowly fill his lungs with Oxygen. He hung there, suspended in the darkness for what seemed like five minutes; it was actually as many seconds. That allowed his inner ear to re-establish its equilibrium; it took the extra time because in the dark, zero-gravity environment of the night ocean his sensory inputs aside from the cold of the water were nil.

The sound of the bubbles faded. Slade reached for his helmet and turned on his infra-red lights. There was a small LCD screen above each eye in his mask; the screens were connected to two diode sized cameras on either side of his mask. Looking around he caught sight of the five other divers of the Delta Force team. They were readying their sleds.

"All right boys time to mount up!" Killer said.

Pulling his sled up and levelling it, Jeremiah aimed it as he would a big machine gun. Hitting one button with his thumb powered the sled up. Hitting two more turned on the sled's more powerful infra-red lights and activated the main screen.

The screen was a multi-purpose display. It automatically displayed what the camera saw; however, the screen also showed the essential mission data required for any military operation: the Zulu time, a chronometer, the compass heading, depth, temperature, and in the lower left corner of the display a navigation display fed by a combination gyro and GPS navigation computer. At the bottom of that display were the latitude and longitude of the sled.

The navigation display showed the outlines of the harbor and the position of the target ship superimposed over the picture of the other divers. The rocks of the breakwater were to his right. They sheltered the old naval harbor of Shahid Bahonor from the sea. That's where the target ship, the *Champion Galaxus*, lay in berth—a civilian ship at the navy yard—the first clue that something was very, very wrong. If the cargo for Soekarno was really just sand and nothing more why wasn't the ship berthed at the more modern civilian port Shahid Rajaee a few miles west?

Slade fell behind Killer, keeping out of his wake but maintaining a few meters behind. He could see nothing but what his sled screen and his helmet camera showed. They ran at eight meters, and at that depth no one, even someone watching for them, would have noted the soft green glow from the sled's tactical displays.

Their only sensory signature was the soft hum of the sled's motors and propellers, but even these were drowned out by the distant yet unmuffled growls of the tugs and ships in the harbor.

Like ghosts they made their way along the breakwater before turning right into the outer harbor. It was nearly a kilometer to the berth where they expected to find the target ship, Soekarno's *Champion Galaxus*. To get there, the sleds had to navigate the outer harbor and whatever traffic it had. That forced them to descend to fifteen meters, ensuring they passed beneath any transiting ships.

The water here was cold and necessarily dark. The sounds of the harbor were many and varied. Engines chugged, propellers whirred, somewhere in the harbor a man was hammering on a steel plate; the resulting blows turned the hull into a huge bell, making the whole harbor ring. Slade got a new appreciation for just how difficult submariners had it when forced to run silent. At one point they passed beneath an anchored ship and Slade swore he could hear singing, very bad singing.

The water changed as they approached the inner harbor. Slicks and globules of oil choked the water. The bottom rose up, strewn with garbage and debris: chains, boots, rags, barrels, anything and everything you might find in a harbor and all slick with sludge and oil. Motoring just over the bottom Slade stuck out a hand. He dragged it across the surface, curious, and came up with a sticky black goo. The harbor waters of Bandar Abbas were disgusting.

"There it is," Killer said through his helmet. The keel of a freighter appeared on the screen behind Killer's sled. The Delta Force steered toward the rear of the ship. Their first goal was the rudder.

Reaching it, Killer searched the large piece of steel for the registration number. It was the quickest way to confirm the identity of the ship. Checking the number against his database confirmed that they'd found the *Champion Galaxus*.

Moving along the hull to a point amidships, the Deltas ditched the sleds on the bottom, mooring them with a simple cable and stake shoved into the goo of the seabed.

Swimming up to just under the surface, Slade and four of the Deltas hung there in the darkness while Killer found the ladder. When he did, he came back and led them to it.

"Secure fins!"

Slade took his fins off and secured them to his vest. Then he swung he KRISS around front and unplugging the barrel. He checked that the silencer was secure and then prepared to follow Killer up the ladder. Killer went first while Slade covered him from below, turning on the reticulated sight, a dim red circle with a glowing dot in the center.

As Killer climbed the welded rebar rungs, Slade scanned the ship's rail, looking for anyone to pop their head over the side.

Pausing at the top, Killer waited before slipping over the side. "All clear, come on up!"

Slade slung the KRISS on his back again, swiftly climbing the ladder. The ladder was not meant for ease of climbing. The rungs were rather too close to the hull, making it easy to rap your knuckles on the steel side. It was sixty feet up the side for Slade, a much longer climb than it would have been ten years ago. He got to the top. The climb warmed him up. Now, peering over the side, he saw Killer crouched in the shadows of a hatch.

The top deck was well illuminated. The dockyard lights shone with a harsh white light. However, this also created sharp shadows of stygian night. Slade rolled over the steel bulwark and into the shadow of the massive hatch next to Killer.

The deck was a busy place. There were four big hatches on the freighter. Only one was open. It was between Slade and the bridge. A crane lowered a railroad car sized container into the hold. Several men were on the deck watching, and beyond them on the elevated bridge Slade saw the captain overseeing the operation. He was a large man, probably six-five or so. It could only be Eva's husband Christian Fletcher.

Jake was about to call up the next Delta Force when there was a commotion on deck. The crane operator was either inexperienced or lazy. He started the container down before having it over the hatch and as a result the container started to swing.

The captain was furious, yelling orders in English. The Iranians on deck yelled back in Farsi and the crane operator stopped the descent of the container suddenly. It jerked around, spinning now, threatening to foul the chain. The captain yelled to the man closest to them, who turned out to be the first mate, directing him to go relieve the crane operator.

The mate ran toward Slade and Killer. They ducked into the shadow around the corner, out of sight. Whether by sight, sound or feel the mate sensed something wrong. They could hear him stop and walk back toward them.

"Johnny!" yelled the captain. "What the Hell are you waiting for?"

The mate stopped and looked quickly around the corner. There was nothing to see except black wetsuits and black equipment enveloped by black night. Slade saw the man's expression, he wasn't ten feet away, but they were invisible.

"Nothing," he yelled back. "I'll be there in a minute!"

Both Slade and Killer breathed a sigh of relief. When the first mate was gone all attention on deck shifted to the hung up container. In less than a minute the other four Deltas were topside.

Leaving the two teams below to secure the deck if need be, Killer and Slade made their way aft to the bridge. With all the attention paid to the wayward container and the sensitive swap of crane operators—the Iranians weren't happy and they voiced it—it was another fifteen minutes before loading could resume. By then Slade and Killer were secreted in the darkness on the roof of the bridge.

Slade leaned over the edge of the steel roof and put a small microphone in the corner of the bridge's port window. Dialing in the frequency of the bug gave them a hollow sounding but clear transmission. The captain was on the phone with someone and he wasn't happy.

"The Iranians are the ones who fouled things up. I'm fixing what they've screwed up; I told them I wanted to use my man but now they've got their panties in a wad!"

He waited, while the person on the other end of the line commented. Whatever was said, it didn't placate him.

"Well I don't like that one bit," he said hotly. "These military guys are all fanatics and they're incompetent to boot. Don't worry. I'll get things back on schedule, just tell them to let me do my job! The sooner we're out of here the better I'll like it."

There was another pause while he listened impatiently.

"I won't breathe easy until we are," he admitted. "Really, all this for a shitload of sand, are you kidding? I think Soekarno's cracked—no offense intended. I mean, I like the wages I make under him, but what I don't like is putting my ship and crew in danger—I don't care how important this is to him—screw his legacy!"

There was a longer than usual pause. When he spoke again, the captain's voice while still incredulous was more controlled.

"Don't listen to me. I'm just torqued because I have to deal with these Iranians—they're like the Nazis for crying out loud—just as arrogant but nowhere half as competent! That and I was just sitting down to watch the replay of the Vikes-Titans game. Now dear, I know it's preseason!"

That reminded Slade of his evening plans. "Damn it, I was looking forward to watching that on the *Enterprise* as well; it'll be over by the time we get back!"

"You two would get along just fine!" Killer whispered incredulously.

The captain continued more gently than he would in any conversation with another man. "Hey honey, don't worry about it; I may not understand it, but if it's important to you it's important to me. I'll make sure the old man gets his special Iranian sand." The captain laughed. "I'm just wondering, why Iranian sand? He wasn't born in Iran; he's Indonesian. What is it about sand from Iran? Well, Okay, I suppose he's rich enough to be eccentric. Hey honey, I got to go. We've got to get these containers loaded."

He said good bye to the woman they guessed to be his wife, and he immediately returned to his walkie talkie, coordinating with his first mate, who had commandeered the crane much to the displeasure of the Iranian dockworkers.

"You tell them I'll come down there personally and knock some heads if I have to; let's just get this done and leave!"

After another hour of complaining he sighed, "It looks like they're done; okay boys button her up! We need to be ready to go tonight!"

The next two hours were all about getting the big ship going. As they attended that, Slade and Killer quitted the bridge and made their way below to the cargo holds. As everything had already been checked it was relatively easy to get into the hold and then very simple to check the three containers.

Climbing on top of the first container, Slade took out his Geiger counter, holding it in various places around the container—there was no reading. He went to the access hatch and looked again; yet again there was nothing. He scowled, telling Killer, "There should at least be some residual radiation no matter how well they hid it."

Carefully Slade opened the hatch a crack. He snaked a small hollow tube in and turned on the spectrum analyzer. It drew in the air from the inside of the container. Once again there was nothing. Frustrated, Slade threw caution to the wind and opened the door, shining his flashlight inside.

He stared at the contents in amazement.

"What is it; what's inside?" Killer demanded.

"You're not going to believe this," Slade told him.

Before Slade could answer a heavy rumbling coursed through the ship. "Whoa! They're starting the engines!" Killer said. "If we don't want a one way ride to Jakarta we better get going!"

CHAPTER 29: Change of Plans

In the situation room the Director of the CIA was getting an urgent call from Slade via the *Enterprise* battle group. He moved away from the dogfight going on between General Mertzl and NSA Chairwoman Carrabolla.

"Slade, I need the status of that cargo in Bandar Abbas and I need it now!"

"I'm in the hold of the ship as we speak sir," he said quickly. "Both the Geiger counter and the spectrum analyzer confirm the cargo is clean, there's no radioactivity, not even medical waste."

"What is the cargo then?" he said with surprise.

"Silicates—sand—sir, it's just as advertised," he replied.

He looked over to Mertz and Carrabolla. They were still arguing, but then the president's face appeared on the situation room screen. "I've got to go; we're about to find out how the president is going to play this—if he plays it at all. Slade, I still think that ship is going to do more than transport sand. We'll play my hunch. Get the Delta Force off the ship but Slade, you stay put! Don't get yourself killed until you figure this out!"

"Yes sir!"

The director approached the screen where National Security Advisor Carrabolla and General Mertzl squared off with the president. If President Oetari looked put out before he was nearly livid now.

"What is so important that my schedule needs to be interrupted," he demanded. "I have very important people waiting for me in Texas. The prospect of me losing the Senate is riding on this and you want me to listen to some vague hunches of yours based on what a submarine heard in the Straits of Hormuz?"

"We know exactly what he Iranians have done; we have the bastards on a meat hook!" the general announced.

"General, Iran is a proud nation; they are our equal," the president said stonily. "I would appreciate you referring to them with the respect due a sovereign nation much older than ours."

"Mr. President the attack sub *Key West* clearly picked up the sonar signature of an Iranian midget sub rendezvousing with the vessel carrying the Iranian Uranium. She tracked the midget sub to the vessel, heard it docking, and then tracked it moving away. There can be no doubt that something took place under cover of the freighter's distress."

"Why didn't the satellite see anything," Oetari demanded. "Why am I asked to make a decision based on a submarine hearing something?"

"The satellite's infra-red cameras were degraded significantly by flares sir," he answered.

"What about visually. Don't we have ships in the area with Night Vision Goggles or something?"

"They could not see into the ship's hold," the general told the president. "We conjecture that's why the Iranians used this particular ship. It has the ability to open cargo doors in the bottom of the hold. It's a large enough opening for an Iranian midget sub to enter the hold where the Uranium is being stored."

"Sir, this is all conjecture, and a bit too much like a James Bond movie for my taste," Carrabolla interjected. "Once daylight arrives we can easily ascertain the status of the Iranian nuclear material. Even if a transfer was made we have UN inspectors in Abu Dhabi. If the general is that concerned we can simply have the containers retested. Rest assured there's no way for the Iranians to pull a fast one. My advice is to let the UN take the lead on this; they know what they're doing. This is their specialty."

"My President, we have the Iranians dead to rights!" General Mertzl argued. "A rendezvous took place; there's no doubt about it. We need to find out what transpired."

"How?"

"The *Key West* is tracking the midget sub as we speak," he replied quickly. It is heading northeast toward Bandar Abbas where coincidently there's a freighter waiting in the navy yard scheduled to head to Jakarta."

"What about Jakarta?" the president asked suspiciously, not hiding his close ties to the island nation of his birth.

"Sir perhaps the Director of the CIA should speak on this matter," General Mertzl told him.

"This better not have anything to do with your wild missing airplane theories," the president said skeptically.

"Mr. President, as you no doubt know Al Qaeda has a firm grip on Indonesia, especially in Jakarta, and combined with the heavy Marxist presence in the islands it makes it a dangerous destination for Iranian fissile material."

"The Indonesians have assured us they have a lid on all of the terrorist cells; their influence and effectiveness is highly exaggerated," the president told him firmly.

"Sir, that runs contrary to every report we have and to every briefing I've given you," the director replied. "I urge you not to discount the danger of this material falling into unfriendly hands."

"How is it to get there?" the president asked. "If the midget sub heads that way—if they even have the nuclear material—can't the *Key West* just sink it?"

"Will you authorize the strike Mr. President?" General Mertzl asked with renewed hope.

"Not without a great deal more information gentlemen," he said, shaking his head. "I'm afraid all you've got is conjecture and boogie men. There's just nothing to this." He paused, seeing that his military men were on the point of rebellion. "All right, wait until daylight. If anything still looks out of place call me and I'll have Turkey ask the United Nations to retest the containers in Abu Dhabi—it won't look so bad then—satisfied? Now, I'm going to Texas."

#

Slade received the director's orders with the steady sense of duty inherent to his naturally taciturn personality. On the bright side, he thought, he wouldn't have to endure another night swim.

The Deltas departed, though not without Killer first securing Slade's sled to the freighter's hull with a magnetic tether.

"Good luck buddy," he told Slade with a pat on the back. "Stay quiet and stay low. We'll be back to get you as soon as we get the word."

"Have a good swim through the Iranian sludge," Slade replied. "Remember to shower before you smoke!"

Killer wrinkled his nose at the petroleum stench emanating from their wetsuits. Climbing over the side he disappeared in the darkness, leaving Slade to the mercy of the *Galaxus*.

The deckhands were almost done securing the main hatches. That meant everyone was busy. Slade slunk through the shadows to the superstructure. He set up shop atop the bridge where he could see everything that was going on as well as listen to his bug on the bridge.

His expectation was that the activity aboard the *Galaxus* would wind down now that the cargo was secured. He was wrong.

The captain, a tall bull of a man, six-five if he was an inch, towered over his crew. He had no patience for the local dockworkers, whom he called lazy and incompetent. From what Slade saw, he was right. Still, now that his cargo was on board Slade was curious as to why the captain should be so overtly demanding. He appeared agitated by something, and nothing anyone could do was good enough.

The explanation for the captain's discomfiture was as amusing as it was surprising. Half an hour later a limousine pulled alongside the freighter. The captain walked down the gangway to meet it. He opened the back door and held out his hand to someone in the car. Slade focused his binoculars on the cabin. The flash of sequins sparkled from the darkness; sequins attached to a dark blue dress. An elegant hand reached out and took the captain's huge paw. The captain grinned widely, helping the slight, elegantly dressed woman from the limousine. It was Eva.

"Well, well, well, the plot thickens," Slade muttered to himself, recording the scene on his digital binoculars. "Why are you personally supervising the shipment of a boatload of sand?"

The captain led Eva up the gangway and into the superstructure. Slade left his position, determined to find out what was so important about the cargo. The captain's quarters were in the superstructure behind the bridge and the adjacent conference room. There was a small back door, actually a hatch, leading out to a small deck on the starboard side of the ship. There were several portholes for the captain's cabin.

Slade dropped off the roof and put a bug in the porthole. Pressing a tiny button activated the transmitter. Their voices came distant but clear into his earbud.

"Not that I'm disappointed to see you dear but Bandar Abbas is a cesspool, especially the military harbor. The civilian side of the house is bad enough but this place— whew—why am I here?"

"Simple, Soekarno has an emotional attachment to this project. He's been dreaming of this since he was a kid."

"Really, this is all about the dreams of a kid from the ghetto?" the captain exclaimed. "That's why I'm in a restricted harbor with Iranians crawling all over my ship and their religious crazies scaring the Hell out of my crew? I don't buy it Eva; what's more I don't like it. I almost tossed one of those fanatic officers overboard for snooping around."

"Don't do that!" Eva scolded him, but in a softer tone she asked what they were looking for.

"I had the Vikes game on the bridge monitor," the captain explained. "When the cameras cut to the sidelines and showed the cheerleaders he about had a cow. He wanted to rip the monitor of the wall! I almost picked his little ass up and tossed him overboard. Really, he was that close to taking a swim!" The captain held his meaty fingers together just short of touching.

Eva laughed and suggested they go outside and get some fresh air.

"If its fresh air you want this isn't the place," the captain told her. Glancing within, he caught sight of the captain and Eva just as they were heading toward the hatch leading out to the deck. Slade smoothly transitioned into the shadows. His black wetsuit hid him as effectively as any camouflage.

The hatch opened and the captain let Eva through first, continuing their conversation. "So are you going to tell me what this is all about or are you keeping me in the dark for a reason?" When she didn't answer immediately he took her by the shoulders and gently but inexorably turned the tiny woman around to face him.

"Eva, we're in one of the most backward, dangerous countries on the planet. We're dealing with people who hate us, hate our lives and hate our civilization—and for what? I'm your husband; I have a right to know why we're here don't I?"

Eva crossed her arms over her bosom and frowned. Shaking her mane of black, perfectly coiffured hair, she emoted, "I hate this place as much as you do! I don't like dealing with these people but there it is. This started as nothing more than what I told you: a shipment of sand for an eccentric billionaire's childhood dream. I'm afraid it's turning into something more than that."

"What's it turning into?"

Before she could answer the hatch to the cabin opened. In the frame stood a tall man in a military uniform. He was tall by local standards but still half a foot beneath the captain. The effect of his presence on Eva and the captain was immediate—and sobering—Colonel Nikahd.

"Good evening Eva. Good evening Captain Fletcher. Here you are." He walked out onto the little deck, passing not three feet from Slade in the long, inky shadows. He smiled, and unknowingly turned his back on Slade. "Captain Fletcher, I expected to find you on the bridge."

"Why?" the captain said carefully. "Our cargo is loaded and secured. We're ready to go as ordered. What's the problem Colonel? I assure you my crew has strict orders to remain aboard the ship. We realize how sensitive this port is; of course, we would rather have used the civilian port."

"Captain, captain, I know you had no desire to come here and risk violating our sensitive military secrets over a load of sand; I completely understand. You have done nothing wrong."

"Then what is this about?"

"It is simply that your mission has changed," Colonel Nikahd informed him.

"Changed, what do you mean?" blurted Fletcher.

"Follow me, you are needed on the bridge—both of you," the Iranian jihadi officer replied suavely. "If you please!"

Nikahd motioned for Eva and the captain to precede him. They re-entered the cabin and headed for the bridge.

Slade switched the channels in his earbud. Then he climbed back onto the roof. Cat footing across the steel structure Slade made his way carefully to the awning over the bridge. He reached it just as Fletcher and Eva reached the bridge. What they saw was enough to have Slade throw himself down flat on the roof of the bridge.

Eva and the captain gasped.

CHAPTER 30: Nikahd Takes the Helm

Slade stifled a curse. His 'vanilla mission' had taken a turn for the worse. Running up the gangway and lining the deck were several hundred Iranian troops. He recognized their black uniforms and green checkered schmaugs: the Republican Guard, the jihadists, the maddest of the mad.

A crane was busy loading a very large container in an empty hold. Captain Fletcher was angry. "What the Hell are they loading on my ship and why are all these troops here? I'm carrying sand for a frigging zoo—sand—what's this all about?"

"Do not worry captain, everything is fine, but we will need your ship for an ulterior mission. We will leave as soon as possible, in fact here is the harbor pilot," Nikahd smiled as an Iranian naval officer entered the bridge. The officer saluted. Nikahd only nodded. He turned back to Captain Fletcher.

"I suggest you get down to the business of leaving port. The sooner you do this the better it will be for you and your very lovely wife."

"My wife?" Captain Fletcher said hesitantly.

The insincere voice of Colonel Nikahd dripped with evil intent. He laughed and said, "Should you not cooperate I will simply have my officer take your ship. I shall of course kill you Captain Fletcher, something that no doubt you are ready for. But are you ready for what will become of the lovely Eva?" He paused to let that sink in. "There is only one of her and I have so many very passionate men!"

He laughed wickedly.

"Whatever you need," Fletcher told him quickly. "We can be under way in fifteen minutes."

"Excellent, Captain Fletcher. I knew you were a reasonable man! First then, I wish you to muster your crew on deck here below the bridge.

There was no reason to refuse Nikahd.

. "All hands report to the aft deck! Repeat, all hands report to the aft deck."

Within ten minutes fifty men were gathered beneath the bridge. The Iranians gathered there as well in two ordered ranks. Colonel Nikahd appeared and addressed the multinational crew in English.

"I am Colonel Nikahd! You are now under my command. My first order is for you all to surrender your cell phones and any other device on your person which could be used for communication!"

Most of the men complied. Some informed the Iranians they didn't have the cell phones on them or they were in their quarters. Nikahd had every man searched.

Seven of the fifty were found to have cell phones or other devices on them. Nikahd had these men separated from the rest and lined up against the port rail.

Slade had enough familiarity with the jihadists to know what was about to happen. He called Director Gann and apprised him of the changing situation. Everyone was watching the port rail as the Iranians gunned down the hapless seamen, shooting them with a flurry of AK-47 fire.

The Iranians laughed, grabbing the bodies and tossing them overboard. A few of the stricken men were still alive when they hit the water.

When the slaughter was over, all Slade could say was a caustic, "Well that's a typical jihadist response!"

Nikahd had the remaining men marched down into the aft hold directly beneath the bridge. It was the smallest of the ship's holds, meant for miscellaneous cargo. Apparently the Iranians would run the ship. The only value of the crew was as hostages; a very temporary value at that.

Slade spent the remainder of the day playing cat and mouse. The Iranians searched the ship thoroughly. They collected all of the crews cloths, books, computers— everything—and dumped all of it overboard. Another couple of crewmembers were shot. The Iranians carried them out of the hold and tossed them overboard.

#

Director Gann took Mertzl's arm and simultaneously cast a glance at FBI Director MacCloud. They convened together apart from Carrabolla, who eyed them suspiciously.

Mertzl was furious. "The *Key West* has them, they have them dead to rights! How can the president not see that?"

"We need hard evidence; evidence the president can't refute," MacCloud said. "Everything points to this being the fulcrum of something big. The mosques are being sent messages to prepare for a great event on the anniversary of Nine-Eleven. This has to be part of it."

"We just checked the cargo of the *Galaxus*," Gann told them.

"And?"

"Sand, nothing but innocuous silicates. It's preparing to leave Bandar Abbas as we speak."

"I'll bet a star that the sub's going to rendezvous with it."

MacCloud shook his head. "All of our satellites are glued to the *Atlas*. We're blind thirty miles away from that ship."

"The damn Iranians are going to make the switch right in front of us and we won't be able to see it," Mertzl growled.

"I have a man on the *Galaxus*," Gann told them. "He's going to stay put and let us know what's going on."

"Good! The *Key West* will continue to shadow the midget sub. By the time the *Atlas* gets to Abu Dhabi we'll know whether the sub has the nuclear material or not."

Now all they could do was wait.

They didn't have to wait long.

"Director!" an aide interrupted. "We have an urgent communique from our operative in Bandar Abbas."

"Slade?"

"Yes sir," he said.

"Jeremiah Slade; the man who murdered President Ataturk's nephew?" Carrabolla heard the exchange and she grimaced.

"Yes young Turgot, who died in the company of his ISIS and Al Qaeda heroes," the director told her, as close to being overtly angry as he ever showed.

"He was a boy, a Human Being," she responded incredulously. The director was about to speak, but she interrupted, asking with a sneer, "Did your precious Slade find contraband on the freighter?"

"No, just sand," the director admitted. "So far Soekarno's story checks out."

"Oh my God," Carrabolla exclaimed with mock panic. "Sand? Say it isn't so!"

The director shook his head, taking the iPad. The director looked at it. Seeing Slade's face, he frowned. "Report Agent Slade?"

"Sorry to bother you so soon, sir, but the situation has changed. The *Galaxus* has been commandeered by the Iranian Republican Guard. Hold on, I better let you see what's going on." Slade's picture disappeared and the deck of the *Galaxus* replaced it. Iranian soldiers were lining up the crew. The image zoomed in on a particular figure. He was a tall man in uniform with a short beard and a craggy, pock marked face.

"Our old friend Colonel Nikahd!" Director Gann said. He nodded to the console operator who put the feed on the big screens.

"Sir, you can bet Colonel Nikahd isn't here to escort sand! We are leaving Bandar Abbas at this time. Whoa, I was afraid of this, here we go," he said in a growl, turning the camera to the rail.

There were seven sailors who were being herded by the Iranians to the rail. Slade zoomed in. The sailors were terrified, but it didn't last long. The four Iranian soldiers lined them on the rail and backed off. Without warning their AK-47's barked.

There was a gasp in the room, led by Carrabolla, as the seven sailors crumpled. Four of them stayed still, lying on the deck or draped over the rail. Three were still moving. The Iranians didn't waste any bullets on them; instead, they unceremoniously dumped them over the side.

"Typical jihadist response!" Slade commented.

"Oh my God!" Carrabolla said.

234

"Don't fret Ms. Carrabolla," Gann said icily, "perhaps the president can explain this to you since he understands these people so well."

Mertzl laughed in a grisly way. "Why don't you get your friends at the EPA to go after the Iranians for polluting the gulf?"

"Slade, stay out of sight; stay out of trouble. Keep me posted!" The director cut the connection and turned to Carrabolla, his voice growing increasingly callous, "Why would Colonel Nikahd, who just met with the president's personal envoy Freddy Waters, commandeer the *Champion Galaxus* if not to rendezvous with the midget sub and take the Uranium? Do you still think nothing is going on?"

Biting her lip, Carrabolla obviously realized that the intelligence agencies had made the connection between the White House and the Iranians. That could be damning for the next election if the Iranians were shown to be lying. If that came out it wouldn't matter how much money the president raised. Fortunately, the president was convinced, and so she was convinced, that the Uranium was still on the freighter—it had to be.

CHAPTER 31: The Shell Game

Captain Bashir looked with concern at the depth gauge and then at the spray of water coming from the ruptured weld in the seam of the pressure hull. The depth gauge read ten meters. The leak came from behind a patch the engineer tried to apply to the crack.

"Can the bilge pumps keep up with it?"

The first officer and engineer shook his head, telling him, "Not for long. In another five minutes we will have taken on so much water that the engines and hydroplanes can't keep us from sinking. We need to surface now while we still can."

"We're not outside the ring of American escorts yet," Captain Bashir said firmly.

"Can we at least go to periscope depth?" the first officer pleaded, fear in his eyes. "It doesn't seem like much but the water pressure is that much less. The pumps might be able to handle it."

"Then we risk being run over by an American warship," Bashir remarked.

"We cannot jeopardize the mission!" the navigator interjected.

"The mission will fail if the boat sinks!" the first officer countered.

"Enough!" Bashir snapped. The two officers stayed silent, waiting on his decision. He took a deep breath of consideration before announcing, "We cannot remain where we are and we cannot surface. Therefore we will proceed to periscope depth and trust to Allah to protect us until we get through the ring of escorts—hopefully undetected."

"Surely Allah will not abandon this sacred mission," the navigator said boldly.

"Not unless we are so stupid that Allah refuses to recognize us!" the first officer muttered, glancing darkly at the navigator.

They ascended to four meters. Water kept leaking from behind the patch but it was not nearly as much. The first officer reported, "Water level is going down in the bilge. We're pumping the water into the dive tanks and then blowing them out using compressed air. We should be able to maintain this depth."

"Can we dive deeper for a limited time if need be?"

The first officer shook his head. "It's risky. If we do that the seam could burst and then it won't matter what we do." He looked at the navigator. "Our sacred mission will rest on the bottom of the Straits of Hormuz."

Bashir stayed at the periscope, gauging the traffic around them. For a tense hour they altered course first one way and then another, weaving through the escorting ships, trying not to get run over or detected. After the hour was up they had progressed only a few kilometers, but the convoy and its shadow ships passed them by.

"I think that's the last of them," Bashir sighed, sweat streaming down his forehead. The crew breathed a sigh of relief.

Without warning the boat heeled over to starboard, rolling so hard that it threw Bashir off his feet and hard into the trim valves of dive tanks. The blow stunned him. He stumbled across the bridge and fell onto the deck, his head swimming. Somewhere in the back of his brain he heard screaming.

Blinking through the blood in his eyes and the confusion in his mind Bashir had the image of the navigator, the zealot of unshakeable jihadist faith, screaming like a little girl. Over his piercing cries was the urgent voice of his first officer yelling, "We're sinking!"

#

In half an hour the *Galaxus* was outside the breakwater. Fletcher turned to Nikahd. "Where to now Colonel?"

Nikahd paused. Then a bright flash shown in the darkness to the southwest. After around thirty seconds a low rumbling boom rolled over the waters. The colonel was busy setting a frequency in the ship's radio. He looked up and pointed in the direction of the fading glow. "Set your course towards the light."

They ran for several hours before a call came over the ship's radio. "Abd al-Rahman hero of the Umayyad! Abd al-Rahman hero of the Umayyad!"

"Go ahead *Rahman!*" Nikahd answered.

"Request immediate rendezvous!" the urgent voice of Captain Bashir answered. "We are close to sinking with our cargo. We are heavily damaged. We do not have much time!"

"Give me your coordinates!" Nikahd told the *Rahman*.

The *Rahman* did so and Nikahd directed Fletcher to proceed there at flank speed. They sailed for another forty minutes, the *Galaxus* heaving in the seas, her engines straining. At last Fletcher reported that they were nearing the coordinates.

Nikahd placed lookouts at the bow of the ship. Shortly thereafter a light was spotted. In fifteen minutes the huge freighter slowed and pulled alongside the *Rahman*. The midget sub was barely afloat. The sea was over her deck. The three containers were half submerged.

Quickly, the deckhands from the *Galaxus* lashed the midget sub to the side of the freighter. The men didn't know why they were doing it, nor did they have to ask. The scores of Iranian soldiers with AK-47's trained on them were all they needed to know.

A small deck crane was enough to upload the three containers. They were then lowered into the same hold as the large container loaded by Nikahd. When that was done the hatch was closed.

"What are we going to do about the sub, I can't drag it to Indonesia. Besides, she won't stand our towing. Our wake would break her up quick!" Captain Fletcher asked.

Nikahd simply smiled and got on the radio. "*Rahman*, you have accomplished your mission. You may now return to Bandar Abbas. May the Prophet be with you!"

"No!" came the desperate reply. "We must be fifty kilometers from Bandar Abbas; we'll never make it!"

"The Prophet will guide you!" Nikahd said firmly and he switched the radio frequency back to the normal frequency used for international waters. Turning to his lieutenant, he said, "Have the men cut the *Rahman* loose!"

"Yes sir!"

To Fletcher, he said, "You may continue your voyage captain." Glancing at Eva, he added unnecessarily, "I would keep your lovely wife out of sight, but remember, if you fail to satisfy the needs of my mission she will satisfy the needs of my men—all of them. Do I make myself clear?"

"So I am to set my course for Jakarta as planned?"

"Of course," Nikahd smiled. "We must get Mr. Soekarno his Iranian sand!"

#

Captain Bashir ordered, "Full ahead! Give me everything you have! Bow planes forty-five up! Aft planes neutral!"

They'd cut away the lines, a necessity to keep them from fouling in the propeller. Now the *Rahman* surged forward, her diesel motor throbbing. Still, it was barely enough to keep her from sinking.

"We won't make Bandar Abbas!" the first officer told the captain.

"I know. Send a distress call. Perhaps someone can reach us in time."

"Impossible," the first officer shook his head, pounding on the radio. "The water is shorting out all the electrical components. The radio just died."

Bashir went to the navigator. He grasped the officer by the shoulder and told him, "Plot me a course to the nearest land. I don't care where!"

The navigator nodded. Now that their mission was over he was all for survival over dying alone in the ocean. He went over his charts and shouted, "Course zero-two-four! We are nine-point-two kilometers from shore!"

"Helmsman steer heading zero-two-four!" Bashir shouted to the man barely two feet away. "If she can hold together for an hour we may yet live through this!"

#

Captain Mars aboard the attack sub *Key West* watched the *Galaxus* cast the *Rahman* adrift. "Okay, they've transferred the cargo to the freighter. We'll follow the freighter. Send word to Washington that we believe the Uranium is now on board the freighter *Galaxus* bound for Jakarta. We will follow the freighter and await further orders."

Captain Mars shook his head. "I have half a mind to sink that freighter now. With everything that we've seen already who knows how long that stuff will remain on that ship!"

#

As far as the fourth ship in the game was concerned, the *Atlas* was under tow and as the sun came up the eyes of every intelligence agency and news agency were upon her.

In the situation room, all eyes were glued to the satellite feeds. During the night the freighter was hooked up to a destroyer and put under tow. As it moved out from under the smokescreen it appeared that the cargo was intact. When dawn finally broke over the Straits of Hormuz it became clear that there were three containers in the hold of the freighter. The *Atlas* would dock in Abu Dhabi in five hours.

"You see general, all of your hand wringing was for nothing," National Security Advisor Carrabolla gloated. "We put three containers on that freighter and there are still three containers. Where's your national emergency now? Would you like me to get the president on the phone?"

General Mertzl was conferring with Director Gann, nodding gravely. He looked up at Carrabolla, and said, "There are three containers there all right but are they the same ones?"

"What are you talking about now?" she asked, sipping her latte. It was getting late and she wanted to be home.

The director nodded to an aide. After a few keystrokes two images appeared on the big screen. They were both satellite pictures of the Iranian freighter. The containers were circled. It was obvious that they had moved. "Our analysts at the CIA have concluded that the cargo containers were moved. This is patently impossible for any simple engine malfunction. Each one of those containers weighs over two tons; that includes the lead shielding."

"If it's impossible then what's your point?"

"My point is that something happened," the director said simply. "I have my suspicions, and General Mertzl's midget submarine must be checked out. At the very least we need to repeat the entire inspection process for each container when they arrive at Abu Dhabi."

"What are your suspicions?" Carrabolla asked doubtfully.

The director shrugged, and said, "The Iranians chose this ship because of its hollow hull; it was designed to be loaded with stones and drop them through the bottom of the ship."

"You think the Iranians dumped their nuclear material on the sea floor?" she said dubiously.

"Not on the sea floor Ms. Carrabolla, on the midget submarine."

"For what purpose?"

"We're working on that," he said.

"Well you keep it up," she laughed. "As I told the president, this isn't a James Bond movie. The simple answer is almost always the best." She pointed at the screen. "What I see is three containers in the before photo and three containers in the after photo. That tells me that those are the same three containers we started with. I don't need the wild imagination of some submariner whose been cooped up in his boat for months to tell me different."

"And the inspection by the UN at Abu Dhabi?" the director asked calmly. "The president agreed to it; wouldn't it simply confirm to the world what you already know? Here's your chance to shut us up Ms. Carrabolla."

"The president said we would do that so we will," she said, nodding. "The president will enjoy roasting your science fiction theories. Maybe you'll finally learn your lesson. The world's not full of bad people gentlemen; it's just full of people—period."

"Thank you Ms. Carrabolla," the director said.

#

As the tow began, Captain Mustafa summoned his first officer to the bridge. "Now that we are out of our smokescreen we will see if we have indeed fooled the Americans."

"What do you mean captain?"

Mustafa pointed upward. "They will be studying us with their satellites. If they have any doubts as to what has happened we will hear a response. If the ruse worked then we should dock in Abu Dhabi by afternoon."

An hour later the first mate of the freighter hurried down to the deck, informing the captain of an important message. "You are wanted on the bridge immediately. Colonel Nikahd is on the radio. He says it is urgent."

The captain waved for the first officer to follow him. As they entered the confines of the bridge he picked up the hand mike, snapping to attention. "Captain Mustafa here sir!"

"Captain, we have a development in the operation," the voice crackled over the radio. "The American's have grown suspicious and are requesting that the United Nations inspectors meet you in Abu Dhabi. There they will re-inspect the cargo and ensure that these delays incurred because of the malfunctions on your vessel have not affected the cargo. Do you understand?"

"I do sir," the captain replied gravely. "We will make preparations."

"I do not need to ask if you and your men are prepared for this final phase of your operation," Nikahd said soberly. "This is an important moment in the inevitable ascension of our faith and our people. I expect all will be carried out properly."

"We will not disappoint you sir!"

"Allah be with you," Nikahd finished.

"Allahu Akbar!" Captain Mustafa finished.

The first officer looked at Mustafa, mystified. "The inspectors cannot fail to discover that the Uranium is gone," he said. "These containers are filled with medical waste; they will only pass a cursory inspection."

"There will be no inspection," Mustafa informed his officer. "Muster the crew on deck. Colonel Nikahd has given us an opportunity for paradise! This voyage will end the only way it could have."

"How is that?" the first officer said, still not understanding.

"With martyrdom!"

#

In the situation room, several hours passed before Carrabolla approached the general and the directors again. She smiled thinly, and said, "The president wasn't happy but he was willing to call his friend the President of Turkey—they share parenting tips."

"The President of Turkey is a big supporter of Hamas," the director said.

"He's no friend of Israel, that's for sure," General Mertzl added.

"The President of Turkey takes a very progressive view of the world," Carrabolla told them. "He's a staunch NATO ally."

"In what way?" General Mertzl asked. "How much help did we get from Turkey in Libya, Iraq, Syria—you name it? They've been radicalized, and the president is a sympathizer of terrorists not the West."

"I do hope you mean the President of *Turkey*, general," Carrabolla said. When the general shot a disdainful expression, she added, "Either way your assertion is errant. There's no greater friend of the United States, and he strongly supports Israel's right to exist."

"That's not what he says," the director reminded her. "We have extensive incidents on tape of him calling for the destruction of Israel, the Jews and the support of jihad and a worldwide caliphate. You know that, or you should; that's part of your job isn't it?"

"I've seen those reports," she sneered. Shaking her curly blonde head. "In my opinion you are taking political rhetoric as policy. There's a difference. We do that during our own campaigns all the time."

The general laughed, telling Carrabolla, "Oh yes, the Democrats and Republicans are routinely talking about driving each other into the sea and about how nice and peaceful the people in Hamas, Hezbollah and Al Qaeda are to their neighbors."

"Your sarcasm is noted general," Carrabolla replied coldly. "It's right there with bigotry. Some people consider these groups freedom fighters."

"Like who?" he demanded.

"Believe what you want Ms. Carrabolla," the director said, bringing up the latest images from ISIS's rampage in Mosul. It showed dozens of heads mounted on the fence posts of a bridge. He nodded to the image, telling her, "I think these gentleman would disagree with you if they could."

"You simply don't understand that part of the world," she said. "The president understands these people; he knows what makes them tick. I advise you to watch and learn. The president has a firm handle on the situation; he's not going to panic the way you are."

"Panic?" the general echoed with contempt.

"Panic, general," she asserted with a steadfast expression. "In another few hours the Iranian Uranium will be safely locked away in Abu Dhabi. There will be no funny business, your conspiracy theories will be discredited. In a few weeks, once the Israelis have satisfied their bloodlust by dropping bombs on civilians, things will quiet down."

At the height of her gloating, there was a strident call from the operations officer. "General, you better come take a look at this! There's a problem with the *Atlas*!"

Carrabolla looked up to the satellite feeds to see the *Atlas* swerving away from its tow ship, the aft end completely engulfed in thick black smoke. As they watched. The ship capsized and sank in a matter of seconds.

"What just happened?" Carrabolla demanded.

"The freighter just blew up Ma'am; it just blew up," the officer monitoring the convoy reported. "I don't know what else to say. The Iranians are broadcasting that the freighter struck a mine."

"Struck a mine?" General Mertzl exclaimed. "They were in the middle of a convoy—under tow—how could they strike a mine?"

"It could, it could happen," Carrabolla snapped defensively.

The director leaned over the console and brought up the CIA display, ordering the operators to, "Bring up the explosion. Give me a running analysis."

The screen showed the freighter under tow, nothing out of the ordinary, except, as the analyst reported, "They were heading west to Abu Dhabi at five knots—not unusual for a tow—however, the crew was mustered out on deck."

"They had nothing to do," Carrabolla argued. "They were under tow."

"Actually the crew is quite busy under tow," the analyst responded. "There are strict maritime procedures for vessels under tow. The crew has a great deal of responsibility; mustering for the captain is not one of them."

The feed continued and it became clear that the crew responded to whatever the captain was saying, raising their arms in celebration time after time.

"Allahu Akbar!" the director muttered.

"Now you're grasping at straws," Carrabolla retorted, albeit nervously.

A blinding flash blanked out the screen. The assembled staff looked on in surprise. It was the director who recovered first.

"A mine wouldn't flash so brightly," he muttered. "We'd see a geyser of water, not an explosion."

"Unless it hit a fuel tank," Carrabolla interjected.

"Fuel fumes explode, fuel burns," Mertzl said gravely, shaking his head. "That looked like a magazine going up; only the freighter isn't carrying ammunition, or rather it shouldn't be."

"Could the Uranium have reached critical mass?" Carrabolla speculated.

The military men looked at her with amusement and concern; disturbed that the advisor to the president on national security was so ignorant, doubly so that she'd voice that ignorance.

"Run it back to the point of ignition," the director said calmly.

The image backed to a point where there was a small pinprick of flame at the stern of the vessel. It erupted through the smokestack and then engulfed the bridge.

"Stop the tape!" the director ordered. He turned to Carrabolla. "The explosion happened at the rear of the ship; in the engine room. When was the last time a mine caught up to a ship; even a ship under tow?"

"They scuttled their own damn ship," General Mertzl said.

"Why, why would they do that?" the National Security Advisor demanded.

Again the director and the general looked at her with disdain, answering together, "To get rid of evidence! Now it will take weeks to prove they didn't have the Uranium on board!"

"Look at that, look at the destroyer," MacCloud noted, running the tape back. "They cast of the tow line just before the explosion. They didn't want to be afoul of the freighter when she went down—even they knew! Damned sloppy, I'd have thought the Iranians would sacrifice their destroyer for appearances at least!"

Carrabolla stood in stunned silence, but the stares of the military men forced her to action. She took out her phone and called the president.

When President Oetari came on line he wasn't even attempting to be diplomatic. "Carrabolla, I hired you to take care of international emergencies, not to bother me with them. What is it now?"

"Sir, the Iranian freighter with the Uranium on board has just blown up." She glanced at the screen with the taped feed. Gann had the crew replay the sequence again. "We're watching the film of it sink."

"Did we do it?"

"No sir!"

"What are the Iranians saying?"

Carrabolla was startled by the question, and she stammered, "Immediately after the explosion the Iranians claimed the freighter ran into a mine; however, our preliminary examination of the video suggests," she hesitated before continuing, taking a deep breath before she did so. "Mr. President, our examination of the video suggests sabotage possibly by the Iranians themselves."

"That's not what the Iranians say—they were there—why assume it's something so farfetched?" the president countered.

"Sir, at this point I don't think we can," she hesitated again, and repeated herself, "I don't think we can trust the Iranians. There's too much going on. The stakes are far too high."

"Yes they are Ms. Carrabolla, and I am not about to go rocking the international boat when so much is at stake," the president replied angrily. "You want me to go and accuse the Iranians of duplicity at a time when the peace of the world is balanced on the edge of a sword—I will not do that!"

"What are your orders Mr. President?" she sighed.

"Begin with lending any and all assistance to the Iranians," the president told her. "Then have our Ambassador to the United Nations consult with the members of the Security Council. We'll see where that leads."

"We're going to wait on the United Nations?" she asked anxiously. The abandonment of so much authority caught Carrabolla by surprise—not because she hadn't thought of it, dreamed of it before—but because hitherto, she'd not been so completely troubled by the prospect. Now, with three tons of Uranium missing, she was not so certain that leaving it to the irresolute halls of the United Nations was all that good an idea.

She opened her mouth to speak but the president cut her off. "There you go Carrabolla," he said curtly. "I expected you to implement that. It's not so hard. You have to be decisive! Write that down. Now let me get to my fund raiser without any more international emergencies. Problem solved."

He hung up.

"Problem solved?" the general and the directors exclaimed at once.

"So it seems," Carrabolla sighed.

The general watched Carrabolla turn and leave, seemingly too embarrassed to continue the discussion. "God help us!" he sighed. With a hard eye he turned back to the Gann, and said, "I've got the *Key West* shadowing that sub. We'll know pretty soon if they rendezvous."

"Good, my man on Soekarno's freighter will keep an eye on the Iranians," the director told him. "The Iranian military now controls it. How much you want to bet the freighter and the sub cross paths?"

"If that midget sub has those cargo containers on board she can't go far; they're not open ocean boats. It makes sense. So the Iranians and Soekarno want the Uranium in Jakarta—right into the hands of Al Qaeda."

"Your man on the freighter; you left him there?" the general asked.

"It's a big freighter. He'll be fine," the director told his ally. A sudden chill ran down his spine at the thought.

The director instantly regretted his comment.

CHAPTER 32: Confirmation

Slade watched the takeover of the *Galaxus* from atop the bridge roof. The bug on the bridge window explained everything except why the Iranians were taking over the ship. That explanation came after they left port and rendezvoused with the midget sub.

Slade had to admit that for all the faults of the Iranians the plan was slick. If their idea was to transport the Uranium to Jakarta then it would be immediately available to Al Qaeda for worldwide distribution.

He downloaded his recorded film and conversations from the bug, and then called the director on the satellite. True to his word the director himself was on the line in a few moments.

"Slade, we are shadowing the freighter with a *Los Angeles* class attack sub, the *Key West*. The skipper was keeping tabs on the midget sub and documented the transfer of the Uranium. Unfortunately the powers that be don't put a lot of stock in acoustic data, they only believe what they see.

"It took an act of God for the president to agree to have the UN inspect the cargo on arrival in Abu Dhabi, but someone must have tipped the Iranians off. They blew up their own ship and crew so now everyone thinks the Uranium is at the bottom of the Arabian Sea."

"One torpedo and we make that story come true sir," Slade replied. "We can't let that Uranium get on the open market in Jakarta."

The director whistled, "The president will have an aneurism if we ask to sink a civilian freighter."

"I'll try and get the captain and the crew off the ship," Slade said.

"Get me verification that the cargo is the missing Uranium and I may be able to do something."

"Yes sir, they've only got two hundred Republican Guards watching the cargo. It's a piece of cake."

"I understand Slade," the director said with laugh, "Good luck! Just get through this with as few bullet holes as possible."

"That's always my goal," he said tersely.

Slade spent most of his time hiding in the lifeboat. It was a freefall type boat, completely self-contained, designed to freefall off the back of the ship. In it were supplies and emergency equipment.

Slade helped himself to the rations and the water packs. They were much better tasting than the military stuff he'd gotten used to. He even allowed himself a nap. When night fell things had quieted down and he made his way to the cargo hold.

Slade reached the amidships cargo hold, a huge space one hundred and fifty feet square. He entered carefully via a side hatch. It opened onto stairs lit by a single protected bulb. The stairs led down to a small antechamber with another hatch. Slade hurried down, taking out his forty-five and attaching the silencer just in case.

When he reached the hatch he listened for a moment. Hearing nothing, Slade turned the latch and opened the hatch a crack. He saw no one standing on the catwalk but there were two guards making the rounds of the dimly lit hold. There were four lights illuminating the cavernous space. Each light was placed halfway along the bulkhead just behind the hatch structure. This lighted the center of the hold well but left the corners in darkness.

In the hold were the three containers for the Uranium, each about eight feet cubed, and one long cargo container next to them about half the length of the hold, twenty feet wide and twenty feet high.

"What in the world can they have in there?" he wondered but that was a secondary consideration. Slade needed to get down there and fast. There was no telling when Nikahd would send more men. He waited for the men to make their circuit beneath him before stepping through the hatch. Slade closed the hatch behind him and descended the stairs, keeping a close eye on the guards. Their backs were turned and there was absolutely no chance of them hearing him.

This was a dry goods cargo vessel, so it didn't carry oil; therefore, there was no need for a double hull. The waves beat upon the hull without mercy, making the interior of the hold a ringing, banging drum. That was fine as long as you weren't inside it.

By the time the guards turned the corner Slade was on the floor. He slunk to the cargo containers, sliding into the shadows between two of smaller containers and the big one. It was almost pitch black there and Slade was nearly invisible in his black wetsuit. Taking out his test kit, Slade ran through the same radiation tests that the UN inspectors used: testing the exterior levels and then opening a small door in the container that gave him access to a valve.

The valve had a nipple designed to accept a fitting for a detector. Slade screwed his detector on it and opened the valve. Once he got a reading he closed the valve back up. This allowed a minute amount of gas from within the container to be analyzed by the detector.

It took only a moment for the detector to display the results: the cargo container had gas that had been exposed to Uranium 235. There was no longer any doubt.

He packed up his kit and secreted it within his belt. It was time to leave. First though, he wanted a look in the big container. What could the Iranians have in there?

A quick inspection showed that it was locked. He could cut through it with his tungsten cutter, but the sparks would alert the Iranians. It would have to wait. Slade had to get word to the director as quickly as possible.

Repeating his ingress in reverse, Slade climbed the stair swiftly and then exiting through the access hatch, at least that was the plan. As he reached for the latch on the hatch Slade heard voices on the other side. As he placed his hand on the latch it began to move.

Slade looked wildly around; there was nowhere to hide.

CHAPTER 33: Showering

Trapped, Slade turned off the single light, drifted back into the corner and drew his forty-five. The door opened and one man stepped into the darkness, barely visible from the dim light outside the hatch. He stopped and made a comment in Farsi about the darkness.

He waited, not wanting to give himself away unless he absolutely had to. The man fumbled for the light switch, found it, and turned it on. His back was to Slade. He turned away and headed down the stairs. A second man came in, closing the hatch behind him. He followed the first man, not glancing to either side, not noticing the dark silhouette of Slade in the general dim light. Both men disappeared into the hold.

They were the relief guards for the two downstairs.

Slade ducked out the hatch. The deck outside was empty. He made his way carefully back to the roof of the bridge but once there he was in for an unpleasant surprise. He tried to call the director on his satellite phone but all he got was static. No matter what channel he tried he got the same thing.

The Iranians had learned to jam.

How was he going to let the director know what he found out? The answer was almost too easy. The ship's locker was easy to find and even easier to break into. He quickly found what he needed: a large brush and a pail of white paint. He took these back to the middle hold, easily avoiding the one patrol Nikahd had on deck, and then he dropped over the side.

As part of his harness Slade had a built in rappel brake and a hundred feet of nylon rope. He secured the black, rubber coated carbine to the rail and rappelled down the side. Then he got to work. It wasn't true art, but Slade was certain he got the message across. He rappelled back up and returned to the bridge, quite pleased with his ingenuity.

The next part of his plan was to wait. Perched on the bridge with the dark coast of Iran blotting out the stars on one horizon and the coast of Oman on the other horizon, Slade was without friends, except for the *Key West* which he assumed was shadowing the *Galaxus*. Fortunately, out in the Arabian Sea was the *Enterprise* and her Task Force. They were friends indeed.

Nikahd was on the bridge with an all Iranian crew manning the helm and providing guard duty. The only other visible guards were the two men patrolling the deck and two men standing watch over the entrance to the crew's prison.

He crept to the back hatch that opened onto the captain's private deck and peered through the port hole. The captain was not to be seen, but Eva was there getting ready to shrug on her nightgown. The momentary sight of her naked, nubile body was almost enough to make the entire ordeal worthwhile.

In the space of a moment she was clothed again. She crept into bed, looking beautifully composed considering there was no way out for her, her husband the captain or anyone else on the crew. As soon as Jakarta was within view their value as hostages would be nil; their lifespan thereafter would be almost as short.

#

At dawn, twenty-six hours after the *Key West* started to shadow the *Galaxus*, the first officer of the American submarine woke Captain Mars up.

"Sir, you're going to want to see this," he said.

The captain pulled on his uniform and joined the first officer on the bridge. He went straight to the periscope which was already pointing at the *Galaxus*. He took one look and said, "What the Hell? That wasn't there yesterday!"

"No it wasn't," the first officer replied.

"We got pictures right?"

"Yes sir!"

"Well send them to FLEETCOM pronto!"

On the *USS Enterprise* Admiral Norman and Captain Buckminster were in the conference room with Captain 'Killer' Kincaid. Director Gann was on speaker. All parties were staring at a picture taken from the periscope of the *Key West*; a picture of a big freighter. Captain Buckminster was briefing everyone.

"The *Galaxus* is a Suezmax with a length of 307 meters and a beam of 68 meters. Her empty weight is slightly over 150,000 tons. She is a bulk carrier. Her holds normally carry raw materials. However, we believe after the *Key West*'s observations that she's now carrying the missing three containers filled with three tons of Uranium 235; the new paint scheme would tend to confirm the *Key West*'s findings."

Amidships on the black hull someone painted a very large "U^{235}". Above it were painted the numbers "7500 (200)." Below the numbers there was a rude but recognizable bullseye.

The voice of the director came over the conference line. "I would say that Agent Slade has confirmed our suspicions. They have the Uranium 235 on board."

"What's the '7500' mean?" said the admiral.

Killer explained, "It's an aviation transponder code used to alert air traffic control of a hijacking. We're guessing the number in parentheses is the number of hijackers—Iranian military no doubt."

"Two hundred!" the admiral started. "That takes storming the ship out of the equation."

"Sir, these are Iranian troops, they are predictable," Killer said with calm confidence. "A ship is a tight battlefield. Careful use of force can easily negate numbers. We just need to carry enough ammunition."

"I would have expected as much from a Delta Force," the admiral replied with a frown. "Captain, I need a realistic assessment. I know your record; bravado is not necessary."

"With all due respects sir, I just finished an operation in open country with a four man team, myself and Agent Slade against a force of about a hundred Tangos." Kincaid said seriously, but then he smiled in an unpleasant manner. "The only hitch in the mission was getting Agent Slade to stop hogging the Tangos all to himself. If we leave him to it he'll get it in his head to do this by himself, mark my words."

The admiral looked to Kincaid and then to the picture of the director, who frowned and sighed.

"Captain Kincaid has extensive experience with Agent Slade, but in this case it's not the Tangos that concern me: it's the cargo. We now know the *Key West* wasn't chasing what the Administration called 'an illusion.' This is what we were afraid of. By the ship's filed route she's bound for Jakarta which has as many Al Qaeda cells as it has mosques—a lot."

The admiral chewed on his pencil, saying after a moment of reflection, "There's the Indian Ocean between the Arabian Sea and Indonesia. That's about eight or nine days of sailing; a great deal can happen in that time if we give the word." He looked around the table and finished his thought. "The Iranians want us to think that the Uranium is at the bottom of the sea. Why not make it real? Instead of calling the Iranians on their lie why don't we make it come true? The *Key West* could make this problem disappear—literally."

"What about the freighters crew?" Sorensen interjected.

"If they're not dead already they soon will be," the admiral said gravely. "We know how these Islamists operate. There's no need to keep the crew alive if they can run the ship."

"You're right," Gann replied with a serious and troubled expression. "That is the way the Islamists and jihadists operate. However, in this case there is a good chance the crew will be kept alive for a while at least as hostages. One thing these Islamists have learned is the West's almost insane desire to secure the lives of its people. If they run into trouble they'll have the hostages as bargaining chips."

"An insane desire you say?" the admiral asked.

"Admiral, they have no problem killing their own people whereas we will move Heaven and Earth to save one," Gann said stoically. "The Israelis just traded a thousand killers for one Israeli. We let these very Iranians hold our people for over a year before brokering a deal to get them back. Believe me, we've taught them the value of keeping hostages."

"You don't approve?" the admiral pressed.

Gann answered immediately and forcefully. "When I consider the repercussions of three tons of enriched Uranium in the hands of terrorists, no, I do not approve. The hostages are expendable. So is Slade and he knows it."

"Then we're back with the *Key West* solution," the admiral sighed. He pointed to the screen and the bullseye painted in the ship. "Your boy's even given us the location of the uranium—nice job—Captain Mars can probably sink the ship precisely enough to keep the Uranium intact in their containers. We can salvage it with a deep sea submersible with no one the wiser."

The director brought up the white elephant in the room, saying with accumulated frustration, "The current administration—meaning the president—will never, and I say never, allow the navy to sink a civilian freighter no matter what the threat or the cargo."

"We'd have an easier time convincing the Pope to let us sink it, that's for sure," Kincaid agreed.

"The Pope's already given us his blessing to stop these people," Gann commented. "However, it took six months to get permission for a limited strike, SEALS, Deltas and CIA on ISIS leadership—six months! We have ten days or less before the freighter enters Indonesian waters."

The admiral spread his arms wide, and growled, "So what's the plan? We can't just sit back and do nothing."

"Let the Deltas secure the Uranium," Killer said.

"They're sure to kill the hostages as soon as they get wind of it," the admiral said.

"You're forgetting we have a man on board," the director told the admiral. "That will be something our agent will be working on. If he can affect the escape of the crew then this will be a much easier sale to the White House."

"I assume you're briefing the president as soon as you're through with us."

The director smiled mirthlessly at the admiral. "It's the middle of the night in D.C. I've already informed the White House Chief of Staff. He's scheduled five minutes for me in the morning. The president is of the firm opinion that the Uranium is at the bottom of the Strait of Hormuz and that considering the sensitivity of the area it is unrecoverable."

"He wants to drop this?" the admiral said, incredulous.

256

"In the worst way," the director replied. "He wants the problem to just go away."

"Then we should make it go away," growled Kincaid. He took the admiral's eyes with his own steely gaze. "Let Slade get the hostages off the ship and then give my team the green light. We'll get that Uranium out of there with no one the wiser."

"Then the crew can return to their ship," Gann nodded. "We can blame pirates from Oman. No one needs to know."

The admiral squirmed, and said, "That's going rogue—isn't it? I've served four presidents with stars on my shoulder. I don't know if I can go that far."

"Hopefully we won't have to," the director said quickly. "That's pushing the boundaries; however, I have hope that the president will see the necessity of keeping the Uranium from ever getting to Jakarta."

"Let's hope so," the admiral agreed. Then he shook his head. "How's your boy going to get the crew off? That's fifty people he's got to move under the nose of the Iranians."

"I'm sure he's working on it admiral," the director said confidently, hoping inwardly that Slade was indeed thinking along those lines.

#

As it was, Slade was indeed thinking along those lines, albeit in his own way. He'd waited until Eva and the captain were asleep before stealing into their cabin and hiding in the bathroom. The shower stall wasn't huge but it served as a makeshift bunk; he'd had more uncomfortable nights before.

It was Eva that woke him up in the morning, or rather her exclamation, "What are you doing?" that roused him. Slade jumped to his feet before realizing the bathroom was still pitch dark. So it wasn't him that she was audibly upset with; was it Nikahd or some of the Iranians? His blood boiled.

No, it wasn't any of those.

The hardly audible sound of a TV commentator buzzed in his ears. He knew the voice—Paul Allen—the voice of the Minnesota Vikings. Slade was now fully awake.

"Do you have to watch the game at five in the morning?"

"Dear, it's on live!" Christian Fletcher responded.

A groan of exasperation approached the door. "You and your Vikings!"

She turned the light on in the bath, did her business and brushed her teeth. Tucking her flowing mane of black hair under a yellow shower cap blotched with bright green leopard spots, she hung up her gown and opened the shower curtain to find Slade appraising her nakedness with a smile.

"Hello Eva, it's good to see you again," he said in a soft voice.

Eva was too surprised to say or do anything for a moment; then she snatched her gown from the hook and covered herself.

"You!" she started to say, but Jeremiah took one step and covered her mouth with his hand. Holding a finger to his lips he brought her into the shower and closed the curtain.

To her consternation he turned on the shower, holding a finger to his lips. "Keep it down!" he whispered in her ear. "Nikahd's a clever fellow. I wouldn't put it past him to have your cabin bugged." He took her gown from her and hung it back on the hook. "You're supposed to be showering; so shower."

She glared at him, whispering harshly, "What are you doing here—Mr. Slade—are you the one behind this?"

"Actually until a few hours ago I thought you might be involved with this yourself."

"Me? You saw what they did to those poor crew members out there didn't you?"

"That's what these people do to everyone who doesn't believe as they do Eva!" he said seriously. "I would have warned you about Nikahd if I could have. As it is, I'm going to try to make sure it doesn't get any worse. I'm going to need your help, but first things first, we need to keep up appearances. That means you shower," he told her firmly, handing her the soap. "Get to it. Nikahd will expect you to be nice and clean." When she hesitated, he scowled. "Come on, I'm serious. We've already got nine dead friendlies; we don't want any more. Nikahd is not one to be trifled with."

"All right," she said, turning away from him and dutifully scrubbing up. "Who are you really; and what's this all about?"

"I'm CIA and this is all about the Iranians using your ship to get three tons of enriched Uranium to Soekarno," he said gravely.

"Soekarno, surely you don't think he's involved in this!" she said sternly.

"Keep it down!" Slade told her ardently. He shuffled around the tight shower so he could see her face and read her eyes. It was close, very close. Dark eyes locked with Eva's deep brown orbs, he continued, "Why wouldn't Soekarno be involved? You don't know him like we do Eva. International terrorism is new to Soekarno, maybe, but he's one of the great manipulators of this world. His file at the Company reads like War and Peace!"

"Then you should know he draws the line at these terrorist scum!" she said with surprising violence. "He wouldn't acquire Uranium for terrorists, not for all the wealth and power in the world! He hates them!"

"Don't try and convince me that he has a conscience," Slade told her emphatically.

The accusation appeared to stun Eva, but she countered with logic and not emotion. "What good would it do him if terrorists like ISIS triumph? He's a capitalist. Soekarno doesn't want to give up his wealth to socialists and fanatics. He's spent his entire life trying to get out of poverty. Do you really think he'd give that up to hand over power to a bunch of unwashed imams who would behead him for his lifestyle? Think about it Slade!"

"Are you telling me this ploy with the sand was for real?"

"That's what I'm telling you," she said.

"So it's Nikahd and the Iranians who are using Soekarno for cover," he said soberly. "They want the Uranium in Jakarta—why?"

"I have no idea," Eva told him. "What are you going to do?"

"I'm going to try and prevent the Uranium from getting to Jakarta," he said. "First things first. Step one is getting you, your husband and the crew off this freighter!"

"How are you going to do that? There are forty of us and hundreds of them!"

"I don't know yet, but we've got to get you off this ship," he told her emphatically. "I've got to talk to your Mr. Christian first."

"Don't you dare make that joke with him; especially in the shower!"

He sighed, plucking the soap from her dainty hand and scrubbing the diesel oil off the wetsuit, muttering, "James Bond gets all the fun. Somehow I'm in the shower with a beautiful woman and I end up scrubbing myself! Story of my life."

"Get over it Slade! I'm out of your league. You got an eyeful; that's more than you deserve!" Eva snapped, stepping out of the shower and grabbing a towel.

"Okay Eva, thanks, you're right. Any one of the Don Juan's in your life could save you from the two hundred sweaty guys outside who want to shower with you next," he reminded her.

She put a hand to her mouth in surprise. "I forgot about that, sorry," she admitted. "Goodness sakes Slade, you made me forget all about them. I have to admit, you do make a girl feel safe." She dropped the towel and posing coquettishly, telling him, "This you cannot afford; but it'll be worth it if you can save our lives."

"The visual is more than enough to send me to Confession Eva. Now be a good girl and send your husband in," he told her.

Eva shrugged on a robe. Before she left she reached up and kissed him on the cheek. "Are you really that nice a guy Slade?"

"Unfortunately—yes," he smiled. "It's a curse; a bloody curse."

Eva ducked into the bedroom. Captain Fletcher entered the bathroom momentarily. Slade didn't meet him in the shower.

Their conversation was much more to the point, much more professional, and Jeremiah didn't enjoy it nearly as much.

Raised voices stopped their conversation. One voice was Eva's, but there were other voices, male voices, and one was Colonel Nikahd's.

Fletcher grabbed a towel and after a glance at Slade, he hurried out into the bedroom. The voices approached the bathroom door. A moment later Nikahd said, "What are you doing captain? Is there something in there you don't want me to see?"

"No, nothing!" he said.

"Stand aside," Nikahd replied sternly. Apparently the captain didn't move fast enough. "Stand aside or I will have your wife raped in front of you."

The latch turned. Slade had only a single moment to act.

CHAPTER 34: Taking the Plunge

Colonel Nikahd opened the bathroom door. It was dark. He turned on the light. That showed him what the captain had been hiding. Shaking his head, the colonel reached across the small space and picked up the Glock 9mm sitting on the counter next to the sink.

He lifted it, pointing it at Captain Fletcher's forehead. The huge man dwarfed the wiry Iranian. He didn't move, and Nikahd asked him, "What were you going to do with this captain; did you really think you could take over the ship with a pistol?"

"No," Fletcher said soberly. "But when the time comes I can keep my wife from being tortured by you bastards!"

The two Iranians with Nikahd stepped forward in anger, but the colonel shouted at them with surprising fury, "Stand down! I did not give you permission to move!"

They stepped back, smoldering, but not daring to cross the most feared man in the Iranian Army. Nikahd cocked the slide, spitting out the bullets in the pistol until there was only one left. Then he handed the gun back to Fletcher. "There, when the time comes, you will have to decide whether to use that last bullet on me or your lovely wife." He smiled, adding, "I can understand a man like you, Captain Fletcher."

Then they left.

Fletcher and Eva rushed into the bathroom. Slade was nowhere to be seen. The captain threw open the shower curtain—nothing. "Where the Hell did he go?"

A black shape dropped from the ceiling above the shower, surprising them both. It was Slade.

"Holy! You scared the crap out of me!" the big man said. He turned to Eva, and said, "He didn't do that to you did he?"

She blushed and said, "No, and a good thing to!"

Slade exhaled sharply, "Playing Spiderman doesn't get any easier with age, I'll tell you!" He took out a couple of clips from his belt and handed them to Fletcher. "Here, you may need more than one; just in case."

"Don't you want it back?" he said, taking the clips and inserting a full one into the pistol.

Slade shook his head. "If I need something I'll get it from the Iranians; they brought enough for all of us." He went to the port hole and looked out. Turning back to the couple he pointed to the door.

"Lock that. Only open it if Nikahd announces himself. Then be polite. I have to get the crew out now. The lifeboat is the obvious solution. But we have to wait until tonight to go, I'm looking at about 2 am Tehran time; they're circadian rhythm will be low, and we're going to need all the advantages we can get. I'll come and get you, but if I don't then you two just head to the lifeboat—got it?"

"We can't go without the crew," Fletcher told him emphatically.

"Captain Fletcher if I don't show up then you are going to be all that's left of the crew. Get off the ship. There's an LA class attack sub off our starboard side, the *Key West.* They will see you; they'll take it from there." Without another word Slade opened the hatch and slipped out the back.

Fletcher and Eva followed close behind but when they stepped out on the deck Slade was gone.

As the day progressed the coast of Iran fell away to the north and the coast of Oman fell away to the southwest; the Galaxus entered the Arabian Sea. Their course turned to starboard at midafternoon, heading into the open water between the Arabian Peninsula and the subcontinent of India. Slade napped part of the day, staying out of sight and out of mind in the lifeboat. He wasn't looking to make trouble, at least not until he got the crew safely off the *Galaxus.*

When evening finally fell he waited patiently until he had complete darkness. Then he crept out of the lifeboat and scouted out his route. The aft hold where the crew was being kept was a catch all for the ship. It was specifically for dry goods, but it wasn't designed for enormous containers—or people for that matter—but often the ship would store a quantity of spare parts, even spare engines when necessary. It was the primary way for accessing the engine room from the outside. This gave Slade a way in other than the above deck entrance which was guarded.

He worked his way down to the engine room, looking specifically at where the Iranians had their men. It didn't take long to map out his route and the impediments in his way. After that it was simply a matter of waiting.

At 1:30 am, an hour-and-a-half after the guard changed, at about the point where the guards were starting to get sleepy and complacent through inactivity, Slade crept into the engine room. Three men were on duty there, monitoring the engines, the fuel levels, environmental control systems and the like. Two were at a small table playing cards. A third was making the rounds.

Slade waited until the man turned the corner, putting the loud, hulking, green painted starboard diesel between his fellow terrorists and himself. The terrorist walked by, his eyes on the diesel gauges. He never heard Slade creep up behind him. The black shadow wrapped an iron muscled arm around the terrorist's throat and plunged his blade in between the ribs, pricking the heart from behind.

The terrorist lost consciousness almost instantly. He was stone dead before Slade dragged him between the engine blocks and secreted his body beneath the catwalk. Disarming the Iranian gave Slade a P90 submachine gun with a red dot sight—a nice little gun—as well as a Glock 9mm.

His silencer fit both the P90 and the Glock. That made the two card players an afterthought. After sighting them from behind and using four bullets on them, Slade hid their bodies and secured the engine room, locking the hatch and chaining it shut.

There were two entrances into the aft hold. One was a large set of double doors. That was intended for bulk equipment. However, there was also a normal hatch. Slade listened with his ear against the steel before cracking the hatch and peering within. The first thing that hit him was the smell. After a few days the stench of sweat, shit and piss was almost unbearable.

The Iranians didn't furnish the crew with access to latrines. There was no reason for it. They were to be slaughtered anyway. The crew had no choice but to pick an area for their latrine and make the best of it.

It took some effort to get the men moving. They were dazed and confused by lack of food, water and air. Once they were moving, however, they were motivated. Slade armed four of them and led them through the now deserted engine room. Up the stairs they went. He stopped them outside an exterior door.

Turning off the lights, he opened the door and scanned the deck. There was an armed patrol that did the circuit of the ship, completing it in fourteen minutes. By his calculations they should be on the other side of the superstructure and just completing their circuit. Looking toward the bow he lowered the lenses of his Night Vision Goggles—nothing.

"We're going to the lifeboat!" he said. Word went down the line. A renewed sense of hope infused the sailors with desperate energy. Leading the forty-one men along the deck was easy; they knew where they were and where they were heading. They followed Slade at a quick trot.

They reached the freefall lifeboat at the same time Eva and Captain Fletcher reached it. The men didn't wait but piled into the boat through the aft hatch.

"Once you get in the water head away from the ship as fast as you can. The *Key West* should be out there; they should see your launch and be there to pick you up."

"What about you?" Fletcher asked. "You sound as if you're not coming."

"I'm not, my job is to make sure this Uranium doesn't get used by terrorists," he said. "Now get going."

Eva stopped by him and kissed him on the cheek again, "Take care of yourself Slade. I won't forget this; my father won't forget this."

Captain Fletcher held out his hand. Slade took it. "Good luck!" the captain told him.

"Skol!" Slade said, giving the secret Vikings farewell.

"Skol!" Fletcher smiled.

Slade closed the hatch and stepped away from the lifeboat. Seconds later the latch released and the lifeboat plunged down the forty-five degree incline and into the water. The ocean completely swallowed the craft, but it bobbed to the surface fifty yards from where it entered the water with the engine running.

The orange lifeboat disappeared into the darkness.

Every light on the freighter came on. Colonel Nikahd's strident voice sounded over the ship's speakers, calling out, "All hands on deck! All hands on Deck! Alarm!"

CHAPTER 35: The Galaxus Game

Iranians spilled out onto deck armed and angry, driven by Colonel Nikahd's fury. The launch of the lifeboat was automatically relayed to the bridge and the Iranian colonel was none too happy about it. When he discovered that all of his hostages were gone he was livid.

The two deck guards were thrown overboard—alive.

The rest of the troops were mustered on deck. They began a painstaking search of the ship. From the announcements Nikahd made over the ships address system, Slade thought Nikahd suspected someone other than Christian Fletcher and his crew but he couldn't confirm it. So began a dangerous game of cat and mouse.

With almost two hundred men at his disposal, Nikahd could have someone in every section of the ship at once; this made it difficult on Slade, but the darkness helped. He was nearly invisible in his wetsuit. That was good, because Slade couldn't just hide. Soon after the search started the *Galaxus* turned south. It took him a few minutes to figure out why. When the engines revved and the *Galaxus* picked up speed he finally figured it out: Nikahd was after the lifeboat.

The lifeboat was a marvel of modern engineering. It was completely self-contained with its own propulsion system, food, water, and with the ability to right itself if capsized by a wave. It was a true lifeboat, but it wasn't a speed boat. The one thing the lifeboat could not do was to outrun its mothership. The mothership was supposed to be sinking or sunk; it wasn't supposed to be tracking the lifeboat with radar and trying to run it down.

That's exactly what the *Galaxus* was doing.

Slade intervened, shooting the thick cable running from the radar to the bridge. That effectively blinded the *Galaxus*; but it also told Nikahd he had a saboteur on board.

Despite the ardent searches Slade made it through the night without any serious encounters but when the Sun dawned things changed.

Slade went below deck, taking refuge in the labyrinth of corridors and storerooms, ductwork and mechanical shafts in the huge ship. He didn't go deep into the ship, however, because in the back of his mind was the *Key West*. If Slade were in charge he'd torpedo the freighter, and that thought kept him thinking escape. Of all things that were possible Slade didn't want to end his career or his life going down with a ship. The thought of drowning in the dark, trapped in the bowels of the Galaxus, sent shivers down his spine.

Possibly to cover his growing unease, or possibly because Slade hated being hunted with no repercussions, Slade took advantage of his situation and turned the table on the Iranians at every opportunity.

#

When dawn came Nikahd ascertained the position of the lifeboat visually. He came ten points to starboard and ordered the engines full speed ahead. "We'll ram them! So much for their escape!"

The crew abandoned their search to gather on the bow, eager to watch the destruction of the recalcitrant crew. Everything went according to plan until they closed within a thousand yards of the lifeboat. Nikahd was looking at the lifeboat through his binoculars when the water to the right boiled and turned white.

A great black tower broke the surface of the water followed by the smooth black hull of what could only be an American attack submarine. The boat launched out of the water, pointing directly at the tanker.

A message came over the radio over the international emergency frequency. "*Champion Galaxus*! *Champion Galaxus*, this is the *USS Key West*! Turn away from the lifeboat or we will fire on you and sink you! This will be your only warning!"

"Ram them!" yelled Nikahd's lieutenant.

Nikahd back handed the officer across the face, knocking him to the deck. The helmsman looked stunned and the ship kept barreling toward the lifeboat. Nikahd shoved the helmsman aside and turned the rudder hard over, veering back east and away from the *Key West*.

The lieutenant got up, fuming. "You're letting them get away!"

Nikahd drew his sidearm and shot the man in the face. He glared at everyone else on the bridge. "Does anyone else want to disobey Ayatollah Hayayi's directives and jeopardize our Holy mission?" When no one spoke up, he said, "Good! Helmsman, steer course one-six-zero degrees. Speed twelve knots!"

"Yes sir!" the helmsman said, taking over.

He told his guards to remove the body of his lieutenant and then promoted the next man in line. Then came a call over his handheld radio.

"Colonel Nikahd, we are in the captain's cabin; I think you need to see this sir!"

"On my way!" he said curtly. He hurried off the bridge with his private guard of four men. When he reached the cabin at the aft end of the superstructure, there were a dozen soldiers gathered there, murmuring and looking at the bed.

On the bed were four soldiers. Their mouths were stuffed with bacon. The men looked on in horror, imagining themselves humiliated in such a way.

Nikahd ran his hand through his hair, and said, "Our intruder has a strange sense of humor; a Western sense of humor."

Another call came over the radio. Another man's voice called for his attention. "Colonel Nikahd, sir, you will want to see this. We are amidships on the starboard side."

"On my way," he said curtly, but he was thinking, "Now what?"

When Nikahd got there a dozen men were leaning over the side of the ship. He gazed at what they saw, reading aloud, "Uranium 235! He knows!" He looked up at the long black shape of the *Key West*, pacing them as they sailed southeast.

"The submarine knows as well! By Allah, why haven't they torpedoed us?"

Nikahd returned to the bridge. The *Key West* stayed abeam at about fifteen hundred meters. Nikahd was thunderstruck. "They know what we have on board but they haven't destroyed us; that can only mean one thing: they are awaiting orders! They need permission to fire on a civilian vessel."

"What do we do colonel?" his new lieutenant asked.

"We make sure their weak willed president will not give them permission to fire! Put me on the emergency frequency for satellite, High Frequency and Very High frequency radios!" he replied. Snatching up the microphone he began issuing a distress call.

"Mayday, Mayday, Mayday, this is the cargo vessel Champion Galaxus! We are at the following coordinates. We are transporting sand to Jakarta for a children's zoo, but an American submarine, the Key West has threatened us with destruction. They are following us now. We request immediate assistance! Mayday, Mayday, Mayday!"

When he finished Nikahd grinned. "Now let the *Key West* sink us! The president doesn't have the balls to sink us!"

He turned back to his new lieutenant. "Broadcast that message every ten minutes. Continue the search! Bring me this Crusader alive! We will make sport of him by carving the Crescent of the Prophet on his chest before dispatching him by the Prophet's own direction! We will sail into Jakarta with our cargo intact, our place in paradise assured and this Crusader's head mounted on the bow of our ship!"

#

In the Situation Room Ms. Carrabolla stared down the Chairman of the Joint Chiefs of Staff and the Director of the CIA. She pointed to the news report on the president's favorite news channel, MSNBC. They were playing the distress call of the *Galaxus*.

"This is the *Champion Galaxus*, Mayday, Mayday, Mayday! We are a freighter enroute from Bandar Abbas to Jakarta with a cargo of sand for a children's zoo! We are being threatened with destruction by the American submarine *Key*

West! We request any and all assistance! American agents have already slain members of my crew! I repeat, this is the *Champion Galaxus*, Mayday!"

Carrabolla was beside herself as images of Iranian crewmembers with bullet holes riddling their bodies and mouths stuffed with bacon plastered the airwaves. "Do you have any idea how bad this looks? Do you have any clue what this makes the United States look like?"

"No one watches MSNBC Ms. Carrabolla," General Mertzl said stoically.

"It's on every station!" she shot back. Turning to the director, she demanded an explanation, "The president demands an explanation. That's your man on board the *Galaxus* isn't it? He's the one responsible for this outrage?"

"Outrage?" the director said calmly. "Those very same Iranians slaughtered nine innocent crew members of the *Galaxus*! You saw the film from Slade, himself. Why don't you counter with those videos and charges of piracy—why don't you tell the truth to the world?"

Carrabolla was momentarily disarmed, but said, "The Iranians beat us to the airwaves. No one would believe us."

"Agent Slade and the US Navy have discovered that Iran has pulled a fast one on the world—and the president— they've discovered where the three tons of enriched Uranium disappeared to and where it is heading. We now have the opportunity to solve this crisis once and for all by taking that ship or sinking it."

"In front of the world?" Carrabolla shouting. "Do you have any idea what a PR nightmare that would be? It would undo six years of trying to destroy the image of America the bully of the world!"

"Would you rather deal with the PR nightmare of terrorists having that Uranium and using it?" the director said sternly.

General Mertzl stepped forward and told her, "Captain Mars is ready to fire on the *Galaxus* and sink her. If you don't want that on your conscience we have a Delta Force team ready to storm the ship and seize the Uranium. All we need is the president's green light."

"The president has already given a statement denying any of this; he is not about to reverse his stance," Carrabolla told them.

"Where is he? I want to hear it from his own lips!" the general demanded. "We have a nuclear crisis on our hands. Al Qaeda is about to get their claws on three tons of Uranium! Is that what he wants as his legacy? Is that what you want as NSA?"

"He's given his orders. There is to be no action!"

"Where is he? Where is the President of the United States?"

The calm deadpan voice of the Director of the CIA informed the general, that, "The president is just now teeing off with a prominent basketball star." He showed the data on his PDF to the general.

"This is what our Commander in Chief does during a crisis?" the general stammered.

"General Mertzl, with all due respects, the president is of the opinion that the nuclear cargo is at the bottom of the Straits of Hormuz. A submersible is in route to verify that. We should know in a few weeks exactly what happened to the cargo."

"What about Agent Slade's discovery?" the director asked.

"Agent Slade is in error," Carrabolla said firmly.

"What if he is not?"

"He is in error," she repeated. "There is absolutely no evidence to corroborate his accusation."

"We have the data from his test kit," the director reminded her. "It conclusively identifies the presence of Uranium 235 in the containers."

"He identified contamination," Carrabolla retorted. "Your agent had no opportunity to weight the containers or perform any other tests; we don't even know if those tests were conducted on the containers in question."

"The data is irrefutable," the director told her pointedly. "An investigation will show that you and the president are purposefully ignoring the facts."

Carrabolla looked stunned.

"Why are you so dead set on believing the Iranians over your own people?" the general demanded. "What is it with you progressives?"

"There is no reason to consider the word of the Iranians as inferior to the word of the military," she told them. "That comes from the president himself."

They stared at her in shock.

Carrabolla blushed at the assertion, and tried to downplay it by saying, "We all believe we're speaking the truth but we all have different perceptions; I'm sure that's all he means. The bottom line gentlemen is that the president needs surety and one agent isn't going to give it to him. When the UN ascertains that the containers with the sunken freighter are not the containers in question, when the Uranium is truly missing, then he is willing to consider other options.

"At the moment, the president is confident that we know where the Uranium is. It is secure on the bottom of the ocean waiting for us to retrieve it."

"So what you're telling me is that we are once again going to do absolutely nothing, and you're going to leave my agent hanging," the director said.

"Isn't that his job?" Carrabolla said with a snide expression.

"You better hope I don't tell Agent Slade that," the director told her.

"Is that a threat?" Carrabolla said with fire in her eyes.

"Ms. Carrabolla you're not worthy of a threat from any of my agents, especially a patriot like Slade!" he said, unaware that at that very moment Jeremiah Slade was fighting for his life, and losing.

CHAPTER 36: Taking the Bait

Slade was trapped and he knew it; worse the Iranians knew it. He wasn't quite sure how he got himself into this jam, running into a dead end, but he did. Now he had dozens of Iranians between himself and the only exit and they had him pinned down.

What to do?

He was in the ceiling, invisible, that was his only advantage. The cooling pipes and electrical ducts hid him from view and deflected the almost constant AK-47 fire coming from only a few meters away. That was his only advantage. His little P90 was a good gun unless it had to be stacked against about a dozen AK's; then, it just wasn't enough.

What to do?

Slade tried every trick in the book: taunting, staying quiet, diversion—nothing worked. They gave him no opening to move or to escape. He had nothing left as far as ammunition; only his knife. Now, to make matters worse, it was getting hard to breathe. The Iranians were throwing up so much fire that the burnt gunpowder took up more air than, well, air.

Still they kept firing, and that, only that, was his salvation. Slade prayed, and after he finished an Our Father and three Hail Mary's plus a Glory Be—glory be and halleluiah—he saw light come through the newest bullet holes in the ceiling.

"Who taught you ladies how to shoot?" he yelled in Farsi.

A hail of gunfire answered him, creating more light in the ceiling. The Iranians were actually throwing up so many 7.62 shells that they were shredding the steel plates in the floor above. That gave him an idea.

Taking out his tungsten rotary saw, Slade began cutting the deck between the holes, all the while egging the Iranians on.

"What's the matter? Are your Burkas ruining your aim?"

It kept coming.

"Nikahd's going to cut your balls off before he has you thrown to the sharks!"

Actually, Nikahd had already done just that to two men. Desperation mixed with fury. Slade could feel the barrels melting beneath him. Yet above him an entire section of the floor looked like Swiss cheese. In an eruption of energy he braced himself on the heavy steel pipe that had been protecting him and shoved hard, squatting the floor plates above him, crashing through the floor to the deck above.

Slade rolled off to the side as more bullets flew, but he wasn't alone. Some enterprising Iranians had noticed the same thing he did. They'd climbed up to the next deck in order to shoot down through the floor at Slade. Only now he was right in their midst.

With surprise and animalistic fury on his side Slade and his knife made short work of the four Iranians who tried to surprise him. He couldn't have recounted what he did, who he knifed first or where, it was all pure training and bestial instinct. Once finished he stood upon the trembling corpses of his kills, dully aware that bullets were thudding into the now dead bodies from below.

That irritated him.

Slade yanked grenades from the men's vests and pulled their pins, tossing them down through the hole on the floor. Only when the screams and firing faded away with the drifting smoke did he stop.

That chore done he thought nothing more of it. He didn't consider how close to death he'd been. He didn't consider how fortune intervened to save him from his own stupid mistake. Slade simply re-armed himself and disappeared into the maze of the ship. The war continued.

Only later that evening after things died down did he realize that he'd been hit by ricochets and splinters. The firefight shredded his wetsuit and he had several bullets that penetrated through his skin. He plucked or dug them out, too worn out to feel pain, too desperate in his situation to care.

His only real concern was having to go into the water if the ship were torpedoed. If he bled that would attract sharks.

Slade did not want to be eaten after all this, he really didn't. He hunkered down in the safest place he could think of: on top of the bridge where he could keep an eye on things.

So it was that while an increasingly frustrated Nikahd directed the search for Slade, he was actually not more than a few meters away all the time.

#

The *Galaxus* continued to head east toward Jakarta, but it was no longer alone. The distress calls sent by Nikahd had their effect on the world at large. Few nations liked the United States. Jealousy had its affect but so did the inherent benevolence of the superpower; it was easy to hate a behemoth that for the most part refused to hit back. However, in a dangerous world, even fewer nations liked a weak United States—the beacon for freedom in the world simply could no longer be trusted. The Iranian freighter was now the underdog being threatened by a once benevolent giant.

World opinion turned decidedly against America to the point where a president who was once reluctant to act now steadfastly refused to do anything at all. More to the point freighters in the nearby area joined up with the *Galaxus*, forming a convoy to protect the freighter. The *Key West* had to submerge and now remained a hidden menace.

Slade saw all of this happening from his perch or heard it from the bridge bug. With growing frustration he realized the president wasn't going to do anything about this. It looked as though only an act of God would stop the Iranians from delivering their deadly cargo to the waiting jihadists in Jakarta.

What was he going to do; he couldn't sink the ship? The only answer was to destroy the Uranium. The problem was, of course, that it couldn't be destroyed. He could theoretically disperse it by blowing it up. Short of that there was really nothing he could do. That was the whole point of sinking it before they reached Jakarta.

The only solution left was to take the ship.

That was obviously a possibility that Nikahd considered. Slade was forced off of his perch on the bridge because

Nikahd put a machine gun nest up there as well as snipers. The cargo hold for the Uranium was likewise protected by a double ring of troops twenty-four hours a day.

Even if Slade had Killer and his Delta Force team it would be a hard, dangerous fight. He was in a quandary. As he put it to the director in his nightly communique—the Iranians stopped their jamming now that the world was interested in the plight of the *Galaxus*—Slade felt completely helpless. "I'm a hundred yards from the Uranium. It's not a matter of finding it; it's right there and I can't figure out how to get to it."

"Don't get yourself killed yet Slade," the director cautioned. "We're not that desperate. We still have a few days."

"Sir, I have one suggestion."

"We need any ideas you have," the director admitted.

"Rattle their cage. We're trying to make it look like the Iranians are pulling a fast one; we're trying to smear them and lessen their international power. Nikahd is gloating about turning the tables on us; let's do it to him. Plant the bug in their ear that we really know those containers at the bottom of the Strait of Hormuz are the real deal, but in order to de-stabilize Iran we've come up with this *Galaxus* scheme."

The director caught on. "Let the international community handle the rest; they'll demand we expedite the recovery of the containers, expecting to expose our duplicity once and for all. In reality they'll blow the Iranian scheme wide open. That will force the president's hand—Slade that's good, very good—say, you're not after my job are you?"

"Not under this president sir. I don't have your self-control."

"You've a point there," Gann admitted. "I'll be in contact—stay alive!"

#

At the United Nations Ari Bernstein, the Chief of Mossad, Israel's Intelligence Agency, led the Israeli Ambassador to a place he knew the Turks had bugged—only the Turks didn't know the Israeli's knew the Turk's had it bugged.

It was a little corner in one of the café's that served kosher food. The Israeli's knew better than to say anything vital there unless they wanted the Arab world to know. Sometimes they threw the Turks a bone just to keep the location viable for something just like this.

Ari, who had just gotten off the line with Director Gann, sat down with a huff, and said, "The Americans have sure mucked it up this time!"

"How so?" an aide dutifully asked. "I thought the *Galaxus* thing was a smokescreen anyway. So no one bought it; they haven't lost anything."

"They will lose a lot if the United Nations ever takes the trouble to check those containers. They made a big deal about the Iranians trying to maneuver that Uranium into the hands of terrorists. If the United Nations proves that the Uranium went down with the freighter the US will have more than egg on its face."

"No one will ever trust this administration again," the ambassador shrugged. "Do they now?"

"It's not the administration, it's the military," Ari told him. "The president was never for this intervention. If he were smart, he'd demand an immediate salvage operation and discredit his own military."

"That would make him happy," the ambassador nodded. "He doesn't like military intervention anyway; this would give him an excuse to pull back even further on the world stage. That's what he wants."

"The military is powerful, they have a huge lobby, but they're scared."

"Why?"

"Because their sub got the whole thing on tape—everything."

"The word is they tracked a midget sub to the Iranian freighter and then from there to Soekarno's freighter—a really slick operation."

"Way beyond the Iranian's capabilities," Ari said dramatically. "The Americans tracked a midget sub into the convoy, yes, and then it suffered a malfunction. The poor

Iranian's were just looking for help when they ran into the *Galaxus*. They ended up beaching the boat on the coast. I don't know what happened to the crew after that."

"Then what's with this *Galaxus* story?"

"A smokescreen to discredit the Iranians; to show how they pander to international terrorism, you know, knock them down a bit. They wanted the Deltas to board the vessel and plant the evidence; they didn't count on the captain sending out a distress signal and the Iranians making a bloody international incident out of it *before* they boarded the freighter."

"So now if the Uranium is found at the bottom of the Straits of Hormuz?"

"The US military exits stage left until the next administration," Ari said soberly.

"We need to block any attempt to search for those containers," the ambassador said.

"That would be exceedingly wise," Ari agreed.

#

Later that same day the Turkish Ambassador to the United Nations demanded the United Nations Security Council follow up on the disaster in the Straits of Hormuz. They demanded the immediate recovery of the nuclear containers.

The United Nations Security Council, eager for Iran to be proven correct and so put the United States in its place, voted on the resolution. Strangely, the United States abstained instead of vetoing the resolution to search for the cargo containers from the sunken freighter.

President Oetari was surprisingly supportive considering the actions of the past week. As he said smugly to the press, "If my military is making mistakes, I need to know about it."

Slade noted an immediate change on board the *Galaxus*.

Nikahd was furious. The colonel wasn't concerned on ideological grounds; rather he knew the capabilities of the West. The President of Turkey wasn't in the know on the Iranian nuclear swap; he was still a sympathizer not a collaborator. Turkey thought they were helping the Iranians; Nikahd knew better. He was horrified that the world might actually discover what the Americans already knew.

Despite that, he consoled himself that any submersible capable of salvaging the containers was still weeks away. By then it would be too late. What Nikahd wasn't counting on was a study being conducted by an environmental society. They were looking at the effects of the manmade Palm Islands on the sea bottom in the Persian Gulf. To accomplish that, they had an unmanned submersible that was taking samples and it was only fifty miles away.

The environmentalists were just as eager to see the Americans put in their place and the Iranians vindicated, which was strange, for it was the Americans who were environmentally responsible and the Iranian who couldn't care less how much oil they dumped in the oceans—one of the reasons for the environmental research team being in the Persian Gulf in the first place.

Regardless of their misguided, emotional motivation, the environmentalists volunteered their vehicle to verify the Iranians claims. The Americans dutifully supplied the exact coordinates of the wreck and two days later the submersible was diving on the sight.

One day out of Jakarta, while Slade was wracking his brains trying to think of some way to disable the ship, the environmentalist submersible succeeded in attaching a flotation balloon to one of the three cargo containers. It floated to the surface and was retrieved by the environmental ship which now had the original United Nations inspectors on board.

So confident was the UN and its officials that they agreed to televise the inspection live with news agencies around the world reporting on their every move. There was a party atmosphere on the ship. The inspectors, lined up in their white anti-radiation suits, were treated like astronauts. They were all miked up and more than willing to talk much more than the occasion allowed.

The inspectors looked over the container minutely, pronouncing it sound. All the sensors were in place and there was no evidence of a radiation leak or of seawater leaking into the container. It was pronounced intact.

They weighed it and confirmed that the container weighed exactly what it should. A cheer went up from the environmentalists; America was going down!

The second test was the residual radiation around the container. The inspectors warned the reporters that it should be low—it was—another cheer. Even the reporters were getting into the mood now.

The real test, however, was to open the access panel and sample the atmosphere within the container, just as Slade had done. With exaggerated thoroughness the inspectors opened the panel. They then held up the detector for all to see before plugging it onto the nipple and opening the valve allowing a sample of the inner atmosphere within the container to enter the detector. Closing the valve, again after allowing the cameras to record every movement along the way, the chamber in the detector filled with the gases in the container. Finally they unhooked the detector, took it out of the access panel and read the data aloud.

"The atmosphere inside the container shows—what?" the chief inspector started to read triumphantly. He stopped and showed it to his colleague, muttering aloud, "This can't be right. There's radiation but at much lower levels than we expect; and there's absolutely no indication of Uranium 235 or even Uranium 238 at all. There's no Uranium period."

"What's in there?" a reporter yelled.

The inspectors looked at each other and shrugged, but the chief inspector said, "We won't know until we open it, but these levels are consistent with one ton of radioactive medical waste. We deal with that all the time."

"Where is the Uranium?" the reported demanded.

The inspector shrugged again and gave the world the obvious answer, "I don't know; ask the Iranians."

The United Nations was not so quickly convinced. They spent the next six hours retrieving the other two containers. By the time the world press watched two more negative tests for Uranium they'd switched sides. It was now remembered how the Americans initially thought something fishy was going on;

that is, until the president and the United Nations accepted Iran's ipso facto explanation.

Now, with righteous indignation the shit really hit the fan.

The Security Council unanimously voted to condemn Iran and impose harsh sanctions, with one abstention—the United States Ambassador was too embarrassed to show up. They wanted to know where the Uranium was, and they wanted to know now. The Iranian delegation responded by walking out.

In the Indian Ocean it was the middle of the night.

Members of the Security Council, behind the scenes of course, rooted out and found the US ambassador. The question was asked: would the president consider storming the *Galaxus* or if necessary sinking it, because once the Uranium got to Indonesia, the world's largest Muslim nation, it would in all likelihood disappear.

The ambassador replied soberly that the president was flying to Martha's Vineyard to study the problem.

CHAPTER 37: Skycraning It

As the dark shadow of the large tropical island of Sumatra passed on the starboard side, blotting out the stars of a misty night, it was just the *Champion Galaxus,* the Iranians and Slade. The flotilla of supporting ship evaporated. Once the Iranian lie was exposed no one was willing to protect the hijacked freighter.

Slade was given the go ahead to try and secure the bridge. He was just gathering up his arsenal in order to take one last, desperate gamble. If he could take the bridge, even for a while, he might disable the ship. That would at least buy time.

The plan was for Slade to take the bridge and hold it. The action should draw the attention of the Iranians, making the Uranium cargo vulnerable. Five minutes after he had the bridge the Deltas would hit the freighter.

If the attack failed the *Key West* was to torpedo the freighter.

Slade was ready.

He dispatched the two snipers—amazed that they would take time out for prayers on duty—he had a feeling the praying wouldn't do them any good anyway. The machine gun crew, two men and a Russian made PK, were on the top of the bridge overlooking the ship. They depended on the snipers to cover their back, only the snipers were dead. That made them vulnerable to Slade's suppressed Makarov.

Slade had regained his nest atop the bridge. Only now he had a machine gun and two Dragunov sniper rifles. That put him in a considerably better mood.

The sound of hydraulic motors resounded over the deck, cutting through the moist tropical air. The cargo hatch over the nuclear containers was opening. They were the folding hatch design, allowing the entire hold to be accessed, the problem was that as the hatch folded upwards it blocked Slade's view of the hold. He couldn't tell what was going on down there. Why was Nikahd opening the hold now?

As if to answer his query, the bridge door below him opened and Nikahd himself marched out of the bridge with his security contingent in tow. This was a stroke of luck. The cargo hatch was open so the Deltas could get at the Uranium and Nikahd's security gorillas were not on the bridge.

As soon as the colonel reached the deck four stories below the bridge Slade called the director. "I'm on my way in!"

There were guards at either door. Slade dropped behind the guard on the starboard side, knifing him as he landed. He was in the shadows and no one in the bridge noticed. Taking a second to drag the body away from the door, Slade took stock of the bridge from the safety of the darkness.

There were four men on the bridge and a guard outside the other door. The guard was facing away. Turning the latch slowly, Slade eased the door open and stepped into the bridge. It was rigged for night, so unnecessary lights were off and the bridge was bathed in a dim red glow. Slade was a shadow.

He stepped inside, moving slowly so as not to attract their attention, and slid into the deeper shadows by the plotting table. He centered the red dot of his P90 on the back of the first man's head. He'd go for chest shots for the rest, but he wanted the first man to fall cleanly.

Slade squeezed the trigger. The silencer absorbed most of the report from the gunpowder going off; however, it couldn't do anything about the hollow splash of a head exploding. The man's head waggled forward and snapped back like someone punched him. He crumpled to the floor. The other three men looked toward the sound, not yet comprehending what was going on. Slade gave each of them a squeeze of the trigger.

The killing hardly made a sound, but the cries of men dying caught the guard's ear. He turned and saw Slade. The P90 emptied its magazine through the tempered window, showering the guard with glass and bullets.

The man fell. Nikahd and his men stopped and stared up at the bridge. He had a few moments, only that before they rushed him. Striding to the helm Slade ripped the throttles to full stop. A bell rang and the engines wound down. Replacing the cylindrical magazine, Slade emptied it into the bridge control console, shattering anything and everything that looked like a useful piece of equipment.

He plugged a new cylinder in the P90 and prepared to meet Nikahd's guards. Only they didn't come. They were trotting with Nikahd, heading for the now open cargo hold. Slade couldn't understand why until he heard the unmistakable whine of a turbine engine. All of a sudden it hit him.

"Damn!" he cursed, rushing out of the bridge through the door he entered. He threw caution aside and fired on the first Iranians he saw, trusting to speed and confusion rather than stealth. Several men went down. He rushed past them, firing, changing his magazine on the fly, kicking a wounded man out of the way and pressing on.

Slade skidded to a halt.

There was a high pitched shriek coming from the cargo hold. A pillar of light rose out of the hold and into the night sky. Rising up from the hold, in the center of the shaft of light, was an enormous green helicopter; it looked like some huge insect from an old Godzilla movie.

Slade instantly recognized the machine: a Sikorsky Skycrane, a legendary aircraft that specialized in carrying bulk cargo. Sure enough, strapped behind the cockpit and between the long spindly landing gear were the three containers. The Sikorsky came to a hover, moving forward far enough to allow Nikahd, who was standing on the next cargo hatch, to climb aboard.

"Damn it! I should've checked the crate!" Slade told himself, sprinting through the darkness. Several Iranians looked his way but then all Hell broke loose on deck. Like specters from a horror film black shadows spilled over the ships rails spitting fire. The Deltas had arrived.

The two men barring Slade's path melted to the deck, shot through and through. He pulled himself atop the hatch cover and got up, running hard as the Sikorsky started to rise. Slade leapt, grabbing the edge of the platform on which the containers rode, throwing the crook of his right arm around the frame of the cargo platform. It was a precarious hold at best. Slade slung a leg up and hooked his heel inside a cargo strap.

With his left hand, he grasped the clip for his rappelling line and snapped it onto the D-Ring through which the strap ran.

The Sikorsky banked and Slade lost his grip, falling off the platform. He landed hard back on the cargo hatch cover. He cursed as the pain coursed up his back, but over the cacophony, somehow he heard his name called.

"Slade!"

He looked to his left and saw Kincaid standing there in amazement. "Killer!"

The Sikorsky was flying away, climbing hard, and already taking fire from the Deltas. There was something strange about the sound though. It took a second before Slade looked down to see his hundred foot long rope reeling out like a mad fishing line.

"Oh shit!"

The chopper snatched Slade off the deck like a minnow on a hook.

CHAPTER 38: Phase Two

Abdullereda Hussein awakened to someone shaking his shoulder violently. He awoke with a start, disturbing the two Western slaves that had serviced him the night before.

"What is it, what is it!" he stammered, covering his eyes, shielding them from the light shining in his face. The light of the room snapped on and he focused on a man, the man shaking him, and the two men in black uniforms behind him.

The girls shrank away in fear, but the man addressed Abdullereda again. He wasn't angry or judgmental, he was excited. "Captain!" That's what they all called him. "Captain, it is time! It is time!"

"Time for what?" he complained groggily, looking at the clock. "It's three in the morning. What can it possibly be time for?"

"Paradise!" the man said emphatically.

"Oh!"

"Come, we've brought your uniform," he said, helping Abdullereda out of bed. "Quickly, go in and shower and shave. We have men getting the aircraft ready as we speak."

"Excellent!" he said, still groggy. He stumbled into the bath. The girls were herded in behind him.

"Wash him thoroughly," the man ordered. "He is a Holy Warrior! He must be cleansed for his mission."

The girls did as they were told, scrubbing him down from head to foot, shaving him, and even brushing his teeth for him. When he was cleaned and dried they dressed him. Only when they had him perfect did they open the door and allow him out.

The man surveyed Abdullereda with satisfaction and nodded, "Perfect! Come with me. It is time to go."

Abdullereda followed the man outside. There was a limousine waiting for them. The man opened the door and let Abdullereda in first. He got in and sat down. As he did so the sound of two shots could be heard in the house. A moment later the two jihadists came out. They got in. The smell of cordite was strong in the car. As the limousine pulled away Abdullereda could already see flames licking at the windows and smoke rising up into the sky.

They arrived at the airport in twenty minutes. The limousine drove straight to the hanger where guards stood outside the hanger doors. Stopping in front of the doors, the driver opened his window. When the guard approached he said simply, "We have the captain!"

"Allahu Akbar!" saluted the guard and he stepped away.

The hanger doors opened and the limousine pulled into the brightly lit area. A freshly painted A380 sat there in the white, blue and gold of Singapore Airlines. Around the aircraft in orderly ranks were hundreds of jihadists. They drove past the men. The stare of their dark eyes was palpable; he could feel their envy. Every man wanted to be him at this moment. His heart swelled with pride.

The limousine drove him right up to the airstairs. Waiting there were several men and imams. The driver got out and opened the door, standing at attention when Abdullereda stepped out. He went up to the men waiting for him, all of whom he either had met or knew. They offered their best wishes, kissing his cheeks and shaking his hand.

"Everything is ready then," he said with finality.

"The cargo should arrive momentarily," the imam said. "We need to be ready to go as soon as it is loaded."

"I understand," he answered. He climbed the stars and entered the aircraft. Turning left he walked into the cockpit. Everything was clean. The carpet even smelled new. Everything was as it should be. It suddenly hit Abdullereda that he would never leave this aircraft as a living man.

#

Slade found himself dangling in the darkness on the end of his rope. Fortunately he wore a five point harness over his wetsuit. If he just had a belt the shock might have broken him in two. As it was the helicopter snatching him from the deck of the freighter qualified as a very nasty carnival ride.

The freighter was dwindling in the distance. Everything else was black. He could hardly see the helicopter. It was flying without lights. The only illumination was the ruddy red glow of the jet exhaust from the twin Pratt and Whitney engines.

Slade grabbed hold of the rope and then splayed his legs out, steadying himself. Slowly he climbed the rope, feeding the line through the brake and working his way back up to the payload. When he finally reached the platform he climbed onto it, but there was little or no rest there. Despite the relatively slow speed of the Sikorsky its forward movement still created a vacuum in the slipstream which constantly tried to pull Slade off the platform.

He had to find a better solution. That turned out to be climbing atop the containers. There was about eighteen inches of room between Slade and the bottom of the Skycrane's spine. It got him out of the slipstream and allowed him to rest; and to think.

His phone buzzed. Cradling his arm around his mouth to cut down the wind noise he answered. It was the director.

"Slade where are you?"

"I'm on the chopper, can't you hear it?"

"Are you with the cargo?"

"Yes, I'm lying on top of all three containers. I'm guessing we're on the way to Jakarta."

"The Delta's are leaving the ship and heading to Jakarta," he said. "They cleaned up the freighter without too much trouble. All the terrorists have been neutralized. The ship is back in the hands of Captain Fletcher and he has a Navy security detail and escort to Jakarta. What's your plan?"

"Sir, I didn't know I had a plan."

"The Delta's should be waiting for you. There shouldn't be any more need for heroics. Ride it out and let them secure Nikahd and the cargo."

"That works for me!"

"We'll follow your flight," the director told him. After a long pause the director told him, "Slade, we're not getting a signal through your GPS."

"I'm not surprised, the voice transmission is omnidirectional, but the GPS requires line of sight with several satellites. I'm under the chopper's fuselage on top of the containers. "

"Can you get me a hit?"

Slade crawled to the edge of the container, warning Gann, "It's going to get noisy!" He held the phone out from under the fuselage, expecting the noise from the rotorwash to drown out all sound. What he didn't count on was the force of the rotorwash catching the phone and flinging it out of his hand.

There was a sinking feeling reaching all the way down into the pit of Slade's stomach. He could only call himself stupid for so long before the business of terrorism and survival focused his mind on the near term future.

He tried to convince himself it didn't matter. The chopper was obviously heading to Jakarta, probably to the loading docks where the cargo would be unloaded and dispersed amongst the Al Qaeda cells. From there the terrorists could attack dozens of cities or venues worldwide with terrible effect.

Nikahd had an ingenious back up plan with the Sikorsky, but it was too late. They'd been found out. When he landed the helo Killer and his Deltas would be there to greet them. Game over. Still, something nagged at Slade. No matter how he analyzed it he couldn't shake the suspicion that he'd missed something.

#

Killer scowled. He'd hopped on an Osprey as soon as the fight was over. The Osprey could fly over twice as fast as they Sikorsky so the idea was to get ahead of Slade and be waiting for him in Jakarta.

That part worked perfectly. Killer was in his battle fatigues at seaport; he was an imposing sight. Once the White House talked to the Indonesian President everything was smoothed over and he had the run of the place. There was only one problem, and he told General Mertzl about it.

"There's nothing here," he said in a low guttural growl, his frustration making him forget he was speaking directly with the Chairman of the Joint Chiefs of Staff, not that it mattered to a Special Operations grunt. "I'm telling you that the workers, cranes and trucks are expecting a shipment of three large boxcars of sand—sand, nothing else. We've been through the entire facility; our people are here questioning the workers. None of them are on the Al Qaeda watch lists. Where did Slade say he was?"

"We got cut off, Captain, I don't know where he is now," Mertzl replied, equally frustrated. "He was with the cargo before we got cut off. He thought it was heading to Jakarta; we've got nothing that tells us anything different."

"Damn it, he's expecting help when he lands," Kincaid said, stifling another curse. An Indonesian man stepped up to him, a CIA operative. Killer listened to him for a second and then relayed the information to Sorensen. "Hey, I got one of CIA's people here. He's telling me the workers are all of Soekarno's boys—they're clean—however, they tell a story about some of their relatives working at Soekarno International Airport being strong-armed by some Jemaah Islamiyah thugs. I'm heading over there to check it out."

"Well hurry, because Slade is landing within the next half hour," Mertzl told him. "The chopper has a limited range. So wherever he is, he's about to land."

"On my way!"

#

The Sikorsky started to descend. Slade couldn't see forward but he could see to the sides. There was a city glow ahead of the chopper, a big city glow, but something wasn't quite right. If they were flying to Jakarta then the dark mass of Sumatra should be on his right; inexplicably it was on his left. Was he then headed north and not south?

Slade knew where the ship had been: east of the island of Sumatra about two hundred and fifty miles from Jakarta. So to get to Jakarta the chopper had to fly south and along the coast of Sumatra to the island of Java. Any way he looked at it the chopper had to come from the north; it had to.

He decided he must be turned around, it could happen, but if he was the big island of Sumatra was on the wrong side of the aircraft.

The Sikorsky turned. The city lights came into view and then the airfield. Slade's stomach turned to ice. That explained it. His gut instinct was right—again. The Sikorsky was flying north. It wasn't going to Jakarta; it was going to Singapore. That airport wasn't Soekarno International; it was Changi.

Everyone was in the wrong place. Slade's help was five hundred miles to the south, and Slade had no way to let them know. He was on his own. "Damn! If I'd known that I'd have tried to get rid of this pallet," he muttered to himself. "It's too late now; we're descending."

The Sikorsky was in a left hand descending turn, heading toward the hangar complex north of runway zero-two-right. As they approached it he could see the hanger doors open. Even at a mile away Slade could make out the distinct, bloated, ungainly shape of an A380—suddenly everything fell into place.

"They're flying the uranium out of here; it's only a question of where." The several hundred armed jihadists waiting on the tarmac confirmed it. He couldn't stay where he was. Landing on that tarmac surrounded by hundreds of jihadists was going to mean a quick, painful end to his life.

Thinking fast, Slade guessed the flight path of the pilot and got ready to exit the Sikorsky. Crawling onto the back of the cargo pallet, he stepped off the aircraft.

Slade was still on his rappelling line. Quickly he let himself down, gauging his altitude by the waves breaking on the shore of the beach. Slade guessed he was under fifty feet and that the chopper had slowed to around sixty knots. He ran all the way to the end of his line, waiting for the chopper to slow even further. He waited as long as he dared before releasing the brake.

Slade felt the freedom of nothing but air beneath him; he'd never liked that feeling even during a safe jump. Plummeting from a guessed at altitude, in the dark, into water of unknown depth at a guessed at speed was not comforting. He assumed his entry position with legs slightly bent, ready to absorb the shock of contact with the bottom or a reef—hopefully neither.

His last thought before hitting was landing on a hungry shark.

The water engulfed him and all Slade heard was the sound of bubbles. He stopped in the water without hitting bottom. That was a good sign. Nothing hurt. Nothing appeared dislocated. Good! He struck upwards, controlling his fear. For all Jeremiah Slade had been through he'd never gotten over night dives; he hated them, absolutely, positively hated them. He didn't even like to wade in the ocean at night.

To panic, however, was the last thing you wanted to do in the water. Panic meant prey; it attracted unwanted guests faster than anything except an open wound.

That reminded Slade of the fight on board. He was going to bleed, no doubt about it. The faster he got to shore the better.

Slade got to the surface and took in a lungful of air, getting his bearings. The sound of the surf on shore was clear. He turned and looked, heading for the white line of foam and the airport lights. Slade had to hurry, but he had to swim smoothly.

The shore was a hundred yards away, but it seemed a mile. He kept swimming, regulating his breathing, everything was going fine. He was halfway there. Thirty yards to go. He reached down and touched the bottom with his foot. It felt strangely firm but yielding—then it moved—a thrill of panic hit Slade.

Something blunt and rubbery hit him on his left side. Slade reacted instinctively, and that meant he reacted angrily, through fear, firing back with his left elbow, feeling it contact a big, heavy, rubbery object. The object didn't move because Slade moved it, it was too big. His head whipped around and he saw a shiny black, blunt nose turn to the left at his counter-strike.

The shape and size of the nose left him thinking one thing: tiger shark!

CHAPTER 39: My Kingdom for a Phone

Slade hated many things: jihadists, the Dallas Cowboys, Hippies, former members of the Weather Underground, and right at the top of the list were tiger sharks.

He hated tigers; hated them with a visceral all-encompassing hatred. They were ugly, dead-eyed, trash eating, Great White wannabes who had a taste for people. They didn't hit you like Great Whites; tigers mouthed you, looking at you with those zombie-eyes. They gnawed you and ate you slow. They made Slade's skin crawl.

After everything he'd been through, Slade was not about to be eaten by the *second*-most-dangerous shark in the oceans. He ripped his P90 around and fired it underwater in the direction of the tiger shark. He didn't hope the bullets would hit or hurt it, but the flash and sound might scare it away.

Slade emptied the magazine and then struck out for shore as fast as he could swim. The remaining distance took an interminable time. He didn't try to swim smoothly, the shark knew where he was; it was just a question of whether the shark thought he was worth it anymore. Every stroke took forever, every breath rang in his ears. Slade's heart pounded so hard every shark in the Indian Ocean must have heard it.

Boom, scrape! His knee hit something. Scrape! His other knee hit something. Then his windmilling hands scooped up a fistful of sand, beautiful, yielding, fluffy sand! Slade's feet touched the bottom and he was up, kicking off his fins, and running, sprinting through the surf. He didn't stop until he was above the surf line surrounded by soft white sand that gleamed dully under the stars.

He threw himself down, gasping for breath. Slade didn't wait, running up the beach, but made a silent promise, "Never, never again will I swim at night—never again no matter what. The president can take a quick trip to Hell before I do that again!"

Slade made his way off the beach and through the jungle, heading for the hangers. There was a thin stretch of forest between him and the hangers, which were lit up like mid-day. It took five minutes to reach the fence line. There were armed patrols on the inside and on the outside of the fence. It was very well organized, especially for jihadists.

He waited, timing their patrols, until he had a large gap. Then it was a matter of running to the fence and cutting an entry slit close to the ground where the guards wouldn't notice it. This he accomplish using a battery operated rotary saw with a tungsten blade the size of a small flashlight. In thirty seconds he was through, shoving the loose end of the fence below the thick bladed grass so the gap wouldn't show. Then he was off to the hangers.

Although the area was well lit, there were plenty of shadows in the heavy moist air. Slade melted into the darkness moving from one hanger to another before he found what he sought. Looking through the window next to a back door he spied an A380, he was guessing *the* A380, in Singapore livery being attended to by over a hundred jihadists.

It was a well-run operation. The cargo doors for the A380 were open and already a loading truck was driving up to the open bay with the three containers on board. It stopped in front of a loading platform. The first container rolled from the truck onto the platform. Once they were locked into place the scissor lift engaged and raised the container to the level of the cargo compartment. The container was rolled into the compartment and secured. The platform lowered and the same routine ran its course for the second and third containers.

To his consternation the huge aircraft was already hooked up to a tug. It looked as though the jet was ready to go and just waiting for its deadly cargo.

From his vantage point Slade could see the entire operation. Everything was laid out, as behind the aircraft there was an operations center that took up the entire back corner of the hanger. A bank of four big screen LCD's, large enough for a small stadium were set up like a NASA launch control center. There were mimicking screens set up all over the hanger so that the support personnel and even the military guards could see what was going on. Inset in the screens were a constant stream of clerics and jihadist commanders giving speeches, urging the jihadists forward to the culmination of their cause.

The monitors told Slade everything he needed to know.

One monitor showed the interior of the flight deck where a captain was preflighting the aircraft. It showed three other men wearing jihadist uniforms, presumably his guards.

Another monitor showed the loading of the containers in the cargo hold. The containers were bracketed by wooden pallets holding scores of smaller packing crates; each labelled with three letters: TNT, tons of it. Slade whistled at the dark genius behind the plot. "They're not usinf the Uranium for a thousand dirty bombs, this thing is one huge dirty bomb; it's a poor man's neutron bomb. With the aircraft as a trigger and a few tons of TNT to disperse the Uranium an entire city could be made uninhabitable."

The next large screen had a flight plan on it. The flight plan looked as though it took off from Singapore and landed in Paris.

Paris was the target!

Slade admitted it was a juicy target. Why not destroy the City of Light and revenge themselves on Charles 'the Hammer' Martel for his stopping the jihad at Tours in 732? That was how Islamists thought. The cultural center of modern Western Europe would be a big target, but then again, he thought, wouldn't Rome be better? The Eternal City was the center of the Islamists biggest religious rival in the world, but then again that would quite possibly unite Catholics and all the Christian world against Islam.

Still, the A380 could reach anywhere in the world. Why not finish off what they started in New York or even take out Washington D.C.? Slade was frustrated and mystified. Strategically, no Western City gained the jihad anything. They'd feel awfully good about themselves but they'd most likely unite the world against them. They'd be annihilated— period.

Were they that stupid? Slade had to admit they were—still, it just didn't make sense.

He was right. Conveniently, the face of an imam appeared on the inset to the screens. In Arabic, he explained, "It is a glorious day. Today, September 11th we launch a strike at the heart of evil in the world." A flashing red circle appeared on the flight plan. It wasn't Paris. The red circle was three quarters of the way along the flight plan, right on the flight path: Israel, specifically Tel Aviv.

Slade understood. "Everyone thinks they're flying a simple passenger flight from Singapore to Paris—it happens every day at 11:55 pm with Singapore 334—only they've rerouted to avoid ISIS airspace—with the cease fire with HAMAS conveniently in effect they can fly over Tel Aviv. Israel isn't worried about a civilian Singapore jet flying over their airspace. It's the perfect cover. When they get over Tel Aviv they pull an Egypt Air, put the nose on the Knesset, and boom! Tel Aviv becomes the world's first radioactive city."

The imam continued in extreme animation, waving a scimitar over his head and banging the podium with it. "On September 11th, a Holy Day in the new Caliphate, we will strike the head off of Zionism. We will ask the rocks and the trees to deliver up the Jew and they will cry, "Here he is! Come slay him!" We will strike them on the necks even as the Prophet did, sending their heads into the trench of history! First Zion and then the West. We will, by Allah, celebrate our inevitable victory in the White House and spread Islam through the world as the Prophet, the Blessed One, said, *Slay the idolaters wherever you find them. Arrest them, besiege them, and lie in ambush everywhere for them.*" He slammed his sword upon the podium, shouting in frenzied, maniacal emotion, "*Kill them wherever you find them, and turn them out from where they have turned you out. And Al-Fitnah is worse than killing! Fight them until there is no more Fitnah and worship is for Allah alone!* Remember the words of our Prophet, Peace be upon Him. Hold them in your hearts and go forward to jihad with joy!"

Slade shuddered, knowing the passages from the Quran, knowing that the "Fitnah" reference included him, Helen, the kids, his friends and his civilization.

He had to get to the aircraft—but how?

Slade needed a miracle, a small one, but a miracle.

It came in the form of an off-key wail that made Slade cringe. "Sounds like a cat with a blow torch up his ass!"

The offending noise came over the loudspeakers of the hanger complex: a call to prayer.

Obviously the operations were behind schedule because they were only halfway complete with loading the Uranium. Despite that the crews stopped what they were doing, climbing down from the loaders, the cargo pits, the fuel trucks—whatever—they proceeded quickly to retrieve their rolled up prayer rugs and gathered at the front quarter of the A380 to pray.

The captain and his guards left the flight deck and climbed down the stairs. Prayer rugs awaited them at the foot of the stairs. The video screens switched from the operations within the hanger to a prayer service.

Slade saw his chance. Shaking his head at the irony of it. He rushed to the door. While the entire jihadist force blinded themselves to his presence, he muttered, "If I get this done and it's because they had to take time off for prayers; well, I think I've got all the answers I'll ever need. There's a price to pay for everything, including misplaced piety!"

He had maybe five to fifteen minutes; it all depended on what reading from the Quran they used. A voice began reciting over the hanger speaker—good—it was a long verse, about fifteen minutes then. Slipping through the door, Slade slunk through the equipment, vehicles and sundry things to the aircraft. Sneaking up the airstairs was out of the question. The captain and his guards were at the foot of the stairs and there were literally dozens of jihadists crowded around him.

He headed to the forward cargo pit. With every jihadist facing the other way he climbed the loader and slunk into the cargo pit.

Slade made his way further forward. There, just as on the Airbus tour in Paris, was an access hatch to the electronics and equipment bay beneath the flight deck. He opened the hatch and crawled into the darkness. He went to the ladder with the intention of getting onto the passenger deck and hiding there but the prayer ended.

Shouting resumed and the loaders were turned back on. Boots thumped on the deck above his head. He was stuck, but at least Slade was on the aircraft. Half an hour later the aircraft was towed out of the hanger and the engines started. Soon the huge jet lifted off with Slade on board as well as three tons of highly enriched Uranium, and twenty-five tons of TNT.

He waited for the gear and the flaps to come up. Slade wanted to capture the aircraft while the pilot was busy climbing out, but he wanted a little altitude above the ground. If it involved a fight he wanted time to recover the aircraft before it crashed. Unlike the jihadists Slade had no intention of being a martyr unless there was absolutely positively no recourse.

He firmly believed in Patton's doctrine of making the other dumb bastard die for his country. The jihadists wanted to die; Slade was more than willing to help them along.

After five minutes, he climbed the ladder to the lower deck. He'd done this in Paris. There wasn't any trick to it, other than making sure no one saw him climb up out of the floor.

Slade was careful, cognizant that unlike the other jumbo aircraft in the sky, the Boeing 747, the cockpit was adjacent to the lower deck instead of on the upper deck. He knew the layout for the A380. Besides being incredibly ugly it had a galley between the E&E deck and the cockpit.

Atop the short ladder, Slade reached up and took hold of the flush mounted lever, rotating it counterclockwise. That released the latch and he lifted up the hatch just a few inches. Bracing his shoulder against the hatch, holding his P90 with the other hand left Slade balanced precariously on the ladder.

That was coincident with the A380's climb over the Titiwangsa Mountains, and the turbulence always present at the knees of those hills. The roiling mass of rough air shook the huge aircraft like a leaf, propelling Slade off the ladder and back onto the metal floor of the E&E compartment. That was all he remembered.

CHAPTER 40: Descent Into darkness

"General, it's not here!" Killer told Mertzl, nearly shouting with frustration. He was standing in an empty hanger at Soekarno International Airport in Jakarta. His team and a company of marines from the *Enterprise* had gone over the hanger with military thoroughness. They found that jihadists had been there with what they could only assume to be the hijacked A380 but they were long gone.

"We've interviewed Soekarno's people. They're confirming what we feared. The jihadists pulled hundreds of bodies off the A380 and dumped them in the ocean. The jet was here, but it's been gone for a week."

"Where the Hell is Slade?" Mertzl snapped. "He was with the Uranium—right?"

"We lost contact with him somewhere around Sumatra," he explained. "He thought he was heading to Jakarta. Obviously he was wrong."

"Well damn it, where could he be? That Skycrane doesn't have the speed or range to get much farther than Jakarta."

"He's probably on one of the thousands of islands around here," Killer sighed.

"That can't be where that airplane is. The A380 was obviously in Jakarta, the ship was heading to Jakarta—there has to be a connection."

"General, we know they want the Uranium for dirty bombs, but an A380 isn't a very good way to disperse it. Why not just ship it out in parcels on smaller airplanes. Unless—"

"Sweet Mother Mary three tons of Uranium in the A380!" the general finished. "The A380 is the dirty bomb! Where? We need to know where!"

"The Skycrane was part of the Iranian plan all along, probably as a backup," Killer guessed. "They probably bugged out when Slade became a problem on the freighter. It has to be close general."

"If they are going to mate the airplane and the Uranium then they have to be somewhere that thing can land. There just aren't that any airports that can handle an A380."

Killer took out his chart, marking the spot where the chopper escaped the *Galaxus*. "They could get to Jakarta, we know that." He drew an imaginary circle around the escape coordinates with the radius being the distance to Jakarta.

Together they answered their own question: "Singapore!"

The general swore again. "We sent our Singapore assets to Jakarta! Turn it around! Get everyone to Changi International Airport, Singapore! I'll get on the horn with the *Enterprise* and see if they can scramble some F-18's up there! Go!"

"We're on our way!" Killer replied, already yelling for his men to get back to their planes.

#

Sweat beaded on Abdullereda's forehead as the hijacked Airbus A380 reached the Top of Descent point. This was it; all of the training over the past few weeks, really all of his aviation career culminated in this moment. All of Abdulleraeda's life came into focus at this time. As he turned off the transponder and disconnected the autopilot he saw two things: the pride of his family that their ne'er-do-well father would wash his sins away by becoming a martyr, and that his peers, who tormented him as an adolescent would finally envy him.

The lights of Tel-Aviv rotated up into the forward windscreen. The rush of air buffeting the windows made normal conversation in the cockpit impossible.

"Allahu Akbar!" Abdullereda shouted as the adrenaline rushed into his head.

There was the capital of the Little Satan. The Jews would get their just deserts! Their government would crumble. The promise of the Arabs finally recapturing Al Quds and driving the Zionists into the sea would be realized!

The rumbling of the slipstream grew louder. The airspeed clacker sounded, meaning they were now exceeding the maximum airspeed of the aircraft. He eased the power back; Abdullereda didn't want the aircraft to break up and veer off course. He wanted to bury it in the Knesset! Over the radio the Israeli controllers were shouting at him, vectoring fighters their way.

The Ghost of Flight 666

Abdullereda kept the dive going. No one could catch them now. Even a Surface to Air missile—even the American Patriot couldn't hit them now; and even if it did it wouldn't matter. Their momentum would take the radioactive debris field directly over the city. The lights of Tel Aviv grew brighter, larger, closer, "Die Zionists—die!"

So excited was Abdullereda that he didn't hear his copilot shouting at him, not that he could hear anyway! What did it matter? They were hurtling earthward doing Allah's work! It wasn't until Zafar clutched his arm that Abdullereda paid attention to him. He looked to the sweating face of the co-terrorist. Zafar was yelling but Abdullereda couldn't understand him over the roar. The man's face was straining, sweating; his large white teeth stood out against the dark slick skin and black stubble.

"Use your microphone!" Abdullereda demanded, keying his mike and shouting into it. These half trained terrorists didn't even know the basics of the cockpit. Of what worth were they, joining in the honor of martyrdom but adding nothing to the operation!

Finally over the headset came Zafar's cracking, panic stricken voice. The man was afraid of death; afraid of martyrdom!

"Someone is shooting at us!"

It took Abdullereda a moment to register what Zafar was saying. Shooting at them; were they? He laughed. "Don't worry, we've got enough Uranium to make the entire city uninhabitable!" Abdullereda yelled back. "They can shoot us down. It doesn't matter anymore!"

The altimeter dropped precipitously through thirty thousand feet. He yelled triumphantly. There was no stopping them now. The operation was a success!

Zafar was beating on his arm—coward!

Abdullereda turned a scathing look upon his co-terrorist only to hear Zafar scream through the microphone, "No, someone on the airplane is shooting!" He pointed back at the bulkhead.

"What—it cannot be—Allah would not allow it!" Abdullereda exclaimed in panic, but looking back he saw a mass of bullet holes in the bulkhead immediately behind him. One of the guards was clutching at this arm. The other was at the peephole, looking back in the cabin. All at once his head snapped back and he was screaming. He pulled away from the cockpit door with one hand over his eye. Blood streamed from beneath his fingers.

#

Slade woke up to the howl of electronic equipment and cooling fans. The E&E compartment was a dim, noisy place that smelled like dust mixed with warm electronics. His head pounded. There was dried blood on the side of his temple where he'd hit the corner of an equipment rack in his fall.

Fighting off the fog of unconsciousness, Slade checked his watch. They'd been airborne for over six hours—six hours! It struck him; they were within an hour of Tel Aviv. All weariness and pain washed away in a torrent of adrenaline. Slade got up and headed for the ladder.

Quickly, but with the necessity of caution, he raised the hatch again. The galley area was clear. He could see the cockpit door. It was closed. Damn!

Slade crawled up through the hatch onto the empty passenger deck. He went straight to the cockpit door, listening. He could hear muffled voices but couldn't make out what they were saying. He tried the door gingerly, but it took only a slight turn of the lever to know it was locked.

Slade retreated to the nearest exit doors. Looking out of both sides of the aircraft he tried to gauge his position. It was the middle of the night in Tel Aviv but he thought he could distinguish the dark swath of the Red Sea and the lights of Eilat.

"Damn!" Slade was running out of time.

He ran back to the cockpit door. Like most cockpit doors it was bulletproof, but Slade knew something most people didn't know. Airlines were cheap, their CEO's were even cheaper. They'd spend money on themselves but not on the security of their aircraft, not unless they were forced to.

304

He ducked into the bathroom behind the cockpit. The cockpit door might be armored but the bathroom bulkhead inexplicably was not. Slade pried away the mirror, exposing the thin aluminum skin between himself and the cockpit. He was on the point of cutting a small hole in the aluminum so that he could discover the positions of the crew when the throttles came back.

Muffled shouts of "Allahu Akbar!" reached his straining ears. He had no more time. Slade put the muzzle of the P90 against the aluminum at a forty-five degree angle, aiming down from chest level. He squeezed the trigger. The bullets cut a hot swath through the aluminum. He rotated the gun from right to left, shooting an arc from the captain's side of the cockpit to the first officer's side. There were screams and shouts of anger.

Slade darted out of the bathroom and behind the cockpit door just as a burst of gunfire erupted into the bathroom. It pierced the bulkhead going the other way, ripped through the opposite wall and tore through the flight attendant jumpseats by the entry door.

A light suddenly appeared at the cockpit peephole and just as quickly disappeared as someone looked through to see what was going on. Slade shoved the muzzle of the P90 against the glass and fired a quick burst. The recoil nearly knocked the light automatic rifle out of his hands, but he was rewarded with a high pitched wail. The bullets hadn't penetrated, but they shattered the glass and drove the shards into the jihadist's eye.

Slade ran back to the E&E door and flew down the ladder. He'd studied the schematics for the A380 and toured the aircraft meticulously in Paris. Now that knowledge came in handy. Just like his beloved Boeings, the E&E compartment went underneath the cockpit. In fact, you could see the compartment from the rudder pedal wells beneath the instrument panel; it worked the other way as well.

Standing beneath the deck, Slade fired upward through the floor, spraying the area behind the pilot seats with the remainder of his magazine. Loading the last cylindrical

Christopher L. Anderson

magazine, the buffeting of the aircraft now growing throwing the airplane around and getting so loud Slade couldn't hear the bark of the gun, he wormed his way up beneath the first officer's rudder pedals, only able to get his arms and the gun into the narrow space. Sticking the muzzle of the compact gun through the opening he sprayed the first officer's seat blindly.

A sharp cry came from above.

He repeated the operation at the captain's rudder pedals, thinking he heard a groan but no more. His hammer fell on an empty chamber.

The noise and vibration in the aircraft was now so violent that Slade could see only in a blur. Staggering back, he crawled up the ladder and bounced from wall to wall to the cockpit door. With great difficulty he entered the emergency code.

The entry buzzer was lost in the deafening sound of the slipstream, but a warning light would flash, informing the crew that someone was over-riding the lock. Slade waited. They had thirty seconds to deny him entry; if they did there was no way in short of breaking the door down.

It was the longest thirty seconds of his life.

With agonizing sluggishness the seconds ticked by until finally he felt the lock open. Slade burst through the cockpit door. Two men lay bleeding on the cockpit floor. One man was slumped over in the first officer's seat. The captain, bleeding from several wounds, was just grasping the rotary switch that would emergency lock the door—it was on the first officer's side of the upper panel—he had to unstrap to reach it and was a second too late to deny Slade.

With an inarticulate roar Slade lunged forward and grappled the captain's bloody arm, dragging him from his seat. The captain screamed and struggled, but Slade pounded him in the face mercilessly, once, twice, three times with his fist. The captain was no fighter. He sank into unconsciousness.

The lights of Tel Aviv were close.

Leaping over the center console and into the pilot's seat Slade took the stick in his left hand and eased it back while pulling the four throttles back with his right hand. The A380 protested, already hurtling fifty knots beyond the barber pole, the maximum airspeed on the electronic instrument display.

Slade ignored the warning clacker, continuing to ease the nose up. Slowly the horizon climbed up the display and the speed began to slacken. The aircraft groaned as the metal of the structure, bent by the terrific forces of air pressure, flexed. The sound of the slipstream lessened. After another thirty seconds of gingerly bringing the nose up Slade levelled the huge airplane at three thousand feet and turned it to the west; out to the Mediterranean Sea.

He breathed a sigh of relief, but then heard the unmistakable sound of fury behind him. He turned to see one of the wounded jihadist guards stirring on the cockpit floor behind him. The man was trying to get his AK-47 in line with Slade, cursing, "Die Crusader dog!"

No longer armed, Slade was helpless; but his copilot was not. Slade snatched the Glock 9mm from the dead jihadist slumped in the first officer's seat and shot his recalcitrant comrade in the forehead.

The blood and brains splashed over the unconscious captain's face and into his open mouth. The now dead jihadist finally cooperated and lay still. Just to be sure, Slade put bullets into the other two corpses, but the captain was alive and he wanted to keep him that way; Slade shot him in the knees and the hands. The pain alone would keep him from doing anything untoward.

At long last left to fly the airplane, Slade put on his headset and dialed in 121.5 on his VHF. It was a good thing he did. Looking outside in the predawn darkness he saw the plumes of two Israeli F-16's joining up on him. He caught the latter part of their last transmission.

"Singapore Flight 344 remain on course two-seven-zero! If you deviate from your present heading you will be destroyed!"

"Roger, Singapore 344 acknowledges, boy am I glad to see you guys!"

"Who is this?" the F-16 pilot asked, obviously surprised at the response.

"The United States of America has taken possession of this aircraft from Al Qaeda terrorists," he explained. "Tell Ari Bernstein, your Director for Mossad that his counterpart Director Gann has a gift for him."

"Maintain your course and altitude Singapore 344—standby," the pilot replied.

"I'll try, but this thing flies like an electronic brick; I hate Airbuses," Slade said.

There was a chuckle of amusement from the fighter pilots. Shortly thereafter Slade was instructed to follow them to a military field. He landed without much trouble and taxied in to a wide empty apron of concrete. Fire trucks, hazmat trucks and armored vehicles followed Slade in and surrounded the aircraft.

He shut down and opened the exterior door. Israeli commandos stormed in, passing Slade by like water around a rock. Ari Bernstein was behind them. He held out his hand.

"I understand the people of Tel Aviv owe you their lives!"

"Mr. Bernstein," Slade nodded formally, shaking the Mossad King's hand firmly. "I'm just glad to be on the ground again."

"So what do you have for me?"

Slade gave him his trademark thin, chilling, smile. "How many bombs do you think you can make from three tons of enriched Uranium?"

Ari grinned and said, "How on earth would I know? Israel can neither confirm nor deny the existence of nuclear weapons in our arsenal!"

Slade shrugged, "There's also enough TNT to blow up every Hamas tunnel out of Gaza."

The commando came out of the cockpit. A lieutenant reported, "They're all dead except the jihadist pilot. He's still alive but in a bad way."

"Make sure he gets extra special care will you?" Slade said, meaning it in only the most diabolical of ways.

"Oh you can be sure of that; you can be absolutely sure of that!" Ari said grimly.

The commandos carried the bodies out and Ari led Slade down the stairs into the harsh lights of the tarmac. "We're indebted to you, but I must ask, how is it you managed this? As far as the president is concerned none of this should exist." Ari said, slapping Slade on the shoulder.

Slade winced, and then noticed a neat round hole in his wetsuit. He grimaced. "I must have caught one back there."

"What in the world have you been doing?" Ari said, looking at the man in sudden concern.

"It's just a bullet," he said.

"No, no, not that; what's this?" Ari asked, pointing to a semi-circle of slashes in Slade's wetsuit that went from his left hip to his ribcage.

Slade all of a sudden felt woozy, "That damn shark bit me! Son of a bitch!"

Ari saw Slade turn white, and comforted him, "Now, now Slade it couldn't have bit you on the plane! Sit down in the limousine; I've got a doctor right here!" He waved the paramedics over. "Slade, how long ago was it? You flew from Singapore right?"

"Right, I'm bleeding to death, the wetsuits the only thing holding me together," Slade said weakly. He slumped into the leather seat.

The paramedic stripped the suit off one arm and took his blood pressure. He shook his head.

"That's it right?" asked Slade. "Damn shark! I knew they'd get me!"

"No sir," the paramedic said. "You're blood pressure's a little elevated, that's all. That's to be expected from the stress you've been through. By the way, the bullet's a through-and-through. You'll be fine."

"To Hell with the bullet!" Slade snapped angrily. "What about the shark bite? That tiger chewed me up!"

"Well let's see," the paramedic said. He carefully peeled the wetsuit off Slade's side.

"How bad is it?" demanded the tough as nails CIA agent.

The paramedic uttered a single surprised, "Whoa!"

Slade fainted.

Christopher L. Anderson

310

CHAPTER 41: A Short Drop

Abdullereda Hussein awoke to intense pain in his knees, hands and face. He opened his eyes with difficulty. They were almost completely swollen shut. Forcing them open, Abdullereda witnessed a fuzzy world of light institutional green. It slowly resolved into a hospital room. A doctor and two other people were leaning over him. They wore yarmulkes.

"There we are," said a voice in Arabic. "He is coming around."

"What am I doing here?" he croaked, his throat dry from the oxygen tube in his nose. "Why am I not in paradise?"

A man smiled, and said, "You're in Tel Aviv not in paradise. I'm afraid that journey will be up to someone else." He laughed and said, "Don't worry, you won't have to wait long."

Abdullereda was confused, but he didn't remain so. Shortly thereafter the men from Mossad came. He tried to be strong but they were very persuasive and he was already weak. Soon, he told them everything they wanted to know and more. Once he satisfied their curiosity all they seemed to want was for him to make a full recovery. They gave him excellent care, he couldn't complain, and then they informed him they were sending him home.

Reality hit Abdullereda. The humiliation! The failure of his mission! He consoled himself though; it was really the guards that failed him. He had done everything a martyr could do but actually die. Surely people would understand.

The day arrived and the Israelis gave him a nondescript grey jumpsuit to wear. Abdullereda shuffled onto an Air Malaysian flight with two escorts. They were there, they said, to make sure he got home okay. The short flight, only seven hours, landed in Kuala Lumpur in a driving rain. They got him off the airplane but instead of taking him through the terminal they took him down the jetway stairs and put him in a van, one man on either side.

"Where are we going," he asked, but then he answered his own question. "Oh, right, we probably want to avoid the press."

Undoubtedly there would be questions about his involvement in the jihad. However, seeing as most people were sympathetic there would probably be a time and a place for the press. Maybe he could salvage his pride. Maybe this would all work out.

Still, he couldn't quite understand why the Israelis of all people were so nice to him. He expected to be tortured to death. It didn't happen. In fact, he owed his health to them. He could easily have died.

The van didn't leave the airfield as he expected but instead it drove to one of the airfield hangers.

"Why are we going here?"

"It's the only place big enough for all the families," said one of the men gravely.

"What families are those?" Abdullereda was truly mystified. They drove through the hanger doors and he saw hundreds of people gathered within. There were several portable grandstands and a raised central platform. The platform had a wooden scaffold mounted on top.

His heart leapt. A hero's welcome!

No.

"These are the families of the people you killed on board Malaysian Flight 666," said the man with grave venom. "You've been convicted in absentia and sentenced to hang for your crimes."

Abdullereda went cold and limp. The van stopped and they half carried, half dragged him up the stairs to the platform. He couldn't register what was happening, but he felt the concentrated glare of hundreds of eyes. He looked out at them; and they all seemed luminous, fiery white eyes that burned him with their stares.

The men on either side pulled his hands behind his back and put them in cuffs.

"Tight!" he yelped. "Too tight!"

A hood was pulled over his head, stifling, black, and musty. It stank of vomit and death. Abdullereda started to panic, to hyperventilate. Then a rope tightened at his throat and a voice whispered in his ear.

"I am the man who will hang you! My niece, my beautiful eight year old niece was on your plane. It was your job to take care of her. Now I will take care of you!"

Abdullereda heard him step away. Clarity came to his mind. It was all about to end. Mustering his courage, Abdullereda shouted, "I did it for the sake of Allah!"

"You did it for the Devil!" replied a hollow, distant voice.

He waited, trembling uncontrollably. Nothing happened. The tension was so great he soiled himself, crying out in despair. Now he wanted, he prayed for the trap door to open and end the terrible anticipation, to bring about death, swiftly.

Abdullereda was only partially right.

The trapdoor opened and he fell—six inches—not the four feet needed to snap his neck. The narrow gauge rope tightened around his neck painfully, slowly strangling Abdullereda over the next twenty minutes.

The last thing Abdullereda heard was the sound of a jet aircraft taking off, as if it were a reminder of the respectable life he could still be leading had he not fallen into darkness. A shudder rippled through his body and then Abdullereda heard voices, thousands, millions of voices screaming, shouting and howling. He couldn't see, but he could feel. His body was suddenly immersed in an intense, skin curling heat.

CHAPTER 42: Coffee With Friends

Slade awoke in an apartment and not in a hospital. That was strange, he thought, because he recognized the effects of anesthesia wearing off. He didn't fight it. He allowed himself to drift comfortably in and out of sleep until such time as his bladder told him it was time to rise.

Putting on a robe, Slade took care of things, made some coffee and went out on the balcony of his room and sat down to enjoy the view of Tel Aviv.

Killer and Bernstein met him there.

"Director Gann congratulates you on a job well done Slade," Bernstein told him. "He passes on that even the president was pleased."

"I must have screwed something up then," Slade smirked, sipping his coffee.

Killer laughed, slapping Slade on the back. "Thanks for leaving most of the freighter guys and almost all the jihadists in Singapore alive! You're slipping. My boys finally had something to do!"

"You cleaned everything up then?"

"Sure, you know how badly those guys shoot," Jake said. He dug in his pocket and produced a photo. Handing it to Slade, he said, "Thought you might like this for your trophy wall. It's the shark that gummed you!"

"That tiger almost bit me in two!" Slade protested.

"It was a nurse shark *Jeremiah*," Killer laughed. "Only a six footer at that; you probably woke him up on the bottom. Probably scared him as much as he scared you."

Slade perused the picture of four grinning Deltas holding a six foot nurse shark full of bullet holes.

Killer chuckled, and added, "His teeth were barely long enough to get through your wet suit!" Then he shrugged and shook his head. "You know, it's kind of embarrassing to have a Delta Force scared of sharks."

"I guess you're going to kick me out then," Slade sighed, putting the picture face down on the table.

"Can't," Killer shrugged. "You still killed the shark and an awful lot of bad guys."

"Speaking of bad guys, I got a special cable this morning," Ari told them. "As you may know, in light of the horrific crimes committed by ISIS in its rampage across Syria and Iraq the Pope has approved the use of force to stop them."

"No I didn't know that," Slade said gravely.

"It's significant for it to have gone that far, but the Pope has gone farther," Ari said. "Cardinal Martel contacted me this morning. The Vatican is of course working through diplomatic channels, the Holy Father sees to that, but Cardinal Martel has been instructed to see if there are certain people within the Free World that would be interested in comparing notes, sort of streamlining things behind the scenes."

They all looked at each other. Finally Slade said, "If that will cut the red tape I'm all in. We were close this time; very close."

"That feeling is not so unique. I'm afraid it's not shared by all, however. There are too many in positions of power who seem to blind themselves to the obvious. Perhaps those of us actually fighting the battle can overcome not only the obvious enemy but the blind friend as well."

"We need to," Slade sighed. "The price of failure is too severe. We can't leave that kind of world to our children."

#

The Iranian President Aliaabaadi met Colonel Nikahd in front of the presidential residence. He led the colonel inside. They joined Ayatollah Hayayi for tea in the reception room. The Ayatollah was curt. He got right down to business.

"We cannot allow this setback to further aggravate our plans," he told them both. "I am already hearing it from our ISIS and Al Qaeda confederates as well as the Grand Mufti of Saudi Arabia. Our Shia-Sunni alliance is cracking. The rise of ISIS is not something we anticipated."

"It has, however, created an unexpected strength in our understanding with our Al Qaeda brothers," Nikahd said. "The

ISIS barbarians prey on them as well as the Shia who fall into their hands."

"We should encourage the Americans to view ISIS as a grave threat," Aliaabaadi said. "Perhaps then the Americans can take care of that problem for us."

"That would be a great help," Hayayi assented. "Though I hate the idea of using the Devil for our deeds it is all too clear that our greatest threat is ourselves. We risk various factions even various communities going forward without coordinating with us. ISIS is one example. Had they waited two years they might have done us a great service. Now, however, they risk focusing the West on the threat we pose them. Hamas is another example. Of what use was it to anger the Zionists before we were ready to strike? Their rocket attacks and the ensuing Zionist offensive nearly ruined this latest operation before it got started."

"To that end we have some problems with our brothers in London," Nikahd reported.

"Problems? What problems?"

"The community has implemented sharia in our neighborhoods and conquest by the right hand; they've been taking Western women and girls for their harems. It is all right and well of them to do so, of course, but those in Manchester have been caught. The resultant trial may very well send things out of control."

Hayayi sighed, "It will be the downfall of our people if we do not learn the patience required for conquest. What good is it to wait ninety-nine years when all that is needed is to wait one hundred? We have fallen short many times before. My fear is that if we do so again we may not be given another chance."

CHAPTER 43: A Bumpy Ride

Captain Bashir climbed into the hot cab of the old, rickety truck with his first officer and navigator for the long ride back to Bandar Abbas. It could have been worse. He could be in the back with the fourteen members of his crew that shared the truck bed with thirty goats. So much for the elite of the Iranian Navy!

As they drove, bouncing along the coastal road in the ancient truck, the driver turned on the radio.

The announcer was reading the headlines, "Last night a Singapore passenger jet, the same jet missing from a hijacked flight from Kuala Lumpur two months ago, landed unexpectedly at military airfield in Israel.

"Rumor has it that it was being flown by the captain of the hijacked flight who was himself involved in the plot. Unfortunately all the passengers are now feared dead. In a strange twist, the flight reportedly had on board the missing three tons of Iranian Uranium that was being transported under United Nations auspices for quarantine in Abu Dhabi.

How the Uranium got on board the aircraft and why it suddenly appeared in Israel is unknown. The Israelis have taken possession of the Uranium purportedly for safe keeping. Iran is thus far silent on the matter. The captain is in Israeli custody and awaiting extradition to Malaysia, where he has been convicted in absentia for the murder of hundreds of innocent civilians. He has been sentenced to hang."

Captain Bashir was struck dumb. The navigator shook his head in wonder. The first officer blinked and asked, "Do you mean to tell me we went through all of this just to give the Israelis our Uranium; couldn't we have just flown it there to begin with?"

CHAPTER 44: McLaren

Slade was tired, sore, and grumpy from a semi-circular shark bite that wasn't even going to leave scars. Already the neat row of tooth marks had faded to pink. The doctors steadfastly refused to make them look presentable or even to waste stitches on them.

The Israeli surgeon told the American, "We're at war here in Israel. I can't waste the thread; I've got real casualties. Really, I thought you Americans were made of tougher stuff."

Now he was home—almost.

Helen and the kids were back. The danger wasn't completely over but it was manageable. They'd never again be able to lead the carefree life they once did, but that was the price the world had to pay to wage war against the jihad. It was a burden shared by everyone, whether they knew it or not.

Slade had only his rollaboard. He wore dark slacks with his black boots, a gray shirt with no tie, and a charcoal herringbone coat. September in D.C. wasn't cold, it was cool, and the leaves were just giving a hint of turning. He waited at the curb of Dulles International, waiting for Helen to drive up in his old silver Jaguar to pick him up and take him home.

He looked for the Jag, but it didn't come. Slade checked his watch. As he did another silver coupe pulled up. It wasn't a Jaguar. It was long and lean, with a huge hood and a growling giant beneath the bonnet. The driver's side door lifted up in its trademark gullwing. Slade peeked beneath the door to see Helen grinning from ear to ear.

"I had no idea driving could be so much fun! Get in!"

He tossed his bag in the back and got into the car, stammering, "Do you know what this is? It's an SLS Gullwing! What's wrong with the Jag; don't tell me they gave you this as a loaner? We can't even afford the insurance!"

The door closed and Helen pulled back out into traffic. "I should be mad at you, or at least a little jealous," she said.

"You must have made that woman very happy, very happy indeed!"

"What woman?"

"Eva! She left you a letter in the glove compartment!"

"Slade opened the opened the door and took out a purple envelope with gold leaf edging. Inside was lavender stationary. The note read,

Dear Jeremiah, it may be cliché, but words cannot express my appreciation for everything you did. My father is even more appreciative, and he hopes you will accept this token of his thanks—don't worry, everything's taken care of—enjoy!

Eva

P.S. Give Helen a big kiss for me. I hope she puts out, LOL!

P.P.S Christian sends Skol!

There was a big lipstick kiss below the note.

"Who is Eva?"

"A bored heiress who got herself mixed up the wrong crowd and needed rescuing," he said simply.

"I see she expects me to put out. What did you tell her about us?"

"Not that!" he assured Helen. "We made small talk during dinner in Paris. I wanted her to know I wasn't available so that we could get down to business."

"I see," Helen remarked, ignoring most of his answer. "You saw her in Paris?"

"We had dinner on one of the river boats—business—I have to take you one of these days."

"Is that what this car is for?"

"No, the Iranians hijacked her husband's freighter," he started to say.

"Not the one from the news? The one with the Uranium on it?"

"That's the one."

"You were there Jeremiah?"

He sighed and said simply, "Now you know what I do for a living."

"No wonder she was appreciative!"

"By the price tag of this car, I suppose so."

"This is from her dad," Helen noted. "How did she show her appreciation to you?"

He shrugged, admitting, "She did flash me."

"She flashed you?" Helen started.

"Kind of like you did when you were seventeen," he reminded her.

"I was sixteen," she corrected. Then a scathing look came across her face. "You're trying to change the subject!"

"I was in her shower. It was the only way I could communicate with her and her husband without the Iranians catching on. Don't worry, I was in a wetsuit. Nothing happened."

"I'm sorry," she said quickly. "I don't have any right to be jealous after all you've done for me and the kids. It's not like we're really married; you're free Jeremiah."

There was a long silence.

"Did she look good naked," she asked, coloring.

"Not as good as you."

"At sixteen maybe. I was pretty hot."

"I meant now."

"You don't have to say that Jeremiah."

"No, I don't," he agreed. "But you wanted to know the truth—didn't you?"

Helen smiled, trying to appear like she didn't care when she did—a lot.

He patted her knee.

"Do you want to go to dinner? We're in a nice car and you're all dressed up."

"Tomorrow," Slade said. "Let's get some pizza and head home to the kids. We'll make it a movie night."

Helen hit the gas and the SLR leapt forward, heading home.

Back Cover: The Ghost of Malaysian Flight 666

An airliner disappears over the ocean without a trace.

Three tons of Iranian enriched Uranium disappears in the Straits of Hormuz.

A CIA agent on the edge.

A father desperately trying to reconcile with his son.

A son trying to reclaim the honor of his name.

A woman trying to salvage a future for her children.

A president watching his world fall prey to reality.

An exotic Heiress held hostage by maniacal killers.

The fate of all these things, and the course of the world, depends on the Ghost of Malaysian Flight 666.

www.ingramcontent.com/pod-product-compliance
Lightning Source LLC
Chambersburg PA
CBHW071241170626
46809CB00001B/41